BOOK TWO IN THE RAIDING FORCES SERIES

DEAD EAGLES

PHIL WARD

GREENLEAF
BOOK GROUP PRESS

Published by Greenleaf Book Group Press
Austin, Texas
www.gbgpress.com

Distributed by Greenleaf Book Group LLC

For ordering information or special discounts for bulk purchases, please contact Greenleaf Book Group LLC at PO Box 91869, Austin, TX 78709, 512.891.6100.

Design and composition by Greenleaf Book Group LLC and Bumpy Design
Cover design by Greenleaf Book Group LLC

Publisher's Cataloging-In-Publication Data
(Prepared by The Donohue Group, Inc.)
Ward, Phil, 1947-
  Dead eagles / Phil Ward. — 1st ed.
   p. ; cm. — (Raiding forces series ; bk.2)
  Sequel to: Those who dare.
  ISBN: 978-1-60832-192-6

  1. World War, 1939-1945—Campaigns—Western Front—Fiction. 2. Soldiers—United States—Fiction. 3. Special forces (Military science—Great Britain—Fiction. 4. Special operations (Military science)—Fiction. 5. War stories, American. I. Title. II. Title: Those who dare.
PS3623.A7342 D42 2011
813/.6   2011931380

Part of the Tree Neutral® program, which offsets the number of trees consumed in the production and printing of this book by taking proactive steps, such as planting trees in direct proportion to the number of trees used: www.treeneutral.com

TreeNeutral®

Printed in the United States of America on acid-free paper

11 12 13 14 15 16   10 9 8 7 6 5 4 3 2 1

First Edition

DEDICATION

Randal's Rules for Raiding

RULE 1: The first rule is there ain't no rules.

RULE 2: Keep it short and simple.

RULE 3: It never hurts to cheat.

RULE 4: Right man, right job.

RULE 5: Plan missions backward (know how to get home).

RULE 6: It's good to have a Plan B.

RULE 7: Expect the unexpected.

STRATEGIC RAIDING FORCES' ONGOING OPERATIONS

OPERATION COMANCHE YELL

RAIDING FORCES' ATTACK ON THE RAIL LINES THAT RAN ALONG the coast in enemy-occupied France came about as a direct result of failure. Lieutenant Randy Seaborn, the captain of His Majesty's Yacht *Arrow*, had found it impossible to locate the tiny pinpoint targets they intended to raid with the primitive navigational equipment he had on board the yacht in time for Raiding Forces to go ashore, conduct a raid, and return home before daylight.

One night in the Blind Eye Pub, the bar Raiding Forces shared with two squadrons of hard-fighting Royal Air Force fighter pilots, after Captain Terry "Zorro" Stone ran through a litany of the problems the Commandos had encountered trying to find their targets, Major John Randal declared: "If we can't find the pinpoints, why not quit looking for them? There are two types of targets: point and area. What's an example of an area target we can raid instead?"

"Rail lines," Sergeant Major Maxwell Hicks volunteered. "They run along the coast, and we can attack them at any place and get the same result."

Raiding Forces conducted their first raid on a railroad the next night. Following that initial successful operation, small-scale demolition missions were carried out on a regular basis against the enemy rail transportation system.

OPERATION BUZZARD PLUCKER

The sniping of Luftwaffe pilots at their landing grounds in France was born out of frustration and envy. The Battle of Britain—being, it seemed, entirely fought by fighter pilots—supplied most of the frustration as well as all the envy. There was no way any of the Raiding Forces Commandos were going to get to be fighter pilots, so they sat around evenings in the Blind Eye Pub surrounded by the partying "Gallant Few" celebrating their latest air victories, drowning their frustration in alcohol and kicking around ideas on how to get into the fight.

Raiding organizations spend a lot of time dreaming up wild schemes to employ their unique skills. They have to, because no one else is going to do it for them. The regular services—army, navy, and air force—would have been perfectly happy at this stage of the war, in 1940, if the Commandos had simply faded away and never asked them to support another operation that took up their precious resources of time, men, and equipment. Raiding Forces had to find a mission and some way to carry it out on their own.

The Luftwaffe had a tactical air support problem, Raiding Forces learned from the fighter pilots in the Blind Eye, and they wanted to take advantage of it. The German dilemma was something called "air-loiter time over target." After linking up with the bombers and escorting them across the English Channel, the Luftwaffe fighters usually only had fifteen to twenty minutes of fuel left before they had to turn around and head home. That meant the German bombers were left unprotected from the furiously attacking English fighters. It was believed that the Luftwaffe was losing more fighter aircraft from running out of fuel and crashing into the English Channel than from being shot down.

The simple solution for the Germans to reduce their time-over-target problem for their fighters was to build their landing grounds as close to the Channel as possible to reduce their flying time to Great Britain. Literally hundreds of small Luftwaffe landing grounds were scattered along the coast of France. Raiding Forces' personnel spent many nights in the Blind Eye concocting wild schemes on how to go about taking advantage of what appeared to be a golden opportunity—handy objectives ripe to be raided that were strategic in value.

The problem was that although the German army had made a name for itself as the masters of blitzkrieg, or "lightning war," serious students of German military tactics—meaning those who had faced them in battle and lived to tell the tale—knew that the real Nazi tactical long suit was the counterattack. The Germans were the best counterattack artists in the business and possessed of a military doctrine that demanded an immediate response to any enemy incursion.

That was very important for hard-drinking British Commandos to keep in mind. Especially while contemplating slipping over the English Channel some dark night and pouncing on one of those juicy Luftwaffe landing grounds situated so temptingly close to the coast. The Germans were going to react with the wrath of Thor, guaranteed.

"Butcher and bolt," Prime Minister Winston Churchill beseeched Combined Operations. The problem lay in the bolting. Following any raid, the raiding party would have to reassemble, return to their boats, and re-embark to sail safely home. The talent the Germans displayed for speedy counterattacks almost guaranteed a fighting withdrawal. Attempting an amphibious re-embarkation in the dark of night, while under close ground attack, is a guaranteed recipe for disaster. Suicide missions being frowned on in Raiding Forces by those who would be expected to participate, there was no real reason to plan any. It is always wise to review stratagems concocted over drinks in a bar, pub, or club at a later date.

Still, the best place to destroy an enemy airplane is on the ground.

The breakthrough came one evening in the Blind Eye when Squadron Leader Paddy Wilcox, the Raiding Forces pilot, mentioned that the time it took to build an aircraft could be measured in hours, but it took years to develop a skilled combat aviator. "Battle experienced airplane drivers are worth their weight in diamonds."

"Bingo," Major John Randal announced from the big easy chair where he had been semi-dozing by the fireplace. "We've been looking at this all wrong, boys. What we need to do is quit trying to figure out how to attack the German airfields and go kill pilots."

Once you break a logjam in thinking, thoughts and ideas often come fast and furious.

"We can find a location where pilots congregate and raid it, or we can land sniper teams from the *Arrow* and they can snipe pilots at their landing grounds," the Raiding Forces' commander added.

"Or," Squadron Leader Wilcox suggested, "I can insert and extract the snipers from a nearby lake by light amphibious airplane, exactly the way I used to fly in trout fishermen."

"Where do we obtain snipers, old stick?" Captain Terry "Zorro" Stone inquired. "One would imagine sniping would require a great deal of skill."

"Lovat Scouts," Sergeant Major Maxwell Hicks said. "The most peerless stalkers and snipers in any army anywhere. Lovat Scouts can turn themselves invisible, and if they can see it they can hit it."

Raiding Forces' mission to kill German fighter pilots was born on the spot.

Captain the Lady Jane Seaborn, Raiding Forces' liaison to the hush-hush Political Warfare Executive, briefed them on Operation Buzzard Plucker. PWE immediately saw possibilities. They suggested that the Lovat Scout sniper teams be outfitted with standard issue German army boots. This idea had two benefits. It made it impossible for the Germans to track the scouts because of the millions of Nazi boot prints. And since standard issue German army boot prints would be found in the snipers' hide positions outside the landing grounds after the attacks, the conclusion would be inescapable that people within the German military, members of a phantom anti-Nazi resistance movement, were responsible for shooting the Luftwaffe pilots.

PWE implemented two additional operations of their own—in effect, missions within the mission—in conjunction with Buzzard Plucker.

Operation Limelight

The first PWE extra mission involved Squadron Leader Paddy Wilcox dropping parachutes weighted down by blocks of ice when he flew over enemy-occupied France to either insert or extract the Buzzard Plucker sniper teams. PWE's idea was for the empty parachutes lying on the ground after the ice melted to cause the German security forces to believe that British agents had parachuted into a certain area. The Nazis would have no choice but to conduct manhunts for nonexistent infiltrators, and since they would never find any, live with the fear that British secret agents were running around the country up to mischief.

Operation Whistle

Once again, the PWE envisioned Squadron Leader Paddy Wilcox dropping something from the Walrus amphibian he flew during Operation Buzzard Plucker. This time it involved scattering dead carrier pigeons over enemy-occupied France. PWE placed fake messages inside capsules attached to the dead pigeons' legs in hope that the Germans would find the fallen birds and read the messages. The fake messages were designed to encourage the Nazi security apparatus to believe that an active anti-Nazi resistance movement existed within the German army. It would appear that the resisters were assassinating the Luftwaffe pilots and attempting to report their success to the British Secret Intelligence Service by carrier pigeon.

Currently, all operations had been placed on temporary stand-down. Strategic Raiding Forces had been alerted for a "Most Secret" mission in another part of the Empire. That it was deemed more important was an indication of just how vital the operation was.

STAGING FOR DEPLOYMENT

1

STANDING DOWN
BUZZARD PLUCKER

Somewhere in France

OPERATION BUZZARD PLUCKER, THE SNIPING OF GERMAN FIGHTER pilots at their landing grounds in enemy-occupied France, had been ordered to stand down. Strategic Raiding Forces, the small Commando unit conducting the mission, had been alerted for another operation with a higher priority. The two Lovat Scouts—wearing gillie suits in the hide position from which they now observed Luftwaffe Landing Ground 279—had no way of knowing their mission had been called off. Their only means of communication was a pair of carrier pigeons carried in little cardboard containers, each about the size of a softball. The snipers, Scout Jock MacDougal and Scout Bill Frazier, could send a message back to Seaborn House, Raiding Forces' headquarters located in the south of England, but they were unable to receive one.

The team had been inserted by HMY *Arrow*. They had encountered no problems making their way ashore, both going barefoot, Scout

MacDougal walking backward carrying Scout Frazier piggyback. Any German beach patrol happening along the following morning would see only the innocent-looking footprints of a lone swimmer and have no cause for alarm.

The team laid up for a half hour to see if the landing had been detected or if the beach was under observation.

After determining that everything was clear, the Lovat Scouts found a good hide position and put on German army boots so their prints would blend in with the million or so other pairs of Wehrmacht boots tramping around Normandy. Britain's Political Warfare Executive had wanted to create the impression the Lovat snipers attacking Luftwaffe landing grounds were anti-Nazi dissident members of a resistance movement within the German Armed Forces, not British Commandos. No such anti-Nazi resistance movement existed, but British intelligence hoped to strike at the psyche of the German High Command.

The Lovat Scouts had no knowledge of that. They did not have a need to know. What they were perfectly clear on was that the purpose of the exercise was for them to shoot as many Luftwaffe fighter pilots on Landing Ground 279 as possible when the opportunity presented itself as the squadron scrambled for takeoff.

The pair of snipers moved out toward their objective, taking the normal precautions not to be tracked—walking backward at times, circling, stepping on rocks and wading in streams, carrying each other piggyback for short stretches. They moved inland for a mile.

At approximately 0400 hours they reached the vicinity of their objective. The men moved into an area of thick forest where they waited in deep concealment until daylight gave them an opportunity to glass the German airfield and select the most suitable position from which to take their shot.

The Scouts would take the better part of the day to move into their final position. The Lovat Scouts were peerless stalkers. Raiding Forces, being shot through with men from the King's Royal Rifle Corps and the Rifle Brigade, had a number of men who were as capable marksmen, but no one was in the same league as the Scouts when it came to sneaking and peeking.

The shooter, Scout MacDougal, was armed with a scoped Wesley-Richards 7x57 rifle that his father before him had carried in the Great War as a Lovat Scout Sharpshooter and had presented to his son on his twelfth birthday. The commonplace 7x57 caliber was in fact a German military round ideal for the mission because a spent cartridge case was not a giveaway as to who had fired it. It could be anyone. With a little luck Nazi intelligence would find the brass and believe the sniper was a German soldier.

The glassman, Scout Frazier, the team leader, was carrying the 20X Ross telescope he used in happier days to spy out the wily red stags that inhabited the remote Scottish highlands. He was armed with a captured German MP-38 submachine gun.

Both men were highly trained reconnaissance experts skilled at what the Lovat Scout Regiment called SOS—Scouting, Observation, and Sniping. The glassman carried a Scouting, Observation and Sniping logbook. On each page of the book was a grid for Time, Map Reference, Event, and Remarks. They carefully recorded what they observed, being scrupulously careful not to give their opinions or interpretations of events.

The landing ground before them was laid out exactly as they had been shown in the aerial photos they studied prior to the mission. It was a military airstrip designed for function, not beauty: A single grass strip was surrounded by concertina and razor wire. Twenty-foot-tall guard towers built on telephone-pole stilts were spaced every two hundred yards around the airfield. Several small buildings sat at the far end of the landing ground. The open-topped control tower was mounted on the roof of what they had been briefed to believe was the field operations building. It was sandbagged waist high at the top.

A squadron of Messerschmitt Bf 109s was operating off the field. The snipers could see a total of thirteen high-performance, single-seat fighter aircraft. Each plane had a large red heart painted on the side of the nose just behind the propeller. Each heart had an arrow piercing all the way through it, slanted down from left to right. A sketch of the insignia went in the SOS log that Scout Frazier carried in the billows pocket of his sand green Denison smock.

The two Scouts observed enemy pilots, ground crew, operations staff, and maintenance and security personnel. Guards were manning the front gate and the towers and were roving the perimeter. No sizable number of ground troops to mount a quick reaction force appeared to be stationed at the landing ground. The Scouts thought that was good.

None of the aircraft had an individual guard posted to it, and the perimeter guard towers were manned by only one sentry at all times. An occasional two-man foot patrol strolled around the perimeter road running inside the strands of barbed wire. Nevertheless, the German soldiers appeared to be thorough and professional, taking their time to check for any visible signs of an intruder crossing the fence.

The pilots, the Eagles, spent their time playing with a soccer ball, lounging in overstuffed chairs their batmen had moved outside on the lawn for them, or sleeping on cots beside their airplanes.

The Raiding Forces sniper team expected the German pilots to launch a dawn patrol, and they were not disappointed. Beginning Nautical Twilight, however, was still too dark to allow the snipers to take their shot as the Me-109s took off.

Eventually the squadron returned, landed, rearmed, and refueled. The pilots went back to their soccer, lounging, and napping as per the day before. Ground crews worked on individual aircraft.

"AH-OO-GHA, AH-OO-GHA, AH-OO-GHA," the klaxon sounded at 1023, and the pilots scrambled. The instant the signal went off, one of the ground crew jumped into the cockpit of each fighter and fired up the engine while the thirteen pilots raced to man their machines. Some pilots ran on foot, some rode bicycles, and others hopped on the back of a flatbed truck that drove around the perimeter dropping off the Eagles at their assigned aircraft.

The snipers coolly waited until the pilot selected to be the first target was seated in his aircraft and his crew chief, standing on the wing, had finished helping him buckle up his parachute and safety harness. Then, after the crew chief had jumped down but before the plane had started to taxi, on signal from Scout Frazier, Scout McDougal squeezed the trigger.

With the canopy pulled back on the fighter, it was an unobstructed shot. The high velocity 7x57-millimeter round struck the pilot just below the right ear. He slumped instantly. The Me-109's engine continued to crank over; there was no visible sign of any alarm from the ground crew. As tests conducted by Raiding Forces had proven at a Royal Air Force fighter strip, the scream of fighter aircraft engines on a flight line would effectively drown out the sound of a shot.

By the time the Scouts shifted their attention to their second target the ground crew still had not realized anything was wrong with their pilot.

The aviator in the second Me-109 targeted was waving off his crew chief and preparing to taxi when Scout McDougal lined up the rifle scope's cross hairs on his flying helmet. On signal from his team leader, the Scout took the shot, hitting the flier high in the neck at virtually the same time he released his brakes. The fighter began to roll with a dead man at the stick.

Once again, there was no discernible reaction to the shot from the ground crew or any of the security forces. A great deal of confusion did erupt, however, when the airplane slowly began taxiing slantwise across the infield of the landing ground into the oncoming traffic pattern, nearly colliding head-on with another ME-109 halfway through its takeoff run. The plane with the dead pilot continued on across the perimeter road, ploughed through the barbed-wire fence, and out of sight, the mainte-nance crew in hot pursuit on foot. Crash wagons, fire trucks, and an ambu-lance roared in, as other ground personnel responded, and the rest of the fighter planes in the squadron continued taking off.

The Me-109 forced to dodge the out–of-control ground-looping fighter lifted up before gaining sufficient airspeed, veered right, clipped one of the guard towers with its right wing—knocking the startled guard over the side—lost more airspeed, wobbled unsteadily for a moment, then cartwheeled into the forest and exploded in an orange fireball.

The remaining aircraft continued to scramble. Approximately three minutes passed, the Scouts carefully noted, before the distracted ground crew of the first pilot shot realized their man was not taking off. A mad frenzy of activity took place around his aircraft, but it was not clear whether the German ground staff actually understood at this point if or how they had been attacked.

The Lovats stayed put in the shoot position and continued to observe the target for approximately half an hour. While there was a great deal of pandemonium among the ground personnel, with people and vehicles frantically coming and going, nothing in the way of an organized response to the attack developed.

The two raiders moved off slowly, taking the normal precautions. Initially, they traveled in the opposite direction of their extraction location, which was a small remote lake inland rather than on the coast as the Germans would expect.

The two men were not surprised to hear the sound of dogs baying in the distance. Apparently some effort was being made to come after them. No problem. Each man simply produced a small silver canister that had been supplied to him by Captain the Lady Jane Seaborn. The men used the secret ingredient in the canisters to salt their back trail. The formula, which had been provided by Captain "Geronimo Joe" McKoy, a Wild West showman and firearms expert who trained Raiding Forces from time to time, consisted of cocaine laced with black pepper and dried chicken blood. It was one favored by the Apache Indians, or so he claimed. In trials at Seaborn House, with Security Police from the Vulnerable Points Wing acting the role of Nazi pursuers and hounds borrowed from the Home Guard, it had worked every time. The tracking dogs were in no mood for man hunting once they sniffed the magic dust.

Being very stealthy the Scouts exfiltrated for a distance of seven miles, employing every trick in the book to throw off trackers, with no further sign of pursuit. By then the sun was beginning to go down. They found a secure hide deep in the forest that offered good concealment. Taking up position, the team remained in place under cover until it was time to move out to the extraction site three miles away.

When it was the appointed hour, the team patrolled to the lake. The extraction aircraft, a Supermarine Walrus Mark I amphibian nicknamed "The Duck" (as in ugly) piloted by Squadron Leader Paddy Wilcox, arrived on schedule almost to the minute and splashed down silently. Signals were exchanged, and the airplane's rubber dinghy, paddled by a Lifeboat Service man, beached where the Scouts waited.

By the time the team climbed on board the gently bobbing float plane, they were already wearing their dark blue Lovat Scouts berets with the blue-and-white dicing and their silver regimental badge—a Royal Stag emblazoned with the words JE SUIS PREST, which when translated meant "I AM READY." The Scouts were pleasantly surprised to find their commanding officer, the American, Major John Randal, MC, The Rangers, sitting in the copilot's chair.

"Hop in, men," he said. "Let's get the hell out of Dodge."

Neither Scout could have agreed more.

The Lovat Scout Regiment has a saying: "It is all right to take soldiering seriously in peacetime, but you should never do so in war." Strategic Raiding Forces was the perfect unit for fighting men with that kind of military outlook.

As the little amphibious Walrus leaped into the purple sky and banked sharply for home, Major Randal ordered over his shoulder, "Give me a report."

"One ME-109 destroyed, sir, two buzzards plucked."

2

RANDY'S NEW TOY

THE WALRUS SPLASHED DOWN INTO THE SMALL BAY AT SEABORN House—the vast estate south of London that Raiding Forces used as their base of operations—like a plump greenhead duck. The sun was coming up fuzzy pink over the horizon. For once there was not a cloud in the sky and it was a beautiful sunrise, but in the distance, the fog was beginning to roll in.

Raiding Forces' sniping officer, Lieutenant Harry Shelby, Sherwood Foresters, was standing by at the dock to greet his returning Lovat Scouts team. Royal Navy Lieutenant Randy "Hornblower" Seaborn, DSC, was also there—pacing back and forth like a caged tiger—waiting impatiently to see Major John Randal. The youngest officer in his grade in the Royal Navy, the first naval officer to earn parachute wings, and the holder of the prestigious Distinguished Service Cross, which is only awarded for valor, he was the skipper of HMY *Arrow*, a 40-foot yacht that had belonged to his parents, Commodore Richard and Brandy Seaborn, before being activated for National Service at the start of the war and assigned to Raiding Forces.

When he arrived on the dock, Major Randal called to his young naval officer, "Well, Mr. Hornblower, I can see you have a story to tell me."

"Yes sir, I most definitely do!'"

"Let's go take a look."

Lieutenant Seaborn and Major Randal strolled down the pier to admire Randy's new toy.

"Before I forget, sir," he began, "my mother asked me to extend an invitation to you to have dinner with her this evening at the Bradford."

"My pleasure, Randy," Major Randal replied. Brandy Seaborn was a glittering golden girl and one of the most likeable women he had ever met. Which reminded him that her sister-in-law, Captain the Lady Jane Seaborn, the drop-dead gorgeous widow who owned Seaborn House, was conspicuously missing, along with her platinum blonde bombshell of a driver, Royal Marine Pamala Plum-Martin. Captain Lady Seaborn worked for Special Operations Executive. For reasons never quite clear, she had decided to adopt Raiding Forces as her personal project and was a tireless supporter and promoter of the small Commando unit. She had arranged relationships with several intelligence agencies that had need of an action arm that could go across the Channel and perform certain tasks. So popular was she with the men that the troops had privately begun to refer to Raiding Forces as "Lady Jane's Own."

Major Randal and Captain Lady Seaborn were in the early stages of a romantic relationship that he did not fully understand. She was fabulously wealthy, with a long list of suitors that included at least one international movie star. The two had been attracted on first sight, but the exigencies of war had made their courtship problematic. Major Randal wondered briefly where she was at this moment, but those thoughts were dispelled by the imposing sight of the Royal Navy motor gunboat docked at the end of the pier. "MGB 345" was painted on the bow by way of identification. The warship was crammed with weapons.

"What is this?"

"Sir, this is a Fairmile C-Type gunboat," Lieutenant Seaborn explained, almost beside himself with joy. "A skeleton crew from the 15th Motor Gunboat Flotilla brought it up, said 'Compliments of Combined Operations,' and then departed for their home station on the next train."

Major Randal was so taken back by the sheer magnificence of MGB 345 all he could say was, "This has to be a mistake." The deadly, sleek motor gunboat bobbed innocently but gave off the ambiance of a napping Doberman pinscher. To his eye she looked like a destroyer. "Randy, are you sure you know how to operate something this big?"

"Sir," Lieutenant Searborn protested. At this juncture in his brief but meteoric career, he probably would not have been intimidated by being offered command of an aircraft carrier. He continued in a slightly hurt tone, "You are jesting, right?"

"What are her armaments?" Major Randal asked. "She's got guns sticking out everywhere!"

"There's a 2-pounder on a power mount forward, a 40-millimeter cannon manually operated aft, two 20-millimeter Oerlikon automatic cannon amidships, and a pair of .303 Vickers machine guns on the bridge. There are mounts for six additional .303-caliber MGs, but we shall have to scrounge them somewhere."

"Okay, break it down for me."

"Sir, the 345 is 110 feet overall, 17 feet 5 inches at the beam. Shallow draft—only draws 6 feet—which means she can work close inshore. That's perfect for our operations. Fully armed and equipped she weighs 72 tons and is powered by three Hall-Scott supercharged petrol engines, 1,200 horsepower each. The auxiliary engine is a Stuart 20-volt lighting set. She has side exhaust.

"Top speed is 32 knots with a cruising speed of 22 knots and a range of 500 miles at a speed of 12 knots.

"MGB 345 carries W/T radio, echo sounding sets, and smoke-making apparatus. The echo sounding gear is going to be a tremendous aid to navigation, sir. Brings us into the twentieth century, finally."

"What's her crew?"

"Two officers and fourteen men, none of which we have, sir."

"That's a problem, isn't it?"

"Yes sir, it is. Coastal Forces, the gunboat command, are saddled with the lowest priority in the Navy. Since Raiding Forces is not officially in the Navy, our priority is even lower, not that it matters very much. There are not enough sailors in Great Britain to man all her capital ships, much less the 'mosquito fleet.'"

"Mosquito fleet?"

"Sir, the *345* may look like a battleship to us, but to the Navy she is a mosquito."

"Well, you're practically an admiral now commanding your own flotilla," Major Randal said. "There's the *Arrow*, the French fishing schooner you captured for transporting military stores over to the French Resistance for SOE, and now the 345. What's your plan, Mr. Hornblower? You have only four sailors."

"It is a problem, sir," the young officer admitted. "I am twenty men and three officers short, bare minimum."

"I know you have a plan, Randy. You always do."

"Yes sir, but you are not going to like it."

"Let's hear it."

"First, I intend to try to identify reserve officers still in training but not yet assigned who would like to volunteer for special service. I shall go looking for former yachtsmen who have not been called up yet and pensioners who have recently retired but want to go back on active sea duty in small boats.

"Then, staying as far away from the 15th MGB Flotilla as I can, because we'll have to rely on them for our support service, I shall try to recruit individual active duty sailors one at a time. To be honest, sir, rounding up a full crew is going to be difficult. The Navy is short qualified seamen."

"How do you plan to work out the transfers for the ones who want to join?"

"All hands will have to volunteer for SOE, and Aunt Jane will have them reassigned to Raiding Forces. She and I have already discussed how to arrange it. Pamala said she would help too."

"Plum-Martin should be a real asset when it comes to recruiting sailors," Major Randal said dryly. "What's the part I'm not going to like?"

"I intend to use Sea Rover Scouts to crew the French schooner."

"Are you nuts?"

"No sir. I see no other option."

"But Sea Rover Scouts—"

"Major, I am never going to be able to recruit all the men I need short of a miracle. The Sea Rovers are excellent sailboat handlers. Saltwater is in their blood; they've been sailing under canvas since they were in diapers. The Royal Navy has always had the rating 'Boy' for sailors fourteen to seventeen years old. My plan is not to recruit any Rover under seventeen—well, maybe sixteen if they are really good. The lads will be called up for National Service the minute they turn eighteen anyway. I want to get them first."

"I don't know—"

"Sir, your regiment, the King's Royal Rifle Corps, has a 70th Battalion made up exclusively of boys under the age of call-up. What I plan to do is not all that much different."

"They only guard static positions," Major Randal protested. "They don't go on secret missions in the dark of night."

"Yes sir, but once Nazi paratroopers start dropping in," the young swashbuckler pointed out, "the 70th shall have to maneuver like the regular battalions."

"You got me there, Randy. What about missing school?"

"You can write them a note, sir," Lieutenant Seaborn said with a straight face. "Commander Tweedleton has volunteered to go along on operations with us to doctor the engine."

"You're kidding!" Commander Tweedleton was a long-retired Royal Navy officer who commanded a volunteer team of on-the-beach sailors that maintained the *Arrow* and were modifying the captured French schooner to carry out clandestine SOE missions.

"No sir, all the retired Navy pensioners on our support team have been begging me for a berth."

"We're going to need to think about this . . . "

"Shall we proceed aboard, sir?"

Randal stepped aboard the craft and began an hour-long inspection tour. MGB 345 was even more impressive close up. Having been developed as an escort vessel, primarily for east coast convoys, the motor gunboat had a mess deck below and sleeping quarters for the crew.

"Are you planning to have your crew stay on board or at Seaborn House?"

"On board, sir. It builds unit cohesion," Lieutenant Seaborn replied. "Live together, fight together."

"You've come a long way, stud."

"Ahoy, 345!" The two officers looked out and saw Royal Navy Commander Richard Seaborn, OBE, standing on the dock. "Ahoy, MGB 345!" he repeated.

"Ahoy, Father."

"Permission to come aboard?"

"Permission granted, sir."

Commander Seaborn nimbly navigated the boarding plank. He moved with the ease of a lifelong sailor. "What is this boat, Randy?"

"MGB 345, sir."

"I can see that. What is she doing here? "

"The *345* is my new command, sir."

"Don't be ridiculous. MGBs are a lieutenant commander's berth."

"Not this one, sir."

"Combined Operations Headquarters assigned her to Raiding Forces," Major John Randal explained. "She's one of three MGBs the Admiralty provided COHQ for raiding operations. General Bourne promised it to me some time back."

"You have a MGB with no crew?" Randy's father shook his head in wonder. "Well, that is typical of the Admiralty when they are compelled to do a thing they do not actually want to do. What are you planning on doing for a crew? There's no possibility of ever having one assigned from the Navy."

"Actually, Father, I intended to talk to you and Grandfather to see if either of you has any suggestions for me."

"My advice was to ship out on the *Hood*, remember?" the commander blurted. "Randy, you must have been born under a lucky star . . . command of a warship at your age and grade is unheard of . . . at least in the peacetime Navy. I am simply staggered, as will be your grandfather. Of course we'll help you in any way we can."

"You two sailors work out our naval strategy," Major Randal said. "I'm going to grab a couple hours of sleep before heading to London to get our marching orders. And don't forget, Randy, we're on alert for immediate deployment. We'll have to postpone your recruiting safari until we find out what our future holds."

"Sir!" Lieutenant Randy "Hornblower" Seaborn responded cheerfully. "And remember, mother at the Bradford tonight."

Major Randal should have noticed, but did not, that Commander Seaborn studiously avoided making direct eye contact when his son mentioned the dinner engagement. Walking down the gangplank he heard the commander say, "You are going to need two sub-lieutenants as watch officers, a midshipman, three engineers, at least one electrical rating, two petty officers . . . "

3

BLUE BOOT

A LOT OF LOOSE ENDS NEEDED TO BE TIED UP AT SEABORN HOUSE before Raiding Forces deployed, and time was short.

Walking up from the dock Major John Randal decided it would probably be a good idea to pay a quick call on the Field Security Police detail that would be remaining behind to secure the property.

Security around Seaborn House was a three-layered proposition. The third and final layer had been added recently by Captain the Lady Jane Seaborn when she assumed the role of Raiding Forces' Intelligence Officer prior to Operation Tomcat. One of her first acts was to bring in a team of specialists from the elite Vulnerable Points Wing, Field Security Police, to guard the area immediately around the mansion. Their mantra was "Be professional, be polite, and have a plan to kill everyone you encounter." They were motivated and armed to the teeth, they had attack dogs, and they lived their motto.

On paper the Security Police worked for Major Randal, but in practice they were answerable only to themselves.

Overall security for the county in which Seaborn House was located was the responsibility of the 2nd Battalion Somerset Light Infantry. The

Somerset's primary mission was to repulse the Nazi assault from the sea that was expected at any moment. The battalion was woefully small and lightly armed for such a major undertaking. But they were all that was available.

Backing up the Somerset Light Infantry and forming the first layer of security was the local unit of the Home Guard. Primarily intended to be used in an antiparachutist role, the local Home Guard unit was composed of volunteer boys too young and men too old for active service, with a few members being officers of various grades up to the rank of general biding their time in the unit while awaiting assignment.

The HG operating on the Seaborn estate was an eclectic band of merry men armed with every conceivable type of weapon imaginable, from pikes to elephant guns. They wore makeshift uniforms that dated back to the battle of Khartoum. One private was a long-retired lieutenant general in his eighties whose weapon of choice was a seven iron.

The local wags nicknamed the Home Guard the "Dawn Patrol" because of their early morning sweeps looking for any signs of enemy parachutists who might have dropped in overnight. There were three types of aerial invaders the Dawn Patrol looked to encounter.

The first and most likely were Luftwaffe personnel who bailed out of shot-up aircraft. During daylight hours the Home Guard maintained observation posts scattered around the county connected by landline communications, and woe be to any enemy pilot or aircrew seen floating down.

RAF personnel who had to parachute to safety had best make their identify known quickly, because the Dawn Patrol had a propensity to shoot first—or more accurately pitch fork first—and ask questions later.

The second type of aerial invaders was agents of the dreaded enemy Fifth Column. Though rumor had it the Abwer's favored method of inserting its operatives was to disguise them as nuns, not a single incident of one actually being apprehended anywhere in England had been recorded to date. That inconvenient fact did nothing to quash the rumors, and the Dawn Patrol was particularly vigilant in their quest for nuns wearing jump boots.

The last group of aerial invaders consisted of the clouds of *Fallschirm-jägers* who were expected to be dropped in advance of any seaborne landing to secure the area immediately behind the beachhead. When that happened, the Home Guard was in trouble. The German jumpers were hardened combat veterans trained to a razor's edge and would come in hot.

Military security is conducted on a "need to know" basis, and the operational plans for combating German infiltrators were highly compartmentalize. A Most Secret operation, called Operation Blue Boot, was in play to identify and trap Nazi infiltrators. This was known to the Field Security Police, the Somerset Light Infantry, and the local Home Guard but not to members of Raiding Forces except Major John Randal.

Major Randal had been briefed on the operation, but had thought it was a joke. Counterintelligence was the last thing on his mind as he made his way up from the dock to Seaborn House. Sergeant Major Maurice Chauncy, Green Howards, his former butler who had been recalled to the colors though he was long past the age for active service, was there to greet him when he came in the main entry of the manor house.

"Good morning, sir. Would you care for a cup of tea?"

"Can you run me up to the Security Police checkpoint, Sergeant Major?"

"Certainly sir," the Green Howard responded crisply. "I shall arrange for the Bentley to be brought around straightaway."

As they rode up to the checkpoint, Major Randal asked, "Any word from Lady Jane?"

"No sir, she and Royal Marine Plum-Martin appear to have vanished from the face of the earth."

"Whatever they're up to, it's probably trouble."

"Captian, Lady Seaborn does have a way of keeping life interesting, sir."

"Yes, she does."

When the limousine approached the checkpoint, the officer commanding the detachment of the Field Security Police, Captain Malcom

Chatterhorn, stepped out of the small guard station that had been con-structed to keep the sentry manning the red-and-white barber's pole out of the elements. The shack also housed a pair of Bren light machine guns and a store of ammunition. Two more Bren gun positions were covering the checkpoint, one out in plain sight and one not. The station was sand-bagged, and concertina wire had been strategically placed around it to channel anyone approaching into preplanned fields of fire.

Major Randal stepped out of the Bentley and returned his chief of security's salute. He did not know the thirty-six-year-old former member of Scotland Yard, Security Branch, well, but in the short time the Field Security team had been assigned he had come to admire the officer for his dedication, attention to detail, and professionalism. They stood in the road chatting as the sun broke through the early morning fog.

In the distance across the fields a small troop of the Dawn Patrol could be seen making their way toward the road after completing a rou-tine early morning anti-infiltrator sweep. Walking beside the road at a point where he would soon intersect the patrol's path was a lone trooper of the Somerset Light Infantry. The soldier was bareheaded and appeared to be unarmed.

One of the Security Police standing behind the striped barber's pole was routinely studying the Home Guard patrol through a pair of binocu-lars. Then he swung over to inspect the Somerset Light Infantryman.

"Blue boot on the road, sir," the guard barked, There was a rattle of equipment as the other security policemen instantly roused themselves and went on a state of full alert.

Captain Chatterhorn abruptly stopped what he was saying in mid-sentence and demanded incredulously, "Give me those bloody glasses!"

Without knowing why, Major Randal clicked on.

Out in the field the Dawn Patrol seemed to take notice of the soldier strolling along. The trooper waved at the Home Guardsmen. The patrol raised their weapons and without any advanced warning, commenced fire. One ragged volley, which apparently missed, was followed by a second that did not.

"What the hell?" Major Randal had no idea what was going on. Had he just witnessed a cold-blooded murder? Had the Home Guard gone mad?

He and Captain Chatterhorn, accompanied by two members of the Security Police, jogged up the road to where the shooting had occurred. The Home Guard charged across the muddy field and surrounded their downed victim. The patrol members were waving their weapons and shouting in jubilation.

The shot-up soldier looked like a piece of hamburger. The man was riddled with everything from fine No. 8 birdshot to a .566 solid. He was dead.

"Notice anything unusual, Major?" Captain Chatterhorn inquired as they slowed to quick time and walked up on the body now surrounded by the celebrating band of Dawn Patrol men.

"A KIA Somerset," Major Randal said. "How are we going to explain that?"

"Take a gander at that man's boots," the Security Policeman prodded. "What do you see?"

"One of them is blue. Looks like he stepped in a vat of paint."

"Operation Blue Boot," Captain Chatterhorn explained, lighting a Player cigarette and blowing out the smoke in a long slow stream. "I never expected it to produce any actual results.

"Nice work, lads," he called to the Home Guard patrol. "A ruddy great story to tell the grandkids, only you shall have to wait till it's declassified after the war."

"Operation Blue Boot?" Major Randal dimly recalled having heard the name. "Refresh my memory?"

"Counterintelligence is feeding Jerry the story covertly, through back channels, that every soldier in the Invasion Zone has one of his boots painted blue as a rapid identification device," Captain Chatterhorn explained with a perfectly straight face.

"I see."

"The idea was to trick the Germans into dropping their secret agents into England with one of their boots painted blue. It's an authentication symbol all right. Our orders are to shoot anybody wearing one blue boot on sight, no questions asked."

"You're kidding."

"Nobody actually believed it would ever work, especially PWE. We never thought the Germans would fall for it.

"Blue Boot," Major Randal. "I thought it was a joke."

"So did we, sir." Captain Chatterhorn agreed. "You are looking at a dead Nazi infiltrator, Major. I bet he was surprised."

"I sure was," Major Randal said. "Whoever came up with the idea is a genius."

The Home Guard patrol leader was a distinguished looking gentleman in knee-high rubber boots and a tweed jacket. He was a major general who had commanded a division on the Western Front in the last war, and it was rumored he was in line to be given command of a mechanized corps in the Middle East—when it was formed. The patrol leader saluted, "One German Fifth Columnist deceased, Major."

"You really lit him up all right," Major Randal said, returning the old soldier's salute. "We've got a dozen or so Enfields sitting in our arms room gathering dust. Do you think you Guardsmen could put 'em to use, Corporal?"

"Absolutely! Increase our firepower, what? Most generous of you to make the offer. We shall accept with pleasure."

"Raiding Forces is preparing to move out on a training exercise," Major Randal lied. "When we get back, what if I have a couple of my men come down to work with your troops. Fine-tune their infantry skills, maybe go along on some of your patrols?"

"Marvelous! Joint operations in the field. Jolly good! We shall look forward to it, Major."

"I'll have the rifles sent round this afternoon. No need for you boys to be carrying any more golf clubs."

"Let's not be too hasty about retiring the bludgeons," the old warrior retorted with a twinkle in his rheumy eye. "One would hate to stand down all that arduous practice we have laid on at the club designed to polish one's swing on the pretense of training to put the wood to a Jerry, what!"

"Right," Major Randal said. "Carry on."

4

COMMAND GUIDANCE

ON IMPULSE, MAJOR JOHN RANDAL STOPPED BY THE OPERATIONS Room. The debriefing of the Lovat Scouts sniper team had been concluded by the time he arrived. The team was where he wanted to be right this minute—asleep.

Lieutenant Karen Montgomery, the officer on duty, was the only person in the room. He had not seen her since the night Raiding Forces took off from the departure airfield on Operation Tomcat.

Captain the Lady Jane Seaborn had recruited the confident, vivacious woman from the Parachute Training School where she was working as a parachute rigger and had arranged to have her commissioned in the Royal Marines. The original idea was for Raiding Forces to have its own self-contained parachute packing section. Now she was also pulling duty as one of the watch officers.

Always ready with a quick comeback, which made her the center of a lot of teasing that she could take as well as dish out, the officer was a lot of fun to be around. In her short time with Raiding Forces, she had proven tremendously capable at any task assigned.

"Good morning, Major," Lieutenant Montgomery gushed.

Major Randal did a double take to see if she was as emotional as she sounded. "I'd like a quick briefing, Karen, on your end of Buzzard Plucker, then I'm going to have a hot shower and a couple hours' sleep before heading into the city."

"Yes sir," the usually high-spirited Royal Marine officer responded with what sounded like a lump in her throat. "Before I begin, sir, I simply have to tell you how terribly dreadful it was to stand idly by and watch Raiding Forces fly off on the Tomcat mission."

The girl actually seemed teary-eyed. This was not good.

"Karen, are you okay?"

"Yes sir, only I never actually witnessed anything like that before. The Raiders looked so brave and determined when they climbed on board those airplanes. The scene was dreadful but magnificent. And now the lads are barely back and have already been put on alert for another mission to who knows where."

"Well, that's what we do."

"I know, sir. I feel anxious when the Lovats launch too. I always worry they might not come back."

Major Randal realized he was in a military situation he had no training for. No women had been in his old outfit the U.S. 26th Cavalry, The Rangers, or Swamp Fox Force. It was clear Lieutenant Montgomery required some command guidance, but he did not know exactly how to proceed, and right now he was exhausted.

Nevertheless, Major Randal gave it his best shot.

"Karen, here's how it works in Raiding Forces. Terry Stone recruited our first intake of men. Since he was from the Household Cavalry he went after cavalrymen. Naturally Raiding Forces took on a lot of the traditions of a cavalry regiment. That is until Sergeant Major Hicks arrived, and then we started doing some things like the Grenadier Guards."

"'If you are on time,'" Lieutenant Montgomery quoted, "'you are five minutes late.'"

"Right. In cavalry regiments, the officers call each other by their first names—everyone, that is, except for the regimental commander, whom they address by his rank."

The striking cinnamon-haired beauty nodded, wondering where this was going.

"So here's the deal, Karen. In Raiding Forces, all the officers call each other by their rank when they're performing military duties involving the troops. They call each other by their first names at all other times, regardless of rank; except for me, who they call either Major or sir, got that?"

"Yes sir."

"Now, I didn't feel that was exactly fair. So I modified the protocol slightly. Since Raiding Forces is not a cavalry regiment and since I get to make the rules, what I came up with is a policy that if there is just one or two of us officers alone, they call me John. Got it?"

"Yes sir . . . I mean John."

"Except I can't get Randy to do it."

Lieutenant Montgomery laughed.

"Now, Karen, what the hell are you so worked up about?"

She could not help but be amused at his abrupt change of pace and the cut to the chase. "John, it was frightful to watch Raiding Forces board the airplanes and fly away not knowing what was going to happen to all of you. I cried. Jane cried after the planes took off . . . John, she cried a lot. Even Pamala wept a bit, and I never thought I would ever see her shed a tear over anything. A few of the RAF airmen at the airfield looked like they had cinders in their eyes too."

"Karen, how many jumps have you made?"

"Seventy-four."

"Did you know the day we first met that I had a really bad case of the pre-jump jitters?"

"You did?"

"Absolutely. Then I saw you wearing jump wings, passing out parachutes, and saying things like 'Bring it back if it doesn't work.' I thought to myself, if she can do it I can do it. There's no telling how many people you've inspired by example."

"I never knew that!"

"Your role, among other things, is to see the troops off on dangerous operations. But Karen, *you're* not sending the men on the mission. *I am.*

"Keep in mind, you're not doing anyone a favor if you let you them see you sad or in tears. Be the high-spirited rigger girl who tagged Terry with the nickname 'Zorro.'"

"That was an accident. He does look like Errol Flynn, but Errol Flynn never played the role of Zorro."

"Well, it's too late to straighten it out now."

"Major . . . ah . . . John, thanks. I guess I never realized the amount of responsibility you have to carry around. Promise, I will never let you down."

"See that you don't."

"Are you simply devastated one of the Raiders was killed?"

Major Randal knew he was supposed to be, but the fact was he felt nothing; he only felt cold. That was it. Taking such heavy casualities at Calais had taken its toll on his emotions. He would not have wanted her or anyone else to know the truth: He did not feel a thing.

"By the way, Karen," Major Randal said, wanting to change the subject. "That day when you told everyone Jane said Terry looked like Errol Flynn you never got around to saying how she described me."

"I promised Lady Jane," Lieutenant Montgomery began, beginning to get her old Parachute School personality back, "I would never tell, even under torture."

"Right. Where is Jane now?"

"Shortly after Raiding Forces went wheels up, she was summoned to take a phone call in the airfield operations center. Then she and Pamala dashed off in her Rolls Royce. I have not seen or heard from either of them since."

"Okay, give me a quick report."

"Yes sir," Lieutenant Montgomery said, suddenly sounding crisp and professional. "We currently have four Lovat Scout teams available for operations. To date, there have been thirteen Buzzard Plucker missions resulting in nineteen confirmed enemy pilot kills.

"There are no teams in the field at present due to Raiding Forces being on alert for an upcoming operation.

"The Scouts report beefed-up security at the landing grounds as a direct response to our attacks. The Luftwaffe's reaction to Buzzard Plucker has been to add more security personnel to the flight lines and around the perimeter of the airfields, and to place additional guards in the watchtowers. However, none of their efforts has significantly curtailed the Scouts' ability to continue the mission.

"To adequately secure even the smallest landing ground, best estimates are it would require the efforts of at least two full companies of infantry. Since we have already identified more than twelve hundred Luftwaffe landing grounds in occupied France, with more under construction, the number of German troops needed to prevent us from striking them would be something like four hundred thousand men, which is impossible. The Nazis do not have that kind of manpower to devote to guarding static positions. Not only are we killing valuable pilots, Raiding Forces is making the Germans tie down valuable troops they could use elsewhere."

"What do you attribute all our good luck to?"

"The Lovats are marvelously talented at what they do, the landing grounds are vulnerable targets, and careful target selection all play a part.

"Operation Limelight may be distracting the Germans away from the Scouts' real target. I think dropping parachutes weighted down by blocks of ice is outrageously funny and totally brilliant. The idea of forcing the German Security Forces to conduct massive search operations for phantom parachutists is marvelous. Talk about melting away into the night."

"Those PWE people are geniuses," Major Randal agreed, thinking about a certain dead Nazi infiltrator wearing a blue painted boot.

"PWE even conduct their own private pre-mission briefings and post-mission debriefings of the Lovat teams, sir."

"Why would they do that?"

"Compartmentalization. PWE is giving the Lovats additional secret tasks to carry out on a need to know basis. Only the Scouts on the team have knowledge of what those specific tasks are for any given mission, in case anyone on another team is ever captured and interrogated. The PWE portion of Buzzard Plucker is a Most Secret operation within a Most Secret operation. It's all very hush-hush."

"Karen," Major Randal demanded, "you know there aren't that many secrets in Raiding Forces. What kind of tasks?"

"Well, I have heard the Scouts are being asked to leave behind certain items after they pull out of their hide position when they move to the extraction point. Things like a metal button off a Wehrmacht uniform, some pigeon feathers, field gray thread that looks like it came off a Nazi uniform, a crumpled letter written in German, and other odd bits and pieces of enemy rations or equipment.

"PWE may be trying to fool the Reich Security Forces into believing dissident German soldiers are shooting their own pilots—it's probably an add-on to Operation Whistle, and highly classified. I should not be discussing it."

"That's okay," Major Randal said. "We're not having this conversation."

"What conversation?" Lieutenant Montgomery asked with a conspiratorial wink.

"Anything else I need to know?"

"Carrier pigeons. Every team of Lovats now carries two birds. Each bird rides in a little round cardboard container that looks something like the can tennis balls come in, except holes have been punched in it so they can breathe. When the Scouts want to send a message, they simply write it out, place it in a tiny capsule, attach it to the bird's leg, and release the pigeon.

"When the bird flies home, it goes into its little apartment up on the roof here at Seaborn House, causing a buzzer to sound and a red light to come on here in the operations room to alert us to retrieve the message."

"Whose idea was that?" Major Randal asked. *Were the live pigeons with real messages a PWE stratagem intended to set up the ploy of the dead ones with fake messages being dropped by Squadron Leader Paddy Wilcox during Operation Whistle?* The spy-versus-spy intrigue could be confusing. Thinking about it gave him a headache.

"I am not quite sure. Lady Seaborn simply arrived one day with a truckload of pigeons in crates, accompanied by a professional pigeon fancier, and we were in business."

"Carry on, Lieutenant," Major Randal ordered in a tired voice as he turned to leave.

"John, is it true you shot five Germans on Tomcat?"

"I wasn't supposed to."

Out in the hall he almost crashed into a tall shapely Royal Marine lieutenant swishing along in her jodhpurs and riding boots.

"Welcome back, John."

"Parker, what are you doing here?" Royal Marine Lieutenant Penelope
Honeycutt-Parker, universally called Parker by her friends, was Brandy
Seaborn's close friend who had served as her deckhand when the two of
them took the Seaborn houseboat to rescue troops from the beaches of
Dunkirk. Having made five such forays, she and Brandy were legitimate
national heroines.

"I work for you now, and this is my first day on duty. I'm on my way
to relieve Karen."

"I see."

"Jane needed help at the exact same time the War Ministry announced
they were inaugurating a draft of women under the age of forty. Somehow
I simply could not picture myself changing a tire on a truck or chauffeur-
ing some boring brass hat around London all day," Parker drawled. "So
here I am . . . besides, my Royal Dragoon husband received his marching
orders for Egypt and I was at loose ends."

"Have much experience cleaning out pigeon cages?"

"You know better than that."

"Anyone else Jane recruited besides you and Chauncy?"

"Brandy declined on the grounds it would probably be bad form for
Raiding Force's only naval officer to have his mother serving in his unit,
particularly if he outranked her. We have to hurry and find something for
her soon before she gets drafted. Can you imagine the damage loading
one of those ack-ack guns would do to one's nails?"

"You'll come up with something, to keep her out of the trenches."

"Thanks for allowing me come on board, John," Lieutenant Honeycutt-Parker smiled.

"Jane's MIA. Do you have any idea where she is?"

"I was going to ask you. I haven't heard from her in ages."

"The last time I saw her was just before we flew off to jump on Tomcat," Major John Randal said. "Have you been issued a sidearm?"

"A Colt .38 Super automatic," the Royal Marine said. "A lot easier to shoot than my father's old service pistol."

"Good, go put it on and keep it on."

"Yes sir."

Command has its privileges, but it also carries responsibilities. Exhausted as he was, Major John Randal went in search of his former butler one more time before going to his room.

"Sergeant Major," he ordered, "while Raiding Forces is on deployment, I want you to make sure the female Royal Marines carry personal weapons at all times."

"Sir!"

"Have them spend one hour per day on the pistol range. You supervise, make 'em work hard, and don't let anyone pull rank on you to get out of it. I'll put it in writing."

"That will not be necessary, sir."

"Yeah, well, probably not, but I'll have the order drafted anyway. I want those Marines armed and able to defend themselves. Any woman can't handle a full-sized service pistol, issue her one of the High Standard .22's without a silencer."

"I shall see to it personally, sir," Sergeant Major Maurice Chauncy vowed. "Request permission to provide the ladies the details of Operation Blue Boot, sir?"

"Go ahead," Major Randal said. "We'll just have to hope nobody around here accidentally steps into a bucket of blue paint."

5

LEAD OFF HITTER

BRANDY SEABORN HAD ARRANGED A QUIET, PRIVATE DINNER FOR Major John Randal and herself at the Bradford Hotel in London. Discretion at the Bradford was something the hotel staff had refined to an art form, and they could have given the secret services of the world's major nations lessons on the subject. The moment the turbaned waiter had poured their wine and vanished, the golden girl cut straight to the chase.

"John, I am what you Americans would describe as the leadoff hitter for the Seaborn family tonight. Since everyone in the family knows how particularly special I feel about you, it was agreed I would be the best of the mob to undertake this little powwow."

"I see," Major Randal replied carefully. A master of the art of laying ambushes, he had the uneasy feeling he might have walked into one tonight.

"John, the Seaborns are a member of what is described as the Six Hundred, an exclusive group of British families of the upper-upper class who control the empire and are defined by their enormous wealth, incalculable influence, and unflinching service to the crown. One does not volunteer to be a member of the Six Hundred; it is virtually impossible to achieve your way in. To be a member one must be born in.

"Mostly we in the Six Hundred tend to marry within our circle, which accounts for why the number of families remains more or less constant. There are two branches of the Seaborn family tree: the branch I married into and the branch Jane married into. Both of our own families, of course, were already counted among the Six Hundred.

"Jane's husband, Mallory, and my husband, Richard, were first cousins and best friends, though Mallory was younger than Richard and junior by one grade. Both of them dearly loved serving in the Navy. When Mallory was lost at sea, Richard was completely devastated. I am not certain, to be perfectly honest, if he is ever going to fully recover."

"I see," Major Randal said again, wondering what Brandy was building up to.

"Being a member of the Six Hundred can be a high-risk proposition at times," Brandy pressed on, not allowing herself to be diverted with small talk. "Quite a lot is expected of our men—to rule the empire, to be captains of industry, and to lead in battle. Unlike nearly all other countries, Britain expects men of the ruling class to serve in time of war and to do so at the sharp end.

"Eleven Seaborn men either failed to return home from the last war or came home so badly broken they died within a few years from their wounds. We Seaborns cannot afford any more victories like the last one.

"Mallory was the last male under the age of sixty surviving on his branch. Richard and his brother were the last two on his side of the family. Seaborn men have a bad habit of getting bowled over like tenpins. There will simply not be enough of our men left to sustain the family name. That is why I worry so much about Dickie."

"Dickie?"

"Richard, my husband."

"He has a nice safe staff job. You don't worry about Randy?"

"Randy may bear the Seaborn name, but he is really a Ransom, which means he is a born fire-eater. Randy will thrive in this war. He is like my father, the 'Razor.'"

"He's a hard charger, all right," Major Randal agreed.

"As for the Six Hundred women, we are not permitted to complain, grieve much, or act like we have any real feelings at all. We are expected to keep a stiff upper lip, to cope no matter how difficult it gets and to simply get on with it. And never ever, under any circumstances, are we to show any overt emotion in public other than joy.

"In our tightly cloistered society, John, we do things differently than you are used to in America. Many marriages in the Six Hundred, meaning virtually all of them, are arranged for expediency, advancement, to combine great estates or to continue the line. Love does not play all that much of a role. The important thing is to make the right marriage. One has one's responsibilities and one must not let the side down.

"From the time she was a little girl, it was accepted that Jane would marry Mallory. He was twelve years older and, of course, they had known each other all their lives. They were a good match; it was a sensible union. And in the end, that is what really matters.

"Jane and Mallory were married two years before the war began. Mallory's ship put to sea the day hostilities broke out. He never returned home. Stuka dive-bombers caught his destroyer, the HMS *Wind*, off Norway and sank her with all hands. There were no survivors.

"I can still remember the day Jane received the telegram from the Admiralty as if it were yesterday. The experience was simply ghastly.

"Which brings us to the point in my story where Mallory's dead, Jane is a widow, and you arrive on the scene. I suspect you wonder where I am going with this." Brandy stopped talking suddenly and blazed away at him with her spectacular golden girl smile.

"You do have my attention," Major Randal admitted.

"Has Jane ever mentioned her uncle to you—Colonel John Henry Bevins?"

"The stockbroker?"

Brandy laughed. "To describe Johnny Bevins as a stockbroker is comparable to describing a Rolls Royce as a family automobile. Johnny is one of the financial advisers to the royal family and a close personal friend and intimate of Winston Churchill. Johnny also advises several European nations—and possibly China, I believe—on their investment portfolios."

"Jane said he was a stockbroker."

"She would! Johnny won the Military Cross while serving with the Hertfordshire Regiment. He is one of only three survivors of the Great War from his entire class at Eton. Nowadays he is back on active duty again, in charge of intelligence for the Western Command after returning from active service in the Norwegian campaign. The colonel is like a father to Jane and he worships her.

"Johnny has managed her affairs since her parents were killed in an airplane crash in Kenya years ago, and he is currently in the process of sorting out Mallory's estate."

Brandy reached across the candlelit table and took his hand in both of hers. "Jane is going to invite you to have dinner with him sometime in the very near future.

"You should understand, John," Brandy pressed on, "that when she asks you, it is not a casual event. In our circle, when a man—but most especially, when a woman—brings someone with whom they have a romantic interest to meet the family, it is a serious matter indeed. When Jane takes you to meet her uncle, the Seaborn family wants you to go mindful that you have our full Good Housekeeping Seal of Approval."

If Mrs. Brandy Seaborn had taken out a hand grenade, pulled the pin, and plopped it in a soup bowl on the table, he could not have been more completely blown away.

"Well, Brandy, you just threw me a curve ball," Major Randal said. "It sounded like you were getting ready to tell me Jane was out of my league."

"While I do not have even the vaguest idea what a curve ball is, John, the family *was* afraid that you might draw the conclusion we would feel that way. In the past we would have. But this war has largely changed how we feel about the future to the point of our even wondering if there is going to be a future. Who knows how long it will last or how many more Seaborns are going to die defending our way of life, not letting the side down? The family talked it over and our wish is for Jane to be happy."

"I see," Major Randal repeated once more, something he always said when he did not have a clue what to say.

"John, we had all better live life right now while we have the chance. If the Germans invade and conquer England, as it appears they most certainly will, the Six Hundred have quietly been informed we have been placed on Hitler's death list. Something evil called the *Sonderfahndungsliste G.B.*

"The Nazi plan is to deport us to the Continent where we will be handed over to Dept. IV B.4 of the Reich Security Office, put into concentration camps, then liquidated. We Six Hundred are literally fighting for our lives."

"How did your husband vote?"

"Dickie, ah . . . Richard, officially abstained as I recall," Brandy responded with a distant look in her golden eyes, not ducking his question. "One cannot blame him, actually. Remember, Mallory was like his younger brother. What is important to note is that Richard did not object.

"My advice, as your dear friend, is to take your time with Jane. She has experienced more heartbreak and tragedy than most. Trust in long-term relationships is not easy for Jane; hers have had such calamitous endings."

"Brandy, what makes you think Jane has any interest in me?"

"I have known Jane for her entire life. She is like my beautiful little sister. Trust me on this, John; women know these things."

"You mean like intuition?"

"Well . . . you make her laugh. Laughter is very important in a relationship. Jane did not smile, hardly ever, after Mallory was killed. Randy says when she is around you she laughs nearly all the time. Believe me, we all took notice at Randy's promotion party. "

"That seems fairly thin, Brandy."

" She gave you Mallory's watch. The reason Jane gave you the Rolex, you know, was so you would think about her every single time you look at it. Women do things like that; it's how we think."

"Still doesn't mean Jane wants to introduce me to her uncle," Major Randal objected, "for any other reason than so that he can meet the village idiot."

"If a woman makes a man feel foolish—like the village idiot, as you put it—the man would be wise to take it as a sign she is paying close attention to him," Brandy explained. "All women like to see men they are interested in struggle."

"They do?"

"Oh, yes," Brandy explained with a sparkle in her eyes. "Particularly men like you who do not seem like the struggling kind. We like that the best of all."

"Are you poking fun at me?"

"Oh no, John! Well, maybe a little."

"You're just guessing," Randal said. "Jane hasn't actually told anyone what she thinks about me."

What Jane had told Brandy was that she really enjoyed being with the American officer, but she was not sure if he was very smart. Neither she nor Brandy considered not being very smart much of a drawback in a man, however.

Since she definitely could not tell him that story, Brandy said, "I cannot reveal anything Jane told me about you directly. That would be breaking a confidence. On the other hand, it would not be violating a trust, would it, if I tell you something Jane said to someone else about you and then that person told me?"

"You sure you didn't go to law school?"

"If I do tell, John," Brandy leaned forward and whispered conspiratorially, "you have to reveal to me some Most Secret, 'if you tell anyone else you have to kill them' kind of thing, that has happened between you and Jane."

"Like what, Brandy?"

"Has she ever caused you to do something completely crazy, or have you two ever done anything that was totally out of character, where you felt like you were spinning completely out of control?"

"Well, I . . . . ah, stopped a train to call Jane."

"How could you possibly make a train stop?"

"A secret code word—it's a long story."

"All right, you stopped a train, then what?"

"Then I got off and phoned her office."

"This is terrific, John. Did you have something hugely important to say to her?"

"No."

"Really, what happened?"

"Well, instead of being impressed, Jane just started giggling."

Brandy's sparkling eyes got big. "Oh, that's good."

"That I stopped a train to make a phone call?"

"No, John," Brandy exclaimed breathlessly. "A giggle is a dead giveaway."

"It is?" Major Randal asked doubtfully. "Well, I don't know—"

"Take my word for it. A woman does not giggle at a man unless she is head-over-heels about him or does not care about him at all, and I happen to know she is mad about you, John. This is good," Brandy repeated solemnly. "Trust me, this is definitely good."

"Now, want to hear the crazy, out-of-control part?" Major Randal asked, looking straight into Brandy's golden eyes. "After I got back on the train, a few minutes later it was all I could do to keep from stopping it again and calling her back from the next station just to hear her giggle one more time."

"Oh, I love you, John Randal," Brandy laughed, her eyes dancing in the candlelight. "I do. It took a real man to tell that story. I am having the most fun!"

"You're not going to make me regret this, are you?" Major Randal asked, already regretting it.

"I shall accept the cigarette, they will have to give me a blindfold, naturally, but even when they stand me against the pockmarked wall, I shall never tell." Brandy put her hand over her heart. "Girl Guide's honor."

"Somehow I have a hard time picturing you in a Girl Guide uniform. Your turn, Brandy," Major Randal said, wishing he had not told her the whole story. Brandy Seaborn had that kind of affect on him; she was like a hypnotic drug.

"John, you have to promise me you will never reveal to a soul what I am about to say to you," Brandy pleaded. "If you do I shall be a dead woman."

"You have my word."

"Pamala told me you were the most terrific looking man she had ever seen," Brandy said, nodding her wheat-colored head. "Now that is a BIG compliment coming from her."

"Royal Marine Plum-Martin said Jane told her that?"

"No, that's what Pamala said about you," Brandy laughed. "She and Jane met you at the train station when you came back from Commando exercises in Scotland. You were wearing your new green beret and must have been through some really rugged training because she said you looked 'tough as hell' and without a doubt you were 'the sexiest man alive.'"

"What does that have to do with Jane?"

"When you were getting off the train, Jane told Pamala that being around you always made her feel dizzy."

"Does Jane know we're having this dinner?"

Brandy artfully dodged the question. "I have been trying to talk to Jane for two days but have not been able to get in touch with her, which is very unusual. I was surprised she was not at Seaborn House to welcome you home. Where is she, John?"

"I have no idea."

"Well, too bad for Jane. She is missing great fun tonight."

"Tell me something, Brandy. If you don't understand what a curve ball is, how did you know what a leadoff hitter was?"

"Richard told me to explain it to you that way."

"Brandy, you didn't make that dizzy part up, did you?"

"No, I most certainly did not!" the golden girl retorted indignantly. "I have the clear impression, Johnny Randal, you have had quite a lot of experience with women but you do not know the first thing about relationships. I believe you and Jane are perfect for each other. I thought it the first time I saw you two together. Everyone knows it . . . except you. Quite possibly you may be the village idiot!"

6

AIR RAID

AFTER DINNER MAJOR JOHN RANDAL HAD ESCORTED BRANDY BACK to her room. Then he returned to his suite, turned off the lights, pulled back the heavy blackout curtains, and took in a panoramic view of wartime London at night. Relaxed in a big overstuffed chair with his feet propped up on the coffee table, he sat well back from the wall-sized picture window just to be safe.

Major Randal was not worried about bomb blast from the nightly air raids that had been going on for several months now. The hotel was not a target. The Luftwaffe had only been attacking strategic targets in the dock area. What concerned him was some overzealous Air Raid Warden patrolling the street below spotting the glowing tip of his cigarette and drawing the conclusion he was a Fifth Columnist trying to signal the streams of German bombers flying overhead. It was a ridiculous idea, but the warden might charge him with a blackout violation, a serious offense. Stranger things had happened.

Wartime London was a spectacular light show. Hundreds upon hundreds of tall stately shafts of silver-white searchlight crisscrossed the ink-black night as far as the eye could see, swaying back and forth hoping to pinpoint an enemy aircraft. Occasionally, one beam would pick up something—or seem to—and then the other tall pencil-thin beams would race each other across the sky to investigate.

After a few minutes, the operators of the searchlights would lose interest and go back to their random searching pattern, but occasionally they did manage to capture a hostile intruder in their beam; then the fireworks began. Immediately, an intense barrage from light and medium antiaircraft guns erupted. The action was terribly exciting for a few minutes, working up to a crescendo; then, just as quickly, the ack-ack would die down and trickle off to the occasional WHAM! of a lone antiaircraft artillery piece firing a defiant shot.

Overhead, high-performance engines screamed. Machine guns mounted on the rooftops of tall buildings crackled, emitting dazzling strings of tracers. Bullets are thought to fly in straight lines, but these always seemed to curve in one direction or the other. Some flew sideways and others zigzagged wildly.

Nothing ever appeared to be hit, though how any aircraft could fly through such an impenetrable wall of steel would be anyone's guess. Major Randal sat swirling his drink in a deep-cut Waterford crystal glass and took in the show.

Suddenly, directly in front of the hotel approximately half a mile out, a stick of bombs came down and detonated with a massive WHUUMP-WHUUMP-WHUUMP-WHUUMP! Shock waves emanated from each blast as they marched straight toward the Bradford.

A siren wailed.

"Incoming," Sergeant Major Chauncy announced.

Major Randal was caught woefully unprepared, wearing a pair of the Bradford Hotel's monogrammed silk pajamas and the elegant monogrammed silk robe Sergeant Major Chauncy had laid out for him. He had humored the old fellow by actually getting into it. Now he frantically pulled on his Bloods-made Wellington dress boots, grabbed his Colt .38 Super in its shoulder holster off the mahogany coffee table, slung it over his arm and ran out into the hall. The sergeant major was already there waiting with a hooded flashlight.

Outside, the air attack intensified. In the hall there was pandemonium in the yellow dimness created by the interior lighting. A human stampede was going full bore.

"Walk, do not run! Move to the east staircase," hotel staff waving hooded flashlights were instructing the guests calmly amid the chaos, the epitome of buttoned-down calm in the eye of a storm. "Walk, do not run. Do not take the lift. Move to the east staircase. Walk, do not run . . . "

Frightened guests in various stages of undress were screaming and running blindly for the exit, ignoring the instructions. For most this was their first actual experience at being bombed, and they were trampling each other in the novelty of a real air raid aimed at them, not some distant target.

As Major Randal moved rapidly with the crowd toward the east staircase, he bumped shoulders with a good-looking woman. It was Brandy. "Brandy, are you okay?"

"I rather twisted my ankle, John," she replied calmly, in obvious pain. Badly it seems—someone stepped on it."

"Can you walk?"

"No. It hurts!"

By now they were alone in the deserted corridor. The mindless thundering herd of frightened hotel guests had all disappeared down the stairway.

"We have to go, sir," Sergeant Major Chauncy implored urgently. "Now!"

Major Randal quickly picked up the slim woman and threw her over his shoulder. Her surprised reaction sounded like "whooof."

"Sorry, Brandy, hang on."

Down the corridor they went, fast, and Major Randal took the stairs two at a time. Sergeant Major Chauncy was right behind him, matching him step for step all the way. Brandy shrieked at every bounce for the entire six flights down to the lobby, plus the one to the bomb shelter in the basement. Once there, Major Randal carried her over to a couch positioned along one wall of the shelter and laid her on it.

"Quite the fashion statement," Brandy quipped, beginning to recover her famous sense of humor. "Silk robe and shoulder holster—do you always wear your pistol to bed, John?"

"Little insurance against parachuting Nazis disguised as nuns."

Having already been summoned, the hotel doctor arrived shortly thereafter and began examining Brandy's injured ankle. Sergeant Major Chauncy brought Major Randal a tall glass of water.

"You looked pretty good there, Sergeant Major," Major Randal said, lighting a cigarette with his old battered Zippo, which sported the crossed sabers of the U.S. 26th Cavalry embossed in gold. "I thought you were going to pass me when we hit the second landing."

"Amazing, sir, what one can do with aerial bombs pranging away."

"You got that right."

The all clear did not sound for three hours. Major Randal was really glad he had drawn the line at wearing the white silk Bradford hotel ascot, with its large gold monogrammed B.

7

WILD AND CRAZY GUY

BRIGHT AND EARLY THE NEXT MORNING MAJOR JOHN RANDAL was sitting alone in the breakfast room of the Bradford Hotel waiting for Major Lawrence "Larry" Grand, Chief of the Special Operations Executive Section D (Destruction), to meet him.

Since the hotel staff were going out of their way to treat him like a long-favored guest, he did not really feel alone. People flocked to his table: a waiter refilled his coffee cup; the doorman left his post and brought him an unsolicited newspaper; the concierge asked if he would like a bootblack to be summoned to give him a shine at the table; the manager inquired if the "evening dinner with Mrs. Seaborn" had been satisfactory. The lift operator even waved at him from across the lobby.

He was getting royal treatment, and he had no idea why.

Major Randal felt as though a time machine had taken him back to the eighteenth century as he looked around the luxurious dining room. Had it not been for the presence of RAF pilots and officers wearing modern Royal Tank Regiment insignia, the illusion would have been complete. The Bradford Hotel was a pleasant place to spend time.

"Morning, John. Sign your chit, the brigadier wants to see us straight-away," the tall major ordered cheerfully as he strolled up to the table, a custom-rolled cigarette in an ivory holder clenched between his teeth.

As usual, Major Grand was impeccably dressed: He was wearing a Saville Row double-breasted, pale gray, pinstriped suit, his signature red carnation in the buttonhole. Topping off the ensemble with dark glasses, he looked, dressed, and acted exactly like the spymaster he was.

The two officers walked out of the Bradford, around the corner, and down the street to the St. Ermins, a building to which Captain the Lady Jane Seaborn had once taken Major Randal. The lift was as rickety as he remembered.

"Go right in, gentlemen, he is waiting for you," the secretary informed them as they entered. "Nice to see you again, Major Randal. We are all quite proud of you, sir."

Brigadier Colin Gubbins, Director of Operations for Special Operations Executive, bounded around his desk to shake hands. "Congratulations on a splendid operation, Major. You definitely obeyed our mandate to set Europe ablaze . . . ha ha! Good show, old boy!"

"Anyone ever find out what caused the lighthouse to go up like that?" Major Randal asked.

"Acetylene," Major Grand explained, "fueled the light. Acetylene burns clean and is not known for its explosive qualities, but it is highly, highly flammable . . . I wish I had been there to see the fireworks."

"Imagine Mount Everest up close, exploding."

"Must have been impressive!"

"Very."

"I know Lawrence has a full morning planned for you, Major, so I shall be brief," Brigadier Gubbins interrupted, cutting straight to the business at hand.

"Strategic Raiding Forces has been tapped for a delicate operation of national importance, one fraught with extremely sensitive political ramifications. If you succeed, no one will ever acknowledge the operation took place. If you fail, it will be front-page news worldwide, and we shall deny we know you. In fact, we shall do our best to make the case you are a rogue mercenary operating freelance, presumably for profit."

Major Randal immediately clicked on.

"Success means that you will save hundreds, if not thousands, of British servicemen's lives and keep our side in the war a while longer. Failure means death or imprisonment in horrible conditions similar to, or worse than, Devil's Island." The brusque brigadier was boring holes in Major Randal with intense eyes that burned as bright as a fire-breathing dragon's. "What say you?"

"Sounds like failure isn't much of an option, sir," Major Randal said.

"With small-scale raiding it seldom is."

Silence hung heavy in the room. "Good man! Failure not an option, I like that—positive thinking, what!"

They were out of the brigadier's room almost as fast as when he and Lady Jane had paid their initial courtesy call. In the lift on the way down, Major Randal remarked, "My two meetings with Brigadier Gubbins together have not totaled ten minutes."

"They say he is a wild one at his club, though," Major Grand replied. "Has a reputation with the ladies."

"Really?"

"Hates meetings!"

They proceeded straight to the major's office next door at 2 Caxton Street. Major Grand did not waste time either. He launched into his briefing immediately.

"To refresh your memory, John, I command Section D, Special Operations Executive. The D stands for destruction, but sometimes we do other things too. Originally, Section D belonged to the Secret Intelligence Service, MI-6, who . . . ah, used to be my employer. Following a vicious backroom power struggle waged at the highest levels of government, Section D was uprooted and transferred to Special Operations Executive after SOE was given the charter to "set Europe ablaze." SIS has remained a purely intelligence-gathering organization, which is their forte.

"A constant battle between the two secret services is being fought out in the thick-carpeted corridors and private, oak-paneled anterooms of Whitehall. One organization has been around three hundred years and the other has not even been around three hundred days, and—ah, well—some feel like Section D was hijacked from SIS in a coup d'etat, causing certain rather hard feelings from the cloak and dagger set at Broadway.

"The old-school SIS conduct clandestine intelligence operations of high sophistication, while SOE is experimenting with bombs disguised as horse droppings. The two cultures clash. One organization takes pains to avoid trouble; the other goes to equally great lengths to cause it.

"Strictly off the record, John, SOE is a frightful potpourri of amateurs, and it is immensely unpopular with the other intelligence services. Somehow we have managed to attract every crackpot in Europe, if not the entire world, to our ranks. SIS is trying to swallow us like a python, and neither the Navy nor the RAF wants to support our operations. Rather hard for one to imagine a worse mess, actually, but we have to press on, muddle through, keep a stiff upper lip, sort it out and all that rot."

Major Randal said, "That's not good."

"Let me give you just the latest example of idiocy I have had to contend with. By official Royal Air Force estimate, in any given twenty-four-hour period, on average, 160 German medium bombers are dropping bombs over London. An elite German Pathfinder squadron made up of the Luftwaffe's most experienced bomber pilots and navigators, called Kampfgeschwader 100, guides the bombers to their targets and then marks the targets for them with high-intensity magnesium air-to-ground flares.

"SOE pinpointed the Pathfinders' airbase outside of Vannes in Brittany, and I developed a plan to ambush the Pathfinder pilots while in transit by bus from their hotel to their airfield prior to a mission."

"Sounds like a great target," Major Randal said. "That why I'm here?"

"No, what I am telling you is old news. We intended to use Free French parachutists for the job, had a team trained and ready to be dropped in. At the very last minute the RAF backed out, refusing us the use of their troop transport aircraft for the mission. The RAF decided, and I quote them as nearly as possible, 'Seems unsportsmanlike to drop armed men in civilian clothes to attack members of a uniformed military force and is not the type of an operation with which the Royal Air Force wishes to associate itself.'

"Naturally we had no choice except to cancel the mission," Major Grand concluded ruefully. "What say you, John?"

"Combat experienced pilots in one bunch are the ultimate high-grade target," Major Randal said. "Exactly the kind I'm looking for."

"Another example of inner-service intrigue—the Navy gave SOE a motor gunboat to do the same kind of cross-Channel stuff you have been doing with your yacht. Guess what? It caught fire and burned up during trials.

"SOE has yet to put a single agent ashore in France by sea, and the rumor is, if the Navy has its way, we never shall. No one actually believes a Royal Navy motor gunboat caught fire in harbor during broad daylight and burned up without some help."

"You think the Navy sabotaged its own boat?"

"No comment. Naturally the Navy has been reluctant to provide us another MGB to incinerate.

"While the whole nation is being bombed into the Stone Age and standing by to be invaded, our response to the onslaught of the evil Nazi peril has been to ramp up inner-service rivalry to a previously unknown fever pitch. The regular military establishment clearly does not wish to support what they contemptuously refer to as 'spy versus spy' adventures. Actually, I do believe there are indeed some misguided individuals who would sabotage what they view as a competing service—hold that thought."

"Roger."

"Now, the reason I have been going to such lengths to bore you with this unhappy tale is because we are planning to send you into a situation where inner-service rivalry, local politics, private agendas, and other competing interests will be more of a direct threat to the success of your mission than the Axis Powers."

"Are you serious?"

"Absolutely. Now, to the main point," Major Grand declared. "Scattered around the globe, John, are a handful of neutral nations. Dotting the world's oceans are islands claimed by these noncombatant countries. Those islands too small to be accorded colony status by the claiming nations are designated 'protectorates.' Most neutral protectorates have at least one port.

"At the outbreak of the war, a number of German and Italian ships were, in the normal course of their duties, caught docked in neutral ports, as were some of our own vessels. They all had to put to sea or face internment.

"Under international law, a ship from a combatant nation may not stay in a neutral port longer than seventy-two hours. If for any reason a ship from a combatant nation does not leave within the proscribed time, it is automatically interned in the port along with its crew for the duration of hostilities, no questions asked and no exceptions made.

"Off the Gold Coast in West Africa is located the tiny Portuguese protectorate of Rio Bonita. The island is so tiny it looks like a flyspeck on the map. Located on it is one little harbor town named San Pedro. Interned in San Pedro Harbor are three merchant ships, two Italian and one German.

"The German ship, *Ems*, has been of considerable interest to us. We put an agent aboard her, and he reported that she is powered by two 6-cylinder, 2-stroke MAN diesels that develop 3,820 horsepower each. John, that's the exact same type of engine the Kriegsmarine uses to power its pocket battleships. Hmmm!

"The decks of the *Ems* are made of special reinforced steel. She carries gun mountings and is capable of doubling as an auxiliary cruiser. Her captain is a hardcore, fanatical, card-carrying member of the Nazi Party.

"The question we asked ourselves was, 'Why would the *Ems* make a high-speed run straight to Rio Bonita on the first day of the war, overstay the seventy-two-hour limit, and allow herself to be interned for the duration when she had been purpose-built and carefully pre-positioned to function as an armed commerce raider astride one of the most strategic sea-lanes in the world?'"

"Doesn't make sense," Major Randal said. "Burned a good asset."

"Off West Africa are about fifty thousand square miles of ocean the Navy calls the 'Southern Sea-Lane' . . . The Royal Navy has only a handful of ships to patrol it, with the predictable result of the Navy being vastly overtaxed. We are losing a significant, and I do mean significant, number of our priceless merchant fleet to U-boats and surface raiders out there.

"Sometimes, in an attempt to fool the Germans, our merchantmen do not always stick strictly to the convoy system. On occasion we let captains sail alone, relying on speed and the element of surprise for protection. It is a mighty big ocean.

"We have even tried letting some of our merchant ships sail with sealed orders not to be opened until they were out to sea, like Royal Navy warships, to eliminate any possibility that 'loose lips' might actually 'sink ships.'

"Nothing works. Whether in convoys or sailing singly with sealed orders, either the U-boats find and sink them or the armed commerce raiders show up and get them.

"It is painfully clear the Germans know each ship's course and speed. Quite often, when the U-boats surface at night and attack a convoy so large the U-boats do not have enough time to sink them all before daylight, they simply go through the convoy and sink the ships with the highest-priority cargo. That tells us they know the name of the ships and what goods they are transporting."

"The German navy must have a crystal ball."

"Well, actually, they have a little help." Major Grand continued. "Our Y-Service has located a high-speed radio signal emanating from San Pedro. The code-breaking boffins were able to read the signals and—bloody surprise—it was the sailing data of allied merchant ships sailing from ports located along the West Coast of Africa. The signal is sent in German navy code from a high-speed transmitter, which was an indication to us it might be coming from the *Ems*. Finally, the Y-Service triangulated the signal and confirmed our suspicions—the transmissions are originating from the *Ems*. No question about it.

"Suddenly it becomes clear. The ship intentionally sacrificed herself in order to establish a strategically located radio station in a safe harbor."

"The Portuguese allow that?"

"No, the Kriegsmarine is running a clandestine operation. In accordance with international maritime law, the Portuguese made all three ships dismantle their radios as a condition of internment, and the vessels are currently subject to periodic inspection to make sure they stay dismantled. Theoretically, all radio traffic has to go through the port authorities in order to be transmitted. We believe the Portuguese do not have any idea the Germans have a secret radio hidden aboard the *Ems*."

"How does the *Ems* obtain our shipping information?"

"That is the BIG question. We are going to be working on the answer, that's for sure. As of this moment, all we know is that the signals are sent

directly to the U-boats and commerce raiders at sea and they immediately act on the information. The transmissions are occurring three times
per week as regular as clockwork. You could set that good-looking Rolex
watch of yours by them."

"What's all this have to do with me?"

"Major, you are to expedite an immediate move of Strategic Raiding
Forces to the port city of Accra in the Gold Coast colony. From there
you will mount a cutting-out operation to board the *Ems* and the two
Italian ships interned in the port of Rio Bonita, then sail them to international waters, where you will effect handover of all three ships to the Royal
Navy." Somehow, the British spymaster managed to make the whole idea
sound sane.

"You want me," Major Randal said, "to invade a neutral country to
commit an act of piracy?"

"And you can never tell a soul," Major Grand confirmed cheerfully as
he fitted another custom-rolled cigarette into his ivory holder. "Sound like
your cup of tea, John?"

"Why bring out the two Italian ships? Why not just take the *Ems*?"

"We suspect the Germans may have hidden a backup radio on one of
the Italian ships in the event anything happens to the one on the *Ems*,"
Major Grand replied. "Or in the unlikely event the locals discover the
primary set on one of their periodic inspections."

"In that case, why don't you simply inform the Portuguese and have
them shut down the *Ems*'s secret radio, and if the signals start back up
again get the port authorities to search the Italian ships?"

"I am not at liberty to answer that question," the SOE man responded
vaguely. "I may or may not have direct knowledge of the exact reason. Sufficient to say, even if I do, am not authorized to discuss it with you at this
time. Probably it would be fair to speculate MI-6 obtained the intelligence
about the *Ems* from some source we cannot reveal to the Portuguese. And
they would be certain to ask."

"Just to get this straight, Major: British intelligence wants me to take
Raiding Forces out to Africa without my having confidence you know all
the answers about why you're sending us?"

"Here is what I am authorized to tell you," Major Grand explained carefully. "The Secret Intelligence Service has an operating agreement with Special Operations Executive in the Gold Coast. Our firm has a presence there, and since MI-6 does not, from time to time we perform certain tasks for them. Because of my, ah, former relationship with SIS, this one landed on my desk.

"Raiding Forces will be acting on behalf of, and with the full knowledge of, MI-6. In addition, this operation has been sanctioned at the very highest level of the government. That, by the way, John, will be confirmed to you in writing at some point before you proceed with the final execution of the mission."

"You realize this could result in Portugal declaring war on Great Britain," Major Randal pointed out. "Don't we have enough problems already?"

Blowing a large smoke ring at the ceiling and then shooting another through it, Major Grand answered deadpan, "That is why you can never tell."

"When is this supposed to happen?"

"You will be flying out to the Gold Coast tomorrow. Your men are going to be put on a fast troop transport to arrive there within a week to ten days."

"In that case, I want my deputy commander, Terry Stone, to travel with me. Also, I will need one of my officers promoted to captain so he can take command of Raiding Forces during the troop movement."

"You certainly don't ask for much. That's what I like about you, John. I shall make the arrangements straightaway. I shall have Captain Stone sent for immediately. Provide me the details on the officer you want promoted. Do not worry unduly about your troops. I intend to have a man on board the troop transport armed with the proper credentials to ensure that your people arrive in Accra thinking they have been on a pleasure cruise."

"You're a wild and crazy guy, Larry."

"I was thinking the same about you, John."

"Tell me the truth. Did the RAF actually say, 'not sporting' about ambushing those German Pathfinder pilots?"

"In truth, yes, they did."

"You really think our side is trying to win?"

"Coming from an American volunteer who came to England's aid in her darkest hour, I suppose that is a fair question. Since we are not having this conversation, I confess that from time to time we wonder the same thing around here. My best answer to you is that most of us are giving it everything we have."

"In Raiding Forces our first rule is there ain't no rules," Major Randal said. "The old school tie network running this war needs to learn that fast."

"Our side has to take the gloves off," Major Grand agreed, nonchalantly inspecting the tip of his cigarette. "And that is exactly why we called on Raiding Forces, John. You do not ask many questions; you just go get the job done.

"Now, how would you like to tag along and observe firsthand a board and seize operation this very night to see how it's done before you go out to Africa?"

"Love to."

8

FIGHTING THE FRENCH

MAJOR JOHN RANDAL, MAJOR LAWRENCE "LARRY" GRAND, AND captain Terry "Zorro" Stone were on board the Raiding Forces' Walrus, piloted by Squadron Leader Paddy Wilcox. The men were inbound to Devonport. The daylight was fading fast as the little amphibian sputtered through the sky at its top speed of 130 miles per hour. As they flew, Major Grand turned in the right front seat of the airplane to talk to the two Raiding Forces officers riding in the back to brief them on the coming night's festivities.

"Here is the situation," Major Grand shouted over the noise of the Duck's engine. "When France surrendered to Germany, it violated the terms of a treaty, which specified that neither Great Britain nor France would enter into independent peace accords with the Third Reich. According to the agreement, in the event France was overrun, England was to rebuild our joint military forces and continue the fight from here, Canada, and the African colonies. Instead, spineless French politicians formed the Vichy regime under Marshal Pétain. France became what amounted to an occupied province of Germany and, though claiming to be neutral, is in fact a wholly collaborating government."

"France has gone Nazi?" Major Randal asked.

"Formally it's called a satellite of Germany," Major Grand clarified. "The French people, they simply end up victims in this ugly drama. The corrupt French politicians who will do whatever is necessary to preserve their personal power are to blame. Some are reportedly so ambitious they have committed to turning France into the 'best state' in the Third Reich."

"As you say, John," Captain Stone quipped, "sounds like we have some new bad guys."

"The current flap, and it goes all the way to the White House, echoed by President Roosevelt, is the fear the Vichy French government will allow the ships of the French navy—most of which sailed to safe haven in Great Britain and the French colonies in Africa—to fall into German hands. The Royal Navy rules the waves, but should the Germans ever manage to gain operational control of the French fleet, which is the fourth largest in the world after those of Great Britain, the United States, and Japan, they will achieve naval parity. Gentlemen, that is something we cannot and will not stand by and allow to take place."

"How do you plan to stop 'em?" Major Randal asked.

"The Vichy French have given assurances to both the United States—which is, ah, officially neutral at this point in time—and Great Britain that they will never allow their ships to be taken over by the Kriegsmarine. The French want us to trust them. More the pity, since no one seems to want to take the word of Nazi collaborators."

"Why should we?" Captain Stone snarled. "A firing squad is the proper medicine for collaboration with the enemy, particularly with murderous scum like the Nazis. In Norway our policy for dealing with Fifth Columnists was 'Catch in the act, shoot on the spot.'"

Major Randal glanced at his deputy, the black sheep son of a duke, the man who had recruited him into the Commandos and who was the best-rounded army officer he had ever served with.

The movie-star-handsome Life Guardsman sounded uncharacteristically bloodthirsty today. Normally Zorro was as cool as a cucumber, a professional who never seemed affected by the dark side of the war. Major Randal guessed that as a member of the Six Hundred, the Stone family had been warned recently, as had the Seaborns, that their entire clan was on the German death list. Knowing something like that could make a man mad-dog mean.

"The French sailors have been given an ultimatum with three options," Major Grand continued. "Rally to the Free French led by General Charles de Gaulle, scuttle in place, or abandon ship immediately because the Royal Navy is going to sink them."

"Fight the French?" Captain Stone drawled. "Unbelievable. We have not fought the Frogs since Waterloo. How did it ever come down to this? Certainly their entire navy cannot have gone over to the Nazi side?"

"The determination has been reached at the highest levels of government that the French fleet poses a grave threat to the national security of the United Kingdom," Major Grand intoned. "They can rally to the Allied cause or be sunk, right now.

"This is an extremely distasteful point in time. However, if one hopes to ever achieve final victory over the Third Reich, now is the time when the English people and the rest of the world, in particular the citizens of the United States, have to be shown that His Majesty's Government is ready, willing, and able to make the hard decisions, take whatever bold decisive action is necessary for victory, and damn the torpedoes, so to speak."

"Scuttle or get sunk," Major Randal repeated. "The harbors will be out of operation until you can dredge 'em back up."

"That is why we cannot afford to give those particular alternatives to the French-flagged ships anchored here in Great Britain," Major Grand replied, tranquilly lighting a cigarette and staring out the window of the Walrus. "We are not about to precipitate any naval engagements with broadsides lobbed back and forth in our own seaports. The scuttling or sinking options apply only to Vichy warships taking refuge in the African colonies."

"I doubt the French Navy will cooperate," Captain Stone observed. "Frogs can be damned hardheaded, and they have some bizarre concepts of what constitutes honor."

"Exactly, so tonight the Vichy French ships berthed in the UK will all be boarded and secured by elements of the Royal Navy and Royal Marines, by force of arms if necessary. And that, gentlemen, is what we are flying in to observe," the SOE man concluded casually. "You may learn something from observing the exercise useful for your own cutting-out operation when you go out to the Gold Coast."

Or, maybe not, said Major Randal to himself.

The ungainly Duck touched down smooth as silk on the water inside the port and taxied up to the dock.

"Have your aircraft serviced, Squadron Leader," Major Grand ordered briskly. "Stand by here; we will be taking back off immediately upon conclusion of the night's enterprise. We have a tight deadline to keep."

The deadline was tight indeed. The Royal Navy was not just going to take over one French ship but every French ship in English ports. Operation Catapult was going to be an extremely complex operation.

Major Grand led the way to an empty port warehouse facility dockside that was serving as the clandestine command center for Operation Catapult. Inside they found a combination of hundreds of Royal Marines, senior officer cadets from Britannia Royal Navy College at Dartmouth, and Royal Navy bluejackets going about the business of preparing for the raid. The atmosphere was intense, as was to be expected from men committed to going into action.

The Raiding Forces officers exchanged glances. Two things were immediately apparent: The Royal Navy was definitely preparing to board and seize control of the French ships, and no one in the building, from the admiral in charge to the youngest naval cadet, had the slightest idea what he was doing. To veteran Commandos who had acquired the skills of their trade by trial and error on actual operations, the preparations bordered on slapstick comedy.

The diminutive Commander in Chief of Western Approaches, Admiral Sir Martin Eric Dunbar-Nasmith, VC, KCB, KCMG, a daring submariner in the last war, was the officer in command of Operation Catapult. A take-charge old school Royal Navy type, he was going to personally conduct the seizure of the French dreadnought *Paris*. He was reported to be an avid reader of the wildly popular Horatio Hornblower novels by C. F. Forrester found in the sea locker of every naval officer worth his salt nowadays. Quite possibly, the swashbuckling Hornblower character had influenced the admiral to lead the way into the breach on Catapult.

Leading a boarding party requires a set of skills entirely different from those of a submariner. No one seemed to have thought of that.

More than two hundred French warships were docked in various ports in Great Britain. The Royal Navy had to take them all down simultaneously while coordinating the timing of their assault with those in Africa, where there was a two-hour time difference. As always the Royal Navy was steadfastly unwilling to accept any help from any military organization not directly under its command umbrella. Unfortunately the Royal Marines, the only assault troops who met that criterion, were spread thin guarding ports, providing seagoing detachments, and manning guns on capital ships at sea worldwide. Merely a handful of leathernecks were available for Catapult, and not all the Royal Marines on call for the mission tonight had completed their basic training. They were basically armed civilians.

To offset the serious deficiency in manpower, the Royal Navy had elected to also use senior Royal Navy officer cadets, commanded by their instructors from the Britannia Royal Naval College at Dartmouth, for the night's work. Royal Navy bluejackets reinforced the Marines and cadets. The end result was a strange blend of troops typical of the British method of conducting improvised war.

Royal Marines and a contingent of Dartmouth officer cadets under their instructors were detailed to board the *Paris*. Major Grand had made arrangements to accompany them. The *Paris* was a Courbet-class dreadnought battleship. A powerful capital fighting ship, she weighed 23,000 tons and carried six to a side 12-inch guns as her main battery, six more to a side 5.5-inch guns, and a total of twenty-two 5.5-inch guns and four 4.7-inch guns scattered around her heavily armored decks.

Moored on the starboard side of the *Paris* and connected by a single gangplank was the largest submarine ever to sail the seven seas, the *Surcouf*. She boasted the most massive cannon ever carried by any undersea craft in the history of naval warfare, sporting twin 8-inch guns normally not found on anything lighter than a cruiser. The sub had a waterproof aircraft hangar mounted on the deck for a small Marcel-Benson reconnaissance seaplane. If either the *Paris* or the *Surcouf* resisted and got her main battery working, the result had the potential to be devastating. Innocents at home asleep in their beds within a twenty-mile arc of the port could suddenly find themselves blown apart by monster shells.

The *Paris* had a crew of 600 sailors; the *Surcouf* boasted 140 hands. Now, eleven days after the formal signing of the armistice ending the war between France and Germany, the French sailors wanted to go home. Virtually none of them had stepped forward to continue fighting the Third Reich. General Charles de Gaulle, whose nickname the "Giant Asparagus" dated from his days at the French military academy St. Cyr, apparently did little to inspire them.

Major Lawrence "Larry" Grand introduced Admiral Sir Martin Eric Dunbar-Nasmith to Major John Randal and Captain Terry "Zorro" Stone. The little admiral was embroiled in the details of getting a hastily improvised mission up and running, and time was short, but he took a few minutes to talk to them.

"Impressive raid you chaps carried out. Hit Jerry for six, jolly good. Glad to have you aboard for this one. Move around, make yourselves highly visible; give the lads a little added confidence, what? But stay out of the way; this is a Navy show, not Combined Operations. Tonight is not a Commando raid. Whatever happens, make bloody sure you do not to give any interviews to the bloody press taking credit when it's over—that's an order."

"We are not here, Admiral," Major Grand responded with a wave of his cigarette holder. "And even if we were, we will be gone by sunrise. Not to worry, these two thrusters will be out of the country incommunicado on a high-priority mission of their own before nightfall tomorrow. They will not be providing any stories to the press."

"Fair enough. Let me introduce you to our Marine commander, Colonel Edward Noyes. Now, gentlemen, if you will excuse me I need to get back to my duty."

Colonel Noyes, long in service as a seagoing fighting man, gave them a quick briefing on the operation. "When we launch, we are going to board the *Paris* directly from portside over the gangplanks in hopes that a massive show of force will take the fight out of them. With any luck the Frenchies will be asleep when the balloon goes up. One can only hope. The boarding party will have officer cadets from the naval college and sailors, many of whom will be artificers armed with tools of the seagoing vocation, like wooden mallets or wrenches, to augment my woeful lack of a full complement of trained Marines."

"Why tools instead of weapons, sir?" asked Major Randal.

"Most bluejackets have never received any formal small arms training. A number of them will be armed with pickax helves, though, which may come in handy for subduing the odd recalcitrant Frenchmen. More to the point, the ratings may require the use of their specialist equipment when they take over the engine rooms or to open watertight doors. All the officers and petty officers will be carrying Webley .455 revolvers. Some of the seamen and all the Royal Marines and officer cadets will be equipped with Short Model Lee-Enfield .303-caliber rifles with bayonets."

"Roger," Major Randal said. The idea that the sailors might find the tools helpful in order to take over an enemy ship made sense. He made eye contact with Captain Stone, who gave him a small nod. Not something either officer would have likely thought of.

"Fully trained professionals are thin on the ground tonight," Colonel Noyes added, misinterpreting the exchange between the two Commandos. "All the Marines who have actually fired their rifles in training have been included in the assault troop complement, and care has been taken to seed the maximum number of NCOs and old soldiers throughout the composite platoons."

"Some of the Marines have never fired their rifles?" Captain Stone queried in disbelief. "Has it really come to that, sir?"

"Alas, it has indeed."

Major Randal asked, "How do you plan to attack the submarine?"

"The Navy has elected not to assault down the plank from the *Paris*," Colonel Noyes explained. "They will be coming in from seaside in three motorized launches. The boarding party will be made up of half Marines and half sailors under the command of Commander Denis 'Lofty' Sprague, the skipper of HMS *Thames*, one of our submarines. The sailors will consist of a complement from his crew on the *Thames*. The thinking is submariners will know their way around a submarine, even if it is a French boat."

"Why not hit her from both sides at once, sir?" asked Major Randal.

"Marines provide troop support for Catapult," Colonel Noyes replied, "not the planning or the tactics."

"May prove problematic," Captain Stone observed. "For maximum dynamic shock effect, it is always advisable to strike from as many directions as possible all at once."

"Too true," the colonel agreed.

"Mallets, wrenches, and ax handles just might be more effective at close quarters," Major Randal said, still reflecting on the choice the of each sailors' individual equipment. "Anything's better in close quarters than battle rifles with 14-inch bayonets on 'em."

"You gentlemen are welcome to go on board with my command party after the main assault party has launched," Colonel Noyes offered. "I shall be making an immediate inspection to check on the performance of my men. And I do mean immediate."

"Thanks, Colonel," said Major Grand. "Let us all pray your operation goes off smoothly, as hoped, without degenerating into a skirmish with people we do not wish to fight."

"Peculiar business," the grizzled saltwater soldier agreed, clearly troubled about the night ahead. Royal Marine officers were famously concerned about the welfare of their troops. "Boarding our former allies by whose side we have gallantly fought a common enemy twice in the last twenty years, in our home port. A sad night's work, upon my word."

"Too bad," Major Randal said, "you don't have cutlasses."

9

TAKEDOWN

MAJOR JOHN RANDAL AND CAPTAIN TERRY "ZORRO" STONE circulated through the clumps of Dartmouth officer cadets, bluejackets, and Royal Marines as they cleaned rifles, sharpened bayonets, and made last-minute adjustments to their personal gear. The sounds and smells and sense of urgency were chillingly familiar. The Raiding Forces officers, by far the most experienced Special Operations veterans present, were strangely tense. In fact, though they did not show it, the two Commandos were highly keyed up, even more so than if they were slated to be going on the mission in a fighting role, not merely tagging along as noncombatant observers. It is one thing to go into battle; it is something else entirely to stand on the sidelines and watch others getting ready to.

The men of Operation Catapult looked upon the Raiding Forces officers moving reassuringly through their ranks as military stars; they were awed by the "Tomcat Raiders," the daring commanders of the first parachute raid of the war, the "hands of steel from the sea that snatched" an unwary German general from his post. The famous Commandos, wearing their forest green berets and parachute wings on their chests, had the look of the fighting man's professional, hard enough to cut glass.

The presence of Major Randal and Captain Stone was confidence building. The Royal Navy had gone to the trouble to bring in the best raiders in all England to ensure that nothing went wrong with tonight's show. Everything was going to be all right. If they only knew. Neither Major Randal nor Captain Stone had the foggiest idea how to capture a warship.

Major John Randal made it a point to spend time with the Dartmouth officer students. Only senior cadets had been selected to take part in the night's operation. That meant they would be commissioned sometime in the near future. The youngsters were mad keen.

"Any of you men have small boat experience, there's openings for naval officers in Raiding Forces," he said. "We're looking for can-do operators."

"How does one go about volunteering, sir?" inquired one of the Dartmouth instructors, a Royal Navy Volunteer Reserve sub-lieutenant, eagerly. "I'm a yachtsman and would delight in the chance to get into the active war, if the offer is available to staff."

"Contact Captain Lady Seaborn care of the Bradford Hotel, London," Major Randal said, studying the young officer closely. "She'll expedite the transfer."

"Poaching, John?" Major Lawrence "Larry" Grand queried with a frown. "Best not get caught. The powers that be are sure to take umbrage. We would not want the admiral to maroon us from Catapult at this stage."

"Hornblower requested permission to recruit Sea Rover Scouts to haul SOE's stores of arms and demolitions across the Channel, Larry," Major Randal said, "so you can set Europe ablaze."

"Ooof," Major Grand grimaced as if he had taken a punch to the solar plexus. "By all means, press-gang away, and good hunting! Scouts conducting clandestine maritime operations—can you be that desperate?"

"We have three boats, one officer, and four naval ratings. You do the math."

Zero hour was 0430, just before first light.

Nearly everyone in the attacking force wore a tin hat, and the officers and petty officers each carried a Webley .455 revolver. In addition, every officer was armed with a single sheet of paper upon which were written the four French phrases deemed to be most appropriate for the night's work, the last being "Levez vos mains"—"Raise your hands."

"It may prove a bit tricky," Captain Terry "Zorro" Stone pointed out, "during the heat of a high-speed, close-quarter boarding operation, conducted under cover of darkness, for one to whip out a paper, peruse the list, select the proper message, and read it in a foreign language to an armed opponent who may or may not be intent on ventilating you at the time."

"Poor prior planning," Major John Randal said, "produces poor results."

Admiral Sir Martin Eric Dunbar-Nasmith had his own note that began, "The French nation has fought gallantly to a standstill" and ended "any resistance can only cause unnecessary bloodshed." Again, how he was supposed to be able to see it well enough to read it, in French, during the period of Beginning Nautical Twilight was never clearly explained.

The Royal Marines and the Navy bluejackets moved into their assault position on the dock. Considering the incomplete state of their training, their lack of experience in working together, and a total absence of rehearsals, they carried off the movement from the assembly area to the line of departure as skillfully as if they performed that sort of complicated maneuver every day. The men were very stealthy. Over the ages, many a surreptitious military endeavor has been compromised by an accidentally discharged weapon or some other egregious violation of light or sound discipline that gave away the show. Not so tonight.

At the appointed time, Admiral Dunbar-Nasmith charged up the boarding plank followed by a host of heavily armed Royal Marines carrying Enfield rifles at the high port, with bayonets fixed, and demanded in no uncertain terms for the sentry on duty to summon the ship's officer of the deck "RIGHT BLOODY NOW!"

The *Paris*'s watch officer pulling the duty happened to be making his rounds not far away. He repaired to the boarding gate to see what all the commotion was about and was presented with the short note. Since the French officer recognized Admiral Dunbar-Nasmith from a previous courtesy call on the ship's commander, Admiral Jean Cayol, in happier times, he wasted no time hurrying to his admiral's cabin to present the document to him.

The instant the duty officer departed, the Royal Marines and bluejackets stormed the *Paris*, taking a page right out of Raiding Forces' "Rules of Raiding"—"It never hurts to cheat."

The boarders were very quick and the *Paris* was secured without resistance. In fact, most of the ship's complement was conveniently asleep in their hammocks when the British struck. Admiral Cayol was sitting up in his bunk wearing an expensive pair of monogrammed pale yellow Chinese silk pajamas—a gift from his mistress—when the ship's watch officer arrived bearing the note.

Pacing back and forth outside Admiral Cayol's cabin, Admiral Dunbar-Nasmith grew increasingly impatient waiting for a reply to his invitation to surrender peaceably. Unable to restrain himself any longer, he suddenly burst in on his pajama-clad counterpart, who was studying the five-paragraph letter. The French flag officer was visibly distressed.

"I could have ordered my ships scuttled," Admiral Cayol lamented, "but that would have merely obstructed your harbor and been an inconvenience to your future operations against our former common enemy."

Upon hearing that tepid response, the Commander in Chief of Western Approaches realized he had, exactly like his fictional hero Horatio Hornblower, actually captured a foreign battleship by boarding.

Major John Randal, Major Lawrence "Larry" Grand, and Captain Terry "Zorro" Stone had stepped on the main deck within seconds of the Marines and sailors piling aboard. They witnessed the extraordinary sight of more than six hundred of the French crew marching up under armed guard, filing off the ship onto the quay, and being herded into a convoy of waiting canvas-topped Bedford trucks. The boarding operation had gone down like clockwork. Militarily it was a thing of beauty.

But why had virtually the entire crew of the mighty French dreadnought been taken unawares snug in their rack asleep? It was passing strange. After all, there was a war on, even if the Frenchmen's hearts were not in it anymore.

"I'd expect more men standing watch on a party boat," commented Major Randal.

10

THE BRITISH ARE COMING

THE AMPHIBIOUS ASSAULT ON THE *SURCOUF* WAS SLOW GETTING off the mark.

On board the French submarine, the radio operator was monitoring the channels designated on the duty watch list. Suddenly, a priority incoming message from naval headquarters in Bordeaux, located in the French unoccupied zone, arrived. The signal was marked "officer only," which meant the radio operator could take it down and record it, but because the message was in code, he did not have any idea what it said.

When the signal arrived, the boat's officer of the deck was in the wardroom drinking coffee. On being summoned, he hurried down to the cramped radio cabin with the key to the safe, opened it, and pulled out the relevant codebook. Decoding the message, he discovered to his distress that the *Surcouf* was to be scuttled immediately.

The duty officer dashed off to inform the submarine's skipper, Capitaine de corvette Paul Martine, of the news, shouting, "The British are coming" like a latter-day Paul Revere. But it was too late; a sixty-man boarding party, half Royal Marines and half sailors from the British submarine *Thames* under the command of Commander Denis "Lofty" Sprague, had already come calling.

At the United States Cavalry School, Major John Randal had been taught never to use the word *assume*. The old horse soldier NCOs instructing at Ft. Riley gleefully liked to point out that any officer who ever used the word, or even so much as thought it when planning a mission or doing anything else of a military nature, would "make an ass out of you and me"—not a good thing. Unfortunately Commander Denis "Lofty" Sprague had never attended the U.S. Cavalry School.

The *Thames*'s skipper's attack plan was based on the assumption that the four hatches on the French submarine's deck would be open for circulation, allowing the boarding party to swarm down all four more or less at once. They were not. Capitaine Paul Martine had ordered three of the four deck hatches battened down to make it easier to secure the *Surcouf* in the event they had to put to sea in a hurry. The only hatch not locked shut was the one nearest the submarine's bow. It was left open to allow the two sentries stationed on deck easy access to get back inside fast if they ever needed to for any reason.

On board the *Surcouf*, the officers and crew were fully aware there was a war on. Capitaine Martine was also aware that their former ally, the British, might one day decide to commandeer their boat in order to prevent the submarine from falling into German hands. He did not intend to allow that to happen if he could prevent it, and he made his feelings known to the crew. The honor of France was at stake.

The two sentries on deck were thoroughly briefed on their night's assignment. Especially, they knew what was expected of them in the event they sighted any unusual activity in the harbor; they had been ordered to be particularly alert to the possibility of British sailors making an effort to board. Since the only way to reach the *Surcouf* from dockside was across the *Paris*, one sentry was stationed at the foot of the gangplank that ran down from the monster-sized dreadnought that towered over the submarine. His instructions were to give early warning of any sign of trouble on board the *Paris*. He would, in essence, be the canary in the coal mine.

The other sentry, the petty officer, carried out a roving patrol along the length of the *Surcouf*, occasionally climbing up onto the top of the conning tower to visually check to see if there was any sign of a waterborne force moving toward the submarine. Each of the French sailors was armed with a big 8-millimeter Lebel service revolver buckled around his waist.

Despite the vigilant sentries on watch, the boarders from the sea side arrived unannounced in three motor launches. They had been lying flat between the thwarts, hoping that in the faint pink light of Beginning Nautical Twilight all that could be seen were the MLs' coxswains manning their tillers. The boarding party was totally exposed in the open boats, but somehow against all odds, the boarders achieved the element of surprise—the gold standard of all raiding operations.

The first man to swing aboard the *Surcouf* was Lieutenant Francis Talbot of the *Thames*. His crew of bluejackets got on deck rapidly without firing a shot and silently captured the sentry by the plank. (He had, reasonably enough, had his eye fixated on the *Paris* as instructed, not the starboard side where the MLs came in.) The petty officer on roving patrol also failed to detect the motor launch's approach, but he proved too fast for the raiding party and avoided capture. Lieutenant Talbot watched helplessly as the French sailor ran along the casing forward, hammering on the hull by the conning tower with the steel butt of his pistol to sound the alarm. Like a rabbit diving into his burrow, the sentry scurried down the fore hatch, which was slammed shut after him and battened down.

Now the *Surcouf* was completely buttoned up. The British sailors and Royal Marines were locked out. Few things on planet Earth have ever been built more watertight than a submarine. Commander Sprague's plan to attack down all four hatches and put a quick end to any resistance was clearly not going to happen. What to do?

Lieutenant Talbot was a bold young submarine officer who did not wring his hands or get all weepy when things did not go according to plan. Having him lead the boarding party was the Royal Navy equivalent of the Raiding Force rule, "Right man, right job." He immediately scrambled up the *Surcouf* conning tower ladder to investigate, but when he reached the top, he discovered that the conning tower hatch was also locked shut.

He noticed, however, that the catches on the hatch looked remarkably similar to the ones on the *Thames*. And, in an emergency, those could be opened from the outside by rescue divers. By any definition of the word, the situation clearly constituted an official wartime emergency. Lieutenant Talbot coolly popped the hatch and led his men inside. Commander Sprague followed a few minutes later.

Down below, the duty officer, clutching the scuttle order, reached the command post where the periscope was located. The CP was the submarine's equivalent of a surface ship's bridge. There he encountered one of the deck sentries, the petty officer who should not have been inside.

"Armed Englishmen," the petty officer reported breathlessly, "have landed on the *Surcouf*, sir."

"Secure the hatch," the officer of the deck ordered unnecessarily. "Sound General Quarters!" he shouted and turned back to go warn his captain.

Things on the *Surcouf* rapidly became confused. When Capitaine Martine, in receipt of the scuttle order, arrived in the command post to carry out his instructions, he encountered Commander Sprague and his merry men already inside taking over the boat. British sailors were trying with varying degrees of success to herd the French matelots up onto the main deck. Some of the crew were sleepy and others surly; none were being overly cooperative. The engine room artificers defiantly refused to budge.

Commander Sprague ordered all the French officers to muster in the wardroom located on the deck immediately below the command post. Once in the wardroom, the French officers and a number of sailors lined up on one side of the long gray-linoleum-topped dining table that took up most of the room. The British invaders lined up on the other side of the table in a face-off.

The wardroom had a number of private officer quarters built off it, screened by canvas curtains. Though the largest room on the sub, with everyone crowded in, it was a tight fit. Congregating there proved to be a mistake.

Commander Sprague produced a note, which he read aloud, purporting to be from Admiral Jean Cayol urging the *Surcouf* crew to "rally to the Free French cause and to continue to fight against the common enemy until victory was achieved." Capitaine Martine did not believe a word of it. He knew full well that his admiral openly despised de Gaulle. He asked to be allowed to go to the *Paris* to confer with his boss. Permission was granted, and the French submarine commander immediately departed under armed escort to attempt to clarify the situation.

The rest of the French and the British remained in the wardroom standing on opposite sides of the table. The four hatches were now open, but despite that fresh air the submarine was a hot sticky place. The tension in the room was like a pressure cooker. Everyone was very uncomfortable. The Frenchmen were clearly indignant, bordering on combative. This was not how the operation was supposed to go. Boarding was intended to be a rapid takedown, not end up in a Mexican standoff.

One of the French lieutenants realized the British were not going to allow Capitaine Martine back on the ship. Acting on his own recognizance he discretely passed a note to an electrician's mate, ordering him to proceed to the engine room, throw the switches to cause a blackout, and tell the crew to wreck as much of the *Surcouf's* machinery as they could. The French sailor made an excuse about going to the head and left the room to carry out his orders.

He didn't notice, however, that he was followed by one of Lieutenant Talbot's petty officers armed with a large wooden mallet and a suspicious nature. When the French sailor threw the power switches, shutting off the lights, the British petty officer struck the French sailor with a meaty thwack and turned the electricity back on.

Meanwhile, in the brief period the wardroom was pitch black, the submarine's surgeon slipped into his sleeping room and retrieved a small .25-caliber Model 28 Armes automatic, which he slipped into his pants pocket.

When the lights came back up, Commander Sprague saw the French surgeon as he tried to surreptitiously step back out of his cabin. The *Thames* skipper reacted by immediately throwing a red-hot temper tantrum, screaming in rage that he had been betrayed. The commander immediately ordered all the *Surcouf* officers off the boat.

The French submarine's executive officer, the senior man now present, defiantly refused, saying, "The crew of the Surcouf will only take orders from our own captain, when he returns!" Then to everyone's astonishment, he stepped out of the wardroom into his adjoining cabin, retrieved an 8-millimeter Lebel service revolver, buckled it on, and stepped back out into the wardroom.

"I have my orders," announced a clearly frustrated Commander Sprague in schoolboy French, and he pulled out his Webley .455 for the first time. "If you people don't file off the boat immediately I shall kill you!"

Commander Sprague made this threat based on a second assumption, namely, that, as on British ships of war, only the duty officers and certain sentries were armed at any given time and at all other times individual weapons were secured in a central arms locker. Not so. Nearly all the French officers present were carrying private-purchase pocket pistols or had them in their cabins, and in most cases the weapons were loaded.

Then the *Thames* skipper did something really stupid. He turned to one of his sailors and, incredibly—still speaking in French—ordered, "Shoot that man."

He should not have done that.

The Royal Navy sailor had no idea what his captain had said, but the French officers did. One of them pulled out a MAB .32 semiautomatic pistol and began firing.

He shot Commander Sprague, the lieutenant standing to his right, and the two sailors standing to his left. All four went down. Commander Sprague squeezed off a harmless round from his sidearm into the steel deck as he fell, but the others were too stunned to open fire. Hearing the shots, a Royal Navy chief petty officer leaned down the stairwell from the command post, his Webley .455 in hand, and shot the French shooter, knocking him off his feet with a single round that shattered the shooter's arm and ratcheted into his chest.

The French gunman, bleeding profusely, managed nonetheless to remove his empty magazine and reload as he struggled to regain his feet. Commander Sprague was down, dying, as was the lieutenant who was shot through the liver and had somehow fallen into a chair. The two British seamen were wounded, but less seriously. Now all the Frenchmen in the wardroom had their weapons out, but no one else was firing. There was no need to. None of the British personnel was capable of fighting.

The *Surcouf* ship's surgeon ducked back behind the canvas curtains of his cabin, pulling his own handgun, the .25 Armes, from his pocket as he went. His bunkmate was sitting on the lower bunk tearing up a technical manual; he was ready to burn it in a trash receptacle, if need be, to avoid its capture. He looked up so see what was happening.

Two British sailors who had arrived upon hearing the shooting followed the doctor into the compartment: the first one was armed with a Short Model Lee-Enfield .303-caliber rifle with saw-toothed bayonet affixed, and the other carried a Webley .455. The surgeon emptied his weapon into the leading seaman, hitting him eight times in rapid succession at virtual contact range. All eight tiny little .25 bullets completely penetrated his body and struck the Webley-toting sailor behind him around the head and shoulders.

Hard hit, the leading British seaman nevertheless continued moving forward in the on-guard attack position. He veered off to run his bayonet through the startled officer who had been sitting on the bunk tearing up the technical manual. The hard-charging bluejacket succumbed to the barrage of pistol shots without letting go his death grip on the rifle.

Amazingly, the other British sailor suffered only superficial wounds, but he had a lot of them. He was out of the fight.

11

THE GENIE

SATISFIED THAT THE ROYAL NAVY, THE ROYAL MARINES, AND the Dartmouth cadets had things well in hand on the *Paris*, Major John Randal, Major Lawrence "Larry" Grand, and Captain Terry "Zorro" Stone decided to pay an impromptu call on the *Surcouf* to see how the boarding operation was going there. They had seen the French sub's captain come on board the dreadnought hoping to confer with his admiral, only to be unceremoniously whisked off squawking like a startled chicken to a waiting truck. A trickle of prisoners from the submarine had already begun moving up the plank to the *Paris*. From all outward appearances, the seaborne assault party had been successful.

Everything on the French sub was quiet as the three observers worked their way down the plank from the *Paris*. They climbed up the conning tower ladder and went down into the command post. It was empty. From there they proceeded down the ladder to the wardroom, Major Grand leading the way.

Suddenly the intelligence officer pulled up short, exclaiming, "Bloody hell!"

Instantly Major Randal went from being a tourist to clicked on full. He stepped around Major Grand with his Colt .38 Super at the ready, conjured up as if by magic in both his hands, moving fluidly like a big stalking cat. What he saw was a massacre. Dead and dying men were strewn everywhere. At the sight of the armed Commando, the French sailors dropped their weapons, raised their hands, and promptly surrendered. For them, the war was over.

Captain Stone brushed Major Grand aside, his Colt automatic leveled. He moved up to where he could help cover the line of *Surcouf* men wedged in tight along the opposite side of the table. The Frenchmen had expressions on their faces that ranged from outright horror to what could best be described as the cat that ate the canary.

By now Major Grand had his Enfield .38 revolver out to back up the Raiding Forces officers, who to his mind had responded with remarkable sangfroid. The unmistakable sound of the slide on a pistol slamming into battery came from behind one of the two canvas curtains behind the captured Frenchmen. With two tiny compartments side by side in the immediate vicinity of the sound of the automatic being charged, it was impossible to tell which one contained a Frenchman with a loaded weapon. Major Randal made eye contact with Captain Stone and cocked his head toward one of the cabins; then he immediately moved around the table and prepared to step through the curtain of the other.

Without hesitation, Captain Stone pushed through the curtain and found a nightmare scene more macabre than the one in the wardroom. A wounded British sailor leaned against a bulkhead, bleeding from multiple head wounds. Another British sailor was frozen in death, lurching forward in the long thrust and hold position. He was clutching a rifle with his bayonet sticking into and protruding out the back of a dead French officer who had a startled look on his face. The French ship's surgeon was trying frantically to reload his miniature little pocket pistol and making a bad job of it.

Again without hesitation, Captain Stone took one short step forward and slapped the doctor across the face with the flat of his Colt automatic, obtaining a most satisfying result. He would have preferred to use some of the exotic gutter-fighting techniques Captain William Ewart Fairbairn had taught them at the Special Warfare Training Center, like the "tiger claw" or the "thunder clap." But since not one of Fairbairn's hand-to-hand combat techniques involved holding a loaded pistol, he had had to improvise.

Just as Captain Stone struck the French surgeon, Major Randal stepped through the other canvas curtain to face three French officers with pistols drawn standing-to. If the trio were expecting a speech from him like Commander Sprague's, they were badly mistaken. Major Randal did not speak French, he did not have a card to read from, and he did not care to make threats.

"Blammm, Blammm, Blammm," the Colt .38 Super roared in the close confines, dropping all three armed officers to the ground before they got off a single round in return. "Blammm, Blammm, Blammm," again, after the pistol-toting submariners were down. "Blammm, Blammm, Blammm," to make absolutely sure they wouldn't get up again. "The first rule is there ain't no rules." Major Randal said through clenched teeth, looking down at the dead men.

The French sailors covered by Major Grand in the wardroom visibly flinched at the roar of each gunshot. A flash lit up the draped compartment with the blast of every round. Then came the metallic sounds of the Raiding Forces officer leisurely changing the magazine on his weapon.

"Any of you other men," asked Major Randal causually, ducking back out through the curtain, pistol in hand, "feel the need to defend the honor of France?"

Apparently not.

After that there was no more armed resistance on board the *Surcouf*. The price of glory has its limits.

"Events did not have to unravel the way they did," Captain Stone commented as they made their way off the submarine. "A tragic waste of good men on both sides."

"Even the French sailors agree the first shots should never have been fired," Major Grand concurred; he was equally troubled by the carnage. "But then some of our survivors admit the Frenchmen were provoked. Why Commander Sprague chose to give his 'shoot to kill' order in French will never be known. What a debacle."

"Once the genie gets out of the bottle in a gunfight," Major Randal said, "it's hard to put it back in."

12

ENIGMA

AT THE STICK OF THE DUCK, SQUADRON LEADER PADDY WILCOX turned to Major Lawrence "Larry" Grand and informed him, "I am in receipt of a radio message Code Word Brilliant ordering us to divert our flight to a new landing port where we will be met by ground transportation to deliver our party to an undisclosed location. The sender identifies as 17F."

"Reply Wilco," Major Grand snapped, white lipped. "Crank this museum piece up!"

"Brilliant" was the second highest priority a message could carry in the British Empire, the first being "Cromwell," which would announce the German invasion of England when it came. The "17F" was the code name of the personal assistant to the Director of the Naval Intelligence Department. Major Grand did not share that classified information with the other three on board the airplane.

"Picked up a couple of little friends," Squadron Leader Wilcox noted casually. A pair of Supermarine Spitfires had swooped in and taken up station off each wing of the Walrus, flying in tight formation.

"I knew we'd pay a price for shooting those Frogs," Captain Terry

"Zorro" Stone intoned to Major John Randal under his breath. "You really do need to work on your form for taking prisoners, old stick. First Tomcat, where you shoot five men because you failed to remember two words of German, and now—"

"Well, I don't speak French either."

A police car with two motorcycle escorts was standing by quayside when they landed.

"Under arrest," Captain Stone shook his head. "There went the rest of the inheritance. It's always darkest before pitch black."

All four officers piled in. The car and outriders raced through traffic with red lights flashing. Their destination turned out not to be Scotland Yard or the Tower of London but the exclusive men's club Whites.

Groom, the hall porter, immediately whisked Major Grand to the billiard room, where Colonel Stewart Menzies, DSO, aka "C," the Director of British Secret Intelligence, was waiting with Rear Admiral John Godfrey, Director of the Naval Intelligence Division.

The porter returned to the foyer shortly thereafter and led the three Raiding Forces officers to a small side room where a tall, urbane, chain-smoking Royal Navy Volunteer Reserve lieutenant commander, sporting a nose broken years before in a rugby match, was pacing like a caged tiger.

"Hello, Ian," Captain Stone greeted him. "What's a Boodles man doing here? Aren't you supposed to be a subaltern in the Black Watch, or have you come up in the world?"

"Quite right, Terry, reversal of fortune," the officer replied suavely. "Naval Intelligence came to have a greater appreciation of my modest talents than the regiment. As you know I was the most horrible cadet in the storied history of Sandhurst, though I do seen to recall you may actually still hold the record for accrued demerits. I'm merely visiting your club today, my good chap; no cause for undue alarm or despondency.

"Fleming," he announced, turning to Major Randal. "Ian Fleming."

"Eton, I presume," Major Randal said.

In the billiard room, Colonel Stewart Menzies explained to Major Lawrence "Larry" Grand the purpose of his being diverted to Whites. "As you are aware, Lawrence, the Germans have a coding machine called the Enigma that they use to scramble all their communications. Looks like a typewriter and functions similar to one. Our side is working on defeating the device, but it is an almost impossible task.

"Our boffins have recently had some luck with the Army model, but the version the Navy uses has proven impenetrable. As you know full well, eliminating the U-boat menace is our top national priority. We have to be able to read Kriegsmarine messages to pinpoint the exact location of their U-boats so the Royal Navy can go there and sink them in order to have any real hope of winning the U-boat war. Right now that is not possible.

"The way the Enigma system works, a message is typed into the machine on one end, which encrypts it, and then it is transmitted to a receiving machine, which decrypts it. The infernal things have millions of possible combinations of ciphers. The arrangement is virtually fool-proof, but its security is also its vulnerability because an Enigma device is required at both ends, thus increasing the chances one of them might fall into our hands. And, let it be said we shall stop at nothing, pay any price, to see that one does.

"Along those lines it has been brought to our attention that the Kriegs-marine air-sea rescue launches working the Channel to pick up downed Luftwaffe pilots all carry an Enigma machine on board. Lieutenant Commander Fleming has come up with an ingenious plan to capture one of the boats in order to steal the device. The operation was laid on, all set to go, but at the last minute the Royal Air Force backed out.

"When he found out about the mission being stood down, Alan Turing, the senior scientist at Bletchley Park working on the project to defeat the Enigma, nearly had a nervous breakdown. He says we absolutely have to get our hands on an Enigma device at the earliest or it could be eons before they can crack it by themselves. No need to tell you, of all people, how vital this project is to the war effort."

"I understand completely, sir."

"We thought it might be a good idea to have our leading expert on small-scale raiding in to give us the benefit of his views on Fleming's scheme to see if there is any possibility we might be able to resurrect the mission to go and pinch one."

"Very good sir," Major Grand replied. "Major Randal has a way of, ah, cutting straight to the heart of a subject. You can expect a direct answer from him."

Groom reappeared in the small side room. "Major Randal, if you will accompany me, please, sir."

The porter led the commander of Raiding Forces to the billiard room. Colonel Stewart Menzies was sitting at a heavy Chippendale table next to the fireplace; Rear Admiral John Godfrey and Major Lawrence "Larry" Grand were sitting across from him, under the heavyweight Belt of England mounted on the wall. Not sure of the protocol, Major John Randal assumed a modified position of parade rest.

"Major Grand has been apprising us of your night's work," Colonel Menzies said in his whispery voice. "Very nicely done, John."

"Should have shot them all," harrumphed Real Admiral Godfrey with a sinister sneer. "Bloody Nazi-loving Frogs!"

The Director of NID was a sea officer in an intelligence assignment, not a career naval intelligence officer. He was proving uncommonly good at his new job, but at heart the admiral was a fighting saltwater sailor.

Major Grand gave Major Randal a thin smile.

"John," Colonel Menzies steered the conversation back on track, speaking to the young Commando as if he were a member of his cavalry regiment, the 2nd Life Guards, where all the officers called each other by their first names except when on parade. "Raiding Forces have been alerted for a most vital mission of national strategic importance along the Gold Coast, which we all have a vested interest in seeing you complete at the earliest. However, a competing operation with an even higher priority has been proposed. The men and material to carry it out have been gathered and trained and are standing by, ready to launch. But at the last minute, the Royal Air Force pulled out, leaving us high and dry, using what we feel is a rather flimsy excuse.

"What we would like is for you to review the operational plan and give us your unvarnished professional opinion of its feasibility."

"Yes sir."

The SIS director produced a thin red folder stamped MOST SECRET and handed it to Major Randal. "Take your time. We want your best assessment." What "C" did not say but was thinking was that the future of the British Empire might very well be resting on what Major Randal reported back.

Apparently summoned by some silent signal, the hall porter reappeared. "We shall have the other officers in now, Groom."

Major Randal joined the three other junior officers and the four of them retreated to a cluster of heavy leather chairs in the far corner of the billiard room. He opened the thin red folder the SIS director had given him and took out a single sheet of paper. The other three lit up cigarettes.

```
OPERATION RUTHLESS

EYES ONLY: Rear Admiral John Godfrey

From: Lieutenant Commander Ian Fleming, Dept. 17

DNI,

I suggest we obtain the loot by the following
means:

1. Obtain from Air Ministry an air-worthy German
bomber.

2. Pick a tough crew of five, including a pilot,
W/T operator, and word-perfect German speaker.
Dress them in German Air Force uniform, add blood
and bandages to suit.

3. Crash plane in Channel after making S.O.S. to
German rescue service in P/L.

4. Once on board rescue boat, shoot German crew,
dump overboard, bring rescue boat back to English
port.

In order to increase the chances of capturing an
R. or M. with its richer booty, the crash might be
staged in mid-Channel. The Germans would presumably
```

employ one of these types for the longer and more
hazardous journey.

Since the attackers will be wearing enemy uniforms,
they will be liable to be shot as franc-tireurs
if captured, and incident might be fruitful field
for propaganda. Attackers' story will therefore
be "that it was done for a lark by a group of
young hotheads who thought the war was too tame
and wanted to have a go at the Germans. They had
stolen plane and equipment and had expected to get
into trouble when they got back." This will prevent
suspicions that party was after more valuable booty
than a rescue boat.

"When was this set to take place?" Major Randal asked.

"Any night we could pinpoint a rescue launch," Lieutenant Commander Ian Fleming replied. "Only we never could locate one. Then the bloody RAF pulled the rug out from under us. Claimed if we landed a Heinkel 111 in the Channel, it would probably sink—which is the general idea."

"So, you have a flyable German bomber?"

"We have in our possession several that have crash landed virtually undamaged."

"Your name is penciled in next to the bit about the German speaker. You planned on going on this raid?"

"That was the idea."

"Done much of this kind of work?"

"Actually, no. Rejected, of course—the admiral would never let me go."

Major Randal handed the sheet of paper to Captain Terry "Zorro" Stone. Then he stood up and walked back to the table at the other end of the long room, where the three most dangerous men in England sat waiting. They seemed surprised that he was ready to make his report so quickly.

"Good idea," Major Randal said, "bad plan."

The pronouncement was received with inhospitable silence. It was, after all, a proposal both "C" and the DNI had signed off on. "Would you care to elaborate, John?" Colonel Menzies prompted at last.

"What's the loot, sir?"

"We could tell you, Major," Rear Admiral Godfrey growled, "but then we would have to take you down in the wine cellar and shoot you. And I, for one, would hate to do that to a man Razor Ransom speaks so highly of."

"Some piece of high-value German equipment that's transportable?"

"Reasonable to presume," Colonel Menzies conceded vaguely. "Let us not press the point; suffice it to say you have all the information we intend to provide you in order to give us an opinion on the viability of Fleming's proposal."

"Capture the German boat, then sail it home, and no matter what cover story you come up with, the Nazis will know you have the loot."

"That is a problem," "C" replied acerbically. "How would you propose to go about it?"

"E-boats are the largest craft you can target," Major Randal said. "Even they have a twenty-five-man crew, which is a lot to expect your team to handle. The R boats have at least 40 sailors on board and M boats over 100. Five men, no matter how tough or well trained, do not stand a chance against that many bad guys."

"A remarkable amount of information about the German Navy," Rear Admiral Godfrey observed, "for a man from The Rangers to have at his fingertips."

"When you spend as much time out in the Channel in the dark of the night in a forty-foot yacht as we do on the HMY *Arrow*, sir, you know about those things."

The officers at the table sat mute. Colonel Menzies and Rear Admiral Godfrey should have reached Major Randal's conclusion themselves before the mission had progressed this far. The importance of obtaining the loot had blinded them to the limitations of reality. Both "C" and the DNI were thinking it was a good thing the RAF had stood down when they did. The RAF had averted a disaster.

"Fleming's plan called for this raid to take place at night," Major Randal continued. "That won't work."

"Why not?" Rear Admiral Godfrey demanded defensively. "Cover of darkness enhances the element of surprise!"

"German boats don't pull air-sea rescue patrols at night, sir; they hunt for shipping targets. What you want to do is put up a spotter airplane at first light, locate an E-boat, shadow it, launch the Heinkel 111 with your five tough crew wearing their bloodstained uniforms, have an MGB standing by just over the horizon with a party of heavily armed Royal Marines on deck, then crash-land the Heinkel in broad daylight right next to the E-boat. While the Germans affect the rescue, have the MGB race up and board it. Put your loot on the MGB, sink the E-boat with a big public bang, and come home. Nobody will be the wiser."

Silence was thick on the ground.

"A Nazi air-sea rescue boat will witness a Luftwaffe bomber crash in plain sight in close proximity," Major Grand mused thoughtfully. "The crew will have no reason to question what they have seen with their own eyes. A sure bet they fall for the ruse."

"Elegantly simple," Colonel Menzies agreed. "The Germans will have no thought but to rescue the downed airmen; that's what they are out there for. They will simply react as we thought all along and be distracted as the MGB comes up. Anything else you might care to suggest, John?"

"Me, I'd try to arrange for the spotter plane to strafe the E-boat while they're rescuing the Heinkel crew as a diversion to cover the MGB attack, sir."

"You managed all that in less than three minutes?" Rear Admiral Godfrey growled. "We have been working on this for over a month. That business about sinking the E-boat is the perfect conclusion for this operation. How would you like a transfer to my staff, Major, when you return from the Gold Coast?"

"Commander Fleming originated the plan, sir," Major Randal said. "He had a good idea, I just added a couple of details."

"How long do you believe we can delay Major Randal's flight on the Flying Clipper?" Colonel Menzies asked Major Grand, "without raising eyebrows?"

"Seventy-two hours easy, maybe more if necessary," Major Grand replied. "British Overseas Airways Corporation can always experience mechanical difficulties with a seaplane, even the big one. The airline will have to wait for a part to be flown in. That sort of delay occurs all too frequently during wartime."

"Make it happen, Lawrence."

"Sir!"

"Major Randal," Colonel Menzies announced, "we are going to postpone your departure to the Gold Coast temporarily so that you can personally take command of Operation Ruthless. Lieutenant Commander Fleming will be detailed as your liaison officer to the intelligence community for the duration of the mission. Anything you need in the way of material and support will have to come from DNI, SIS, or SOE. Rear Admiral Godfrey will make sure you receive whatever you need."

"In that case, sir," Major Randal said, "I'd rather use my own people for the boarding party. Raiding Forces has an MGB but no crew. Can you supply gunboat sailors for the duration of the mission?"

"Admiral?"

"A veteran crew from Coastal Command will arrive at your station by this afternoon, Major."

"It's Randy Seaborn's boat, the 345, sir," Major Randal added. "I want him in command."

"Done," Rear Admiral Godfrey agreed without reservation. "I've known 'Hornblower' since he was in knee pants. He sails under a lucky star, a lad after my own heart."

"Anything else, John?"

"Squadron Leader Wilcox can fly the spotter mission, but if you want to increase our odds of finding a German E-boat, arrange for an entire squadron of Walruses. The more eyes we have in the sky, the better our chances of pulling this off fast."

"Actually, the bomber pilot is something of a problem," Colonel Menzies admitted. "The one we had was RAF. Unfortunately they pulled him from the operation. Would it be possible for your pilot to fly the Heinkel 111?"

"No problem, sir. Squadron Leader Wilcox has always wanted to go on a raid."

"We might be able to arrange to have the original RAF pilot

reassigned," "C" added. "However, it would tip our hand that we are pressing on with Ruthless. One can never discount the possibility of the Air Marshals doing something foolish if they find out. Interservice rivalry at times can be more of a hazard than the Nazis."

"Paddy can fly anything with wings," Major Randal said, "but I'll need to take a look at the four volunteers Fleming picked for the mission, sir."

"You shall find them qualified men," Colonel Menzies assured. "Achnacarry trained."

"I'm still going to want to check 'em out, sir."

"One thing Fleet Air Arm is free with is Walruses," Rear Admiral Godfrey injected, reflecting on Major Randal's earlier suggestion. "We can put a swarm of the things up, blanket the Channel. Guarantee we find an E-boat."

"In that case, gentlemen," Major Randal said, "let's go get the loot."

13

MISSION PREP

RAIDING FORCES' HEADQUARTERS AT SEABORN HOUSE WAS A beehive of activity. The Commandos were simultaneously on alert to conduct an immediate highly classified small-scale raid while organizing for imminent deployment by sea on another highly classified operation somewhere off the coast of Africa. A drumbeat of anticipation was pulsating through the command. Men moved with a purpose.

Specialist personnel for Operation Ruthless began arriving. First on the scene were a crew of combat-seasoned Royal Navy Volunteer Reserve motor gunboat men. The sailors had been precipitously yanked off operations on their own boat, assigned to Coastal Forces Command, where they had been going out nightly to do battle with their opposite numbers—the German E-boats. The officers and men reported to Lieutenant Randy "Hornblower" Seaborn. He ordered them to set about storing their gear on board and familiarizing themselves with MGB 345. A team from the firm of Randal and Boot arrived with a 10-centimeter Type 271 radar set to be installed on MGB 345 to help the crew pinpoint the E-boat the Raiders intended to board. Commander Richard Seaborn, who was still in residence at Seaborn House at the time, was pressed into service to act as the 345's navigator for the mission since he was familiar with the technology of the radar navigational equipment. He reported aboard to supervise the installation. The commander was one of the most experienced navigators in the senior service, having served in that capacity on HMS *Hood* prior to his assignment as a convoy router.

Swarms of signals personnel under the command of a full colonel from the Royal Corps of Signals descended on Seaborn House and began setting up a bank of long-range radios to handle the communications necessary to coordinate the complex air-sea operation.

A string of Supermarine Walruses, made by the very same firm that built the Spitfires and Seafires, winged in, looking like ruptured dragonflies and plopped down in the bay. The Walrus was an ugly-as-mud bi-wing, pusher-type amphibian armed with two Vickers .303 externally mounted machine guns. Today each had a pair of 250-pound fragmentation bombs mounted on the hard points on their wings. In total, fourteen planes flew in, more than normally found in a full-sized squadron. When word got round that a combat mission was in the offing, every Walrus pilot on flying status and all qualified amphibian pilots assigned to staff duties on the naval station where the little amphibians were based showed up to fly. Finding planes to accommodate the pilots was no problem. The Royal Navy had more of them than they did aviators assigned to fly them.

Lieutenant Commander Ian Fleming briefed the Walrus drivers. They were to fly a grid over the Channel looking for a lone German E-boat at sea out of sight of the enemy coast. The pilot that found one would radio the location to Seaborn House and remain on station, keeping it in visual contact. In turn, the Signals Station at Seaborn House would transmit the E-boat's location to Lieutenant Seaborn on the 345 and to Squadron Leader Paddy Wilcox, who would take off in the Heinkel 111 once the MGB reported she was in position to begin her attack. Squadron Leader Wilcox would make a simulated crash landing near the E-boat in order to trick them into rescuing the Commandos on board.

When the other Walrus pilots heard the transmission to Seaborn House giving the location of the E-boat, they were to immediately turn, fly in that direction, and take up a combat air patrol designed to cordon off and isolate the targeted German boat. Their orders were to attack any

Kriegsmarine craft attempting to approach it while the mission was in progress. Once the boarding party had returned on board the 345 and the MGB was away, the Walruses were to form up line astern and bomb the E-boat "into an oil slick."

Squadron Leader Paddy Wilcox was familiarizing himself with the Heinkel 111 he had ferried in, landed, and parked on a straight stretch of the country lane leading to Seaborn House. The German bomber was hidden under a half acre of camouflage netting.

The highly professional Raiding Forces Field Security Police from the Vulnerable Points Wing closely guarded the site. A ring of Raiders was pulling security in a tight perimeter two hundred meters in circumference encircling the Security Police. Outside the Raiders, one half mile deep around the concealed aircraft, a company of the Somerset Light Infantry was standing guard, and outside that the ever-vigilant Home Guardsmen had been called out and were on patrol in strength.

Inside Seaborn House Lieutenant Commander Fleming put up a large diagram of a German E-boat in the briefing room. Major John Randal briefed a ten-man team of Raiding Forces, backed up by a four-man reserve team, selected as the boarding party on their individual assignments. The Raiders were to capture the boat, with or without the assistance of the crew from the Heinkel 111. Special emphasis was placed on speed, violence of action, and the importance of rapidly securing the radio shack before any of the equipment inside could be destroyed. Captain Terry "Zorro" Stone was entrusted with that specific task.

Once the signals room had been cleared of enemy personnel a two-man technical team was to go in and obtain the loot. The pair had showed up at Seaborn House in the uniform of petty officers in the Royal Navy Volunteer Reserve, but to the trained eye of the sailors and raiders they were clearly civilians who had never worn a military uniform before. Not even Major Randal, who would be leading the boarding party, knew they were from the super secret Bletchley Park. What he did know was that he had been ordered to assign each of the two petty officers a handpicked Raider bodyguard for the duration of the mission. In the presence of the Raiding Forces commander, the two Raiders selected for the escort team, Sergeant Mike "March or Die" Mikkalis and Royal Marine Butch

Hoolihan, were briefed privately by Lieutenant Commander Fleming. His orders were succinct.

"In the likelihood of capture, shoot the individual you are escorting in the head, twice. You are licensed to kill."

Rehearsals for Operation Ruthless began immediately.

Squadron Leader Paddy Wilcox was in the cockpit conducting a detailed inspection of the Heinkel 111's instrument panel. Four tough-looking men in Luftwaffe uniforms were lounging under the wings, cleaning their Walther P-38 pistols. Each man carried two. Lieutenant Commander Ian Fleming was pacing back and forth, on tenterhooks, under the camouflage netting that covered the Heinkel 111. Major John Randal would be arriving at any moment to "meet" the four pseudo-Germans who were going to be on the Heinkel 111 flown by Squadron Leader Wilcox. Any time an outside player was brought into a tight-knit team of highly trained men, it was best to tread lightly or speak from a position of great authority backed up by strength. There was no telling how the Ruthless assault troops would react to a new mission commander. The men might not be on their best behavior.

To be perfectly honest, the four German-speaking soldiers scared Lieutenant Commander Fleming. They were dangerous men, a law unto themselves. He wondered how Major Randal was going to handle it. If it were up to him, he would arrive with an entourage of big tough Raiding Forces personnel armed to the teeth.

In the distance, the sound of a powerful engine thundered. Over the rise on the blacktopped country lane, a lone rider on a Norton motorcycle appeared. The cycle skidded to a stop at the top of the hill, its motor rumbling, as the man on it studied the scene below for a moment before lazily rolling down to the concealed Heinkel 111. Major Randal had come all by himself.

He was wearing his green beret and sand-colored parachute smock. A big scarlet cravat was wrapped around his neck and tucked into the smock. The scarf caught the eyes of the men in the German uniforms.

They scowled, having encountered military posers before. They had no use for them.

Lieutenant Commander Fleming had a sick feeling as Major Randal rolled up on the Norton and dismounted; this could all go terribly wrong.

"Men," Major Randal began as the Commandos reluctantly gathered around, "I've wanted to meet studs who think they can climb on board an E-boat and kill half a dozen Germans each, no problem."

One of the troopers, who looked like a Neanderthal, sneered. "I could snap your neck like a twig right now, Major, and there is not one thing you could do to stop me."

Since the giant was going on what amounted to a one-way mission within the hour there was not much in the way of punishment anyone could do to him if he did any worse than that and everyone present knew it.

"Well, go ahead," Major Randal said. "Then you'll have to follow Commander Fleming's, Ian Fleming's, original plan, which guarantees we'll all have supper in hell."

This was greeted by a long awkward silence.

"No one bloody explained it to us like bloody that," another of the Commandos piped up cheerfully. "If they bloody well 'ad, we'd 'ave 'ad the bloody royal red carpet all rolled out waitin' for you like, sir."

The Commandos in the Luftwaffe uniforms broke into guffaws. Not a pretty sound, but a good sign. Lieutenant Commander Fleming relaxed. It was the only time he had ever heard these hard-case individuals laugh other than when they were talking about killing something.

"We're not taking any prisoners," Major Randal said, removing the thick red cravat from around his neck and separating it into the five individual scarves he had borrowed from Captain the Lady Jane Seaborn's wardrobe maid. He handed one to each Commando and tossed the last to Squadron Leader Wilcox, who was standing off to the side observing the proceedings with a sardonic grin and holding a cocked Walter P-38 behind his back.

"When my Raiders storm the E-boat, we'll shoot any man not wearing a red scarf."

There was a murmur of appreciation from the troops. Someone should have thought of that detail before. No one had given one moment of thought to their welfare on this operation prior to the major having arrived. That fact did not pass unnoticed.

"Now listen up: Suicide missions being frowned on in Raiding Forces, we don't plan any. Every man that goes in comes out. Is that clear?"

"Clear, sir!"

"I'll see you men on board the prize."

14

THE TYPEWRITER

AFTER A FINAL BRIEFING AT SEABORN HOUSE AT O4OO HOURS, attended by all personnel participating in Operation Ruthless, the MGB 345 set sail. Just before sunrise the Walruses passed overhead in single file en route to taking up their stations. Almost immediately, one of the pilots spotted an E-boat leaving harbor on the French side of the Channel

A coordinate was passed to MGB 345. Commander Richard Seaborn huddled under the lantern over the radar set, studied the screen, and announced, "Target acquired."

Lieutenant Randy "Hornblower" Seaborn ordered a course change to the azimuth indicated by the radar contact. The sleek motor gunboat heeled over and powered on the compass bearing "Full Speed Ahead."

Squadron Leader Paddy Wilcox roared into the predawn sky and aimed the Heinkel 111 in the direction of the German E-boat. His passengers on board, the four German-speaking Commandos, were now covered in buckets of fresh chicken blood and wearing Lady Seaborn's bright scarlet scarves prominently around their necks.

"Ten minutes to target," Lieutenant Seaborn announced.

"Stand by Raiding Party," Major John Randal ordered.

The Walruses began converging to establish an aerial screen designed to isolate the E-boat.

The MGB 345 was pounding like a greyhound toward the German radar contact located out of sight over the horizon.

The Heinkel 111 screamed low overhead, rocking its wings. Then Squadron Leader Wilcox activated the smoke bomb attached to the tail of the fuselage, and dark black smoke started billowing out in a thick stream behind the German bomber.

"Enemy in sight," Lieutenant Seaborn read out, cool as ice.

"Lock and load," Major Randal commanded.

The Walrus that had made the initial contact with the E-boat turned in toward it and lined up to make a gun run on the enemy craft.

"Prepare for impact!" Squadron Leader Wilcox announced over the intercom to the Commandos.

The Heinkel was streaking straight as an arrow at the German E-boat. The W/T operator urgently started calling "Mayday, Mayday" in German.

"Bloody fantastic," Lieutenant Commander Ian Fleming shouted exuberantly observing the action through a powerful pair of binoculars. "The Heinkel managed to clip the radio antenna clean off the E-boat with its wing. That pilot of yours is a maniac!"

"Three minutes," Lieutenant Seaborn called.

After clobbering the antenna, the Heinkel careened past the E-boat. The Kriegsmarine crew could be seen standing on the deck looking up in awe as it sailed over. Then Squadron Leader Wilcox made a tight turn, streaming black smoke, came back around, and headed toward the German craft. He flashed his landing lights and brought the bomber in for a belly landing within one hundred yards of the air-sea rescue boat.

The pilot of the Walrus lined up on the E-boat began his attack run. The two Vickers machine guns began hammering. A stream of bullets splintered the deck of the German boat.

Squadron Leader Wilcox and the Commandos wasted no time abandoning ship. The Heinkel was going down like a rock. The five men made it out of the bomber but had trouble getting into the small rubber raft in the swell. The German sailors were lowering a net for them to use to climb aboard the E-boat, but the crew scattered when the craft suddenly came under aerial attack from the Walrus.

"Commence firing," Lieutenant Seaborn ordered his gunners as the 345 pounded toward the E-boat, closing rapidly. The volume of fire was staggering. MGBs packed almost the firepower of a small destroyer. Every weapon converged on the E-boat, and it appeared to blur in a hail of tracers, shot as full of holes as a cheese shredder.

The Walrus pilot bore in on his attack run, hammer down on the firing button. This was his first attack mission. His normal duties were to serve as the aid to a flag officer. Today in the cockpit, with an enemy in his sights, he reverted to the warrior he had trained to be. His fangs came out, his eyes narrowed, his pulse slowed, and against all orders he toggled his pair of 250-pound bombs. Fortunately both bombs missed; the last thing anyone wanted was to actually sink the patrol craft before it could be boarded. But they hit close enough to lift the stern of the E-boat completely out of the water, and when it slammed violently back down, the impact broke the crankshaft. Unfortunately the concussion also swamped the rubber raft that the Commandos and Squadron Leader Wilcox had just managed to board.

The German E-boat was dead in the water, but the little ship was not toothless. The starboard antiaircraft gunner, though a badly shaken sailor, promptly shot the attacking Walrus out of the sky.

The MGB 345 roared to within fifty yards of the E-boat, with all organic weapons blazing. The first Walrus had crashed a short distance away, and another Walrus was lining up to make a gun run, while yet another swooped in to rescue the crew of the downed floatplane.

Major Randal ordered, "Let 'er rip." On his command, every one of the ten men in the assault party, plus the four men of the reserve team and the two licensed-to-kill bodyguards, raised his Thompson submachine gun as planned and emptied a magazine into the E-boat point-blank. Then the Raiders quickly changed magazines and stood by ready to board.

Lieutenant Seaborn drove toward the E-boat at full power. His father, Commodore Seaborn, turned to look at him in alarm; they were in imminent peril of ramming. At the last possible second, the young skipper made a hard turn to port and sang out, "All astern, full."

The MGB 345 laid up against the E-boat amidships in a controlled crash.

"Boarding party away—follow me," Major Randal shouted, leaping onto the flush deck of the enemy ship and firing his Thompson from the hip.

The Raiders crossed over and boarded the E-boat in a single bound then exploded out in all directions. The men blasted their way to their assigned objectives screaming Comanche yells, Highland war cries, and other improvised screams at the top of their lungs. Surprise was complete. The Germans were overwhelmed. Too many things were happening to them at once.

Major Randal and Corporal Jack Merritt headed for the bridge. Firing on the move, with their Thompsons locked against their shoulders, the two gunned down the E-boat's captain and his executive officer and chopped the bridge into matchsticks in a hail of .45-caliber slugs as big around as cigars.

All over the E-boat the Raiders raced to carry out their individual assignments. The dead and dying German crew littered the deck. There was very little resistance.

Squadron Leader Wilcox and the Commandos finally arrived on board the E-boat. Straightaway the pseudo-Nazis ripped off their German blouses. They were not taking any chances, red scarf or not. Raiding Forces were on a rampage.

"Had to show off," Major Randal said to a thoroughly soaked Squadron Leader Wilcox when he reported to the bridge, "didn't you?"

"We did not want the Hun to be sending out radio signals," the rotund pilot replied with water dripping from his black eye patch. "Now did we, Major?"

"Well, you made sure of that."

Minutes after the attack began, the two civilians in Royal Navy uniform were escorted aboard the E-boat by Sergeant Mike "March or Die" Mikkalis and Royal Marine Butch Hoolihan. They proceeded directly to the radio compartment. Once there the two began disconnecting the Enigma machine.

Lieutenant "Pyro" Percy Stirling, the legendary exploder of lighthouses, came aboard with Private Ned Pompatus, each man lugging oversized Bergen packs stuffed with guncotton. Lieutenant Stirling had orders to blow the E-boat into the Kingdom Come. The only problem was he didn't know how he was going to do it, exactly. E-boats ran on nonexplosive diesel, not gasoline or the acetylene that went up so dramatically at the lighthouse during Operation Tomcat.

Lieutenant Stirling disappeared belowdecks while Private Pompatus repaired to the torpedo tubes mounted on the bow. Lieutenant Stirling had decided to blow the diesel tanks in hopes that diesel would spark off within a confined space. He likewise hoped that the explosion would detonate the torpedoes and obliterate the ship. An aerial bombing of a ship at sea was too uncertain for this critical mission. Captain Terry "Zorro" Stone came up on deck and announced, "Loot secured."

"Move it to the 345," Major John Randal ordered. "Nice job, Terry."

Sergeant Mikkalis and Royal Marine Hoolihan trooped by on their way back to the MGB, their wards in tow. Major Randal called out, "Get me a headcount, Sergeant Mikkalis."

When everyone was off the E-boat and Sergeant Mike "March or Die" Mikkalis reported a "good count," Major John Randal shouted down into the engine room. "Light it off, Percy!"

Lieutenant "Pyro" Percy Stirling set the five-minute time fuses and burst on deck shouting, "Fire in the hole, fire in the hole, fire in the hole!" He jumped onto the MGB, followed closely by Major Randal, the last Raider off the E-boat.

The 345 thundered toward Seaborn House, kicking up a big rooster's tail in her wake as she executed that age-old military maneuver known popularly in Raiding Forces as "getting the hell out of Dodge." Captain Terry "Zorro"Stone and Major Randal sat cross-legged on the stern cradling their Thompson submachine guns. Captain Stone produced a couple of Players from his sterling silver cigarette case that they lit with Major Randal's battered 26th Cavalry Regiment Zippo.

"You know what the loot was we went to all this trouble to obtain, old stick?"

"No."

"A typewriter."

"Really?"

Behind them the charges on the E-boat cooked off with a loud crack, then a massive explosion, followed by a shockwave that rocked the motor gunboat, causing the Raiders and sailors to shout in surprise. A fat gray column of smoke with a mushroom-shaped top magically appeared where the German craft had been an instant before. The men on the 345 cheered. Apparently diesel fuel in a confined space did have explosive powers.

Once again Lieutenant Stirling had delivered a masterpiece. The Raiders began chanting "Pyro, Pyro, Pyro . . . "

"A typewriter," Major Randal said. "You're sure about that?"

"Too true," Captain Stone drawled. "Electric model."

The Raiders did not enjoy the heroes' welcome they had experienced after Operation Tomcat. No crowd of dignitaries, beautiful women, or Marine band greeted the 345 when she pulled into her berth at Seaborn House. A staff car was waiting to whisk the loot to Bletchley Park, a pair of stone-faced, Tommy-gun–toting Royal Marines standing on the running boards. Lieutenant Commander Ian Fleming piled into the car, clutching the canvas bag with the loot inside, and roared off to Bletchley Park.

Rear Admiral John Godfrey personally conducted the debriefing of the mission in Seaborn House immediately after the Raiders disembarked from the MGB 345. It was short and to the point.

"Now here this, gentlemen. What took place today never happened," Rear Admiral Godfrey bellowed at the group of pilots, sailors, Commandos, and Raiders assembled. "Forget this raid. Erase it from your minds. Discussion of Operation Ruthless is a violation of the Official Secrets Act and any breach, however minor, will be prosecuted vigorously."

The officers and men in the room sat completely silent, most of them looking down at their boots. The adrenaline was beginning to wear off. Post-mission wind-down was starting to set in. Nevertheless, they were a happy bunch.

"Having said that," the admiral continued, "your country owes you a great debt, one it can never adequately repay. You men have performed an invaluable service for King and Empire, greater than you will ever know. Much of intelligence value was gained by your efforts. More's the pity, since you shall never be given official credit for it, not in this lifetime.

"Unfortunately," he lied, "the specific item we were looking for was not, I say again NOT, on board the E-boat."

"You reckon," Captain Terry "Zorro" Stone leaned over and whispered to Major John Randal, "Godfrey simply felt the need of a new electric typewriter for his personal secretary? Fleming says he has an eye for the skirt; even gave the order at NID recently to only hire the pretty Wrens on the grounds they keep secrets better."

"If a typewriter's what the man was after," Major Randal said, "we sure as hell kidnapped it for him."

ADVANCE PARTY

15

A CLIPPER COCKTAIL

THE REGAL BOAC BOEING-BUILT B-314 FLYING CLIPPER made a long takeoff run across the water and became airborne in slow motion. Pale yellow moonlight reflected off the waves passing below. Overhead, a fighter escort of twin-engine, long-range Bristol Type 156 Beaufighters circled protectively. The fighters would cover the Clipper until it was well out into the Atlantic.

On board in the sixth compartment, Major John Randal and Captain Terry "Zorro" Stone settled in for a long, over-water flight. The sixth was the smallest compartment on the plane, snuggled next to the stewardess galley located in front of the deluxe suite in the tail. It sported two reclining loungers that would fold all the way back into a semi-bed. Curtains could be pulled around the compartment for privacy.

Travel in a commercial flying boat, especially a Clipper, was luxurious in the old-world style and rivaled the elegance of the finest ocean liners. In prewar days, a one-way ticket from the United Kingdom to the United States on the Clipper cost the equivalent of $10,000 US.

Every passenger on board was either a very important person or operating under the illusion they were. Only thirty-six passengers were allowed on overnight flights. Competition for a space was vicious among the flag-set. Rank has its privileges, and travel on a Flying Clipper represented the ultimate status symbol. Only the crème de la crème of the top echelon of military officers, minister-level government officials, and ambassador-level diplomats were even aware the Clipper was available for military transport. The run-of-the-mill VIP thought a seat on a Royal Navy Catalina was as good as it gets.

To rate a berth on the Clipper required what was referred to as a "God-high priority." There were more than a few raised eyebrows when Major Randal and Captain Stone came on board at the very last minute before takeoff. If either of the Raiding Forces officers noticed those eyebrows, they gave no sign of it. Both the young officers were wearing exquisitely cut Pembrooks-made lightweight khaki drill service tropical uniforms with all qualification insignia and decorations removed. The only markings were regimental badges indicating that one of them was in The Rangers, now the 9th Battalion of the King's Royal Rifle Corps, and the other was a member of the Life Guards.

The two made their way straight to the lounge chairs in compartment No. 6 and immediately pulled the curtains shut. Each compartment, or "lounge" as the aircrew preferred to call them on the Clipper, was decorated in a different color. No. 6 was a soothing pale blue-green with matching turquoise carpet.

"The exact colors you would expect to find in a loony bin," Captain Stone observed laconically. "I feel like I need to spend some time in one, after the events of the last twenty-four hours."

The stylish art deco lights, thick pile carpeting, heavy soundproofing behind the burled-walnut paneled walls, and comfortable upholstery were all an attempt to create an elegant style of air travel suitable for the titled, rich, and famous. BOAC had spared no expense for its super-wealthy prewar clientele. Now, with the war on, the effect came off as overdone. In point of fact, to the Commando officers, the Clipper gave off the charm of an airborne cathouse.

The captain switched on the intercom to announce they would be "flying at 13,000 feet, with a cruising speed of 185 miles per hour."

Major Randal unlocked the briefcase attached to his wrist. Both officers took off their KDS tropical uniform blouses and hung them up. Under the blouses they were both wearing Colt .38 Super automatics in shoulder holsters, which they left on.

Just at that moment, the curtains swished open. A stunning redhead— one of the elite who were handpicked for their jobs from a legion of experienced BOAC stewardess applicants because they looked like fashion models and exuded that world-famous Clipper Girl personality—sprang into their lounge to plump up their pillows and spread some good Clipper cheer with no small amount of Flying Clipper glamour.

Two things then happened more or less simultaneously.

First, the Clipper Girl noticed that the young officers were neither members of the royal family nor admirals, though she did have to double-check to make sure the one with the cute blond cavalry moustache was not the heartthrob movie star Errol Flynn.

Second, she saw the pistols. In less time than it took Superman to make a costume change in a phone booth, she went from being Miss Clipper Congeniality to the Wicked Witch of BOAC. Weapons were not allowed on board unless stowed in carry-on baggage, unloaded.

"You cannot have those guns on our passenger deck!" the stewardess hissed, trying to keep her voice under control. She was following her training and attempting to stay calm, contain the situation, and not cause a panic among the other passengers. BOAC was very clear on the issue of passengers carrying weapons, even in time of war when all officers were routinely armed.

Major Randal, having noticed that something was amiss, looked up at her and said, "Frogspawn."

"WHAM!" The curtains slammed shut and Red was gone.

Captain Stone glanced at him curiously and inquired, "Frogspawn?"

"A secret code word," Major Randal explained. "A trick Lady Jane taught me."

"Whatever is it supposed to do?"

"Anything you want it to. The way it works, you say the secret code word and then brazen it out. Jane says she makes up different ones. I like 'Frogspawn.'"

"Have you ever tried it before?" Captain Stone asked skeptically.

"Stopped a train once."

"You stopped a train merely by saying 'Frogspawn'?"

"Yea, I went to the conductor and said 'Frogspawn.' He looked like he had been brained by a moonbeam covered in pixie dust. Worked like a charm. Give it a try sometime."

"Why would you care to stop a train, old stick?"

"To make a phone call."

"Surely, you jest."

"Negative."

"What could possibly have been so important you would stop a train during time of a war, holding up the hundreds of officers and troops on board so that you could use the blower."

When he saw the look on Major John Randal's face he shook his head and started laughing until tears came to his eyes. "You called Jane, you lovesick fool. You are a lost cause, a goner that's for sure."

"I was testing it out."

"Well, I have the distinct impression," Captain Stone laughed, "'Frogspawn' failed to do the trick on Red."

"She must not be cleared for high-level secret code words."

"Well, neither are we."

The curtain sprang open again and the stewardess, flanked by the Clipper's captain, was standing there. The pair did not look happy. The captain was middle-aged, tanned, and going to fat, but he was clearly a take-charge kind of guy, one of the most experienced flying-boat pilots on the BOAC roster

He took one look inside compartment No. 6 and ordered straight-away, "Give these gentlemen anything they desire. Consider them my personal guests for the duration of the flight. Is that clear?"

"Sir?" squawked the startled Clipper Girl.

"Who is the most exalted passenger you have ever catered to?" the captain demanded, sounding suspiciously like a man harboring a dangerously short fuse. "On any flight, ever?"

"I had the Prince of Wales on board once, sir."

"You give these two officers the exact same royal treatment you gave the Prince of Wales. Make sure the rest of the staff understand my instructions to do the same. I repeat, these officers are my personal guests for the duration of their time on board this aircraft."

Red looked as if she had swallowed a fishbone.

"Gentlemen," the pilot said, "I would consider it a personal favor for you to come up to visit the flight deck whenever you find it convenient. My flight crew would love to have a chance to visit with you. Enjoy your flight, and if you need anything do not hesitate to ask. It is an honor and a privilege to have you aboard.

"Oh, and should you have to shoot someone, hit what you aim at. Try not to puncture any vital parts of my airplane. We will be a long way out to sea for most of the flight."

Captain Stone could barely contain himself until the curtain was fully shut, and then he blurted in amazement, "Wow, that 'Frogspawn' stuff really did the trick! I sure am impressed."

"I don't think so, Terry." Major Randal said. "When we boarded, I saw the captain reading a two-day-old copy of the *London Times*. Our pictures from when we got back from Tomcat were on the front page."

Red came back almost immediately, and now she looked as if she had taken a happy pill. "Sorry about the misunderstanding. I had no idea you were national heroes. No hard feelings, I hope?"

"You are forgiven this once," Captain Stone said magnanimously. "Do not let it happen again."

"I try not to read the paper because the news is always so depressing," she confessed. "The rest of the girls are all simply dying to come back and meet you, but I told them you were too busy. How would you like it if I whipped up a couple of Clipper cocktails as a peace token?"

"Clipper cocktail," Captain Stone perked up, "whatever is that?"

"Our official Clipper concoction," Red explained, back in full Miss Clipper Congeniality mode. "It is a yummy drink that consists of one-half ounce golden light rum, one-half ounce vermouth, and one-half tablespoon of grenadine poured over cracked ice. It's smashing!"

"I shall be willing to drink one of your Clipper cocktails," Captain Stone offered charitably, "if you agree to try a Black Strap."

"What's a Black Strap?" Red asked in her bubbly Clipper Girl voice.

"A secret mixture of brandy and port; it's the regimental drink of the Life Guards Regiment."

"You are a member of the Life Guards?" She sounded impressed. "Why in the world would a Life Guardsman be on a Commando raid? Shouldn't you have been home protecting Buckingham Palace?" Red clearly knew her regiments.

Captain Stone gave her one of his deadliest lady-killer smiles while tapping a Player's Navy Cut on his elegant sterling silver cigarette case and drawled, "I was merely along to lend tone to what would have otherwise been a vulgar brawl."

"So, if I agree to drink your drink," the spectacular Clipper Girl laughed, "then you will drink mine . . . is that the deal? How fun!"

"I wouldn't be too quick to accept that Black Strap challenge if I were you," Major Randal warned. "Tradition dictates you drink it standing on your head."

Red's beautiful, pale blue-gray eyes fizzed. "Sorry boys, I am not allowed to imbibe on duty," she said in her official Clipper Girl tone—cool as the North Pole and about as remote. "However," she continued without missing a heartbeat, "I will try anything once if you give me a rain check."

"Bring on that Clipper cocktail!" Captain Stone semi-shouted. "Peace in our time."

"How about you, Major?"

"I'm not drinking any Black Strap, but you might as well make it two."

Red went off to make the drinks.

"Well, that was certainly impressive, Captain Zorro . . . 'I'll try anything once.'"

"Did you see that thing with her eyes?" Captain Stone asked. "Where they went buzz?"

"Yes, I did."

"What do you think that was about?"

"I have no idea, but I'm confident you're going to give me a full, in-depth report as soon as you find out."

"Consider it done."

They settled in for a long flight. The locked briefcase was packed with documents, and the plan was for the two officers to study them thoroughly before the Clipper reached the Gold Coast. As the evening turned out, they had to spend several hours explaining the details of Operation Tomcat to their spellbound fellow passengers before they were able to press on with their homework. Everyone on board was thrilled to hear a rare bit of good news about England's war effort.

The two young officers were modest. But not so much so that it kept Captain Terry "Zorro" Stone from discreetly accepting the telephone numbers of a couple of the other Clipper Girls. After all, that was one of the perks of being a celebrated warrior.

When the last of the callers left their lounge, the Life Guards officer summed up his estimation of the situation, tongue firmly in cheek. "I would have to say it is better to be a live hero than a dead one."

"You're already a dead man," Major John Randal laughed. "After Red gets through jumping your degenerate bones there won't be enough of you left to bury."

"'Into the Valley of Death rode . . .'" Captain Stone quoted. "You know I quite enjoyed that Clipper cocktail."

"Ride boldly, ride."

"I fully intend to."

"Do you really believe Rear Admiral Godfrey meant what he said?" Major Randal asked, changing the subject.

"You mean his idea that good-looking Wrens are better at keeping secrets?"

"No, about the loot not being on the E-boat."

"John, when those two 'specialists' saw that funny-looking typewriter," Captain Stone replied, "you would have been convinced they had laid eyes on the Holy Grail. Have no doubt, whatever it was, we got the loot."

"That's what I thought."

16

PYGMIES AND PROSTITUTES

FINALLY MAJOR JOHN RANDAL BEGAN READING THE DOCUMENTS inside the briefcase. They told a strange and fascinating tale. When he finished with a page, he handed it to Captain Terry "Zorro" Stone, who was reclining on the other lounger. As the Commandos read, the sensation of being transported into the great unknown on a desperate venture grew.

The island protectorate of Rio Bonita was first claimed by a Spanish navigator in 1473. Spain sent settlers to the island, named after the spectacularly beautiful river that ran through it and emptied into a tiny harbor they called San Pedro. But most of the settlers died of scarlet fever.

In 1785 Rio Bonita was ceded to Portugal for reasons not made clear. The Portuguese brought in more settlers, set up cacao plantations, and leased timber concessions. Prior to the arrival of the Spaniards and Portuguese, the only inhabitants of the island had been a tribe of playful pygmies who hunted in the mountainous triple-canopy jungle that covered the western third of the island and frolicked on the white sandy beaches on the eastern side.

Being hunters, not gatherers, the pygmies refused to work for the Portuguese on the cacao plantations or to harvest timber. Manual laborers, primarily from the East African Bone tribe, were imported to supply the workforce. These new laborers were housed in conditions approaching those in the most unspeakable prison camps and were treated as virtual slaves. The Bones, a tribe with skeletons in their closet so to speak, eventually took culinary matters into their own hands. They ate pygmy.

The result was a greatly diminished pygmy population to the extent the little people became well-nigh extinct except in the isolated western third of the island, which was cut off by the breathtaking Rio Bonita River. Reports that some highly antisocial pygmies inhabited the western bank of the river went unsubstantiated because no one who crossed it ever came back alive to confirm the sightings. Equally uncorroborated were lurid accounts that the surviving pygmies were headhunters who had turned into cannibals themselves.

Emissaries out from Lisbon made an inspection tour of Rio Bonita in 1805. They reported to the Portuguese Colonial Department there were not enough "white women" on the island for the Portuguese and few remaining Spanish men who had survived the scarlet fever epidemic. Miscegenation had occurred, resulting in a high number of mulatto children. It was not the kind of report an expansionist colonial European country like Portugal wanted to acknowledge, much less publicize.

What to do? Being a practical-minded people, the Portuguese simply introduced a policy that they had used from time to time in other colonies, protectorates, and territories around the globe—with varying degrees of success. They shipped every white woman in Portugal who had been convicted of prostitution to Rio Bonita straightaway. Problem solved. Well, almost.

There was a finite number of hookers in Portugal. Their sudden departure to darkest Africa created an outcry from the sporting element of the male citizenry. To quiet the local unrest and simultaneously resolve the harlot supply-and-demand problem, Portugal adopted an entrepreneurial approach.

The government advertised throughout Europe for "white prostitutes who would like to resettle on Rio Bonita, all travel expenses paid, and become honest women." To everyone's delight, the first group of volunteer strumpets who traveled out to the island actually liked the place and wrote letters home to that affect. Some of their girlfriends visited, liked what they saw, and in short order there were plenty of European women to go around.

"Do you think SIS or NID is making this up?" Captain Terry "Zorro" Stone demanded incredulously. "This is outrageous!"

"Why would they?" Major John Randal said, passing him another page. "Didn't England stock Australia with convicts? What's the difference?"

"Excellent point," Captain Stone said going back to his reading. "The original Australian settlers used to shoot aborigines for sport. Now that I think about it, the Portuguese may have had the superior plan."

On Rio Bonita the terrain consisted of two-thirds flat, lush cacao plantations. The timber concessions were mostly closed down. Nearly all the hardwood had been harvested long ago and the land converted into more cacao plantations. The other one-third of the terrain was the unsettled triple-canopy jungle, mountainous country—inhabited by headhunter pygmies, possibly cannibals—previously mentioned.

The climate was mild, if a tad humid. The sun shone virtually 365 days per year. There was only one large town, and it was located around its namesake, the tiny harbor San Pedro.

Approximately three thousand Europeans, primarily Portuguese plus a few Spaniards, lived in San Pedro. The major industry besides the cacoa trade was tourism from West Africa, primarily from visitors coming over from the British Gold Coast or the French colonies adjoining it to party in the bars lining the harbor. The British and French colonists liked to stay at the small, quaint hotels in San Pedro because of their European flavor. The architecture, an eye-pleasing Spanish-Portuguese-Tuscany blend, gave San Pedro a mellow ambience.

Most tourists arrived in San Pedro by private yacht, the occasional touring steamer, the flying boat that serviced West Africa biweekly, or the daily ferry from Accra, eighteen nautical miles away on the Gold Coast. It was a common event for private boats and fishing craft of various sizes to call on San Pedro at any hour of the night or day.

An immigration official was stationed in the port of San Pedro. His primary responsibility was not immigration, however, of which there was very little; it was to collect docking fees from the tourist steamers and merchant ships. Docking fees were a major source of revenue for the port.

Even so, the inspector was on duty only during the daylight hours. If a ship came in at night he collected her docking fee the next day.

The system was very casual. No real attempt was made to inspect passports or to log the comings and goings that took place round the clock. What would be the point?

Rio Bonita did not have an army, a navy, or an air force. But the protectorate did station a fifty-man Defense Force in small outposts dotted along the length of the west bank, non-pygmy side of the Rio Bonita on anti-headhunter patrol. Though the force did not see much action, successive governors-general of Rio Bonita felt it was better to be safe than sorry; you just never knew.

A single Defense Force antiaircraft battery of three Oerlikon 20-millimeter towed guns guarded the Port of San Pedro. The air-defense weapons could also serve in the ground-defense role in the event of an amphibious assault from the sea, though none was anticipated. Mainly, the cannons were used for ceremonial purposes.

The San Pedro Police Department was ten men strong. There were no other military, paramilitary, or police forces on the island except for a few individual police constables in one-man posts dotted around the eastern, civilized two-thirds of the island to handle domestic disputes.

Somewhere between 180 and 200 German and Italian sailors from the *Ems*, *Egadi*, and *Giove* were interned on their ships in San Pedro Harbor for the duration. Under international law, they were not armed. Theoretically, some authority in Rio Bonita had disarmed them, but exactly which one was not clear.

Not to worry, the interned sailors were purported to be civilian merchant marine types who did not pose any threat. But then again, they were supposed to be idly vegetating on the beach until the war was over, not operating a highly effective clandestine naval intelligence radio station.

Aerial photos showed the three Axis ships anchored bow and stern. All three were permanently moored, their anchors encased in concrete as stipulated by international mandate. In the photos, the ships had their boarding ladders down, presumably so water taxis could ferry their crew to and from the shore at all hours.

Knowledgeable sources reported that many of the Italian sailors were broke most of the time because Italy had to send money to them via neutral Lisbon, which took a long, long while to accomplish. Generally the men had already spent all of their pay before it arrived, leaving them in a vicious never-ending cycle of debt. The intelligence report stated "some of the Italian crew members are barely able to sustain themselves."

The captains of the *Egadi* and *Giove* had jumped ship, moved ashore, and taken up residence with local women. The two ship's captains were clearly no longer interested in the health or welfare of their sailors. In fact, the report claimed they virtually never set foot on board their ships.

Discipline on board the Italian flagged ships was rated nonexistent, morale low. The crews had stripped their two vessels of all their brass fittings—along with anything else of commercial value—and sold them at fire-sale prices to buy food and supplies. Some of the Eyetie sailors had been forced to take part-time, menial jobs in San Pedro in order to earn enough money simply to eat. The locals generally looked down on the Italian seamen and treated them as second-class citizens. Only the Bones were lower on the social pecking order.

On the German ship *Ems* it was a different story. Captain Wolf Steiner was a practicing martinet. The aerial photos showed his men standing inspection, chipping paint, mopping, splicing ropes, making repairs, and working like galley slaves. She was clearly still operating as a warship with a purpose, and her skipper was not going to tolerate any decline in efficiency. If there was going to be a problem Major John Randal knew it was going to happen on the *Ems*.

After he had completed reading the intelligence dossier, Major Randal discovered a small pamphlet that Major Lawrence "Larry" Grand had thoughtfully included. The title was "How to Use High Explosives." A handwritten note scrawled on the margin said, "Our brief is to set Europe, not Africa, 'ablaze.' Thought you might find this material helpful. Bon Voyage—G."

He handed the booklet to Captain Terry "Zorro" Stone without comment.

"We are never going to live that lighthouse down," the movie-star-handsome cavalry officer observed ruefully. "He makes a good point, though. We need to be very stealthy. I for one would not want to spend any more time than absolutely necessary on that little slice of tropical island hell."

"Yes, we do," Major Randal said. "Have any thoughts on how we're going to pull this off?"

"I've got to admit I'm baffled, old stick. Do you?"

"Not a clue. I brought you along under the pretense of being my operations officer. Come up with a plan, Captain."

"Boarding is one thing; getting three ships out of the harbor is something else altogether. I shall need to give this some serious thought."

"Well, I'm going to get some shut-eye. Wake me up when you have one."

"John, I'm a Life Guardsman. We're not known for being brainy, remember?"

"How could I forget?"

"One thing is for sure, though."

"What's that?"

"This trip is not shaping up boring."

"Try to come up with a plan."

Eventually the big Boeing B-314 Clipper splashed down at Accra, Gold Coast Colony. Normally it did not land there. The flight plan had been diverted to deliver Major John Randal and Captain Terry "Zorro" Stone to their destination. If there was such a thing as being in the middle of nowhere, they had just plopped down into it. The Gold Coast was where people were sent when whoever it was that assigned them there could not think of anyplace worse to maroon them in.

A tanned, extremely fit man in his mid-thirties boarded the plane and was immediately escorted to compartment No. 6 by the magnificent Clipper Girl, Red.

"Ahoy, anyone home?" he called as he poked his sun-bronzed bald pate through the curtain. "Don't shoot, men. I am not hostile."

"Who might you be?" asked Major Randal.

"A friend."

"In that case," Captain Stone ordered, "advance, friend, and be recognized."

Slipping into the small compartment, the man in the khaki bush jacket carefully shut the curtains and explained in a stage whisper, "Our mutual acquaintance in London, a man who generally wears a red carnation in his lapel, asked me to meet your plane. My orders are to show you this as my first official act of business." He produced a sealed envelope from his jacket with one hand while conjuring a knife, seemingly out of thin air, with the other. There was a metallic "click" as the blade switched open at the touch of a concealed button.

The bald man watched discreetly to see if the two young officers were suitably impressed as he slit the envelope open with the razor-sharp blade. They were. The sleight of hand with the knife was a genuine attention getter.

Using the tips of his fingers he gingerly extracted a letter written on flimsy paper from the envelope, opened it, and held it up so the two could read it but he could not see its contents. The Raiding Forces officers read: "MISSION APPROVED BY PRIME MINISTER STOP GOOD HUNTING STOP SIGNED G STOP"

"Got it?" Baldie asked. "Make sure you do before you say so."

"Got it," said a stone-faced Major Randal.

The switchblade clicked shut, vanished, and a lighter appeared in its place. Baldie flipped it open with one hand, flicked the wheel, then touched the flame to the corner of the flimsy message. "Poof"—it disappeared in a bright white flash without leaving a trace of ash.

"A good thing Red did not see you do that," Captain Stone opined.

"Yeah," Major Randal agreed. "You're probably not supposed to ignite stuff on an airplane."

"Gentlemen, if you will follow me."

They did with alacrity.

17

DEAD END OF NOWHERE

MAJOR JOHN RANDAL AND CAPTAIN TERRY "ZORRO" STONE followed the bald man off the Flying Clipper. They were the only passengers disembarking in Accra.

Captain Stone winked at Red as they went out the door. "Call you as soon as we return to London."

"If I happen to be flying, leave a number," the lovely Clipper Girl said, giving him a quick kiss on the cheek as they exited the airplane. "I am so looking forward to your Black Strap. Do try to be careful."

"Careful, of what?" Captain Stone protested over his shoulder as he went down the steps. "We're here on leave."

"Sure you are, hero."

"It's a vacation."

"Right, one would be wise to presume the Gold Coast, aka the 'white man's grave,' is called that for a reason. Have fun, boys."

"Black strap?" Baldie asked with a cocked eyebrow. "What's that?"

"Long story," Major John Randal said. "The short version is it's a drink."

"For a second there I was beginning to get a little nervous, at least about one of you." Baldie held his hand out palm down and rocked it back and forth. "Sounded a little, you know—"

"Oh, there's plenty of cause to have concerns about Captain Stone's moral turpitude. I sure do. Red knows she has to drink her Black Strap standing on her head."

"You don't say."

He led them to a clay-brick-yellow-colored 1935 Chevrolet four-door sedan. Then Baldie trudged back to make sure their stowed luggage was being unloaded from the B-314 Flying Clipper's cargo bay. In a short while, he returned with a muscular African BOAC baggage handler who was lugging all their gear. The bulging bags were loaded into the car's trunk.

"Normally the Clipper never lands here," Baldie explained. "You two made an unscheduled stop and I bet there are some very unhappy, very important people on board right about now."

They watched the big, elegant flying boat taxi out to open water for its takeoff run. The brilliant sunny day was a startling contrast to the cold, fog, mist, and incessant rain they had recently been experiencing in the British Isles.

"Someone sure wanted you shooters out here fast and well rested," Baldie observed, "or they were trying to make a statement."

"Why not both?" Captain Stone responded.

They climbed into the Chevrolet, with Baldie at the wheel and Captain Stone in the passenger's seat. Major Randal sat directly behind his fellow Raider. "Welcome to the Gold Coast, gentlemen, the dead end of nowhere. I hope you lads have come out to make my life interesting and exciting."

"Why would we do that?" a poker-faced Major Randal asked.

"Accra is a jungle backwater. Life travels a lot slower out here than what you men have been used to. For example, our newspapers run behind the UK but we do eventually receive them. Seen ours today?"

In the front passenger seat Captain Stone turned and held up the *London Times* edition Baldie had been reading while waiting for their plane to arrive. The bold headline screamed "BRITISH PARACHUTISTS CONDUCT DARING RAID." There was a large black-and-white photo of Major John Randal in his beret and parachute smock stepping ashore from the HMY *Arrow*. A warlike-looking Captain Terry Stone was at his side carrying his Thompson submachine gun casually over his shoulder by the Cutts compensator on the muzzle.

"Now I ask myself, what could bring a couple of thrusters like you two to sleepy old Accra, the same two blades who captured a real live German general a while back, as I seem to recall."

"We're going on safari," Major Randal said.

"Major, that is exactly what the movers and shakers in the colony are going to be afraid of. What kind of game are you after, exactly? You two have a reputation for going for the really big stuff."

"We're tourists."

"Right, you two gentle sightseers might as well understand, if you are hoping for any support from the Gold Coast authorities for whatever enterprise it is you have in mind out here . . . forget it right now.

"Why, you might ask? Have either of you looked at a map? The Gold Coast is completely surrounded by Vichy French–controlled territory." Baldie glanced sideways at Captain Stone and then looked over his shoulder to address Major Randal. "We should be at war with them; they are, after all, the enemy, but the colonial administrations on both sides of the wire have a live-and-let-live policy in effect out here that amounts to a private, wholly unauthorized, completely illegal ceasefire."

"Charming," drawled Captain Stone.

"No one will come right out and say it, but the official unofficial policy in the Gold Coast is to try not to antagonize the opposition and pray they reciprocate. All parties concerned, friend and foe alike, would dearly love this war to simply pass right on by, except for the parts where they can make some money off of it."

"It's not going to," Major Randal said.

"That's right, Major. Most of the colonial officials are so dumb they can't read a newspaper, but they do look at the pictures." Baldie laughed. "Now, the Clipper diverts to drop two famous raiding specialists off in sleepy old Accra. Even the Colonel Blimp types we have running this glasshouse are going to be able figure out that what happens next is not going to be good for them."

"We're tourists," Major Randal repeated. "I'm planning to work on my tan."

"No one will believe that." Baldie laughed again. "'Don't create waves' is the order of the day in the Gold Coast Colony, and you two have the look of world-champion wave makers."

"What about you? Where do you fit in?" Major Randal asked to shift the attention off of them.

"I report to the same firm as our mutual friend with the red carnation, which means I work for you, according to my most recent marching orders. In the Gold Coast I am the man to see. Just don't expect too much from me. I am not the most popular citizen out here myself."

"What does that mean," Captain Stone inquired, "*exactly*?"

"Means I am not allowed to do anything that will upset our frog-eating neighbors. Under no circumstances am I ever remotely to take any action large or small that might provide the Germans the slightest possible excuse to intervene militarily in the Gold Coast region. I hate this bloody job!"

"What's your name?" Major Randal asked.

"Oh, sorry, I never quite got around to introducing myself, did I? In my business names are not all that important." The SOE man grinned. "I'm Jim Taylor, and that may or may not be my real name. You can call me Baldie; everyone else does."

"Do you like to be called Baldie?" Captain Stone queried.

"No bother to me."

"In that case, Jim," Major Randal said, "where are you taking us?"

"To a safe house for a clandestine meeting with some of the local intelligence, police, and colonial office movers and shakers, Major. I had it laid on before I saw the newspaper. *Clandestine*. That's a joke now, haha. With your pictures on the front page, I might as well hire a marching band for an escort. Hey, I have an idea. Why not hold a press conference to announce your intentions?

"Hand that paper back to me, will you? Let me read you something—I bloody love this part."

Steering with one hand, Baldie held the paper up with the other and read, "According to Captain Terry Stone, MC, who has the colorful nickname 'Zorro,' 'When the firing broke out on the objective, red, green, and silver tracers were flashing back and forth, hither and thither, like 300 miles-per-hour fairies—'

"Did you really say that, 'Captain Terry Stone, MC, nickname 'Zorro'? Is that what tracers look like to you . . . fairies?"

"Evil fairies," Captain Stone replied facetiously. "I would have said so, too, except I was concerned about frightening the young readership."

"Fairies hither and thither, that is bloody great hyperbole—"

"Do any of these people we are meeting have an idea why we are out here?" Major Randal cut him off.

"Not the slightest notion. No one in the Gold Coast has any idea what you are planning, including me. And *I* have a need to know. We are all tremendously interested, though, for different reasons of course."

"What's your angle, Jim?"

"Major, I am a professional intelligence officer. At least I used to be until they formed SOE and transferred me to that bughouse zoo along with the rest of Section D. Somehow I managed to get myself exiled to the Gold Coast. For the record, mark me down as sick and tired of the pink gin on the veranda, everybody watching the sun go down, playing croquet on the manicured lawn, don't rock the boat, hope the war ends soon, give peace a chance out here. Life in the Gold Coast is making me stir crazy!"

"Really."

"True. I like arranging for things to go boom in the dark when no one is around and to make bad people disappear in the trunks of cars. Whatever it is you have going, count me in. Maybe if we handle this right, whatever it is, I can arrange to get myself kicked out of the colony after it's all over."

Captain Stone looked in the rearview mirror and made eye contact with Major Randal in the backseat. "What makes you so sure the colonial officers are concerned about our coming out here?"

"Commandos with a penchant for daring operations against all odds are exactly what the local politicos have been staying awake nights sweating bullets about. Now you are out here and on the front page of the *London Times*. Bloody great timing! For the record gentlemen, this has to be the worst operational security in the history of covert operations!"

"How do you recommend we go about establishing an understanding with the locals," Major Randal asked, "if only to keep them from interfering with us?"

"Going to be difficult," Baldie answered thoughtfully. "No matter what, you are never going to be able to trust anyone out here. Not ever, not for one minute. The politics out here are a special brand of corrupt, bordering on outright treasonous. I do not exaggerate."

"That bad?" Captain Stone asked.

"Unfortunately, the people in the government out here do not see themselves as a part of the day-to-day war effort and resent having to participate," the SOE station chief explained. "If you had some way to prove your mission is not raiding for the sake of raiding—or, even worse, some kind of economy-of-force ploy designed to draw German troops out of Europe and into West Africa—that might help.

"Or if you could produce written confirmation you two are here on a mission sanctioned by the Prime Minister, something like that would get their attention. Otherwise, the authorities are going to treat you like lepers. Expect them to try to find some way to checkmate whatever it is you are out here to do and justify their actions as being in the best interests of the colony."

"Well, Jim, you burned up our only proof," Major Randal said. "And we did come out here to do something pretty crazy."

"Crazy?" Baldie's voice cracked. He locked eyes with Major Randal in the rearview mirror.

"That's right!"

"Absolutely insane, old stick," confided Captain Stone. "Without question the maddest thing I have ever heard of."

"Coming from the guy who thinks tracer rounds cracking past look like 300-miles-per-hour fairies, it's got to really be something completely nuts!" Baldie responded, sounding eager. "My best advice, in that case, is not to tell a soul—simply do it. That's what I recommend. Go right out and execute your mission straightaway, the quicker the better. What's the plan, gentlemen?"

"Pull in at that tailor shop," Major Randal leaned forward and pointed over Baldie's shoulder.

"Yes sir, Major, sir."

Captain Stone took his and Major Randal's khaki drill service blouses and disappeared into the shop.

"Come on, Major, it's time to ante up your bona fides," Baldie begged. "What's your crazy plan?"

"Terry is going to be the operations officer on this project," Major Randal said. "You'll be working directly with him. Tell me right now if you think you'll have any problems with that."

"Working with Captain Stone a problem, are you kidding? I have already had the pleasure of seeing him in action." Baldie chortled. "You know, I read somewhere BOAC has eight or nine hundred applicants for each Clipper Girl position. Movie stars and millionaires hit on them all the time—no luck. Zorro had Red eating out of his palm. Maybe he can teach me a few tricks. Now, about the plan, Major?"

"I'm going to need a cover story before our meeting. One that will divert the local authorities' attention away from the coast. Got any ideas?"

"What you really need is a plausible story, one the locals should believe but never do because they instantly recognize it as a lie," the SOE station chief responded. "Your plausible story keeps them guessing what your real intentions are but at the same time forces them to go through the motions of reacting to it as if it were true. Get the picture?"

"I see."

"What a plausible story does is buy us time," Baldie elaborated. "Then, later, we feed them a second, more believable story in bits and pieces, which is in fact our cover story, and we let them put the puzzle together for themselves. That will cause the locals to be convinced beyond any doubt that the second story, the cover, is actually the true story—because they figure it out for themselves.

"It won't be, of course," the covert operator continued, rapid fire, "but by then we will have done whatever it is you came out here to do, or we'll be so far along with it, it will be too late for them to interfere with us."

"Sounds like you know your stuff, Jim."

"I'm a professional, Major. It would help if I knew the real plan, but how about this? What if we say you two came out here to put a stop to the cross-border cattle trade with the French Ivory Coast colony? That kind of thing is illegal in time of war; you are not supposed to trade with the enemy, but hey, business is business with these slime, and 'just because we happen to be giving aid and sustenance to the enemy—not to mention making a big fat profit off our Nazi-loving neighbors—does not make us bad people.'"

"Why won't the colonial officials believe that story?"

"Because, Major, you happen to be a float-down-a-river-on-a-log-with-a-knife-in-your-teeth fighting soldier, not a policeman. The Gold Coast crowd won't buy that story for one minute. Not with your reputation."

"Okay, then, that's the way we'll play it. You'll have to come up with the cover we feed them in bits and pieces."

"No problem."

"Jim, can you find a place for us to stay? On the beach . . . far enough out of town where we'll be totally isolated?"

"I have exactly the spot. Come on, Major, what is this fruitcake plan of yours?"

"We need a boat and we need it tonight."

"I have a twenty-eight-footer I use to fish for sharks—great whites. Will that do?"

"Perfect. Now, eventually we're going to require support from the local Royal Navy commander. Can we count on it?"

"The Senior Naval Officer Commanding Port Facilities Accra is a strange bird . . . an ingratiating type who likes to stay in tight with the sun-downer set. I would not rely on the man. No one gets assigned to the Gold Coast because they graduated at the top of their class," Baldie explained. "The best way to get stationed out here is to annoy your superiors."

"Who did you annoy, Jim?"

"Major, in my case it was practically everybody."

"I'd like to hear the story," Major Randal said. He was not exactly asking.

"At the beginning of hostilities, I was working for an unspecified agency that does not officially exist, in a country where we do not operate, doing things we would never do. In that unnamed country was a five-hundred-year-old national treasure, a historic landmark noted for its spectacular arches, which spanned a certain scenic terrain feature; it formed the world's most perfect choke point.

"German Panzer Mark III tanks manned by murderous Waffen SS storm troopers were driving straight for it—killing, raping, burning, and pillaging everything in their line of march.

"On the night immediately prior to the Panzers' arrival, the aforementioned scenic historical landmark disappeared in a cloud of smoke with a great big unauthorized bang, leaving the Nazis high and dry on the far side and buying enough time for a lot of fleeing refugees to make their way to safety.

"Less than a week later I found myself counting monkeys out here in the Gold Coast," the agent concluded. "Now are you going to tell me what this is all about?"

Captain Stone came out of the tailor shop with their blouses. The black and silver thread RAIDING FORCES flash was neatly stitched back on each of the uniforms. The jump wings and the Military Cross decorations were pinned in the correct places. Both officers opened their canvas bags and pulled out their green berets.

"The authorities have been expecting Commandos," Captain Stone said with a grin. "So let's give them Commandos."

"Oh, that's great," Baldie said grimacing. "You guys are going to be a barrel of laughs."

"Jim, are you familiar with the island of Rio Bonita?" Major Randal asked.

"The Portuguese protectorate. I've been over there a few times, why?"

"There happen to be three enemy ships, two Italian and one German, interned in San Pedro Harbor."

"I am aware of them."

"The German ship, the *Ems*, has a hidden radio transmitter on board transmitting shipping data about our convoys to Nazi U-boats and surface commerce raiders operating off the West Coast."

"Now that I did *not* know."

"My orders are to go into San Pedro, board all three ships, kill or capture the crews, and bring the ships out of the harbor," Major Randal said in a conversational tone. "Sound crazy enough for you?"

Baldie sat perfectly still, silently staring out the window, for a long time. Finally he burst out laughing. "You're right, Major. It's the wildest thing I have ever heard. Really bloody beautiful, though. Want to know why? Because, whether you pull it off or go down trying, I am going to be persona non grata in the Gold Coast for eternity. The Colonial Office will have me booted out of here within forty-eight hours. This is great news. I love you guys. Whoever dreamed this idea up is a total moron. There have to be a hundred reasons—no, make it a thousand reasons—why the idea is absolute complete lunacy.

"But, if you do go into San Pedro Harbor and cut out those ships, the Gold Coast authorities will go totally berserk," Baldie enthused. "Politically, it will have the same effect as a volcano erupting during a major earthquake while the colony is being hammered by a typhoon during a stampede of killer elephants caused by a native uprising. I love it!"

"Any particular reason why you can think we can't pull it off?"

"For a couple of raiding aces like you two, none that I can think of . . . provided you bring in some outside talent. You lads are definitely not going to get any quality help here, not from the military side."

"On the way."

"Great, I love you guys!"

"You said that before, Jim."

"Yeah, Major, but now I really mean it."

18

HOUSE LIZARD

WHEN THEY ARRIVED AT THE BUNGALOW, THE GOLD COAST colonial officials who greeted them were a seedy-looking group of middle-aged men dressed like Boy Scouts in their matching khaki shirts, khaki shorts, and tall khaki stockings. Most of the deputation had cropped little toothbrush mustaches and fat knees. They all wore polished Sam Brown belts but no sidearms.

Clearly the event was orchestrated for the sole purpose of divining why two Commando officers had landed unannounced and uninvited in their sleepy environs. The Gold Coast administrators did not learn much, though the subject of the cattle trade did manage to make its way into the conversation peripherally. Major John Randal and party explained they were there to take the sun, but they also professed a mild interest in going to the northern border, where the bulk of the illegal cattle trade occurred, to hunt elephant. Fortunately, the meeting did not go on for long. Since everyone was lying, the atmosphere was strained.

Back in the Chevrolet, Major Randal took out a small writing pad and scribbled a message. "Jim, can you arrange to have this message go out emergency priority?"

The communiqué read: URGENT STOP REQUEST COM-MANDER RICHARD SEABORN BE ASSIGNED TO COORDI-NATE NAVAL ASSETS REQUIRED STOP TO ARRIVE ACCRA AS SOON AS POSSIBLE STOP EXPECT NO HELP FROM LOCAL MILITARY AND POLITICAL STOP INTERFERENCE FROM LOCALS LIKELY STOP TEMPORARY PROMOTION FOR COM-MANDER SEABORN HELPFUL STOP SIGNED RANDAL, MAJOR STOP RAIDING FORCES STOP.

"It'll be sent out tonight, Major."

"Is it true, Baldie," Captain Terry "Zorro" Stone inquired, "the Gold Coast is called the white man's grave?"

"When an Army officer was being sent out here a while back," the SOE man began matter-of-factly, "he asked a friend who knew the colony what equipment he should bring. You know what the answer was?"

"What?"

"'A casket; that's all you are going to need.'"

Jim "Baldie" Taylor put them up in a safe house eight miles outside of Accra. The cottage was a thatched-roof bungalow on the beach. As they arrived, the incandescent globe of the sun was glide-bombing itself into the southern sea-lane. When it slammed into water, the ocean turned the green color of a parrot's breast. After that it got dark fast.

The whirling ceiling fans in every room of the hut swished through the warm, semiliquid air in a vain effort to create some resemblance of a cool breeze.

Moths the size of sparrows race-tracked crazily around the lights covered with green shades. A colorless, motionless gecko clung spread-eagled high up on one wall. "House lizard," Baldie explained. "Eats mosquitoes."

The three men sat around a glass-topped wicker table studying a map of Rio Bonita. They could hear the sound of the waves lapping at the shoreline.

"I know exactly where that beach is. In fact, I am fairly familiar with the entire eastern side of the island," Baldie stated confidently. "Now, the western side where the head-hunting pygmy cannibals are alleged to be, that's another story. I have never been ashore over there."

"Why not?" Captain Terry "Zorro" Stone asked.

"Never cared to run the chance of getting zapped by a poisoned dart," Baldie said. "That's why."

"Good reason."

"How long will it take," Major John Randal wanted to know, "to reach the beach?"

"About two hours. The sea is generally calm this time of the year unless a squall blows up. We should have a pleasant trip."

"We're supposed to be there any time after 2200 hours." Major Randal added. "I'd like to arrive at least an hour early."

"Good idea, Major. That way we can lay offshore and watch to see what develops. Who are we meeting?"

"My instructions are a little vague. I'm to meet an 'agent or agents known to me,' whatever that means."

"Means you recognize them. You know anybody on Rio Bonita?"

"No."

"In that case, this should prove interesting. If we are going to arrive early we need to leave right away."

The men boarded the SOE chief-of-station's fishing boat. Khaki shirt with sleeves rolled up, shorts, and canvas rope-soled deck shoes were the uniform of the evening—just what the respectable tourists they were pretending to be would be wearing. Everyone was doused with mosquito repellant.

Under their khaki bush shirts Major Randal and Captain Stone wore their silenced High Standard .22 semiautomatic pistols in lightweight canvas shoulder holsters. Laced to the holsters were their Fairbairn fighting knives. Baldie took a professional interest in the weapons, neither of which he had ever seen before.

A full moon was out and it was a beautiful, if somewhat muggy, African night. As advertised, the boat trip was pleasant. They arrived on station off the beach with plenty of time to spare. While the two officers napped, Baldie studied the shore through a pair of large Royal Navy–issue night glasses he kept on board. He watched a lone vehicle approach with its lights on. The car stopped, and several people exited and walked down toward the water.

"We have company," Baldie announced softly and was surprised at how quickly the two Commandos came fully awake. It was a neat trick. They watched as a large bonfire was lit on the beach.

"Run downwind about a quarter of a mile, drop me off, then bring Terry back up here and put him ashore," Major Randal ordered. "We'll let him make the initial contact with the shore party."

To minimize engine noise, Baldie pushed the fishing boat down the shoreline at quarter throttle, out of sight of anyone on the shore. Presently he pulled in close to the beach and Major Randal slipped over the side and waded ashore in the dark.

The fishing boat slowly putt-putted its way back to the vicinity of the bonfire.

"The Major is a careful guy," Baldie observed.

"Yes, he is."

Taking their time, they hove to off the beach opposite the bonfire. Captain Stone waited a while before easing over the side. It looked like three people were sitting in canvas folding chairs around the bonfire. From all outward appearances, they were having a small beach party.

A voice bellowed, "HALT, WHO GOES THERE?"

Captain Stone recognized the ancient challenge of fighting men dating back to the days of the Roman Legion, and there were only two possible responses to that question: "Friend" or "Foe." He seriously doubted anyone in the history of armed warfare had ever actually responded "Foe."

"FRIEND!" he sang out.

"ADVANCE, FRIEND, AND BE RECOGNIZED," came the distinctly accented male voice.

"PASSWORD?" a female voice demanded militantly.

Uh-oh! He did not know any password. One had not been supplied for this mission.

Just at that moment Major Randal stepped out of the shadows directly behind the man in the canvas chair. He placed the bull barrel of his pistol against the back of the man's neck and cocked the hammer. The metallic clicking sound of the mechanism seemed unnaturally loud.

"Frogspawn."

Everything became very still. The only noise to be heard on the beach was the crackling of the bonfire. And, like the sound of the pistol being cocked, it sounded exceptionally loud in the tense moment.

"I sure do hope that's the business end of a custom silencer screwed on the barrel of a High Standard .22-caliber Military Model D semiautomatic pistol," Captain "Geronimo Joe" McKoy rattled off, "or we're in a heap of trouble."

"Well, Captain McKoy," Major Randal said, "would you mind explaining what it is you're doing here on this beach tonight?"

"Toasting marshmallows, John," the ex-Indian fighter, Rough Rider, Arizona Ranger, et cetera, replied. "Would you care for one? It's not nice to be sneaking up on your old friends like that; you might scare somebody."

"Terrified me," admitted Royal Marine Pamala Plum-Martin in a small voice.

"Me too," seconded Captain the Lady Jane Seaborn. "I thought my heart was going to explode! Who is that out on the beach?"

"Come on in, Terry."

"Hello," Captain Stone said casually when, pistol in hand, he stepped into the circle of light cast by the fire. "Should I have brought wine?"

"Captain McKoy," Major Randal said. "I asked you a question."

"Collecting stamps, John. Did I ever tell you I was the Secretary-Treasurer of the Southwestern Cattlemen's Association's Chapter of the American Philatelic Society? Rio Bonita is a stamp collector's paradise. She's a Portuguese protectorate but prints her own stamps and is world famous for her insect stamps. They got themselves a little fire ant stamp with a double watermark that is about the purtiest—"

"Will you put a cork in it," Major Randal snapped.

"That's our cover," the old Arizona Ranger persisted in a hurt tone. "I'm supposed to be a rich Texas oilman rounding up stamps for an exhibition at the annual Southwestern Cattlemen's Association Symposium entitled 'Stamps of the Non-Belligerents.'

"This here is my niece, Pamala Sue McKoy, and her best friend, Martha Jane Canary."

"As in Calamity Jane. Well, you got that part right," Major Randal said, staring hard at Captain Lady Seaborn. She blushed and looked down at the sand.

"Now hold on there, young major, don't you go gettin' yourself all riled up," Captain McKoy ordered. "You ain't got a monopoly on this here war; there's plenty to go around. We don't have much time so let's get down to brass tacks."

"Why don't you do that?"

"The ladies and I are doin' a forward reconnaissance for our mutual friend Larry Grand. For the last two days, Pamela Sue and Martha Jane have been paddlin' around the harbor in a canoe, in their bathing suits, takin' a lot of pictures. They've been doin' a little fishin' too. Ain't caught much since both of 'em had lead sounding weights on the end of their lines instead of fishhooks. They charted the whole dang harbor.

"We brought you the rolls of undeveloped film and the depth charts in an airtight waterproof bag in case you accidentally drop it overboard on the way home, but try not to drop 'em. You boys sure won't find any surprises when you come a-bustin' into San Pedro Harbor after you get through studying the photos.

"Everything we've seen on the ground pretty much squares with the intelligence you've already been provided," the cowboy showman concluded. "The only thing I might want to add to it is that the morale of the interned Italian sailors is probably even lower than reported. Those boys barely have a pulse. Watch out for the *Ems*, though, John. Her Hitlerite skipper rules his ship with an iron fist. You may run into some trouble with his Nazi sailor boys."

"We'll do that."

"When are your troops expected to arrive in the Gold Coast?" Captain McKoy asked.

"Six days."

"Good. Can you be ready to attack next Saturday at midnight?"

"Why then?" Captain Stone inquired.

"The moon will be down before midnight, giving you the advantage of the cover of darkness. I don't know if it's in your report or not, but to save energy, meaning money, Rio Bonita's authorities turn the electricity off every night, rain or shine, at midnight. The whole island gets blacked out.

"I want you to begin your operation the instant the lights go out Saturday night."

"What's special about Saturday night?"

"We're goin' to be throwin' a couple of parties that night: one is for the bigwigs—the mayor, the civil defense chief, ships' officers of all three interned ships, the police chief; everybody who counts will be there. And to be on the safe side, I'm organizin' a second party, a beer bust on the waterfront in San Pedro for the Axis crews of the interned ships.

"Right after the lights go out at midnight, the grand finale of both parties will consist of touching off the biggest fireworks bonanza in the history of Rio Bonita. We've bought up all the fireworks on the island and are shippin' in a whole bunch more from the Gold Coast.

"The reason we're goin' to all the trouble is you're goin' to have to cut the anchor chains on the three interned ships with demolitions. There ain't no way to haul 'em up because they're encased in concrete. The fireworks just may give you enough cover not to alarm the Port Defense Force too much when you go to detonatin' your charges to blow them suckers."

"Terry?" Major Randal turned toward his second in command.

"Raiding Forces will be coming through the entrance to San Pedro Harbor the instant the lights in the town go out Saturday night, Captain. You just make the harbor look like Guy Fawkes Day, New Year's Eve, and the King's Birthday all rolled into one, old stick," Major Stone said.

"Bank on it, buckaroos," Captain McKoy declared. "One more little thing. I need you to have whoever brought you over tonight be back here Saturday night, a-standin' offshore from 2400 hours on to pick us up. I intend to pie-yie out of here right after the party. There ain't no sense in waitin' around to see if the locals can add two plus two."

"A boat will be here at midnight, Captain McKoy," Major Randal promised. "Make sure you're on it."

"We will be, that's for dang sure," the ex-Arizona Ranger laughed. "And we might be bringin' you a present."

"Any chance I could sneak back into town with you tonight and observe the harbor for a day or two?" Captain Stone inquired unexpectedly.

"Martha Jane, what do you think?" Captain McKoy deferred the question.

"We can arrange for the housekeeper to have a few days off," Captain Lady Seaborn said. "Best to keep you out of sight, Terry."

"In that case, Baldie and I will pick you up here at this time in three nights," Major Randal said.

"John, can I have a word with you in private?" Captain McKoy asked, sounding mysterious.

The two stepped away from the circle of firelight out of earshot of the others.

"I have another little diversion plan laid on to help whittle down the odds a tad more in your favor, but I don't want the ladies to know some of the more intimate details," Captain McKoy explained in a loud stage whisper. "This here is on a need-to-know basis and the girls don't have any legitimate need to know, if you get my drift."

"I got it."

"I've contracted out the whole entire red-light district for Saturday night. I've hired every hooker in San Pedro. Like I said, we're throwing a beer bust for the sailors of the interned ships and everything is going to be on the house, and I mean the whole shee-bang."

"What is it you don't want Jane and Pamala to know?"

"Well, that I've hired every hooker in Rio Bonita for the big show. There's a couple coming out of retirement just for the party and some more coming over on the ferry from Accra. I even have some fancy French girls coming over from the Ivory Coast."

"Hooker warfare," Major Randal said. "I'm surprised at you, Captain."

"Remember, John," the flamboyant showman explained in a semi-embarrassed tone, "you're the one with the rule 'It don't hurt to cheat.'"

"I thought I stole that one from you!"

"Well, it's a dang good rule."

"How do you plan to write it up when you account for your funds?"

"We ain't going to tell a livin' soul, and let history work it out for itself. You and me ain't even havin' this conversation."

"Captain McKoy, I'm not exactly clear on why it is you're here. We need to have a heart-to- heart talk when this is all over. Watch yourself, cowboy. I'd hate to have to come back after the raid to break you out of jail."

"Thanks, John. I believe you just might do it too."

"Make sure we don't have to find out."

"You boys made the newspaper, you know that?"

"The *London Times* is available over here?"

"Yeah, it came in on the evening ferry from Accra. I'm goin' to need to get you to autograph me a copy so I can mail it back to the Southwestern Cattlemen's Association to let the boys at home see what you done with all those Thompson guns they sent you. They'll get a kick out of it.

"I sure woulda loved to have seen some of them 300-miles-per-hour fairies ol' Zorro was describin'—sounded downright colorful."

"Looked a lot like tracers."

"I figured as much."

When it was time, Captain the Lady Jane Seaborn walked Major John Randal down to the edge of the water. "I was dreadfully disappointed not to be able to be there to welcome you home from Operation Tomcat. I wanted to, John. I am quite proud of you, you know."

"I heard you cried when my plane took off," Major Randal said. "Is that true, Jane?"

"What if I did?" the drop-dead gorgeous spy responded defensively. "Pamala cried, too, and she never gets emotional. Watching you and the rest of the lads flying off to invade France all by yourselves was simply dreadful. After the Whitleys took off, Tomcat suddenly seemed like an incredibly stupid idea."

"Did it occur to you I might not feel so great about sailing off and leaving you behind on this island tonight?"

"Oh, John." She flung herself into his arms. They locked tight as the waves lapped around their knees.

Time stood still. The two might have stayed there all night if Jim "Baldie" Taylor had not finally eased the fishing boat in to the beach.

Before he stepped into the boat Major Randal reached into his pocket and produced the profusely engraved pearl-handled Walther PPK 7.65 automatic he had taken from the German general captured on Raiding Forces' very first raid. "Put this in your purse and keep it there," he ordered. Two could play the game of giving a present that would make the other think about them every time they saw it. Major Randal was pretty sure Lady Jane looked at her purse a lot.

Later, headed back to the Gold Coast, neither man said anything until Baldie broke the silence by observing, "I love it when the intelligence they give you in the initial briefing before you go on a mission turns out to be accurate. Seldom ever is, in my experience, but it was right on tonight."

"What are you talking about, Jim?"

"The part in your briefing where it said you would be met by 'an agent or agents known to you.' You sure seemed to know one of them, all right. I can see it's going to be a lot of fun working with you and Zorro. Does either of you have any more women stashed around the Gold Coast I might need to be aware of?"

"Not that I know about."

19

SOUNDS LIKE A CATFIGHT

THE THIRD MORNING AFTER THE RAIDING FORCES OFFICERS'
arrival in the Gold Coast began early with a drive to the headquarters
of Lieutenant General G. J. Giffard, General Officer Commanding West
African Forces, located on the lovely grounds of Achimota College. Major
John Randal had been invited to a classified briefing on the military situation in West Africa. Baldie drove, and on the way gave him the briefing
before the briefing.

"The thing to remember, Major, is they are going to be trying as hard
as they can to learn why a famous Commando has suddenly turned up out
here. Don't give them a thing! Make the blighters work for every single
detail they pry out of you."

"What can I tell them?"

"Nothing," Baldie said decisively. "If the opportunity to mention the
illegal trade in cattle across the borders with the Vichy French presents
itself, take it. Only do not come right out and voluntarily tell them the
whole plausible story, which is that you're here to put a stop to the traffic in
cattle with our Nazi-loving neighbors. Remember, if ending cross-border

collaboration with the enemy was your real mission, it would be classified. They know that, so be very, very vague."

"Roger."

"Ask the odd question from time to time. The idea is to force the locals to try to deduce what you are up to, so it does not really matter if your line of inquiry does not actually make much sense. The longer you can string out the process, the better. That buys us more time before we have to feed them our second, more believable, cover story and sets them up to fall for it in a big way when they put the pieces together and figure it out all by themselves."

"Any ideas on the second story, by the way?"

"I'm still working on it, Major. You string out this first one long enough, we might not *need* a second story. Keep in mind, General Giffard's worst nightmare is an outside interloper like you gate-crashing his personal bailiwick and setting up a private raiding enterprise not answerable to him. The last thing he wants is a loose cannon operating in his private preserve, so you try to convince him that's exactly what you are."

"You mean calm, cool, and raring to get at the bad guys?"

"Exactly!" Baldie laughed. "Act demented; that's what I do. That always works."

"What's the story on General Giffard?"

"Giffard is an empire builder and has amassed a great deal of power out here. Hates Special Operations Executive because he is not in its chain of command and therefore has no direct control over us. He tried to get SOE disbanded in the colony. As you have already observed because I carefully pointed it out to you, the Gold Coast is completely surrounded by Vichy French territories. Well, General Giffard banned sabotage across any border, which put a definite crimp in my nocturnal activities."

"Why would he do that?"

"He and all the rest of the colonial authorities are terrified our enemy-loving neighbors will use even the slightest cross-border military action as an excuse to counterattack and invade the Gold Coast."

"What are the odds of that happening?"

"Precisely zero. The Frogs don't want to hurt trade either, and militarily the Vichy French colonies are even weaker than we are.

"Now, the thing to keep in mind, Major," Baldie picked back up where he left off before being interrupted, "is that the Gold Coast is broken down into four different governorships, and each one is an autonomous colony. Throw into the mix the Colonial Office, the War Office, the Foreign Ministry, and Special Operations Executive, and you have an evil brew. Each one has its own private agenda, and they all compete for something. Even de Gaulle has announced plans to come in and set up a Free French base of operations so he can recruit volunteers for his Fighting French Forces."

"Sounds like a catfight to me."

"Down to the ground. In reality, there are only two things on the Gold Coast of any strategic value—well, three actually if you throw in gold production—but they are of immeasurable value to the war effort," Baldie explained. "And, they are both at Takoradi.

"First are the airfields: three, thousand-foot-long strips that are being expanded as rapidly as possible. The United States is planning to fly in P-40 Tomahawks from aircraft carriers and give them to the RAF under a program called Lend Lease. The U.S. Congress has not approved the plan yet, but we have been quietly informed that they will sometime within the next six months.

"Second, Takoradi is the Gold Coast's only deepwater port. The U.S. Navy has surveyed it and is planning to use it to off-load additional crated aircraft in the port. The R.A.F. will ship out other aircraft by sea from the UK and also unload it there. As soon as the crates come ashore, the plan is for the planes to be rapidly assembled and flown in hops, along with the planes landing from the carriers, out to Cairo for our Desert Air Force, where they are in desperate short supply."

"That sounds like a big operation."

"It will be. As you already know, the Gold Coast is situated astride the South Atlantic Sea Route. The southern lane runs the length of the colony. With the Suez Canal out of our hands right now, ever since the Italians came into the war and gained air superiority over the Red Sea, it has assumed critical strategic importance. If the Germans can find a way to shut down the South Atlantic Sea Route, or even to choke it off enough, it's endgame; they win the war.

"Major, that's what makes your task of knocking out the clandestine radio station on the *Ems* so critical," Baldie summed up. "Those U-boats and surface raiders are at the point of being able to shut down the South Atlantic Sea Route right now, right this minute. You have been handed a big, and I do mean BIG, assignment.

"You and Zorro can't win the war, but if you manage to pull off the raid on Rio Bonita you might keep us from losing it."

"The mission," Major Randal said, "was never explained in those terms."

"London might not have thought you had a need to know. Quite possibly Larry Grand thought your operation was difficult enough without the extra pressure. Maybe I should have kept my big mouth shut, but I believe a man has the right to know what he's risking his neck for."

They drove onto the beautiful college campus. An overage-for-grade captain in starched tropical khaki battle dress sporting the insignia of the Gold Coast Regiment was waiting outside on the drive. He escorted Major Randal inside.

A staff major from the Royal West African Frontier Force began by giving a pessimistic sketch of the military situation in the colony. "Following the collapse of France, French West Africa remained loyal to the collaborationist government of Marshal Pétain, leaving the four British colonies of the Gold Coast surrounded on three sides by enemy territory, with the ocean to our rear.

"Thus far the war has gone rather badly for the colony," he continued despondently. "Our Gold Coast Regiment has been alerted for deployment to Kenya to participate in the upcoming Italian East African Campaign. Its departure will leave the colony virtually defenseless. Since the Gold Coast Colony is the wealthiest colony in the Empire, it is reasonable to presume the Nazis are constantly putting pressure on the Vichy French next door to invade at the earliest possible moment, most likely when the regiment ships out, which will happen any day now.

"Intelligence has recently confirmed beyond question our worst fear. Hitler has plans to recover the portion of Togoland ceded to Great Britain in the last war as a matter of honor."

The gloomy briefer droned on and on. When he ran out of steam, another pessimist replaced him. Eventually still another briefer took over from the second, and so on, until it was time to troop off to lunch.

After the noon meal the briefing picked up where it left off. By the end, Major Randal had been subjected to a mind-boggling overload of information about the Gold Coast, British West Africa, French West Africa, the Vichy French, German intentions, military strengths in the region, shortages of all kinds, fears, concerns, and estimates of a wide-ranging variety of threats facing the colony. The only place the briefers did not seem afraid of being invaded from was Rio Bonita. In fact, the tiny Portuguese protectorate was never mentioned at all.

At the end of the day, the Colonial Office extended an offer to Major Randal to attend a follow-up briefing on political affairs the next day, which he accepted.

Just as he was climbing into Baldie's Chevrolet, a sharp-looking African soldier in heavily starched khaki battle dress and bare feet ran up and handed him an envelope through the car's window. Inside was an invitation to a reception that evening for Commodore Richard Seaborn, OBE. Major Randal handed the card to Baldie.

"Now that's impressive! I'm going to get you to recommend me for a promotion some day, Major. Getting someone bumped up from commander to commodore is quite a jump up the ladder."

Commodore is a temporary promotion usually given to Royal Navy captains that will be commanding other captains. For a Commander (equal to army lieutenant colonel) to be given the rank of Commodore was very unusual. Commodore comes in two grades: Junior Grade and Senior Grade. Senior Grade Commodores are allowed to wear the rank of Admiral—an even greater distinction for Searborn. Any officer who holds the rank of Commodore for even one day is addressed as Commodore for the rest of his career or until he makes Admiral.

"What do you think it means?"

"I interpret it to be a clear signal London is trying to give you all the support they possibly can; going to a lot of trouble not to be subtle about it too. And Major, that can only mean one thing: This mission is high on someone very important's 'action this day' list, not just some harebrained scheme like most of the jobs I've seen proposed lately." Baldie's voice quivered with mounting excitement. "We may actually green light this one."

"In that case, Jim, we better get it right."

"Along those lines I have a question for you, Major, and I want a straight answer."

"Shoot."

"What is your connection to Lady Seaborn and Pamala Plum-Martin?" Baldie did not take his eyes off the road, but he managed to give the impression he was watching as well as listening to the answer.

"Lady Jane is related by marriage to my naval officer Lieutenant Randy Seaborn, the son of the recently promoted Commodore Seaborn. As you probably know, she is with SOE. Somehow she secured a commission as a captain in the Royal Marines and spends most of her time working with us, meaning my outfit, the Strategic Raiding Forces. She is currently listed on the roster as the intelligence officer, though it looks as if she has abandoned her post. Royal Marine Plum-Martin is her driver.

"I have sort of, ah, well, a personal relationship with Lady Jane," Major Randal continued uncomfortably. "I'm not exactly sure how to describe it, because to tell you the truth, Jim, I don't completely understand it myself."

"Major, Lady Seaborn is a talent spotter for SOE. Looks like she spotted you, huh! Plum-Martin is SIS," Baldie declared bluntly. "Sounds to me like maybe you don't know the whole story. Don't feel bad; you aren't the only one who finds it hard to understand women, either. I should know; I've been married to three of them," Baldie confided man-to-man.

"The word is Lady Seaborn has a good heart. In my experience, when a man gets involved with a woman generally described as 'drop-dead gorgeous' and having a 'good heart,' he is in way over his head. You tired of being a bachelor, Major?"

"That what you did, Jim?" Major Randal asked. "Go for women with good hearts?"

"Hell no, I'm a leg man."

By the time Jim "Baldie" Taylor drove his Chevrolet up to the Colonial Planters Hotel in downtown Accra, Commodore Richard Seaborn's welcoming cocktail party was in full swing.

"I have a few errands to run," the SOE operative said. "Be ready to leave here by 2000 hours. We still have a night's work ahead of us."

"I'll meet you out front, Jim."

Inside the hotel, the power elite of every branch of military service, the police, the constabulary, the Colonial Office, and politicians of every stripe—from the governor of the Gold Coast on down—had gathered for the reception. The event was a required function for most attendees, business not pleasure. The colonists in the Gold Coast were a hard-partying set; they would get around to the pleasure a little later in the evening. They always did.

Major John Randal joined the crowd that was moving slowly toward the receiving line, and when he finally reached it, the governor's aide whispered his name in the great man's ear. The governor's eyebrows pinched together like he had suddenly been zinged by a migraine.

"Major Randal, welcome to the Gold Coast. Accept my heartfelt congratulations on your amazing exploits. Please get together with my aide and schedule time when we can arrange to have you give me a full accounting of your latest thrilling adventure. I admit to being fascinated by all things military."

"My pleasure, sir."

Both men were lying.

The governor's heavily tanned and anorexic wife was dripping in diamonds. "Major Randal, you have caused quite a stir in the colony. All the women are simply dying for a chance to meet you after seeing the newsreel of your raid at the cinema. Let me introduce you to Commodore Seaborn, out from the UK."

"Major," said an unhappy-looking Commodore Seaborn, sporting the brand-new insignia of a rear admiral as senior-grade commodores are authorized to do. "I understand you spent the evening with my wife at the Bradford the night before you flew out. And how was Brandy?"

"Fabulous as ever, sir."

The receiving line grew very quiet. People did everything but cup their hands to their ears straining to hear the exchange. Sounded like the making of a scandal, and new gossip was always welcome in the tiny expatriate set.

"I shall want a word with you as soon as the guests quit arriving, Major."

"Yes sir."

As he was moving away, he heard Commodore Seaborn say to the governor's wife, "Major Randal is practically a member of the family. In addition to being my son's commanding officer, he recently rescued my wife and carried her down seven flights of stairs after she had been injured in a German bombing attack."

The governor's wife gasped, "Oh my!"

Major Randal drifted over to a bar in the corner of the White Hunter Room. Since he had a long, busy night ahead of him, he settled for a tall, cold glass of sparkling water with a thin slice of lemon. From his vantage point, he could discreetly observe the people in the room.

Power, politics, greed, ambition, and sex were simmering. No one came anywhere near him. He might as well have been a leper; so much for the women dying to meet him.

After a considerable time passed, Commodore Seaborn made his way over to where Major Randal waited. The commodore appeared visibly shaken. "My orders state that I am to be met by an officer known to me who will give me my next instructions. Please tell me you are not that officer."

"Sir, are you familiar with a Portuguese protectorate, an island called Rio Bonita?"

"Yes, I have sailed these waters before. Why do you ask?"

"There are three Axis ships interned in San Pedro Harbor, one German and two Italian. Y-Service has determined that a secret radio station located on the German ship, the *Ems*, is transmitting the routes, sailing times, and cargo manifests of our convoys to U-boats and surface commerce raiders operating against the South Atlantic Sea Route."

"Something like that has long been suspected, but we never knew for certain," Commodore Seaborn said grimly. "Appalling news, could not be worse, actually. Rotten luck. The radio is safe and sound in neutral waters."

"Neutral or not, sir, on Saturday night I am taking Raiding Forces into San Pedro Harbor, boarding all three, killing or capturing the crew, and bringing the ships out of there."

For a moment it was not clear whether Commodore Seaborn was having an epileptic seizure or cardiac arrest. He turned several different colors and was having trouble breathing normally.

"Major, do you have the vaguest comprehension of the catastrophic consequences of the mere suggestion of invading a neutral Portuguese territory, Britain's oldest ally?" Commodore Seaborn asked in a tone of resignation.

"Bad, sir."

"If Portugal comes into the war on the Axis side and mounts heavy shore batteries along its coast, which will be the first thing it does if we ever get caught violating its neutrality, we lose the Strait of Gibraltar. Can you even faintly grasp the strategic implications if that should happen? Obviously not; going after enemy ships docked in San Pedro is total lunacy. Politically as well as long-term militarily, the idea is simply mad."

"Commodore, your assignment is to make the naval side of things happen so we can carry out our mission," Major Randal responded calmly. "Mad or not."

Both officers stood studying each other for a moment, contemplating the enormity of the assignment.

"Later tonight I'm traveling by boat to Rio Bonita to pick up Terry Stone, who's over reconning San Pedro Harbor. Want to tag along for the ride?"

Commodore Seaborn stared down at the striped zebra-skin rug he was standing on. "I can live with the fact that my son idolizes you; that my wife is fascinated by you; that my father–in–law, the Razor—whom I have never been able to even remotely impress, not even once in my whole entire miserable existence—respects you; and that my dead cousin's wife has fallen for you. But I am going to hate being your cellmate in a rotten stinking Portuguese prison.

"Bloody right I want to come!"

20

AMATEURS TALK TACTICS

ONCE HE WAS OVER THE INITIAL SHOCK OF FINDING HIMSELF responsible for organizing the invasion of a neutral country, Commodore Richard Seaborn threw himself into planning Operation Lounge Lizard with an enthusiasm and grim gusto that impressed Major John Randal, Captain Terry "Zorro" Stone, and Special Operations Executive's Gold Coast chief of station, Jim "Baldie" Taylor.

The commodore had spent most of the previous year buried deep in the subterranean bowels of the Admiralty, routing convoys. The duty was unglamorous, high stress, twelve-hour-a-day grueling staff work that ground on and on with little reward, not much recognition, and a lot of heartbreak. But it gave him strategic insight into the war available to few men serving.

There is a saying in the senior service that amateurs talk tactics, professionals talk logistics.

Routing convoys was the ultimate game of logistics. It could be compared to playing chess blindfolded against a master opponent who has the advantages both of being able to see the board and of throwing in an extra pair of queens. The life of a Royal Navy convoy router was extremely

frustrating, and over time increasingly desperate, though it might arguably be the most important job in the war. Nervous breakdowns and even
suicides were not unknown in the division.

Logistics depended on the mathematics of supply and demand. For its
survival, England demanded an enormous quantity of supplies. Because
just a tiny percentage of those supplies arrived by air, the only way to take
delivery of the tonnage the UK required was by surface merchant ship
traveling over the northern and southern sea-lanes. While England was
standing by to be invaded at any moment, the fact was Germany did not
actually need to go to all the trouble of launching a full-scale invasion to
win the war. All the Nazis had to do was prevent the UK from bringing
in its required daily tonnage. The country would starve. Hitler knew that.
Right now, the Nazis were winning the war of the numbers at sea by sinking British merchant ships at a rate faster than they could be replaced, thus
choking off supplies. The harsh reality was that if the UK continued to
lose merchant ships at the present clip, it was only a matter of time before
it experienced logistical, mathematical, and unavoidable defeat. England
was teetering on the very edge, like a drunken sailor.

German submarines had tipped the balance of naval power. The single greatest threat England had ever faced in its entire storied history was
the submarine fleet commanded by Admiral Karl Dönitz. The peril was
global. His underwater wolf packs were running wild and there was no
effective defense against them. The German U-boats seemed unstoppable.

The U-boats were successful because the Kriegsmarine had developed the most effective worldwide maritime intelligence system in the
history of naval warfare to support them. Armed with accurate shipping
information, Nazi U-boat wolf packs operated with maximum efficiency
and deadly precision. They knew exactly where to be and when.

German submarines attacked. Then they vanished. Not one counter-
measure the Royal Navy tried had the slightest effect.

The underwater craft were augmented by a lethal surface fleet of
commerce raiders consisting of heavily armed auxiliary cruisers sailing
the world's sea-lanes masquerading as neutral merchant ships, flying false
flags. The German raiders' favorite tactic was to tear into a British merchant convoy unexpectedly, like a rogue collie dog slaughtering a flock of

sheep, and then resuem the role of a peaceful commercial vessel as they awaited more unsuspecting victims to sail blithely over the horizon.

The combination of U-boats, commerce raiders, and pinpoint naval intelligence was lethal.

There was one critical piece of the puzzle that tied it all together; it was the catalyst that made it work. That was the secret worldwide Nazi communications network that flashed the naval intelligence information to the Nazi war fleet in time for them to act on it. Yet, it was vulnerable.

The secret radio transmitter on the *Ems* in San Pedro was the critical link in that vital communications network on the southern sea-lane. Without the information transmitted over it, the U-boats would be throwing darts at a board when it came to locating targets.

Commodore Seaborn understood that disrupting the radio transmissions was the key to overcoming the deadly logistical threat to England, a most necessary first step in defeating the Nazis.

Major Randal, blissfully unaware of the high-intensity melodrama being played out round the clock in the bowels of the Admiralty, had requested then-Commander Seaborn by name for Operation Lounge Lizard for the simple reason that he was the only senior Royal Navy officer he knew personally. He had not asked for him because he believed the man to be a particularly talented naval officer or because he believed the staff officer might have any special insight into the mission. The truth was, the few times he had been around the man he had not been all that impressed.

A good leader knows when he needs help and is not afraid to ask for it. Major Randal had recognized right away he needed a senior Royal Navy officer to coordinate naval support for the cutting-out operation. One of his standing rules was "Right man, right job," and along those lines he wanted someone who would be highly motivated to see Raiding Forces succeed from a standing start. His idea was that the father of one of the officers going on the raid would fit that bill.

By pure, dumb luck Major John Randal had managed to pick a Navy officer in the best possible position to make an accurate strategic assessment of Operation Lounge Lizard.

Commodore Seaborn instantly grasped the magnitude of the threat the clandestine radio station located on the *Ems* posed. The clandestine broadcasts answered a lot of questions about how German U-boats always knew exactly where to be waiting when those carefully routed Most Secret convoys on the southern route steamed straight into their torpedo sights and offered themselves up for the slaughter. The transmissions had to be stopped.

After carefully analyzing the operation, Commodore Seaborn broke the mission down into four vital phases: (1) transporting Raiding Forces to Rio Bonita; (2) boarding and seizing the three enemy ships; (3) moving out of San Pedro Harbor; and (4) handing the ships over to the Royal Navy.

Phase two of the operation was Major Randal's responsibility; Captain Terry "Zorro" Stone, the resident Raiding Forces expert on enemy ship boarding techniques, would develop a tactical plan to capture the German and Italian ships. (In point of fact, the Life Guards officer knew very little about the subject.)

Phases one, three, and four were all seagoing functions, which meant they were Commodore Seaborn's responsibility to plan, coordinate, and set in motion. Unselfishly the naval officer—who had come out to Rio Bonita expecting a command—threw himself into the project even though he was bitterly disappointed with the scope of his assignment—token brass hat. To everyone's relief he did not seem to have any problem working for officers many years and several pay grades beneath him, even prior to his amazing promotion.

After all, as Captain Stone candidly pointed out to Major Randal in private, Commodore Seaborn was "a career Navy man in a rear admiral's suit, reporting to an Army captain, planning a mission that was essentially a Navy cutting-out operation, commanded by an Army major." The commodore had to be possessed of a sense of humor neither of them had previously detected.

Whether or not he had a sense of humor, a lightbulb had definitely gone off in the sailor's heart-of-oak brain. A high-ranking Royal Navy officer such as himself was an absolute necessity if there was any hope of this operation succeeding. That young Major Randal had been able to evaluate the political and military situation in the Gold Coast, conclude he needed assistance, identify what type of assistance he needed, and make the request within about an hour of arriving in theater, even though to do so required him to ask that an officer who outranked him be assigned to the mission, was impressive.

Most young officers given an independent command might have been tempted to try to go it on their own.

Commodore Seaborn began by tackling the problem of moving the three enemy ships after Raiding Forces boarded and seized them. Somehow they would have to travel from where they were anchored in San Pedro Harbor out to the three-mile international limit Rio Bonita claimed. Raiding Forces' Rule 5 read, "Plan missions backward. Know how to get home." The commodore thought it a sensible rule.

Only two options were available. The ships could steam out under their own power, or they could be towed out. Right from the start Commodore Seaborn saw clearly that running the ships up to full speed and sailing away was wishful thinking. He realized that the only viable option was for the boarding parties to go into San Pedro in the dead of night on aboard at least three tugboats, forcibly board the enemy ships, cut their anchor chains, effect tows, haul the ships out to international waters under tow, and hand them over to the Royal Navy somewhere on the high seas.

If once on board the Raiders could manage to get the enemy ships powered up, so much the better. But for planning purposes, he was not going to count on it.

Commodore Seaborn understood the importance of physically moving the ships out of the harbor. It gave Great Britain the cover it needed, making it seem as if the German and Italian crews had decided to escape and simply sailed away. As far as the tugboats went, well, their presence could be seen as part of the German and Italian getaway plan. The ships would be gone and who was to say what had actually happened? Especially since, according to plan, every adult in the port area was going to be highly inebriated on the big night.

Command and control at the point of the handover was crucial. Extensive coordination and cool heads were going to be required to prevent a blue-on-blue friendly-fire incident. Sailors in a hot war zone tend to shoot first and ask questions later. To effect the handover of three enemy ships at night at sea to Royal Navy men-of-war whose gunners had their fingers curled on the trigger was going to be tricky at best.

The commodore wanted to be able to accomplish the entire mission without leaving behind any fingerprints. The Portuguese government had to be given political cover that allowed them an out and not be forced to declare war on England.

Major John Randal, Captain Terry "Zorro" Stone, and Jim "Baldie" Taylor came into the room where Commodore Seaborn was working.

"How goes it, Commodore?" Major Randal asked.

"Not bad, John, not bad at all, actually. However, there is one matter we need to clear up before I can proceed."

"Sir?"

"The question of command," Commodore Seaborn said carefully.

The men became instantly alert. They had known all along the subject would come up sooner or later; it had to. No one was looking forward to discussing it because questions concerning command can be, and usually are, volatile when differences in rank are involved. The fate of the mission might very well rest on how they solved the issue.

"Operation Lounge Lizard has four basic phases after we marshal forces," Commodore Seaborn ticked off crisply. "Transport to the target area, actions in the target area, movement out of the target area, and handover of the prizes the Royal Navy."

The other three men nodded guardedly in agreement, each wearing a poker-faced serious expression.

"No one has explained what is expected of me other than to assist in planning, make the Navy end of things go smoothly, and run interference with the local authorities. I need to know what role you have in mind for me, if any, during the 'movement to and actions in the target area' phases so I can determine where to pre-position myself to be the most effective."

"Sir, I want you to plan and coordinate all sea movement to and from San Pedro, to include the handover of the prizes," Major Randal replied. "Considering that everything we do after we enter the harbor will technically be a violation of international law, it's perfectly understandable if you choose not to accompany us into the harbor. My guess is you'll want to travel with the Royal Navy to supervise the linkup and handover. It's strictly your call, sir."

Commodore Seaborn looked at the young major closely. "Are you are willing to subordinate command of certain phases?"

"Sir, I'm in overall command of Operation Lounge Lizard, and as you know, I can't delegate that responsibility. However, I don't care who commands the individual phases of the operation as long as we put the most qualified person we can find in charge of each task."

Now, Commodore Seaborn was really impressed! He knew, because he had spent a lifetime studying such things, the mark of a superior leader is his ability to also be a superior follower when it best fits the interest of a mission. Major Randal's response had been one of absolute professional confidence.

"Here is the problem," Commodore Seaborn explained, saying the exact words the others in the room most did not want to hear but had more or less been expecting from the time he had arrived. They braced themselves for a treatise on the prerogatives of rank. Royal Navy officers have a reputation for being sticklers about adhering to correct protocol in such matters.

"You appear to have overlooked one vital aspect of the cutting-out phase. It's not enough to simply board and capture those three enemy ships. They have to be moved out of the harbor to the three-mile limit somehow. I believe the best way is by tow, but we might be able to sail them out under their own power. Either way, somebody has to conn each ship."

Since this was not what the other men had been expecting to hear, all the commodore got in return were totally blank stares.

"In plain language, somebody is going to have to stand on the bridge, take the wheel, and drive the prizes out of the harbor whether they are being towed or sailed under their own power. And whoever that person is had better not make a mistake!"

Major Randal looked at the other two as if to say, "I told you we needed a navy type."

"What's your recommendation, sir?"

"Randy has never conned anything as large as our target ships before. I can signal his transport skipper and order the captain to give him some hands-on practice at sea before they arrive in Accra. Randy's CPO spent a couple of years as the helmsman of a tramp steamer, so he can easily handle one."

"Who do we get to conn the third ship?" Captain Stone wondered out loud, voicing the question the other two men were thinking.

"Me," was the naval officer's immediate reply. "I simply needed to find out if it was going to create a command problem for you if I came along on the raid."

"Commodore, I don't mind being a private to and from San Pedro Harbor as long as you agree to be a swabbie from the instant I say 'Boarders Away,'" Major Randal said. "I promise to hand control back to you the very second we secure the enemy ships. At that stage, all I'm going to want is for you to sail us away and gone."

"Never would have figured you for a pirate, sir," Captain Stone opined.

"Chalk it up to temporary insanity." Commodore Seaborn's sick grin showed he wasn't joking entirely.

The other three men could not help but notice he had turned a faint shade of green at the mention of the word *pirate*. Apparently it was not a term he considered beneficial either to his naval career path or to the honorable Seaborn family name.

21

COUNTING CARIBOU
IN ANTARCTICA

"WHAT DID YOU LEARN TODAY?" CAPTAIN TERRY "ZORRO" STONE asked Major John Randal as Jim "Baldie" Taylor pinned up the 8x10 photos he had developed from the rolls of film the Life Guards officer had smuggled out of Rio Bonita by courier the night before.

"Witchcraft."

"What?"

"Since the outbreak of hostilities, the reported number of incidents of witchcraft in the Gold Coast has increased significantly," Major Randal explained. "No one seems to know why."

"Now that is invaluable information," Commodore Richard Seaborn chuckled. "Exactly what are we supposed to do with it?"

"The locals are really laying it on thick," Baldie observed approvingly. "You're doing a great job diverting their attention from what we are up to here at the beach house. Keep up the good work, Major."

The photos were interesting in more ways than one. There was a blowup of a tanned Captain the Lady Jane Seaborn, wearing skintight blue-jean short shorts, on board the Italian ship *Giove* surrounded by a leering group of sailors. In another, taken on the *Egadi*, Royal Marine Pamala Plum-Martin, sporting a black French cut swimsuit, was surrounded by a similar mob of lascivious-looking Italian seamen.

The two Mata Haris had managed to click their way all over both Italian ships, even working their way up and around the upper decks. The luscious secret agents—who appeared to have changed their costumes three or four times a day—took scores of photos. Not going to be any secrets on these ships when Raiding Forces went in for the kill.

Not surprisingly, the women had failed to gain access to the German ship. For instance, there was a shot of Royal Marine Plum-Martin on the small boarding ladder deck of the *Ems* looking up with a startled expression on her face. The next photo, aimed almost straight up, showed a hawk-faced, visibly angry Kriegsmarine officer glaring down over the rail.

"That's the skipper, Wolf Steiner," Baldie stated. "Definitely a no-nonsense kind of guy, diehard Nazi fanatic all the way."

Not to worry. The next blowup featured Captain "Geronimo Joe" McKoy wearing a huge ten-gallon straw hat, holding a fishing pole, and waving stupidly at the camera. Behind him was the *Ems*, dead center.

Major Randal could not help but laugh.

"I think this one is for you, John," Captain Stone offered with a perfectly straight face, handing him a 8x10 photograph of a tanned Captain Lady Seaborn in a tiny white valentine-shaped swimsuit that fit her like it had been spray-painted on. The black-and-white glossy was a full-length shot of her leaning back against a rail looking square into the camera. The erotic impact of the photo was like a body slam.

"Why don't you keep that one, Major?" Baldie suggested, trying unsuccessfully not to grin. "Really does not contain much actionable intelligence, at least as far as Lounge Lizard goes."

"Let's get back to business," Major Randal snapped.

Pinned next to the blowups of each of the three ships in the harbor was a schematic diagram of each vessel. The diagrams were the kind of intelligence information that was worth its weight in rubies to a mission planner.

"Where did these come from?" Major John Randal asked.

"Various places," Baldie answered vaguely.

"These are priceless!"

"Major, I am an intelligence officer. That's what intelligence officers do, provide priceless information," Baldie said in monotone, making it clear he was not going to be drawn into any conversation about tradecraft or sources.

The SOE station chief was not about to discuss any information he did not want the opposition to know, with men preparing to go on a hazardous mission with a high probability they would be captured and interrogated.

"We finally nailed down how the *Ems* obtains the information on the ship movements she transmits," he informed them, moving on to a new subject. "Pretty neat the way it works. As you know, the Gold Coast consists of four colonies, or governorships. The easternmost governorship is called British Mandated Togoland."

He pointed to the Gold Coast map pinned on the wall and began his briefing. "Togoland used to be a German colony. At the beginning of the last war, twenty-odd years ago, the French invaded from the west and we invaded from the east in a well-coordinated pincer attack. We captured the whole of the country in a lightning-fast virtually bloodless campaign. Then we split the German colony right down the middle by drawing a line on the map. After the Armistice, we kept our contiguous half, while the French kept theirs.

"Overnight, the people living in the eastern part of Togoland became British subjects instead of German; those on the west side, French. The annexation resulted in a large number of people, black and white, originally German citizens who speak German and still think of themselves as Germans and who never wanted to be British—living under our flag in the Gold Coast today. More than a few are pro-Hitler.

"We have reason to suspect that the clandestine German Naval Intelligence HQ in Western Africa is based someplace in British Mandated Togoland.

"Now, the German Secret Service, the Abwehr, plant low-level agents in every port facility, every shipping yard, and every passenger or freight shipping company along the coast, casting a giant invisible maritime espionage and intelligence-gathering web over the entire Gold Coast. The Nazi spies are, for the most part, nondescript employees, like clerks, security guards, cleaning people engaged in menial work. Those cleaning staff, maintenance crews, and night watchmen have unlimited access, day or night, to all areas of the port facilities where they are employed. They often work during hours when no one else is around; they come and go as they please; and by the very nature of their jobs no one ever pays any attention to them, which makes them invisible. In other words, the German naval intelligence network is hiding out in plain sight.

"However, by the nature of their jobs they are strategically placed in key positions, thus making it possible for them to discover the names of ships preparing to sail, to know their departure times and routes, to obtain copies of the manifests or bills of lading, and to learn the priority of the cargo on each ship.

"The raw data the agents gather are consolidated, encoded, then given to a courier who hand-carries them to Rio Bonita three times a week by way of the Accra ferry. The courier deposits the coded intelligence in a clandestine dead-letter drop located in San Pedro. An officer dispatched from the *Ems* retrieves it the same day.

"According to our Y-Service boffins, the *Ems* transmits the information promptly at 0200 hours the same night it comes on board and the commerce raiders and U-boats immediately swing into action.

"Gentlemen, the network I have just described may sound childishly simple, but be advised, it is a sophisticated intelligence-gathering operation producing a high-grade product. The results speak for themselves."

"Fascinating," Commodore Seaborn commented. "How long have you known about this?"

"It's red-hot late-breaking news fresh off the press, Commodore. Our plan is to grab the San Pedro courier right after he returns from his run on Saturday. We intend to wait until the last possible second before Raiding Forces launch their attack to reduce the chance of compromising your mission," Baldie explained. "Then my boys are going to squeeze him like a lemon, and with a little luck, he should give us what we need to be able to roll up the entire network."

"Nice work, Jim," Major Randal slapped him on the back. "Your boys are real studs."

"Impressive, old stick," Captain Stone agreed. "Most!"

"I wish I could be there when you chaps interrogate the courier," Commodore Seaborn said regretfully, sounding a lot more bloody-minded than you might expect of your average paper-pushing convoy router.

Captain Stone brought up another subject. "The troopship carrying Raiding Forces will arrive in Accra in two days' time. I am planning to fly out by Catalina tomorrow to link up with it and brief the men on the mission in order to give them as much time to begin mission preparation as possible. Anyone want to go with me?"

"Count me in," Commodore Seaborn said. "After your briefing, possibly, we can fly down and coordinate with the squadron of corvettes I have arranged to rendezvous with us when we bring the three ships out of San Pedro Harbor."

"Marvelous. Takeoff is at 0600 hours, sir."

"While you two are doing that, I should probably fly up to the border in a lightplane with you, John, and make a whirlwind inspection to throw off the locals," Baldie suggested.

"Love to, Jim. I'm getting saddle sores from sitting in on all these briefings."

"Make sure you call and cancel your schedule, being careful to mention at least a couple of times we are planning to travel to the Ivory Coast border. The locals are dense, but you and I going on a border tour will definitely grab their attention."

After making the necessary phone call, Major Randal and Commodore Seaborn left the other two to their planning. They walked outside and climbed into Baldie's Chevrolet; Major Randal took the wheel. They drove to the Navy dock in Accra. Commodore Seaborn had obtained the names of the three most experienced tugboat skippers operating on the Gold Coast and arranged for a private meeting with them.

While they were driving through the dark African night, Commodore Seaborn gave Major Randal a short, completely unauthorized briefing. "What I am preparing to tell you, John, is classified Most Secret, need to know only. The information is not to leave this vehicle. You are not to share it with anyone—even Terry and Jim. In the event of your capture, you will not reveal anything I tell you tonight, even under the most severe interrogation."

"Yes sir."

"In February of this year, Hitler authorized unrestricted submarine warfare. The following are the United Kingdom's shipping losses for the last four months we have the complete numbers on: March—107,009 tons; April—158,218 tons; May—288,461 tons; and June—585,496 tons. Approximately thirty-five percent of the sinkings took place in the South Atlantic Sea Route. Do you get the message?"

"Loud and clear, sir," Major Randal said. "Doesn't take a sailor to understand that's an ugly progression."

"After reading the same intelligence brief you yourself were provided, I was not persuaded it painted a sufficiently grim picture. You, in your role as mission commander, deserve to know exactly how important knocking out the secret radio station on the *Ems* actually is to the total war effort."

"I appreciate that, Commodore Seaborn."

"Be advised I am not authorized to share what I told you with anyone, including you. Those numbers are one of the most closely guarded secrets in the Empire. Do not let me down or we could end up sharing a cell in the Tower of London."

"You have my word, sir."

"Up to now the Royal Navy has been powerless to do anything to slow the number of sinkings. Knocking out the radio transmitter on the *Ems* is a significant first start."

What Commodore Seaborn did not tell Major Randal was that Churchill, the former First Lord of the Admiralty, made it a regular practice to pop into the subterranean convoy routing room unannounced, at all hours of the day and night, to inquire about the state of the convoys at sea.

During one of those surprise visits, the prime minister candidly admitted that the only threat that really scared him was knowing what would happen if the U-boats kept up their onslaught on British shipping. Commodore Seaborn had been on duty, standing at the map table, when Churchill had made his pronouncement. He would never forget it. After the PM departed, Commodore Seaborn's boss had ordered everyone in the room to forget the incident had ever happened on threat of being assigned to a weather station in Greenland for the duration.

When the two officers arrived at their destination in the port facility, Commodore Seaborn went in alone. The Senior Naval Officer Commanding Port Facilities Accra was a Royal Navy captain who had been generous enough to offer the use of his spacious private office for the meeting.

He was clearly curious about what was taking place. Commodore Seaborn had obliquely mentioned he needed to explore contracts with tugboat operators to handle the Lend Lease shipping that would be arriving in the Gold Coast sometime in the future. However, when the commodore made a point of not inviting him to stay for the meeting, the port facilities' senior officer eventually got the message and departed. Major Randal waited in the Chevrolet until the captain had left the building before getting out of the car.

The three tugboat skippers cooling their heels in the lobby had no idea why they had been ordered there, and not being the kind of men who reacted well to being summoned anyway, were clearly disgruntled. They observed the comings and goings with a jaundiced eye.

It takes a special kind of hard luck to end up captaining a tugboat on the Gold Coast of Africa—the kind you had to have worked at. The Port of Accra was a saltwater cesspool inhabited by the biggest losers on the seven seas.

The tugboat captains were middle-aged men, but because their sorry lives had been a long repetitious slow-speed death spiral of bad booze, bad women, barroom brawls, petty offenses, and overnights in jail, they looked a lot older. They blew every penny they made, which was a substantial amount, as fast as they laid their hands on it. All three sported deep dark tans from the deadly hot sun, spiderwebs of broken blood vessels on their noses from the drinking and brawling, permanently bloodshot eyes, and heavily wrinkled brows from the constant pain of the hangovers and squinting into the harsh African glare. These three sailormen did not look like anybody's grandfather.

Mike "Wino" Muldoon was the only one who would even admit to a first name. The other two, "Mud Cat" Ray and "Warthog" Finley, claimed to have forgotten theirs, and maybe they had. The old salts were excellent nonverbal communicators. They made it plain they were not happy when they filed into the office.

"I am Commodore Seaborn. This is Major Randal."

There was no sign of expression from the hard-nosed captains. Obviously they had no intention of being cooperative, much less friendly. They may have been dead-enders and life's losers, but in the rarified world of tugboat drivers, they were emperor-kings.

When a tugboat skipper speaks, admirals and the captains of great ships hang on their every word. When a tugboat captain plying his trade issues a command, the high and mighty and eminently powerful leap to see it instantly obeyed. A tugboat skipper with a ship under tow is the Master of the Universe. No one outranks him.

A long, distinguished naval career can turn to dust in an instant if the ship has a collision or runs aground. What would happen to the tugboat skipper? Not much. What could the Admiralty do—ship him to the Gold Coast? Tugboat skippers are generally not awed by gold braid, rank, or fancy titles. They have the opportunity, the means, and the ability to break captains or admirals on any given day.

"You men may recognize Major Randal from newsreels and the newspapers as the famous Commando raider."

Three sets of hardcase eyes briefly flicked over to Major Randal then drifted back to Commodore Seaborn without much change in expression and zero percent increase in interest.

"Everything said in this room tonight is classified Most Secret. Do not discuss this meeting with anyone not present. If you do, you are subject to immediate imprisonment under the Official Secrets Act, which none of you have signed. There is no need to sign it. To tell the truth, men, in this case we are not going to waste time bothering with the finer points of the law should you breathe a word of what is said here tonight. I do hope you get my drift.

"Does anyone have a question? No . . . very good, then. Major Randal has a proposition for you."

Commodore Seaborn's little speech did not generate a reaction from the skippers, but he had gotten their attention. Being experienced men, they could recognize a threat when they heard one. For his part, Major Randal looked at the tugboat captains levelly, straight into their bloodshot eyes, completely unfazed by their open hostility. They noted that.

"Gentlemen, there are three Axis ships in San Pedro Harbor on the island of Rio Bonita: the *Egadi*, *Giove*, and *Ems*. On Saturday night, my men and I intend to call on San Pedro, board the three ships, kill or capture the crews, and bring all three ships out of the harbor."

Whatever they had expected, this bombshell was definitely not it. It screamed in and detonated right in their booze-addled brains. Each skipper's demeanor flashed from cantankerous to all ahead full apprehensive. They could guess what the major was going to say next. He did not disappoint.

"You men are going to tow 'em out of there for me."

"We ain't in the bleedin' navy," Mud Cat bellowed. "You can't order us what to do."

"Actually, as of now, you are," Commodore Seaborn announced mildly. "You, your crew, and your tugboats have all been called up for National Service. Detachments of Royal Marines are boarding your boats as we speak."

"You can't do that!" Mud Cat protested once more, foaming at the mouth.

"Yeah, he can," Warthog rasped in a whisky-ruined voice. "He's Royal Navy. He can ship us to Antarctica to count caribou if he has a mind to."

"There ain't no blinkin' caribou in Antarctica," Wino taunted him, sounding like the class know-it-all.

"In that case, we won't be doing much countin', will we, Wino?"

Not being accomplished verbal debaters, neither of the other two skippers could think of a retort to counter that logic. All three had a lot of practice at being forced into doing things against their will by some authority they were powerless against. Men living at the bottom of the food chain always do.

"What do we get out of the deal?" a more subdued Mud Cat asked finally. "There ought to be something in it for us."

"The chance to serve your king and country; afterward, England will buy your tugs at a premium price. When this operation is completed, you qualify for thirty days' paid leave anywhere you wish to take it, as long as it is not in West Africa or Portugal. Following your leave, His Majesty's Government will award you a new contract to go back into the tugboat business after you relocate to a new port of call and make sure you are able to purchase boats at a reasonable price, meaning for less than what we paid you for yours."

"We get to pick our station?" Warthog inquired.

"You can relocate anywhere in the Empire, as long as it is not a port along the southern sea-lane," Commodore Seaborn confirmed. "We do not want any loose lips after the mission is completed."

"I have always wanted to get back to Singapore," Mud Cat semi-whispered in a tone filled with mounting excitement as he imagined hordes of golden-skinned Asian girls in silk dresses with a long slit up one thigh.

"Does this deal mean we have to wear sailor suits?" Wino asked petulantly. "I bloody hate Navy dress."

"No," said Commodore Seaborn, "you can wear a Hawaiian shirt and sandals for all it matters. Uniforms are not going to make any difference if we get caught. The Portuguese will hang us for piracy regardless of our attire."

"Why didn't you say so in the first place?" Mud Cat demanded. "I've always wanted to be a pirate. Sign me up!"

"I saw your picture in the newspaper," Warthog rasped to Major Randal. "You say the plan is to go over to San Pedro on Saturday night and tow those three ships out of the harbor? Do you think it will be that easy?"

"Never is."

"You got that right, Major. Count me in. What about you, Wino?"

"I'm going to have to check my calendar, Warthog. But I'm pretty sure I can fit it into my schedule."

Not one of the tugboat skippers even brought up the possibility of being killed or wounded. No questions were asked about who was liable for things like medical coverage. These old African hands were simply not the kind of sailor men to sweat the minor details.

22

TICKET PUNCHING

THE NIGHT BEFORE MAJOR JOHN RANDAL WAS SCHEDULED TO FLY TO the border, he and Captain Terry "Zorro" Stone decided to go into town, considering that they had been living on sandwiches for the past two days at the cottage. They would leave Commodore Richard Seaborn and James "Baldie" Taylor to their work. Acting on a recommendation from the SOE station chief, they drove to the hotel where the reception for Commodore Seaborn had been held the first night he arrived in Accra. The two officers were supposed to be on holiday, and tonight they were going out to act like it.

When they drove into the center of the city in Baldie's Chevrolet, neither man noticed that they were being discreetly shadowed by a police cruiser. There was no reason for them to. They were simply out for a night on the town.

The first stop was the Gold Bar located off the lobby of the hotel. There were enough big green leafy plants in giant terra cotta pots to make the interior of the bar look like it was in the middle of the teeming jungle. As usual, servants in starched white hotel safari outfits were lurking behind every bush. The place was crowded for a sleepy backwater town on a weeknight. A tiny jazz band was playing in one corner. Bronzed couples were crowding the small dance floor.

The two officers stepped up to the end of the highly polished long bar and ordered drinks. A pair of huge ivory elephant tusks, each in the two-hundred-pound range, hung over the mirror behind the bar. The bar stools were covered in zebra skin. Mounted on the walls were the stuffed heads of every known animal that had ever walked. The Commandos had a commanding view of the room.

"The locals appear resolved not to let anyone forget we are in darkest Africa," Captain Stone opined as he pulled out his sterling silver cigarette case with the family crest on it and offered Major Randal a Player. "Not that one possibly could."

"I expected more jungle," Major Randal said. "This place is like California."

"That's farther inland," Captain Stone explained, scanning the crowd. A dedicated lady-killer, he checked out the various single girls in the crowd, purely out of professional interest. In return the ladies were brazenly staring up the newcomers. The local women knew who the two were, namely, the closest thing to real-live celebrities the colony had seen.

The Commandos were not looking for action, but then again, targets of opportunity are difficult to ignore. The only complication was that Major Randal had a semi-commitment to a certain Captain the Lady Jane Seaborn, which though never having exactly been put into actual words, nevertheless had a dampening effect on his enthusiasm for chasing women. Two athletic-looking beauties were toying with their drinks down at the other end of the bar. The pair looked bored, which was always a good sign.

"What do you think?" Major Randal asked, lighting a Player with his old engraved Zippo.

"The game is afoot," Captain Stone replied, studying the possibilities.

"I mean about the mission."

"Why do you ask," the matinee-idol handsome Commando asked, taking his eyes off the two women to stare levelly at his friend.

"Major Grand, Baldie, and the Commodore have all hammered me

privately with their own personal highly classified versions of why raiding San Pedro is a great idea," Major Randal said. "You haven't had much
to say."

"Mine is not to reason why," Captain Stone replied self-effacingly. "I
serve where sent. We Life Guards, we simply follow the crowd in a charge,
though we do strive to maintain our best appearance at all times during
the melee. One does have standards."

"Do you believe this mission is crucial?"

"As it gets, old stick," Captain Stone replied confidently. "On that you
can rest assured. Up to now, most of our operations, with the possible
exceptions of Comanche Yell, Buzzard Plucker, and Ruthless, have basically amounted to live fire–training exercises. Not this one."

"Really? Why do you say that?"

"The Treaty of Locarno," Captain Stone explained, taking out another
cigarette and tapping it idly on his engraved silver case. "Quite possibly
the most incredibly wrongheaded military blunder Great Britain has ever
committed in its entire storied history of blunders, for the worst of all
reasons. A national disgrace of the first water, and virtually no one knows
anything about it."

"Lay it out," Major Randal said. "I'd like to hear what you'd classify as
a worse foul-up than Calais."

"After the last war, the Treaty of Locarno imposed a strict quota on
German naval hardware," Captain Stone said, accepting a light from the
major. "The limitation was a touch troublesome for the Nazis. You see, in
addition to restricting the number and size of the surface ships Germany
was authorized to build, the Kriegsmarine was specifically prohibited
from operating a submarine fleet, which is an absolute necessity for any
expansionist nation whose dictator is seeking world domination.

"The German navy did not have a single U-boat," Captain Stone reit-
erated. "Not to worry, Hitler negotiated for a fleet."

"Negotiated?" Major Randal said. "With what?"

"Well, the Royal Navy was also restricted in the number and size of
the ships it could build, though it enjoyed tremendous numerical superiority over the Kriegsmarine in sea power. However, it, too, was limited by

the treaty, and the Admiralty harbored an insatiable desire for more battleships, many more than it was allowed. With unerring cunning, Hitler
sensed an opening. The man has a gift for spotting weakness and exploit-
ing it. The Führer offered to allow the senior service to construct the
battlewagons it longed for in return for giving the German navy license to
build a modest U-boat fleet."

"How many was modest?"

"The Admiralty pondered that question and then, in its infinite wis-
dom, advised the Chamberlain government to allow the Germans to build
U-boats at the ratio of forty-five percent of the Royal Navy submarines.
As I recall it worked out to be a total of eighty-six Nazi U-boats. In turn,
that concession allowed the Sea Lords to churn out dreadnoughts to their
hearts' content."

"The Royal Navy agreed to that?"

"Indeed," Captain Stone said disdainfully. "Those eighty-six U-boats
are the very ones strangling the life out of Great Britain as we speak."

"So, the Germans have less than one hundred U-boats in action,
right now?"

"And they are on a terrible rampage, old stick; pretty close to completely shutting down the world's sea-lanes. I am told the outcome of
the sea war may well determine the future of the Empire, with the submarines the Royal Navy handed the Nazis on a silver platter being the
deciding factor."

"I thought the Germans had thousands of 'em, the way people have
been acting," Major Randal mused. "What could the Admiralty have been
thinking?"

"Now that's the truly ugly part," Captain Stone drawled. "The Navy
only wanted the additional battleships so senior officers would have more
capital ship command slots—which are a prerequisite for promotion—not
out of strategic necessity. In their arrogance, the admirals believed the
Royal Navy could simply sink the German submarines if it ever came to
it. Those old fools thought they were getting their battleships for free."

"You're kidding!"

"Sinking U-boats has turned out to be a little trickier than the admirals pictured. We may lose this war because of the Admiralty's desire for big surface ships. Which, according to some naval strategists, submarines had already made obsolete at the time this foolishness was taking place."

"Ticket punching," Major Randal said. "Unbelievable."

"Quiet so," Captain Stone agreed, "but true."

"How do you know this stuff?"

"I was in Pop, after all," Captain Stone pointed out. "The boys' club at Eton, as you may recall, whose members go on to rule the Empire. A fellow Pop, a few years my senior, explained it all to me over drinks in the bar at Whites a few years ago. He was, I believe, the aide to one of the delegation at the convention acting on the instructions of our government, following the direction of the Admiralty. My club mate said England would live to regret the Admiralty's conceit. He was spot-on."

23

GET OUT OF JAIL FREE

THE COMMANDOS DECIDED TO REMAIN AND BE SERVED IN THE Gold Bar, where all the action was. The two moved to a table, and shortly thereafter a waiter appeared and produced a menu. Suddenly the table was surrounded a group of big burly men. The assemblage consisted of the entire night shift of the detective squad from the Accra Police Department. The visitors were clearly not on a social call.

"I'll have a T-bone," Major John Randal said looking up from the menu. "Medium rare."

"Gentlemen, my name is Chief Inspector Fowls," the head man introduced himself, producing credentials to back up his claim. "You two lads are under arrest. If you will come along quietly, now, there will be no necessity to make a public scene."

"Arrest?" Captain Terry "Zorro" Stone inquired in feigned surprise, somehow managing to convey the impression of being bored at the same time. "Are you quite sure, old stick?"

"You can come easy or hard," Chief Inspector Fowls continued conversationally, ignoring him. "'Tis of little consequence to us. Things have been slow at the office lately; my men could use the exercise."

"What exactly are we being arrested for?" Major Randal asked politely, but there was a hint of steel in his tone that gave the chief inspector pause. The policeman knew the reputation of these two officers. They were dangerous men. And he was fairly certain both were armed, though no weapons were openly visible.

"We will discuss charges later, Major, at the station. Now, why not come along friendly, like good fellows?"

Across town the governor of the Gold Coast was sitting down to a pleasurable evening of canasta. His partner tonight was the British Consul's wife, a horsey woman with an abrasive laugh but one devil of a cardplayer. A barefoot servant in a starched white jacket appeared at his side, trailing a phone with a long extension cord.

The governor took the receiver, spoke into it, and listened for a few moments. "You have your instructions," he said to the caller—the Accra chief of police—then handed the phone back to the servant and began to shuffle the cards. Across the room at another table, Lieutenant General G. J. Giffard, General Officer Commanding West African Forces, made eye contact with the governor. They had been expecting the call.

Between the two of them, they held virtual dictatorial power over the colony and were comfortable exercising it. The governor and the general had crafted a plan of action to deal with the Raiding Forces' interlopers who had arrived in their private domain uninvited with plans to do who knew what. Tonight the opportunity had presented itself to put their plan in motion, and they had made their move.

Both senior officials were quite confident the night's doings had been calculated to perfection. This was how problems were solved out here in Africa: in your face, but with no visible fingerprints and no recourse.

Meanwhile, at police headquarters, sitting at his desk in the Detective Bureau, Chief Inspector Fowls was ruefully studying the arsenal of weapons on his desk surrendered to him by the two officers he had hauled in from the Gold Bar. There was an evil-looking pair of razor-sharp double-edged stilettos, called Fairbairn fighting knives. He had heard of them but had never seen the real item. Two High Standard .22-caliber semiautomatic pistols, with long cylinders in separate canvas sheaths ready to be attached to the threaded barrels, required some explanation. The young American had produced from the back of his pants—from a skeleton holster, what some people called a Yaqui slide—a 9-millimeter Browning P-35.

These two were packing a lot of heavy artillery for a quiet night on the town. The detective wondered what the lads carried when they went out intentionally looking for trouble.

Speed being of paramount importance to the dirty work at hand, Chief Inspector Fowls decided to move things along. The policeman was not pleased to be doing what was called for, but then in his line of employment, unpleasant business had to be done from time to time. It went with the job. Tonight he had his orders and they came directly from the chief of police.

"Would you mind informing us why you have requested our presence here tonight?" Captain Terry "Zorro" Stone inquired politely. "You are rather interrupting our evening, old stick."

A veteran detective and great solver of mysteries, Chief Inspector Fowls deduced that the Raiding Forces officers seemed somewhat amused, which did not set well with him. He liked his detainees to be at least minimally apprehensive. Tonight they had good reason to be.

Major John Randal and Captain Stone had already been tried, convicted, and sentenced in absentia. Now the chief inspector was about to deliver the verdict. There was no court of appeal.

"You men have been arrested for solicitation of prostitution," Chief Inspector Fowls explained in a stern voice. "We have strict laws governing moral turpitude in the Gold Coast Colony, lewd and lascivious conduct being frowned upon."

"That's not what I hear," Captain Stone drawled. "Wife swapping among the expatriate sundowner set out here famously being the national pastime, second only to the infamous Happy Valley set in Kenya, according to my sources, which are impeccable."

"Hookers," Major Randal said with narrowed eyes, "tonight?"

"I have signed statements," Chief Inspector Fowls continued, holding up a raft of papers, "from two of our most trusted vice operatives, sworn policewomen, who will testify that you solicited them for wicked purposes with a promise of monetary recompense for immoral services."

"When, exactly, is this supposed to have happened?" demanded Major Randal.

"Here is the way it's going to work, lads," the chief inspector pressed on, avoiding the question. "Normally in a case such as this, you would be arrested and held in jail until such time as a hearing could be arranged. Then you would appear before a magistrate, the charges would be read, and you would be remanded to a trial and released on bail. However, the legal system works differently out here in the colonies. The judge has a lot of latitude, but on morals charges the sentence is always the same—immediate deportation."

"How convenient," Captain Stone observed.

"Since you men happen to be national heroes and may or may not have full knowledge of our local laws, what we are going to do in this instance is simply detain you, hold you incommunicado at a private location for a period of forty-eight hours, then put you on a steamer outward bound on passage to the home island."

The policeman added, almost as an afterthought, "After your transport sails, I intend to personally see to it that all copies of the charges against you are destroyed. No permanent file will be maintained; in other words, this little unpleasantness will have never happened and there will not be any stain on your reputations. With any luck, you shall enjoy a nice relaxing sea cruise home."

"So, you want us out of the country," Major Randal said, studying the chief inspector. "That's what this is all about."

"Major, I am a simple policeman," Chief Inspector Fowls pointed out. "What I may or may not want has nothing to do with anything. I have signed complaints from undercover officers and clear instructions on how to proceed, and I fully intend to carry out my orders down to the ground."

"I say," Captain Stone turned to Major Randal, "don't you think this would be the appropriate time to break out one of those magic words of Lady Jane's—what was it you said to Red on the airplane?"

"Frogspawn."

"Frogspawn," the chief inspector repeated, rolling the word around on his tongue and not liking the sound of it. "What the blazes does that mean?"

"It means get the British Consul down here," Major Randal said, reaching inside his beautifully tailored uniform blouse. He extracted a pigskin credentials case and produced a letter he passed across the desk. "Right now."

The detective stared at the document bug-eyed. He had never come across anything comparable to it in his lengthy law enforcement career. The instructions read like something out of pure fiction, only they were under the Imperial Seal of the War Office.

```
To: British Consuls, Senior Naval, Military, Air
Commanders, and Civilian Officials to whom the
bearer may deem it necessary to present this letter:

This is to certify that Major J. Randal, M.C., is
on special duty under War Office direction. Provide
him all assistance in your power, to include
priority transport by sea, land or air. Under no
circumstance impede this officer.

J.M.E. Simpson-Smyth, Brigadier G.E.
For Director of Military Operations & Plans
```

"I should pay close attention to the last sentence if I were you," Captain Stone advised. "Particularly the word *impede*; it means obstruct, hinder, hamper, delay, detain, et cetera. You get the picture. John, are you feeling impeded yet?"

"I'm gettin' there."

The barefoot house servant trailing the phone and extension cord reappeared silently at the governor's side as he was laying down his hand. The houseboy held out the telephone. On the line was the chief of the Accra

Police Department. The governor listened and turned pale. He realized immediately that what had happened might very possibly spell the end of his political career; he could be sacked.

"Release those men immediately," he ordered in a tone bordering on hysteria. "Oh, they already have been, excellent!"

The governor hung up, signaled Lieutenant General G. J. Giffard and the British Consul at the other table, both of whom were looking up curiously over their cards, to join him, and lurched out of the room. The startled players at his table were left speechless.

"What is the problem, Governor?" General Giffard demanded when they were alone. "You act as if you have seen an apparition."

"This night's devil's work has imploded. The Commandos have been set free," the governor sniveled. "I should have never listened to you. My career may be in peril; I could be recalled, or worse. And you could be bowler hatted. No telling how many capital laws we broke tonight."

"Are you mad?" the general seethed. "We implemented a foolproof plan. Why would you allow the rascals to be discharged once we had them in our grasp?"

"The American produced credentials," the governor screeched, wiping his beady brow with his handkerchief, clearly in a state of distress. "The chief inspector had already released Major Randal and Captain Stone by the time he called the chief of police. I had no say in the matter."

"Get a grip on yourself, man. You're the chief executive in the colony," General Giffard barked. "Act like it."

"If I may dare to pose the question," the British Consul inquired in a prissy legalistic tone, "what possible documentation could two Commando thugs possibly have in their possession that would trump sworn affidavits by female vice officers rendered under oath?"

"A 'get out of jail free' card, Major Randal called it."

"That is ridiculous," General Giffard snapped. "No such document exists in our judicial or military system."

"Not only does the major have one, he requires the pleasure of the British Consul's company in the Gold Bar in twenty minutes."

"Are you having me on?" the British Consul huffed, shaken to the very core of his vanity. "I am summoned to a public hostelry by a relatively junior military officer, who by all rights should be under close arrest? Absurd!"

"Better hurry," the governor of the Gold Coast Colony said. "We have already wasted five of your minutes."

24

LEPIDOPTEROLOGY

SINCE JIM "BALDIE" TAYLOR HAD A FEW LOOSE ENDS TO TIE UP, IT was decided that Major John Randal would continue the charade by attending the morning's dog and pony show. Thereafter, the two men would fly up to inspect one of the Gold Coast border police stations around 1200 hours. The morning lecture Major Randal attended, titled "The History of Camouflage," was delivered by a tubby captain sporting wire-rimmed spectacles. The speaker was a lepidopterologist of note—whatever that was—and he was clearly an expert on the subject.

"Prior to World War I the word *camouflage* was not even in the *Encyclopedia Britannica*," the speaker explained, warming to his subject. "The word *camouflage* itself is French and is said to derive from the Parisian slang verb *camoufler* meaning 'to disguise'; or perhaps it came, as the Italians claim, from the word *cammufare*, derived from *capo muffare*, 'to muffle the head.' Who is to say, what?"

Glancing at his heavy black-faced Rolex with the lime green digits, a present from Captain the Lady Jane Seaborn, Major Randal noted that the lecture had been pressing on for a total of three minutes, which meant he had only another three hours and fifty-seven minutes to go. Not counting breaks. His mind wandered from the details of the lecture to thoughts of Jane.

"In the great war, a French portrait painter, forty-three-year-old Second Class Gunner Lucien-Victor Guirand de Scevola, was credited with being the first to mask artillery by covering the guns in his battery with painted sheets to confuse enemy artillery spotters in the trenches. At approximately the same time more or less, another painter, Louis Guinlot, also serving in the artillery, came up with the idea—after his unit had been bombed one fine day—to stretch canvas tarps over the tops of the guns so aerial observers could not see them from the air."

Major Randal rested his chin on his hand.

"Thus the French Army's *section de camouflage* was formed and staffed entirely by artists, sculptors, theater designers, and others of like ilk. To distinguish themselves the men wore a specially designed white-and-red brassard with a chameleon embroidered in silver wire, the chameleon being legendary for its ability to change its color and blend into its surroundings."

Major Randal stifled a yawn.

"In modern war, it was concluded that, as in the insect world, seeing and not being seen is a matter of life and death. For example, when a cabbage white butterfly lands on a green-and-white striped cornus bush, its folded wings perfectly align themselves with and match the ragged pale edges of the cornus leaves, thus . . ."

Major Randal's head jerked as he nearly nodded off.

"The renowned British biologist Edward Bagnall Poulton was the first to note how the white spots stippling the darker shaded side of the Purple Emperor butterfly . . ."

Another peek at the Rolex; two whole minutes more had passed. He was dying by inches.

" . . . khaki first appeared in the Indian Army, and the word is derived from *khak*, the Urdu and Persian word for 'dust colored.' In 1857 British troops serving in India begin dyeing their snow-white cotton tunics and pants with a combination of tea, curry powder, and dirt. By 1885 khaki was universal in the British Army serving in India.

"The U.S. Army, after their experience in Cuba and the Philippines adopted khaki in 1902, and the Japanese followed suit in 1905. The Germans elected to go their own way with field gray. Their cloth was a blend of green, blue, and gray filament . . . "

The lecturer droned on and on. It was like Chinese water torture—drip, drip, drip. Major Randal felt like he was in danger of slipping into a coma. He fantasized about putting the speaker in a rear takedown stranglehold and making him do the chicken.

An eternity later Major John Randal and Jim "Baldie" Taylor were winging their way at treetop level over the African bush in a Aeronca C-3 two-seat private plane that so lacked any semblance of aerodynamics it was officially called the "Flying Bathtub." Baldie was at the stick. The SOE man was an accomplished pilot.

For the first time, Major Randal was getting a chance to see what real Africa looked like. Baldie buzzed a herd of giraffes that lumbered along kicking up a huge cloud of dust. The Flying Bathtub was powered by a forty-horsepower engine, so the plane was not traveling very fast. The two were headed to a post on the border so isolated there was no improved road running all the way to it. To get there it was necessary to fly in and land on an improvised dirt strip or travel cross-country part of the way.

"I have not decided yet if General Giffard is a bad man," Baldie shouted over the engine noise, "or simply a ripping misguided fool with a Napoleonic complex."

"Why doesn't the War Ministry fire him?" Major Randal asked.

"Probably love to but can't. We need every general we have, even the bad ones." Baldie grinned. "The Gold Coast is where they transfer you when they *do not* want you to screw up anything else. The moment they can find some assignment worse than here, he will be gone in a flash."

"Right," Major Randal commented dryly. "That apply to you and me, Jim?"

"Especially us! I already filled you in on my story. Now as far as you're concerned, the hard cold truth is, Major, you and your little band of buccaneers are expendable."

"Expendable?"

"Abso-bloody-lutely!" Baldie said with a big grin. "An American commanding a small irregular unit? If something goes wrong, oh well, fortunes of war. You work for SOE or Combined Operations; no one is sure exactly which. Or maybe you work for MI-6 and even you don't know it, that's called a false flag recruitment

"In the grand scheme of things, MI-6 hates SOE because they see it as a competitor, and the Royal Navy, the British Army, and the RAF all despise Combined Operations for carrying out freelance operations they have no control over, soaking up their precious resources of equipment or siphoning off their best men. Which means Raiding Forces cannot be all that popular, no matter who they work for, so you've gotten shipped out on a mission no one else wants any part of."

"You said the raid was vital!"

"It is," Baldie laughed, "yet no one actually expects you to be able to carry it off. At least you have an operation that lets you go shoot bad people. All I get to do is whisper."

"Whisper?"

"'Subversive Verbal,'" Baldie explained in disgust. "That's the official program designator, a 'diabolical whisper campaign' aimed at the natives in the Vichy colonies. I have a man in each district to run the program. My lads are not allowed to spread rumors themselves. Each one has to appoint a local 'chief whisperer' to disseminate the tall tales. Each chief whisperer operates independently but has to report back what rumors are circulated so we can coordinate them with the whispers spread in other districts."

"You're kidding, right?"

"Only about the diabolical part." The spy shook his tanned bald head. "Each chief whisperer recruits sub-whisperers so we have an official government-sanctioned most secret hush-hush gossip network operating Gold Coast–wide, whispering. And I get to be in charge."

"What kind of whispers, Jim?" Major Randal asked, still not sure whether to believe him.

"How's this? Three Germans died of snakebites—the Snake Societies are vigilant. Or, both a German and a Vichy French officer who infiltrated Dahomey to spy out the land were killed by lightning—the Bariba tribe have a very powerful juju. Stuff like that. Oh yeah, a good one was that the

'German Armistice Commission was superintending the killing of local natives and shipping the corpses to Germany as pig fodder.'"

"Human pig fodder—I like that one."

"My favorite is, 'Three pilgrims on their return from Mecca had a vision near Timbuktu of the Archangel Gabriel sharpening his sword.'"

"What's it mean?"

"I have no idea." Baldie grinned. "But you have to admit it has panache. The whole program is total rubbish. It could amount to something, though, if I were given free rein to be creative, but I am specifically ordered not to allow 'strategic deceit' rumors to go out that have 'any military application.'"

"So that's how you spend your time," Major Randal said. "Spreading nonmilitary whispers."

"I also get to be in the magic lantern business," Baldie added. "Traveling propaganda shows, splashing movies on bedsheet screens outdoors. You will have the opportunity to see one of our current programs this very night."

"Looking forward to it, Jim."

Up ahead a small tent city became visible. There was a tiny strip of grass next to it, and Baldie banked the light aircraft toward the runway. They puttered over at low altitude to let the people in the tents know they were arriving and to check the tiny airstrip for obstructions. It was a good thing they did. A string of zebras was grazing leisurely across the field.

The Flying Bathtub banked around standing on one wing and dived down low to buzz them in a failed effort to frighten them off. After a couple of passes, several khaki figures arrived to herd the animals away. The little plane immediately came in for a perfect three-point landing.

"By the way, John. Learn anything useful at your lecture?" Baldie inquired conversationally as the little airplane rolled to a stop. "You've been real quiet about it."

"Camouflage should be used to confuse, not conceal."

"Major, you just laid out one-half of the mission statement every national-level military intelligence organization worldwide hopes to accomplish against its opposite number—in less than ten words."

25

CINEMA STAR

A BIG STRAPPING LIEUTENANT DICK COURTNEY GREETED THEM when they climbed out of the airplane. He was dressed in razor-sharp machete-creased bush shorts and a khaki bush shirt. The subdued GCBP pins on the collar indicated his position in the Gold Coast Border Police. He looked like one of those eager, clean-cut, wholesome types generally seen on posters advertising movies about the Royal Canadian Mounted Police.

"Welcome to His Britannic Majesty's most remote outpost in the Gold Coast Colony, gentlemen." Staring at Major John Randal, he asked curiously, "Have we met, sir?"

"Don't think so, Lieutenant.

"This is the Major John Randal, cinema star," Jim "Baldie" Taylor explained.

"Quite right," Lieutenant Courtney said with a big white-toothed smile and a dawning recognition. "The pinprick fellow. Fancy encountering you way out here in the bush, sir? The locals will be highly impressed. Never met a real-live celluloid hero before, I'll wager."

Courtney explained that the Ministry of Information operated four cinema vans staffed by members of the Colonial Film Unit that traveled far and wide to all parts of the Gold Coast Colony for propaganda purposes. One of them had made its way cross-country through the bush to Lieutenant Courtney's isolated border post. The CFU showed newsreels, short subjects (usually about the Royal Family, because there was virtually no good war news), and the ever wildly popular Charlie Chaplin movies. To bush natives who did not have electricity, this was an unimaginably fantastic form of entertainment.

"I also have bulletin boards we put information on," Baldie commented idly as they stood on the runway. "Boy Scouts move them around for us from place to place to obtain more readership. Only I have a difficult time getting enough Scouts assigned to move the boards."

"We're planning to use Sea Rover Scouts to augment the crew of some of our small boats," Major Randal said, "for clandestine cross-channel work."

"And I thought I was bloody desperate!" Baldie countered. "The propaganda flick Courtney here has been showing features your Commando raid," the SOE chief of station explained.

"You have a clip of the jump on Tomcat?"

"Afraid not—what we are running is the one where the 'hand of steel from the sea plucks a German general from his post' somewhere in enemy occupied France. You looked really good in that one, Major."

"It's nearly six months old."

"Practically real time," Lieutenant Courtney quipped, "for bush rats like us, sir!"

Two of the Gold Coast Border Police askaris lugged their canvas bags to the sleeping tent the two visitors would occupy for the night. As they unpacked their gear, Baldie gave Major Randal a quick rundown on the duties of the GCBP.

"The Gold Coast Colony has several thousand miles of desolate borders. Some are internal borders, but quite a lot of it runs along the Vichy frontier, which means enemy territory. The French colonies' borders surround the Gold Coast and for the most part are completely undefended. Officers like Lieutenant Courtney patrol the border doing the king's work and keeping an eye peeled for any signs of a once or future enemy incursion. It's a lonely, dangerous job that carries a great deal of responsibility, and it requires a lot of individual initiative from the junior officers who operate all alone out in the blue."

"Who does Lieutenant Courtney rely on for backup?"

"In the African bush, if a GCBP officer gets into trouble," Baldie explained, "there is no one to call—he is expected to get himself out of it. A border policeman has to be thinking a couple of moves ahead at all times."

"On antiguerilla patrol in the Philippines, that's the way it was, too," Major Randal said. "Got dicey sometimes."

"I bet it did, Major. Huks have a nasty reputation. Anyway, Dick is my man in this part of the world, and he is a competent operator, though he hates the job."

"Why might that be?"

"Dickey sees himself paddling ashore in a rubber boat behind the lines under cover of darkness with a knife in his teeth to do battle with the dreaded Nazis, not patrolling a lonely border in the middle of nowhere."

"I see."

"Tough to blame him," Baldie continued. "There is a distinct shortage of quality female companionship out in the bush, leaves are few and far between, and this is hard duty. As the lieutenant sees it, the war is passing him by."

"He has a point."

The first order of business was for Major Randal to conduct an inspection of the squad of Gold Coast Border Policeman, as was expected of all visiting "luminaries." The policemen hastily assembled in bare feet under a Union Jack that waved bravely in the breeze. A large crowd of visiting natives, in the camp to see the night's show, gathered round.

A great twitter of excitement ran through the assemblage when Major Randal marched out wearing his Commando forest-green beret cocked down low over his right eye to begin the inspection. Clearly the people recognized him from the newsreels. The natives craned their necks and jockeyed for a better position to view the hardscrabble parade ground. They noted that the great warrior took the time to speak to each and every man he inspected, which was doubtless a mark of respect.

Though he was not a parade-ground soldier, and he'd forgotten most of what little he'd been taught about drill and ceremonies, Major Randal went at it with professional intent that would have made Raiding Forces' Sergeant Major Maxwell Hicks, Grenadier Guards, proud. Enfield rifles were slapped out of steady black hands and inspected stem to stern with robotic military precision then slammed back at their owners hard enough to crack against their palms. The gleaming weapons were immaculate.

The GCBP troops loved every minute of it.

When the ceremony was complete, Major Randal took the salute from Lieutenant Courtney, wheeled around, and marched rigidly back to his sleeping tent—being careful not to trip over a tent rope. He remembered being advised by one of the drill and ceremony instructors during his cavalry school days at Fort Riley, Kansas, that when in doubt on the parade ground do "something, anything at all, as long as you execute it in a vigorous military manner with a serious demeanor."

Baldie was outside the tent, smoking and observing the performance.

"Nice job of showing the flag, Major," he commented laconically. "Perform much close-order drill in the Commandos?"

"I'm glad Terry wasn't here to see that," Major Randal said. "The Life Guards take their parade seriously."

Next up on the day's program was a briefing by Lieutenant Dick Courtney on the situation along the lengthy, isolated stretch of the border he was responsible for patrolling. He ran through a long litany of petty problems of the type any policeman could expect to encounter during the course of normal day-to-day activities. Then he came to an interesting item.

"Our neighbors across the wire also have a distinguished visitor recently arrived, Colonel Doctor Rudolph von Himmel and his lovely bride."

"When did that happen?" Jim "Baldie" Taylor demanded, unable to mask his clear and present interest. "This is the first I have heard of Count Himmel being in Africa. What kept you from reporting this to me earlier, Dick?"

"I received the information only yesterday, sir," Lieutenant Courtney explained. "Since you were already planning to come up here, I thought it best to wait and brief you when you arrived. Besides, there is not much to tell. The count is on a honeymoon safari with his new wife, and from the reports I have from locals coming over to watch our nightly cinema shows, all he has been doing is riding around the neighborhood slaughtering herds of gazelle with the pedestal-mounted MG-34 machine gun on his Kübelwagen by day and spending his nights drinking buckets of champagne in his tent with Ursula."

"I want everything you can get me on the count's setup," the SOE station chief said in a tone that made Major John Randal click on. "Round up any native on station who has been in the safari camp."

"All I know, Chief, is the German and his party arrived in the area in the last day or two, and ever since, he's been shooting anything that moves," Lieutenant Courtney said. "Unless it's a trophy worth mounting, he never follows up wounded game. The count simply blazes away at the animal with the machine gun while his driver tries to run it down. Bloody murder is what it is, sir."

"Where is his camp located?"

"Not more than five miles from here as the crow flies." Lieutenant Courtney pointed to the map board. "Right about here."

"How many do you estimate in the German hunting party?"

"There's the count, Ursula, four other German men—who are sharing a single sleeping tent, so they may be soldiers—and a squad of askaris. This is a five-star white-tablecloth safari, sir, which means a couple of professional hunters, his and hers, and at least twenty other servants, tent boys, cooks, waiters, skinners, trackers, gun bearers, mechanics, et cetera, and all the trappings."

"How did you manage to obtain the woman's name?" Baldie inquired. "Natives generally do not pay much attention to white women."

"The bride is fast and free with her rhinoceros whip. Apparently likes to lash out at anyone who comes in range, sir. The people who have been in the camp describe her as 'Ursula, the blonde witch.' They all know Ursula right enough."

"Let's get those who have been over there in here right now," ordered Baldie. "I want to interview them."

After the young policeman stepped out of the tent, Major Randal asked, "You know this German, Jim?"

"Colonel Doctor Rudolph von Himmel," Baldie said with a gleam in his eye, "is SD, which as you probably are aware, John, is the intelligence gathering arm of the SS."

"So I've been told."

"In point of fact, the count commands the SS intelligence division. He has the ear of Hitler, which makes him a treasure trove of classified Nazi information plus a lot of high-level gossip. What Count von Himmel is doing out here on the border is anyone's guess."

The SOE Chief of Station, Gold Coast Colony, eyeballed the young Commando. "You would not be opposed to mixing a little pleasure with business would you, Major?"

"I thought you'd never ask."

26

X-RAY AND VANISH

THE GYAMAN TRIBE LIVED PRIMARILY ON THE FRENCH SIDE OF THE border, but they resided on the British side as well. In other words, the border being ill defined—it was not marked at all most places—the tribesmen moved back and forth freely, hunting, grazing their cattle, and visiting friends and relatives as they saw fit. They knew the border was there because there were official crossing checkpoints every hundred miles or so. Most of the Gyaman sensibly ignored the official crossings as an unnecessary bother and simply went around them. Smuggling was an old and much-practiced tradition, to the point where none of the Gyamans even thought of it as a crime. The GCBP pretty much turned a blind eye to the comings and goings of the locals on the principle that they could not arrest everyone and that the smuggling was good for the native economy.

The Gyamans viewed the English and the French as being pretty much equal evils, but all the tribespeople universally disliked the Germans. Tribesmen shared information about the French with the English, and vice versa, but they shared nothing with the Nazis.

By interviewing the natives who had visited their friends and relatives over in the German camp, Lieutenant Dick Courtney and Jim "Baldie" Taylor quickly had a fairly accurate picture of the complete layout of SS Colonel Doctor Rudolph von Himmel's safari base. Getting an accurate head count proved a little more difficult, but in time the two had a reasonably good idea of how many people—including Europeans, native support personnel, and security guards—were there.

For a German semi-military operation, discipline in the safari camp seemed lax. By all accounts, everyone essentially drank himself into a stupor at night and fell asleep. No German guards were on duty past midnight, but an armed squad of tough Ashanti askaris was present as a security element.

"Happens," Lieutenant Courtney explained. "Some bwanas come on safari in the wild mysterious bush simply to get smashed, and they stay shattered the entire trip. Before the war, I spent a couple of seasons as an assistant professional hunter and shot all the trophies for more than a few great white hunters who never drew a sober breath or left camp. The film stars and royalty were the worst; tycoons and millionaires tended to have more desire to get their money's worth."

"I'm going to want to take a look," Major John Randal said.

Lieutenant Courtney cut his eyes at Baldie with an unspoken question. It was one thing to paddle ashore and snatch German generals off sandy beaches or jump out of airplanes in the dead of night over enemy occupied France. It was something else to operate in darkest Africa. The Gold Coast was no place for amateurs—even decorated ones.

"Time spent on reconnaissance is rarely wasted," Baldie intoned. "Teach you that in cavalry school, Major?"

"Roger that."

"King's Royal Rifles abide by the same standard," Baldie continued, rubbing his tanned pate. "Religious about it."

"Yes, they are."

"Dick, why don't you and the major pop over and put some trained eyes on the target, then get back here right quick so we can finalize our plans for the night?" Unsaid was that the young policeman would have an opportunity to weigh up Major Randal's performance in the field. His renown as a Raider had preceded him, but reputations can be overblown and medals do not mean a thing.

"I shall want to take my trackers, X-Ray and Vanish," Lieutenant Courtney responded. "With any luck, we can be back in about three hours."

Major Randal repaired to his tent to organize his gear. He had not brought much with him, so it did not take long. Lieutenant Courtney tagged along. His evaluation was going to start before they even left base. Major Randal, fully aware of what was taking place, ignored him. What the young GCBP officer did not realize was that the commander of Raiding Forces was also sizing him up.

First thing, Major Randal reached around and slipped his Browning P-35 out of the Mexican slide holster in the back. He retrieved the lanyard from his carry bag and snapped it on the ring on the butt of the pistol. (The lanyard had been attached to the Browning at Calais when ex-Legionnaire Sergeant Mike "March or Die" Mikkalis had originally given the weapon to him.) Then Major Randal cracked the slide to verify that a round was in the chamber, inserted the Browning—hammer down—back into the slide, concealed it under the bush jacket he was wearing, and looped the lanyard over his neck.

Next he took his primary Colt .38 Super out of his bag and buckled it around his waist so that it rode high and flat on his right side. Then, he strapped on his High Standard .22 with the silencer. It fit flat on his left chest. Laced to the shoulder holster was his slim Wilkinson-made Fairbairn fighting knife.

Last, Major Randal drew each weapon and taking his time, cracked the slide to make sure a round was in the chamber before he lowered the hammer on each pistol in what is known as Condition Two, then holstered it. Condition Two is not the recommended method of carry. Only fools or professionals pack an automatic pistol with the hammer down on a live round. However it is an extremely fast way to get the gun into action for those who know what they are doing.

Lieutenant Courtney was impressed.

"Let's do it, Lieutenant."

27

LEADERS RECONNAISSANCE

MAJOR JOHN RANDAL CLIMBED INTO THE POLICEMAN'S NEARLY fourteen-year-old dilapidated Ford Model A truck, and the two strikers X-Ray and Vanish took their places in the back. At the wheel, Lieutenant Dick Courtney set off in a direction opposite to the safari camp. They cruised three miles south and then looped back through the bush and finally came to a stop, parking the truck in defilade in a dry stream that may or may not have been a mile over the border, deep inside Vichy French territory.

Dismounting, Lieutenant Courtney raised the hood on the truck and removed the distributor cap before quietly lowering the hood. "The locals are right bloody handy at hotwiring."

Major Randal produced a small jar of dark-green theatrical face paint one of Captain Terry "Zorro" Stone's stage actress girlfriends had donated to the war effort. As the three GCBP men looked on, he removed his beret, tucked it carefully in a bellows pocket (Major Randal always preferred to patrol without headgear), and then striped his face and the back of his hands with the green paint. Without a word, he proceeded to paint stripes on a surprised Lieutenant Courtney's chiseled brow, and then he striped

Vanish and X-Ray. The strikers stood proudly. They were on a mission of war, not a sport-hunting safari for the pleasure of some pampered client.

The four moved out silently: the order of march was X-Ray on point, Major Randal, Vanish, and Lieutenant Courtney. In that way both of the trackers and their boss could keep a watchful eye on the newcomer exactly as they would a novice hunter following up a wounded Cape buffalo. The purpose behind the patrol's organization was not lost on Major Randal.

Though nothing had been said to that effect, Lieutenant Courtney was in command. On small patrols, leaders were sometimes the last man in the column, though it took confidence to do it that way. With the exception of Major Randal, the team had worked together so long they were virtually telepathic. All talking from this point on would be no louder than a stage whisper, and only rarely that.

Lieutenant Courtney was carrying his favorite Rigby 7x57 magazine rifle over one shoulder, holding it casually at the muzzle. The weapon was the caliber of choice, Major Randal noted, of his own snipers and stalkers, the peerless Lovat Scouts. X-Ray and Vanish were armed with well-maintained Short Model Lee-Enfield .303-caliber rifles. The Commando had turned down the offer of the loan of a rifle. This excursion was a reconnaissance job, not a fighting patrol.

Circling overhead almost out of sight an eagle keened a cry that razored the late-afternoon air. Crickets chirped and an elephant trumpeted a short blast in the distance. The four men traveled on azimuth, moving carefully but steadily covering ground. Danger was all around. The little band patrolled for over an hour through tall stands of sharp-edged gray-green elephant grass, heavy clumps of yellow acacia, brachystegia, and an assortment of thorny gnarled laurel mixed with hardwoods.

Suddenly Major Randal sensed they were getting close. He clicked on hard, the enemy encampment was up ahead somewhere. He came to a sudden halt.

X-Ray paused in mid-step and glanced back over his shoulder with an inquiring look. Behind him Vanish froze. Lieutenant Courtney stared with a heavily wrinkled brow. The trio of GCBP watched as Major Randal silently slipped the double-edged Fairbairn stiletto from its sheath. He leaned down and deftly sliced a canopy-shaped fungus the size of an

Eskimo pie from its short fat stem on the ground. Then he impaled it on the razor-sharp tip of the fighting knife and held it up for inspection.

All three Gold Coast policemen watched with curiosity.

The Commando thumped the big fungus solidly with his forefinger. A puff of spores exploded in a small cloud of fine dust, which drifted back into his face. Major Randal smiled. X-Ray smiled, Vanish smiled, and Lieutenant Courtney relaxed. They were downwind of the camp, so their sounds and scents wouldn't betray them to their enemy. The setup seemed about perfect.

The patrol eased into a thick patch of eight-foot-tall elephant grass and huddled up. This was what the staff of the Special Warfare Center at Castle Achnacarry, Scotland, called an "objective rally point." Each GCBP man silently checked his primary weapon, carefully easing open his rifle's bolt a notch to visibly triple-check that a round was in the chamber, and then sliding the bolt closed, careful not to make any metallic sounds.

Major Randal checked his High Standard .22, racking the slide a crack until he saw the gleam of brass. He hoped he would not have to use the pistol today, but if he did he could take advantage of the fact that it was silenced. When fired, the pistol made a sound no louder than striking a wooden match.

X-Ray was dispatched to move forward alone until he could determine the exact location of the camp and then come back to report. Vanish, Lieutenant Courtney, and Major Randal lay in a tiny perimeter facing out, weapons at the ready.

The tension and stress in an objective rally point, by the very nature of its being located in immediate proximity to the enemy, is always almost unbearable. Although Major Randal had done this kind of thing many times before in the Philippines, operating against Hukbalahap guerrillas, his heart was pounding. Vanish and Lieutenant Courtney looked calm, but both of their faces were pinched tight with concentration.

Stalking armed men is exceedingly hazardous, especially when one of the men you are pursuing is a full colonel in the Nazi SS, the most ruthless killers on the planet. SS Colonel Doctor Rudolph von Himmel was a dangerous opponent. And heavily armed SS and tough Ashanti askaris surrounded him, each of whom would just as soon murder as look at you.

Nevertheless, after a while, the waiting in an ORP can be as boring as watching paint dry, because if everything is working out the way it should, absolutely nothing is happening and that can be dangerous. Sometimes it's difficult, Major Randal knew, not to lose your concentration and begin fanaticizing about some girl you knew back in high school or college. In his case that would be the suntanned beach bunny Miss UCLA, his student teacher in English Lit his senior year. She was hard to forget, though it dawned on him that he did not seem to think about her as much ever since he had met the drop-dead gorgeous Captain the Lady Jane Seaborn.

Ever since Baldie had informed him Lady Jane was a talent spotter for the secret services, Major Randal had privately questioned if that was what their relationship was all about. Was she merely recruiting Raiding Forces to carry out clandestine missions and showing a romantic interest in its commanding officer as a way to accomplish that task? It was possible. He forced himself to get back in the moment, which was on full alert, *not* thinking about his girlfriend—drop-dead gorgeous or not. Drifting off like that can get a man killed. Still, he wondered.

There was a whispering sound as X-Ray slithered back into the ORP. Using the tip of a small twig, the tracker diagrammed on the ground the layout of the safari camp, which was located approximately one hundred yards away. He made his report in his native language, and although Major Randal could not understand, he could tell X-Ray seemed disturbed by something.

"Camp is straight ahead," Lieutenant Courtney mouthed, translating semi-silently. "X-Ray says all the camp followers have departed. Except for the Europeans, the askaris, and a handful of native staff, the place is virtually empty. Normally a safari base camp is teeming with visiting locals.

"Let's check it out."

Suddenly a flurry of shots rang out from the direction of the German camp. Major Randal immediately recognized them as shotgun rounds. X-Ray jabbered softly, unalarmed by the gunfire.

"Bird hunting," Lieutenant Courtney mouthed. "Stay right on my heels, Major," he ordered, then crawled out, cradling the Rigby in the crook of his left arm.

It seemed to take an eternity to make their way the short distance to a point where they were able to observe the German position. Major Randal's hammering heart cut out the moment he actually laid eyes on the objective. Once the target came into view, he became very calm, breathing slowly. And, out of old habit, he made it a point never, ever to look directly at anyone in the camp. "Tiger Stripe" and "Hammerhead," the two 26th U.S. Cavalry Regiment master sergeants who taught him the skills required to out-guerrilla the elusive Huks, had firmly held to the belief that if you stared at an enemy or made eye contact they would instinctively sense it, look right down your line of sight directly into your eyes, and spot you—no matter how well concealed you might be.

Maybe that was true and maybe not, but Major Randal was not taking any chances today.

The German safari camp looked exactly like a Boy Scout troop on a weekend jamboree except for the blood-red Nazi flag with the prominent black swastika flying from a small flagpole. The green Egyptian cotton tents were lined up with military precision. They were all the exact same size except for two, which were much larger. Clearly the big tents were the bwanas' sleeping quarters and the safari mess. Smoke was coming out of the tin stovepipe chimney on the mess tent, and native staff could be seen working inside. The motor pool was set off to one side so that drivers would avoid covering the tents in dust clouds when they drove into camp.

Lieutenant Courtney produced a small pair of hunting binoculars, and the two officers took turns scanning the layout. The count and his bride were sitting in canvas chairs outside their tent, firing at every bird that winged over. Most of the birds were not edible, and no one bothered to retrieve them. Dead birds littered the ground and the trees, and scattered feathers drifted in the breeze. It was a depressing sight.

As they continued their observation, Major Randal and Lieutenant Courtney identified two professional white hunters, four muscular SS types who were the bodyguards, with MP-38 submachine guns slung over their broad shoulders, and ten tall natives with bandoleers of ammunition strapped across their chests—the Ashanti askaris. Another six unarmed natives moved through the camp completing their appointed tasks.

X-Ray was right. The safari headquarters was extremely quiet. At long last, Lieutenant Courtney turned carefully to look at Major Randal. The

Commando nodded one time and the two men carefully withdrew, crawling backward until they were out of sight of the camp, and then they made their way back to the objective rally point.

Not wasting any time, the officers picked up Vanish and X-Ray, and, moving out as rapidly as the team possibly could while maintaining noise discipline and security, they returned to the truck as the amber sky blushed crimson from the slowly setting sun. The reconnaissance patrol was not particularly worried about running into anyone as darkness set in. A lot of animals with big sharp teeth liked to come out at night to hunt, so the odd native made it a habit to be where he or she was going long before sundown.

When they drove back into the GCBP camp, Major Randal discovered that all the natives from the German safari camp had trooped over to see the night's magic lantern show. Word had spread by bush telegraph that a famous film star was in camp, a mighty warrior who would be appearing in tonight's feature film. The Gyaman on the Vichy French side of the border could not resist the temptation to come across and see the spectacle. The native population on the Gold Coast side of the border had more than doubled.

Many, many more were on the way. In fact, the entire Gyaman tribe was migrating to the British side of the checkpoint to see what all the excitement was about. But because of the onset of darkness most would not arrive until the next day. Because the same propaganda film was scheduled to be shown every single night that week, the natives were not going to miss a thing.

No one realized it at the time, but a major international political flap was in the making. And it had nothing to do with the wholly unauthorized plan three rogue officers had cooked up to slip across the border and kidnap a senior Nazi SS intelligence official on his honeymoon.

28

RED RUBBER BALL

WHILE THE CROWD OUTSIDE MILLED AROUND WAITING FOR THE film to start, Major John Randal, Jim "Baldie" Taylor, Lieutenant Dick Courtney, X-Ray, and Vanish knelt inside the checkpoint command post tent, drawing in the dirt. A Gold Coast border policeman was standing guard at the entrance and another one was around back. Even so, the men talked in hushed tones. When planning a dangerous enterprise, you can never be too sure; and sometimes there really is a native hiding behind every bush.

Though nothing had been said to that effect, Major Randal was clearly in charge. He diagrammed the German safari camp in the dirt with the tip of his Fairbairn and placed little bundles of broken twigs where the tents were lined up. Small stones represented the vehicles in the motor pool.

"Situation . . ." Major Randal began casually, but doing it strictly by the book, Baldie noted, focusing intently on every word. "Mission, this is a snatch mission, my favorite kind . . ."

The briefing lasted a full half hour. When it was finished, every man present knew exactly what his role in the night's undertaking was going to be, step by step, from the time they rolled out of the checkpoint until they rolled back in with Colonel Doctor Rudolph von Himmel in tow.

"Line of departure time is 0200 hours," Major Randal concluded. "What are your questions?"

"You realize, of course," Baldie pointed out, "everything we do from this point forward is in breach of King's Regulations, as interpreted by the local authorities?"

"We can show the movie," Major Randal said, "and then go straight to bed if you're worried about getting into trouble, Jim."

"Not bloody likely!"

"Lieutenant?"

"In for a penny, in for a pound," Lieutenant Courtney answered enthusiastically.

"Let's do it," Major Randal said.

Lieutenant Courtney served as the master of ceremonies. The Colonial Film Unit's cinema van's generator powered a small string of lights strung up in front of the screen. Arching back in a semicircle the local Gyamans sat on the ground in family groups; behind them were the unofficial visiting Gyamans from across the border. Behind them, outside the ring of light, glowed the lime green eyes of a pack of curious hyenas that had silently crept up to observe the proceedings.

After the newsreel of the first pinprick raid was shown, Major Randal was called on to come forward to make a short speech about the operation and to tell how no German sentry was safe at his post anywhere on the French Coast. Major Randal kept it short and simple, pretty sure they did not understand a single word he said.

Tonight there would be a triple feature, and the cinema crew had been instructed to show all three back-to-back. When Major Randal ended his speech, the first Charlie Chaplin film came on. That was the signal for the Gold Coast police/SOE snatch party to quietly depart.

The plan was as simple as could be crafted: a four-man team led by Baldie and guided by Vanish would enter the tent occupied by Count von Himmel and his better half, overpower the couple, and gag and secure the two with handcuffs. A four-man team led by Lieutenant Courtney would surround the tent occupied by the Ashanti askaris and prevent them from interfering should the alarm be sounded. Last, Major Randal and X-Ray would be responsible for ensuring that the four SS men did not leave their tent in the event the balloon went up.

The signal that Baldie had the prisoners under control and ready to be moved out of the camp was for Vanish to step out of the tent and slap the flat of the stock of his Enfield rifle three times. Poles had been cut and plans made to lash the SS husband-and-wife team to them, with eight men designated as porters, four to a pole, to transport them back to the Ford Model A police truck. The idea was to move fast.

In the unhappy event shooting broke out, Major Randal would take command of his and Lieutenant Courtney's team to cover the extraction and conduct a fighting withdrawal.

A giant rat cheese moon made navigation easy. The Gold Coast border policemen unloaded quietly from the truck. The troops assembled into their teams; then, without a word, Lieutenant Courtney and Vanish stepped off and led the way to the objective rally point. They made good time.

After a last quick leaders' conference in the ORP, the teams moved out, creeping through the bush to their release points. The objective was not hard to find since the camp was lit up like a Broadway musical on opening night. Candles were burning everywhere: on poles stuck in the ground, swinging from improvised candle holders dangling from tree limbs, and flickering in tin cans lining the walkways between the tents.

Actually, it was more like Halloween. Trick or treat!

The order of march by teams was Lieutenant Courtney followed by Major Randal and then Baldie. The lieutenant and his team peeled off, and the SOE man and his team proceeded on to their target. The policemen drifted into the camp one at a time. The idea was that if one of the enemy was awake and looked out of his tent, all he would see was someone wandering around, not a fighting formation.

It was eerie; no one was stirring, but a chorus of snoring rose from the various tents. Everyone appeared to be fast asleep.

Major Randal barely had time to move into position with his silenced High Standard .22 at the ready when the sound of three sharp slaps on the wooden stock of an Enfield rifle sounded.

X-Ray reappeared at his side and they folded in on Lieutenant Court-ney. Both teams then moved rapidly to where Vanish waited at the flap of the Nazis' tent. Stepping inside the SS man's private sleeping quarters was like entering something out of the Arabian nights. Colorful oriental car-pets splashed the floor; two big overstuffed chairs covered in zebra skin sat next to a queen-sized bed draped in acres of white gauze mosquito netting. Sterling silver candle chandeliers swayed, giving off a mellow flickering light.

The porters were at work securing SS Colonel Doctor von Himmel to a pole. He was naked except for a red rubber ball strapped in his mouth. A woman, apparently Mrs. SS Colonel Doctor von Himmel, was already tied to a pole. She was demurely attired in a black leather bra, short black leather skirt, tall black riding boots, and her husband's SS hat with the sil-ver death's head insignia pinned above its highly polished bill. The woman had a rag stuffed in her mouth and was wiggling furiously against the restraints.

"That was quick," Major Randal said.

"Not much to it," Baldie replied, shaking his head. "She had him handcuffed to the center pole of the tent when we came in. The hard part was finding the key."

"Let's get the hell out of Dodge."

"Moving now, Major!"

The Flying Bathtub took off at first light. About half an hour later, they flew over Lieutenant Dick Courtney in the Ford Model A truck trailing a plume of dust as he headed toward Accra with their precious Nazi cargo on board. Ninety minutes later the little airplane flew over a small convoy that was speeding toward the end of the improved road. Lieutenant Gen-eral G. J. Giffard was in the convoy, which was rushing to the border to see what mischief the hated SOE chief of station and Major John Randal were perpetrating. The vehicles were nearing the point where they would reach a dead end and have to leave the road to move cross-country.

"Hope Lieutenant Courtney doesn't run into them."

"Never fear," Jim "Baldie" Taylor said. "Dickey is a very capable lad."

The pilot then scribbled a note, put it in a message sock, and banked low over the convoy. He dropped it in front of the general's staff Buick.

"What did you have for the general, Jim?" inquired Major Randal.

"Sorry we missed you. See you back in town."

When the Vichy French discovered that the entire Gyaman tribe had crossed over into British territory, they immediately lodged an official protest, blaming Lieutenant General G. J. Giffard for "luring them across the border." They claimed, truthfully, that the general was physically present at the checkpoint to welcome them when the tribe arrived. Overnight the governor of Gold Coast Colony, who had dispatched the general to the border to personally investigate Jim "Baldie" Taylor and Major John Randal's doings, had a full-blown international incident on his hands.

The fear and panic in Accra was that the Gyaman crossing might cause a domino effect among other tribes along the border. What would be the Vichy and Nazi reaction? Would that be the trip wire to invade? All eyes in the Gold Coast Colony were locked on developing events inland. No one was paying any attention at all to what was happening at a small bungalow on the beach not far outside Accra.

Had he planned for a year, Baldie could not have come up with a better diversion to serve as cover for Operation Lounge Lizard.

THE MISSION

29

BRING HIM BACK ALIVE

IN AN ABANDONED WAREHOUSE LOCATED NEAR THE END OF A remote pier at the Royal Navy dock in Accra, a handful of officers had gathered. Two private automobiles and a motley assortment of rental civilian truck transports were parked outside. One of the cars belonged to Commodore Richard Seaborn, the other to SOE's Jim "Baldie" Taylor. The latter had arrived with two passengers in tow: Lieutenant Colonel Dudley Clarke and Lieutenant Commander Ian Fleming.

Ostensibly on the final leg of a strategic reconnaissance mission to determine the best overland route from Cairo to Mombasa—which was true—Lieutenant Colonel Clarke was in fact in town to handle the misinformation campaign that would be implemented to attempt to mystify and mislead as to who had actually pirated three interned Axis ships from San Pedro Harbor following the raid. Not really expecting anyone to actually believe the story, Lieutenant Colonel Clarke planned to make the case that the crews had mutinied while most of their officers were away at Captain "Geronimo Joe" McKoy's party and sailed into international waters, where they ran afoul of the Royal Navy.

The Portuguese were going to know that was not true, but the idea would give them a fig leaf to help cover the embarrassment resulting from British Commandos entering one of their protectorates and spiriting away three interned vessels from under their nose. The Germans and Italians were not going to be mystified or misled either, but no one in British Forces really cared how they felt about it.

As the personal assistant of Rear Admiral John Godfrey, director of Britain's naval intelligence, Lieutenant Commander Fleming was on the mission to observe the operation for his boss and assist Lieutenant Colonel Clarke with the post-mission dissemination of misinformation.

The men gathered in the warehouse were there to clandestinely meet a ship.

The Royal Navy fast transport carrying Raiding Forces docked before first light. With their duffel bags over one shoulder, the Raiders disembarked and immediately boarded the small gypsy caravan of trucks waiting for them dockside. The troops were all dressed as seamen to throw off anyone who might be watching. Sailors arrived in port and went on shore leave all the time. Jim "Baldie" Taylor escorted the convoy to the bungalow in his Chevrolet.

Waiting to greet Raiding Forces when they piled out of the trucks at the cottage were Major John Randal and Captain Terry "Zorro" Stone. The troops were genuinely pleased to be reunited with their two senior officers. The salute Sergeant Major Maxwell Hicks rendered when he reported to his commanding officer would have done justice to a field marshal.

Included in the group was the Dartmouth Naval College instructor, Royal Navy Volunteer Reserve Sub-Lieutenant Nigel Perryweather, who had wanted to volunteer for special operations, along with three hand-picked Dartmouth cadets, all veterans of Operation Catapult. The three cadets had been immediately commissioned midshipmen on instructions from Major Lawrence "Larry" Grand, who had taken it upon himself to have the four transferred to Special Operations Executive in time to sail with Raiding Forces.

"Hornblower has had Mad Dog teaching us parachute landing falls for practically the entire trip, sir, getting us prepared for parachute school," Sub-Lieutenant Perryweather quipped to his new commanding officer. "Surely PLFs have to be easier on solid ground than the undulating steel deck of a troop transport ship."

"I wouldn't count on it if I were you."

The four German-speaking Commandos from Operation Ruthless were also in the group. They had volunteered for Raiding Forces and been accepted on a probationary basis, there being some concern that anyone crazy enough to volunteer for a suicide mission might not have the requisite mental discipline to fit into the unit. The men's skill as linguists was so valuable an asset, however, it tipped the balance in their favor for a trial.

Last but not least were nine able-bodied Royal Navy sailors Commodore Richard Seaborn had arranged to have volunteer for the raid based on a suggestion made by Major Randal. The main lesson he and Captain Stone had learned observing the takedown of the French fleet was the value of having experienced seamen along on boarding operations, equipped with the tools of their trade.

"We're going to need rated sailors for Lounge Lizard. Since any who go on the mission with us won't be allowed to return to their ships anyway," Major Randal had suggested to the commodore, "why don't you arrange for them to have skill sets Randy can use to crew the MGB 345, sir?"

"Kill two birds with one stone," Commodore Seaborn mused. "Capital idea, John!"

Jim "Baldie" Taylor was observing and carefully taking stock, as was Lieutenant Commander Ian Fleming, of the officers and men who would be executing the mission. The SOE operative did not fail to note the subtle, almost imperceptible change that came over both Major John Randal and Captain Terry "Zorro" Stone the moment they came in contact with their troops. Particularly telling was the young officers' "command presence": They seemed to stand more erect. When they spoke, their sentences were a little more clipped, their voices took on a slightly sharper ring, and the expressions on their faces tightened. Though they laughed and joked with the men, calling them by name, they were no longer the same happy-go-lucky bachelors he had first met on the Flying Clipper. The transformation was a significant indicator of the two young officers' style of leadership. They took command seriously.

An Operations Order was immediately issued; Major Randal briefed. It was not a complete order, only a fragment of the order, called a "frag order," consisting mainly of the "Concept of the Operation." While another briefing of the mission was not really necessary at this stage, Major Randal believed it was important for him as the mission commander to go over the plan in order to let the troops hear from his lips exactly how he expected it to play out.

"Captain Stone has already issued your Operations Order. There is no change in the military or political situation. The mission is for Raiding Forces and attached personnel to enter San Pedro Harbor on the island of Rio Bonita under cover of darkness tomorrow night, board and seize three enemy ships interned there, and move them to international waters, where they will be handed over to the Royal Navy.

"The *Ems* is the primary target. The Germans have an illegal radio transmitter hidden somewhere on board and are using it to send Allied shipping reports to their surface raiders and U-boats with the purpose of vectoring them in on convoys traveling the South Atlantic Sea Route. As Captain Stone briefed you previously, the Nazis have been using this intelligence information to locate, attack, and sink a sizable number of our merchant fleet.

"I will lead an eleven-man team to board and capture the *Ems*. My assistant team leader is Lieutenant Stirling. Commodore Seaborn will be attached. Two veteran HMY *Arrow* ratings and two Lifeboat Servicemen will be attached, plus Sub-Lieutenant Perryweather, one midshipman, and three of the volunteer naval ratings. The individual task assignments of the team members will be as briefed in the Operations Order. My team will be designated Team 1.

"Team 2 will be composed of an eight-man party commanded by Captain Stone to board and capture the *Giove*. Lieutenant Corrigan will be the assistant team leader. Lieutenant Seaborn and two Lifeboat Servicemen will be attached, plus one midshipman and three volunteer naval ratings.

The individual task assignments of the team members are as briefed in the Operations Order.

"Captain Pelham-Davies will command Team 3, a nine-man party to board and capture the *Egadi*. Lieutenant Shelby will be his assistant team leader. Two HMY *Arrow* ratings and two Lifeboat Servicemen will be attached, plus one midshipman and three volunteer naval ratings. The individual task assignments of the team members are as briefed in the Operations Order.

"Each team will travel to the objective on board one of the three tug-boats. In the spirit of keeping it short and simple, we have designated them as Tugs 1, 2, and 3. My team will travel on Tugboat number one; Captain Stone's team will travel on Tugboat number two; and Captain Pelham-Davies' team will travel on Tugboat number three.

"Upon reaching the buoy that marks the entrance to San Pedro Harbor, Teams 1, 2, and 3 will each off-load their boarding ladder assault party into the tugboat's dinghy. The dinghies will then be towed from that point until they reach their individual designated release points.

"At 2400 hours—or whenever the electricity in San Pedro is shut off and the lights go out—we attack. I say again, the signal to begin the attack is the town lights going out. Under no circumstances do we jump off until lights out.

"At that time, Tugs 1, 2, and 3 will proceed independently to their target ship towing their dinghies. As each tug approaches its target, the boarding ladder assault party in the dinghy will cast off and row to the portside boarding ladder and board the ship via the ladder.

"Each tug will continue on and pass by its target ship on the starboard side. Then each will come about, making a hard U-turn, and pull alongside its target ship, at which point the main boarding party aboard will immediately assault up the starboard side utilizing grappling hooks and lines.

"Upon arriving on deck, each main boarding party and boarding ladder assault party will break down into smaller teams as briefed in the Op Order, and each team will independently proceed on its assigned missions and carry out its individual tasks.

"After dropping off the main boarding party, each tugboat will make fast its towing wire and take its assigned ship under tow immediately upon the anchor chains being blown. Each tug will then proceed to tow its designated ship out of the harbor independently. No tug will stop for any reason until it reaches the three-mile limit Rio Bonita recognizes as the outer boundary of its territorial waters.

"Upon reaching international waters, the tugs, with prizes in tow, will rendezvous with a squadron of Royal Navy corvettes standing by and effect a handover of the captured enemy ships. Raiding Forces and all attached personnel will then be returned to the UK by Catalina flying boat and upon arrival begin that well-deserved leave I promised you after Tomcat.

"Men, you will never, ever mention Operation Lounge Lizard to anyone for the rest of your life because this mission never happened. Is that clear?"

"Clear, sir!" Raiding Forces thundered.

"What are your questions?"

While there may have been one or two men present who had points they might have liked to raise, there were no questions.

Rehearsals began immediately. Each boarding party had a number of tasks that it was required to accomplish once the men were on board their target ships. Raiding Forces personnel went through the standard crawl-walk-run cycle of rehearsal they had perfected at Achnacarry.

Crude outlines of the three enemy ships were scratched out on the beach. Then three groups of Commandos gathered, each group representing one of the boarding parties. Separately each of the three groups huddled together and started marching toward the marker that simulated the flashing light indicating the entrance to San Pedro Harbor. When each tugboat group reached the buoy marker, the boarding ladder assault party that would be traveling in the dinghy detached itself from the tugboat group and the two clusters of men then moved separately from each other.

The two clusters of Raiding Forces men marched on toward the outline of their target ship drawn in the sand. One bunch moved to the right and the other to the left. Then they simulated assaulting the ship from both sides simultaneously.

When the Raiders arrived on the simulated deck of their target, the bunched groups of men broke down into small teams and practiced moving out on their individual assignments.

Raiding Forces ran the exact same drill over and over and over again. To the uninitiated it probably looked silly—like little boys playing army. Truthfully, the first few times they performed the exercise it felt foolish to the Commandos, and the exercise was pretty ragged.

Each and every man knew, however, that there was nothing foolish about it; this was deadly serious business. What they were doing was definitely not a game. The kind of exaggerated attention to detail they were performing is what distinguishes a crack unit from the run-of-the-mill. As time went by, the men became smoother and smoother in their execution as their actions became reflexive.

Raiding Forces simulated every phase of the operation. The men were focused and worked hard. There was no horseplay. The basic building block of the process was repetition, repetition, and more repetition!

The attack on the German ship of war posed the most complicated challenge for a number of reasons. She was the biggest of the three vessels with the largest complement of crew, who were all picked men. The size of what was expected to be only a skeleton crew was going to be a challenge for the tiny band of Raiders to overcome quickly, which meant the capture had to be accomplished by the proper application of surprise, speed, and violence of action. The assaulters were going to have to hit hard and fast.

The *Ems* had two radio cabins: the official ship's radio room and the secret station used to make clandestine broadcasts to the surface raiders and U-boats. Finding the ship's main radio cabin was not going to pose any trouble because it would be clearly marked. The hidden radio was going to be considerably more difficult; it had to be well concealed, otherwise the port authorities would have discovered it long before now.

Lieutenant "Pyro" Percy Stirling was assigned the responsibility of finding and disabling the clandestine radio before it could broadcast news of the raid. He had as his assistant Sergeant Mickey Duggan, the veteran Royal Marine signaler of Calais fame. His team consisted of one of the Dartmouth midshipmen, one of the volunteer sailors to handle any technical problems of a nautical nature, and one of the Operation Ruthless Commandos who was fluent in German.

Sergeant Mike "March or Die" Mikkalis, formerly of the French Foreign Legion, King's Royal Rifle Corps, and Swamp Fox Force, had the mission of securing the German crew members, which did not bode well for the health and welfare of any recalcitrant Nazi sailor. The hulking German-speaking Operation Ruthless Commando who had threatened to snap Major Randal's neck was attached to his team.

Sub-Lieutenant Perryweather, with a team of two of the volunteer sailors and two Raiders, was tasked with securing the engine room of the *Ems* and attempting to get up steam. No one was counting on it, but if the German warship could make way under her own power, so much the better. If she could steam out instead of being towed, the ship could travel faster, which is highly desirable when, as Major Randal so colorfully put it, "you're getting the hell out of Dodge." Two of the German-speaking Commandos were attached to communicate with the Kriegsmarine stokers.

During the first break in the training, Major John Randal assembled all the Navy volunteer personnel for an informal briefing. Jim "Baldie" Taylor, Lieutenant Colonel Dudley Clarke, and Lieutenant Commander Ian Fleming hovered in back of the formation listening in.

Time was short and Major Randal wanted to give the bluejackets an opportunity to spend some time with their commanding officer. Infusing new men into a tight-knit unit that had trained to a razor's edge and fought together was not the best thing to do immediately prior to launching a complex special operation. For Lounge Lizard, Raiding Forces had no choice.

"Well, men, I guess you are wondering why I called you here today?" Major Randal said to the assembled group.

That's exactly what he had said to the Riflemen and handful of Marines destined to become Swamp Fox Force on his first day at Calais. It had worked to lower the stress level then and it worked now. The sailors all laughed; they knew they were going into action. There was no guarantee they were all going to come back. Maybe none of them would come back. Clearly their new commanding officer, who would be sharing the risks, did not seem unduly concerned. Tension in the group ratcheted down precipitously.

Unlike the men of Swamp Fox Force on that day at Calais, the blue-jackets already possessed quite a lot of information about Major Randal; during the voyage down to the Gold Coast, the Raiders had filled them in on everything they needed to know on that score. In addition, Sub-Lieutenant Nigel Perryweather was able to provide a tale of his own about the major's actions on the French submarine *Surcouf*. Both the new recruits and the tough Raiding Forces Commandos, hearing about it for the first time, found it to their liking.

"All of you men are volunteers," Major Randal continued. "Since our mission is Most Secret and involves invading a neutral protectorate, none of you will be allowed to return to your old berths after it's over. In fact, as of now you are members of a secret organization called Special Operations Executive, but you can never tell anyone because even its initials, SOE, are classified."

The officers as well as the ratings looked surprised; no one had explained the implications of volunteering in those terms.

Major Randal's announcement had the effect of binding the newcomers together in a way they had not felt before; they were no longer outsiders. SOE was something big, it sounded dangerous, and now that they knew it existed, being the kind of men who volunteer for hazardous assignments, they wanted to be a part of it whatever it was.

"After Lounge Lizard is over," Major Randal said casually, "the men we invite can continue on in Raiding Forces or stay with SOE at their own discretion.

"For the initial assault, every one of you is paired with a Raider. Stick to him like glue. You are all rated men with certain skills, you've been thoroughly briefed on your individual assignments, and you know exactly what to do. That's why you're here. Focus on your job, do your duty, leave the rest to the Raiding Forces' studs, and everything will be okay."

Upon the conclusion of Major Randal's talk, a middle-aged civilian he had never seen before approached and introduced himself.

"Major, my name is Ray Terhune," he said with a distinct Australian accent.

"Mr. Terhune, would you kindly explain to me how it is you came to be here?" Major Randal demanded sharply. "This is a secure site."

"Yes sir. Major Grand pulled me off my duties as an instructor in naval demolitions and sabotage at a school his firm operates for some people who have a need to know those sorts of things. On the voyage down, I have been teaching your lads the gentle art of naval demolitions. In peacetime I make a living as a naval salvage engineer. Before that I was Royal Navy."

"What is it exactly you've been teaching my people?"

"Breaching charges, mostly; your men are going to need to blow open the metal doors on the ships they will be searching. I have also worked up prepared charges to cut each ship's anchor chains."

"Well, thank you very much, Mr. Terhune. Now if you'll excuse—"

"Major, you have a potential problem that could put paid to your operation right enough before it gets fairly started, and no one seems to be paying any attention to it. It seems to have been overlooked."

"And what might that be?"

"Scuttling charges. I doubt the Italians have them on their two ships, but I'm willing to wager the Germans have scuttling charges in place on the *Ems*, just lurking there waiting to be detonated in the event of an attack like the one you lads are planning."

"Commodore," Major Randal called out immediately. "Sir, would you step over here a moment? Okay, Mr. Terhune, take it from the top."

After listening to the former Royal Navy hard-hat diver, Commodore Seaborn quickly concurred. "Quite right. I should have anticipated scuttling charges myself."

"Well, what's the solution, Mr. Terhune?" asked Raiding Forces' commander.

"Simple, actually. You are going to have to locate and disarm the charges before the Jerries detonate 'em, Major, and I'm afraid I happen to be the only man present qualified for that kind of work."

Major John Randal looked at him closely, "You volunteering?"

"I was Royal Navy for twenty years, a hard-hat diver, *and* a demolitions man," Mr. Terhune repeated. "I reckon I can do one more job for ol' England."

Major Randal signaled Royal Marine Butch Hoolihan.

"Sir?"

"Hoolihan, you know Mr. Terhune?"

"Yes sir."

"I have a mission for you."

"Sir!"

"Mr. Terhune is going to board the *Ems* with the boarding ladder assault party to locate and dismantle scuttling charges that may or may not be on board her. His task has top priority. Starting now, you're his guardian angel."

"Sir!"

"Do not permit anyone to interfere with Mr. Terhune in the execution of his duties. You're not to allow him out of your sight until this operation is over. Is that clear?"

"Clear, sir!"

"Bring him back alive, Butch."

30

PREPARE TO MOVE OUT

THE THREE HARD-SERVICE AFRICAN TUGBOATS *KING KONG*, *Superman*, and *Big Toot* arrived off the beach later that day. Each skipper was rowed ashore in his tug's dinghy, accompanied by a Royal Marine escort from the Port of Accra Base Defense Security Organization Detachment. A pair of Royal Marines remained on board each tug as a precaution, just in case the pilots decided at the last minute to abandon the mission and take off. The Marines had been given the same options as the sailors with one extra alternative—if they elected not to volunteer for Raiding Forces or SOE they would be immediately transferred to some remote base in the far outreaches of the empire.

Although African tugboat skippers are a breed apart, and often hard to figure, Mike "Wino" Muldoon, "Mud Cat" Ray, and "Warthog" Finley were now wholeheartedly committed to their roles in the mission. They seemed to get a kick out of having their very own armed Royal Marine tagging along at their heels. Commodore Richard Seaborn had diplomatically chosen to inform the skippers that the Royal Marines were being provided as their personal bodyguards for the duration of the operation. The Royal Marines, of course, had been given an entirely different slant on the nature of the assignment.

Raiding Forces personnel were suitably impressed by the tugboat captains from the get-go. The trio of sun-baked alcoholics looked exactly like what the men thought African tugboat skippers were supposed to: tough and evil tempered, ready to blow sky-high at any moment. The troops had a good feeling about the boat captains who would be taking them into San Pedro.

Each tugboat skipper was married up with the raiding party he would be transporting. The idea was for them to spend as much time together as possible before the operation. The boat captains showed a great deal of interest in the rehearsals. Drills are something all seafaring men can relate to. With their caps pushed back on their heads, big tattooed arms crossed on their chests, and nasty-looking cigars planted between their stained teeth, the trio acted like they did this sort of thing every day of the week.

One exercise the skippers could really appreciate and thus paid special attention to, since they could see how it was going to have a direct bearing on the state of their personal welfare in the immediate future, was marksmanship. When they observed the skill of the Raiders on the practice range, they nodded to each other appreciatively.

They strolled over to watch Major John Randal fire his pistols after his men had finished and departed the firing line. Just as he began to take aim at the large paper target downrange, the Commando commander asked conversationally, "What was the name of your tugboat again, Captain Finley?"

"The *King Kong*, Major."

Captain "Geronimo Joe" McKoy had replaced the tiny front sights on both of Major Randal's Colts with tall thick blades that looked like they had come off his Peacemakers, each sporting a bright gold bead like you would find on a best grade shotgun. The rear sights were replaced with simple oversized solid steel versions of his own manufacture, which looked pretty much like the original John Browning had designed only a lot bigger, with all the sharp edges filed off. The sights were very easy to see. The Colt .38 Super barked ten times, and then Major Randal repeated the process with his backup pistol.

The little group of skippers, their Royal Marine bodyguards, Lieutenant Colonel Dudley Clarke, Jim "Baldie" Taylor, and Lieutenant Commander Ian Fleming sauntered downrange to inspect Randal's handiwork.

When they reached the target, none of the tugboat captains had much to say. Neither did anyone else.

The skippers had intended to have some fun razzing the young major, planning to give him a hard time about his shooting skills, but what they saw was so uniformly awful, there was nothing to tease him about. The bullet holes were widely scattered, spread out about six inches to the right of the large bull's-eye in a strange pattern two pie pans could not have covered. Simply terrible marksmanship; some of the worst the old salts had ever seen.

All three of them could have done as well anytime after 1800 hours on any given day, which meant dead drunk.

The boat captains, their bodyguards, and the three observers wandered quietly back to the firing line, being careful not to make eye contact with each other and each privately hoping the major was a better leader of men than he was at shooting a pistol. Their confidence in Operation Lounge Lizard had just taken a hit.

When everyone was back, Major Randal produced his silenced High Standard .22, and firing rapidly, emptied a magazine downrange at the target. Then he quickly inserted a second and ran through it.

"Go ahead, check it out," Major Randal ordered, recharging his empty magazines. "Give me a report."

Reluctantly, the skippers trudged back downrange, shadowed by their Royal Marine bodyguards, followed by the three silent intelligence officers, who seemed lost in their own thoughts. The captains were wondering how to break it to the major that he had best restrict his shooting to the sawed-off Browning A-5 with the nifty duckbill device on the end of its barrel or, better still, let someone else handle the gun work.

When they reached the target, a ragged shout of happy surprise erupted from the group. The large .38 Super holes scattered all over the target had been connected by a string of small .22-caliber bullet holes forming a ragged but perfectly recognizable "KK." It was the fanciest trick shooting any of them had ever seen.

"I'm putting that up in my wheelhouse!" Warthog rasped, proudly ripping down the target. "*King Kong*! I'm going to have it framed. What part of Texas did you say you came from, Major?"

"California," Major Randal said, racking the slide on his pistol and lowering the hammer before sliding it into his chest holster.

Captain McKoy would have been proud.

Lieutenant Dick Courtney arrived at the bungalow after having driven all the way from the border with his two prisoners. They had been dropped off and were under intense interrogation by SOE operatives at an undisclosed location. Jim "Baldie" Taylor, Lieutenant Colonel Dudley Clarke, and Lieutenant Commander Ian Fleming intended to sit in on their "debriefing" as soon as Raiding Forces set sail.

Major John Randal pulled Lieutenant Courtney aside. "Jim tells me if you stay on in the Gold Coast they're going to blame you for the Gyaman crossing."

"Bloody likely."

"How would you like a job in Raiding Forces?"

"I should like that, sir," the young Gold Coast border policeman replied eagerly. "Quiet a lot, actually."

"You can tag along as an observer tonight," Major Randal said. "Bring all your gear; we won't be coming back here."

31

URBAN COW-SLUTS

CAPTAIN THE LADY JANE SEABORN AND ROYAL MARINE PAMALA Plum-Martin were having the time of their lives being secret agents on San Pedro. The girls had affected what they thought was a simply fabulous Texas accent by trying to see which one of them could say *y'all* the most times in a single sentence.

Since not one single person in the entire Portuguese protectorate of Rio Bonita had ever actually set foot in the Lone Star State, they had everyone completely fooled. On the whole, it was actually not bad trade-craft; however, the people they were attempting to deceive were very gullible. Their technique would not have worked so well in a more cosmopolitan location, say, downtown Berlin.

The night of the planned attack by Major John Randal et alia on the three Axis ships in San Pedro Harbor, the two sidekicks were in the ladies' room of the San Pedro Rod & Gun Club preparing for their part in Operation Lounge Lizard. Each was dressed in a short, fringed cowgirl skirt, a wide, hand-carved leather belt with an engraved sterling silver concho belt buckle, and peewee cowgirl boots with big white "Lone Stars" inlaid on the tops. The boots featured high, skinny riding heels.

The *dos amigas* wore banana-yellow silk blouses with Western yokes and pearl snap buttons that they had gone to a lot of trouble not to button all the way up. The girls did not look the least bit wholesome: nothing at all, for example, like the "Queen of the Golden West," cowgirl movie star Dale Evans.

The two cowgirls sauntered boldly out to the party room, across the empty dance floor, then outside to the expansive terrace where the well-lubricated power elite of San Pedro were gathered in eager anticipation of the start of Captain "Geronimo Joe" McKoy's knife-throwing, pistol-shooting, and fireworks extravaganza.

The location for the show had been carefully selected. The stage put the guests outside on the back terrace *behind* the Rod & Gun Club, a mile and a half away from the harbor, down a winding mountain road in a spot where they would not be able to see Major John Randal and his team of Raiding Forces' Commandos when they came calling.

The spectacular Rio Bonita River flowed past the back of the club in the valley below, two hundred yards away. The thought that head-hunting pygmies might be watching from the teeming dark jungle on the far bank added a shiver of excitement to the eagerly awaited event. Life traveled dead slow in San Pedro, so any organized event was keenly anticipated.

Except for the unlucky few who had the duty of standing watch on their interned ships, the officers of the *Ems*, *Giove*, and *Egadi* were all taking full advantage of the open bar. They knew their men were tying one on in the red-light district at the International Seaman's Appreciation Street Party, so their consciences were clear—not that the German or Italian officers really needed an excuse. To a man, the Axis officers felt abandoned, out of touch with world events, sick of Africa, and put upon by the vicissitudes of war.

"You ladies sure do look like genuine, urban cow-sluts." Captain McKoy shook his silver mane in approval when the secret agents sashayed up. The two beautiful British spies could not tell if he was paying them a compliment or not.

The captain was resplendent in a tangerine-colored silk shirt with enough white fringe dangling down to flock a Christmas tree. A long white silk scarf flowed from his neck. He wore pale whipcord pants tucked into the tops of his favorite pointy-toed yellow alligator boots outfitted with tall riding heels and big Mexican silver-rowled spurs that jingled when he walked.

Buckled around his waist in a hand-carved, double-holster El Paso rig rode his ivory-stocked, fully engraved single-action Colt .45 Peacemakers. Long, thick snow-white hair hung down, gunfighter style, out the back of his flat-brimmed pearl-gray Stetson hat. He was in rare form tonight.

Royal Marine Plum-Martin had lost the coin toss. While the crowd watched in drunken anticipation, Captain McKoy strapped her to the large, solid roulette wheel table that had been specially constructed to his specifications for the show.

"Would you care for a blindfold?" the ex-Arizona Ranger offered gallantly.

"No thanks, Captain," she replied bravely.

"I'll have one then," announced Captain McKoy, "seeing as how y'all got yourself shortchanged in the dress department. It'd probably be a dang good idea not to get myself distracted a-throwin' these Bowie knives."

The inebriated crowd roared. Every man present, and one or two of the women, was already distracted. The handsome old Ranger manfully whipped off his 10-gallon hat as Captain Lady Seaborn pranced over and tied his scarf over his eyes. Then she pranced back and stood by the spread-eagled Vargas Girl look-alike Royal Marine strapped on the wheel.

"Are y'all ready, Captain?" called Captain Lady Seaborn.

"I was born ready!"

She spun the wheel. Royal Marine Plum-Martin tried but could not restrain herself—she shrieked as she went round and round.

Knives started flying immediately. "Whack, Whack, Whack." They appeared between her tanned, extraordinarily fit legs and between her equally tanned and equally fit arms. A balloon pinned above her snow-blonde head burst.

When each knife found purchase, the lovely assistant tried very hard not to wiggle or scream. The crowd was thoroughly enjoying the action, agreeing that it was great fun and a terrific show.

To be honest, Captain Wolf Steiner, commander of the *Ems*, was a trifle disappointed by the entertainment. He had been waiting to see what would happen to the short, fringed, cowgirl skirt when the blonde whirled upside down. Captain McKoy did not leave him in suspense for long. His first knife pinned the tiny skirt firmly in place between her thighs. The throw drew a gasp from the audience, but that skirt was not going anywhere, no matter how long she hung upside down.

Too bad! Captain Steiner was a red-blooded sea dog. His only real vice was women, of whom he considered himself a connoisseur. Unfortunately, he had been trapped in San Pedro Harbor without any quality female companionship for quite some time now.

Ever since the day the two stunning Texas cowgirls had playfully tried to come aboard the *Ems* to visit, he had been making every effort—fruitlessly until now—to find some way to arrange an opportunity to make amends for his rude behavior in not allowing them aboard his ship, which in retrospect he had decided was a mistake.

Before the war, Captain Steiner had always been a lucky sailor. He held a command in the German High Seas Fleet stationed at the precise place, with the exact weapon, at the right time to make German naval history! Few fighting men have ever been so fortunate, and he knew it. He was destined to be Hitler's pirate.

The Nazi skipper had romanticized about sinking epic tons of enemy shipping. But when the word came down containing his wartime sailing orders, Captain Steiner had been staggered. Simultaneously with news of the outbreak of hostilities, the *Ems* received a priority message ordering her to throw the cannon concealed in her hold overboard, make a high-speed run to San Pedro, and NOT—repeat NOT—depart neutral Rio Bonita within the seventy-two-hour time limit mandated by international maritime law. Which meant the Portuguese would intern the *Ems* and her entire crew for the duration, however long that turned out to be.

Captain Wolf Steiner's war was over before it ever got started.

The *Ems*'s orders condemned him to a never-ending slow-motion living hell. He was limited to passing on intelligence reports while his contemporaries enjoyed what the German Navy was calling the "Happy Time" sinking English ships, winning buckets full of medals in the process.

Tonight all he had on his mind was drinking as much as required to numb his pain and then to cut out one of the Texas beauties, board her, and plant his flag. Captain Steiner was fairly certain of success. Both women had been flirting outrageously with him ever since he had arrived at the club. Clearly the cowgirls were competing with each other to see which would be the one to get lucky. In that he was not entirely wrong. The girls did, in fact, have designs on the *Ems*'s commander.

The shooting portion of the show concluded with Captain McKoy twirling his pistols, exploding tossed glass balls that shattered spectacularly, splitting a bullet on the edge of a knife (which caused two balloons to burst simultaneously), and shooting a cigarette out of the wobbly mouth of San Pedro's greasy-looking, bantam-sized mayor.

From the shark-toothed expressions on the faces of some of the partygoers who were unable to restrain themselves, there may have been one or two constituents present who secretly hoped the Wild West cowboy would have a momentary lapse, miss, and drill the diminutive mayor through his corrupt little brain. Rio Bonita may have been a laid-back, sleepy sort of place, but people played hardball politics there.

32

DON'T STOP AND MAKE FRIENDS

AT LONG LAST, IT WAS TIME FOR WHAT THE RAIDERS JOKINGLY referred to as the "last and final briefing—absolutely!" With operations there always seem to be no end of "final briefings." They are a necessary evil.

Jim "Baldie" Taylor pinned up a map of Rio Bonita. "Each of you has been provided with a small strip escape map. If any of you men find yourself in a situation where you need to escape and evade, head west for the river. Pursuit by anyone from Rio Bonita will cease immediately when you cross.

"As you can see, the western third of the island is cut off from the rest of the island by the river it is named after, the Rio Bonita. Legend has it head-hunting pygmies—who may or may not be cannibals—inhabit this area. I don't know if this is true, but should you see anybody over there, don't stop and try to make friends."

Baldie pointed to a spot on the map. "There will be a motorboat off this beach every night for a week starting the night after the raid, in case any of you goes missing. I will be in it; just don't expect me to come ashore looking for you."

Major John Randal was up next. "Men, that has to be the worst Plan B I've ever heard."

The Raiders all roared. The SOE station chief shrugged his shoulders and held up his hands. "Sorry, lads. Best I could do on short notice."

Lieutenant Colonel Dudley Clarke glanced at Lieutenant Commander Ian Fleming, who simply shook his head.

The men laughed again. The troops liked Jim "Baldie" Taylor. They could tell he was one of them.

"If you haven't figured it out already, let me make this perfectly clear," Major Randal said. "Failure is not on for tonight. When we go in, go in hard and get the job done.

"You've been issued three pairs of handcuffs. You've been issued a hard rubber cosh." He held up one of the rubber clubs. "Supplied courtesy of the London Passenger Transport Board; they're strap hangers taken out of their coaches.

"When you take a prisoner, don't run any chances or waste time. Cosh him, cuff him to the nearest solid object, and continue your mission. Don't let anything detour you from carrying out your individual assignment. Cosh 'em and cuff 'em. Is that clear?"

"CLEAR, SIR!" the troops sounded off in unison.

Commodore Richard Seaborn was next up to speak.

"It has been said 'a picture is worth a thousand words,'" the Commodore explained as he unfolded a map of the West African coast. "Every dot on this map represents one of our ships sunk by a U-boat or surface raider." The room went from quiet to dead solid silent. The map was black with dots, so many it looked like it had been blasted with fine birdshot.

"Every one of these sinkings has taken place since the *Ems* was interned in Rio Bonita. If we can permanently knock out the hidden transmitter located on board the German ship, the next time we prepare a chart of these waters it will have eighty-five percent fewer black dots, maybe less."

Then he sat down, leaving no one in doubt about the importance of the night's work.

"Men," Major John Randal stepped back in front of the formation, "you all know your job. Let's go do it."

The Raiders and attached personnel were ferried out to the tugboats in the dinghies. To get all the men and equipment aboard required three trips per tugboat. Despite their colorful names, the Gold Coast tugboats were the most decrepit, run-down, grimy vessels any member of Raiding Forces had ever had occasion to board. Long service in African waters was apparently hard, dirty duty, and tugboat sailors were clearly not spit-and-polish nautical types. The tugboats looked like they might rot to pieces then and there and that you could catch a disease if you touched something.

"Move aboard quickly now," skipper "Warthog" Finley called out. "There's plenty of room up on the 'head deck.' For you Marines and sailors, that's what tugboat men call the bow. For you soldier mugwumps, it's the pointy end of the boat. Ha-ha."

The little three-tug flotilla made way after the onset of the hours of darkness under a blue-black African sky that was salted with millions of tiny neon white stars. The stars glowed hot in the dark velvet canopy overhead but created virtually no light. The moon was heading down and the wind was dead still. Later, the Southern Cross came out.

After what seemed like the longest three hours in history, Warthog sang out, "Thar she blows! Harbor buoy two points off the starboard head deck. Look lively, lads. I'm going to lay us alongside that buoy with time to spare." Far ahead through the inky night they could barely make out a throbbing blue light. The light marked the entrance to San Pedro Harbor.

Without any orders or prompting, every man in the cutting-out party automatically began the ritual of checking his weapons and equipment, the most reassuring thing a battle-experienced Commando on the brink of going into action can do. The fact that they had probably performed the same personal inspection subconsciously fifty to a hundred times already did nothing to lessen the feeling that it gave the men of getting prepared to go—this time for real.

At minimum, each Raider carried four concussion grenades, two fragmentation grenades, two prepared breeching charges to use to blow open watertight steel doors, a flashlight, three pairs of handcuffs, a hard rubber cosh, toggle rope, a canteen, a first aid pack, compass, map, wristwatch, Colt .38 Super with three additional magazines (or the handgun of choice), and a Fairbairn fighting knife—plus any specialized equipment that their individual missions might call for. Most men carried the A-5 Browning with 50 rounds of 12-gauge ammunition. Thompson submachine guns were forbidden tonight because of their distinctive sound signature.

Rations for one day had been issued in the event things went wrong and they had to escape and evade to the rendezvous—a possibility they were all secretly trying not to think about. Each man carried one canteen.

The Lifeboat Servicemen immediately repaired to their dinghies and performed a final pre-mission inspection. At the same time, tugboat crewmen reported to the stern to check out the towline, or "wire" as it was known in the trade.

Every Raider not going up the boarding ladder had a grappling hook and line that needed to be looked at five or six more times. Attention to detail had a marvelous way of taking a man's mind off the great unknown and unexpected.

At this point, the senior Raiding Forces' officer on each tug gave the order to "saddle up." Upon receiving the order, each Raider took a long strip of white cloth out of his pocket, wrapped it around his forehead, and tied it off in back, creating a distinctive white headband. The orders were to cosh, capture, or kill, though not necessarily in that order, anyone not wearing a white headband. The improvised recognition device made it unnecessary to blacken their faces tonight, which was normally standard operating procedure on nocternal operations.

The teams responsible for cutting anchor chains carried the prepared explosive charges Mr. Ray Terhune had designed, with two backup charges in reserve. Sometimes, with explosives, things do not go according to plan. The Raiders intended to be ready if that happened and the chain did not fall apart as it was supposed to on the first, or even the second, attempt. Mr. Terhune had intentionally designed the charges "to be on the light side." The trick to blowing the anchor chain on a ship that you intend to sail away in is to use the right amount of explosives to cut the chain but not enough to sink the ship. It is important to think about things like that in advance. The last words anyone wanted to hear from the anchor chain demo teams was, "Uh-oh." Lieutenant "Pyro" Percy Stirling would not be blowing any anchor chains tonight.

The Lifeboat Servicemen were all carrying an ample supply of civilian holiday fireworks in their Bergen packs. After the men set the charges in place to blow their designated anchor chain, the plan called for them to light up the fireworks and shoot them off to create a diversion when the anchor chains' charges exploded. Tonight was going to be a big night for the Lifeboat Servicemen; they had a lot of direct-action tasks to perform. For a change, they were not simply going to be seagoing taxi drivers.

On the horizon, the mellow golden glow of the lights of San Pedro could be seen. To men who were used to wartime blackout regulations, it seemed completely unnatural for a city to be lit up at night. In the blacked-out UK you could not even smoke a cigarette on the streets after dark.

Since Rio Bonita was not at war with anyone, there was no reason why the citizens of San Pedro had to observe a blackout. Even in peacetime the city authorities turned the power off at midnight to conserve energy and save money. San Pedro rolled up its sidewalks at midnight every night. The war had nothing to do with it.

Turning off the electricity at midnight, however, did not automatically guarantee that the revelry in the bar district along the wharf would come to a stop. In fact, the bar owners, like all successful entrepreneurs, had a Plan B. They would break out kerosene lanterns and candles and light torches in order to keep the party going.

Every eye on the tugs strained to see inside the harbor. It was wasted effort; no one could see a thing. The port facility was too far off in the distance.

When Major John Randal glanced at his Rolex, he thought it might be broken. The lime-green hands were locked tight in place. They did not seem to have moved at all.

Adrenaline surged through his system. He was clicked on, super alert, and extremely aware. His hearing was accentuated, his peripheral vision had expanded to what seemed like almost a full 360 degrees, and his decision-making process was fluid, seemingly effortless.

The heightened awareness was something that always happened to him on every mission. Even on training exercises it kicked in at a certain point, and he had come to expect it. Major Randal was totally focused on the mission while at the same time fully aware of everything happening around him. To the troops he seemed very relaxed.

Tugboat No. 1, *King Kong*, slid in alongside the buoy and came to a stop with engines idling. The other two tugs pulled in line abreast, with their sides touching, so that it was possible to step from boat to boat.

Warthog pulled out a giant set of German Kriegsmarine night glasses. "Salvage from a Nazi surface raider the Navy worked over," he explained, handing them to the Raiding Forces' commanding officer. "Sailor boys normally pick those ships clean before we take them under tow, but they missed these."

Looking through the binoculars it was possible for Major John Randal to observe the three enemy ships they had come to capture. As expected, the targets were moored exactly the way they were depicted in the photographs. That was good. The ships were anchored stem to stern about 150 yards apart toward the back of the harbor, out of the way of incoming or departing traffic.

The *Egadi* was first in line, the *Giove* second, and the *Ems* way back in the harbor. So far, everything appeared according to plan!

"Captain Pelham-Davies, there's your target," Major Randal said in a crisp command voice as he handed over the night glasses and pointed out the *Egadi*.

"*Egadi* looks exactly the way I expected she would from the photos," Captain Jeb Pelham-Davies remarked, ice cool, taking a long, unhurried look and making a thorough study of the ship before returning the glasses. As usual, he had a thin, half-smoked, unlit cigar clenched in his teeth.

"Captain Stone," Major John Randal said, passing the night glasses, "there's your target."

"I suspect," Captain Terry "Zorro" Stone commented casually, managing to sound almost bored, "Captain Kidd would feel right at home sailing with us tonight." He took an equally long time making a study of the *Giove*.

When Major Randal took the Zeiss night glasses back, he handed them to Commodore Richard Seaborn.

"I hope one of you knows first aid for cardiac arrest," the commodore commented idly while carefully inspecting the *Ems* through the glasses. "I may have a seizure."

"You look all worried as hell, sir," Major Randal said.

"Gentlemen, we attack the instant the lights go out. Rejoin your troops. Good luck and good hunting."

Then Major Randal issued the order to the men under his personal command that fighting officers have given to their troops since the invention of gunpowder: "Lock and load, boys."

The Raiders broke the still of the night as they crammed 12-gauge shotgun shells into their A-5 Brownings with a sharp click, and slammed their actions with a solid kerthunk. They made a tick-tick noise as they inserted magazines into their Colts and High Standard pistols and cycled slides. Finally they put their pistol actions on safe with a click. These sounds are always very comforting to the working Raider getting ready to take it to the bad guys.

The luminous hands on Major Randal's black-faced Rolex said 1145 hours. He wondered briefly what Jane was doing right that minute. He stepped off Tugboat No. 1/*King Kong*, crossed over Tugboat No. 2/*Superman*, and boarded Tugboat No. 3/*Big Toot*. Taking his time but not wasting any, he went round and checked on each and every one of his men.

Still taking his time, he stepped back on Tugboat No. 2/*Superman* and repeated the process. Then he came back to Tugboat No. 1/*King Kong* and conducted a quick personal inspection of his own men, addressing them by name, acting in his role as their assault team leader.

When his brief inspection was completed, he gave the order for the boarding ladder assault party to board the dinghy. The Tugboat No. 1/*King Kong* dinghy would be carrying the heaviest load of the three. On board would be the two Lifeboat Servicemen at the oars; Mr. Ray Terhune with his bodyguard, Royal Marine Butch Hoolihan; Commodore Seaborn with his bodyguard, Royal Marine Jock McDonald; plus Corporal Jack Merritt. Major Randal would round out the party. It was going to be a tight squeeze to fit everyone in with all the weapons and equipment.

Major Randal had pulled the two Royal Mariness off their original assignments and designated them to be bodyguards for the simple reason that both Commodore Seaborn and Mr. Terhune were Royal Navy. He hoped having a Marine instead of a cavalryman or a rifleman as their guardian angel might make the two feel just that little bit more comfortable. Sometimes it is the tiniest detail that tips the balance toward success instead of failure on a small-scale operation.

Corporal Merritt had been Major Randal's wingman during all the tactical training at Achnacarry and the jump on Operation Tomcat. He would play the same role on Lounge Lizard. The two men had trained, jumped, and fought together to the point where they could practically read each other's thoughts.

Tonight the Randal/Merritt individual mission was to initially secure the small boarding ladder dock, then board and seize the bridge on the *Ems*. The capable young Life Guardsman was the target of quite a bit of ribbing from his mates. The troops liked to tease him about being the major's batman, which he was not. The commander of Raiding Forces had not informed him yet, but after this mission he intended to recommend Corporal Merritt for a direct commission.

"You men going to be able to handle such a full load?" Major Randal called down to the Lifeboat Servicemen.

"Abso-bloody-lutely, sir," they responded cheerfully. Coming from two of the best small boat handlers on the seven seas, the answer was comforting.

Major Randal returned to the head deck where the assault team was mustered. "Ready, stud?" he asked Lieutenant Stirling. The aggressive young cavalry officer, holding a grappling line in his hand, was surrounded by the primary boarding party. The Raiders were raring to go.

"Ready as I shall ever be, sir!"

"Merritt and I will take out any radio we find on the bridge," Major Randal repeated for the hundredth time. "You and Sergeant Duggan are on your own when it comes to finding the hidden transmitter. Sergeant Mikkalis will take care of securing the rest of the ship."

"Roger that, sir."

The lights went out in San Pedro.

"See you on the *Ems*, men!" Major Randal called to the assault party.

"Good luck, sir," Sergeant Mike "March or Die" Mikkalis growled with danger in his voice.

The Nazi sailors unlucky enough to have the duty tonight on the *Ems* were in for a rough night.

The rest of the men chorused, "Good luck, sir. See you on the *Ems*." Someone muttered, "Remember Calais."

"Boots and saddles, Captain Finley," Major Randal ordered. "Lead the charge."

Then he trotted to the stern of Tugboat No. 1/*King Kong* and stepped gingerly down into the bow of the heavily loaded dinghy. "Try not to swamp us," Major Randal said to the two Lifeboat Servicemen.

"Not bloody likely, sir," the two men chorused as the tug made way, pulling the slack out of the rope towing the dinghy.

The night air was so heavy and the tension so thick on the tiny little craft that it was difficult to breathe. The passengers on board were afraid to anyway, anxious that if they breathed normally they might tip the cockleshell right over. The Raiders were worried about drowning, pygmy head-hunting cannibals, and carrying out their individual tasks. No one seemed much concerned about the German sailors they were up against.

Raiding Forces was going in.

33

DON'T FORGET NOTHING

TUGBOAT NO. 1/*KING KONG* MADE WAY IMMEDIATELY, WITH THE other two tugs falling in line-astern formation. The little convoy sailed resolutely forward into the blue-velvet darkness of San Pedro Harbor. The moon was down, but the sky was filled with millions of stars. It was a beautiful night for Raiding Forces to come calling.

Because the little craft rode so low in the water, there was not much visibility from the dinghy being towed behind the lead tugboat. Major John Randal and Corporal Jack Merritt crouched in the bow of the dinghy. Immediately to their rear sat Commodore Richard Seaborn with his bodyguard, Royal Marine Jock McDonald; seated next in the boat were Mr. Ray Terhune and Royal Marine Butch Hoolihan. At the oars were Lifeboat Servicemen Tom Tyler and Jimmie Dodds. Their initial objective was the landing dock at the port side ladder of the *Ems*. Once they had secured it, they would launch their attack on the ship up the ladder from there.

On board Tugboat No. 1/*King Kong*, preparing to storm the starboard side of the *Ems*, was a party of Raiders with two HMY *Arrow* Ratings attached, led by Lieutenant "Pyro" Percy Stirling, who was assisted by the pale-blue-eyed ex-Legionnaire, Sergeant Mike "March or Die" Mikkalis.

Sergeant Mikkalis was charged with the initial overall responsibility of subduing the German sailors on duty on the German warship. Once that was accomplished and the secret radio station was located and put out of action, he was to hand off his assignment to Lieutenant Stirling, who would then act as Major Randal's second in command on the ship.

In truth, once the clandestine radio station was out of action and the German sailors under control, the Raiders—from Major Randal on down—would not be much more than sightseeing passengers as Commodore Seaborn piloted the *Ems* out of the harbor. Next in line chugged Tugboat No. 2/*Superman*, towing Captain Terry "Zorro" Stone, Lieutenant Randy "Hornblower" Seaborn, and Lifeboat Servicemen Dennis Horrell and Fred Jones in its dinghy. On board the tug, under the command of Lieutenant Taylor Corrigan, sailed the combined Operation Tomcat teams he and Captain Stone had jumped with, reinforced by four Lovat Scouts participating in their first-ever Commando raid. Their mission was to take down the *Giove*.

Bringing up the rear in the tail-end Charlie position, being towed behind Tugboat No. 3/*Big Toot*, were Sergeant Major Maxwell Hicks, Trooper Nelson Reynolds, and Lifeboat Servicemen Dave Higgins and Matt Riding. On board the tug was Captain Jeb Pelham-Davies with the team he had led on Operation Tomcat, plus two HMY *Arrow* ratings and four Lovat Scouts, also on their maiden raid. Their target was the *Egadi*.

Raiding Forces was a crack outfit. The men were smart, tough, dedicated, superbly trained professional soldiers taught to be swift and deadly. They had traveled more than two thousand miles to carry out this operation. Each man knew his assignment. The suspense was intense, the wait unbearable.

"Thump, thump, thump"; the line of tugs chugged steadily into the dark. There was no sign of life anywhere in the harbor except on deck at their targets. The enemy vessels were the only major ships in the harbor. All three were sporting strings of naked white light bulbs in their riggings run off the ships' generators to allow the sailors to navigate the deck. The necklace of lights gave the ships a party-boat look that no one on board any of the three craft even remotely felt. And the white light destroyed the night vision of every sailor on the deck.

Tugboat No. 1/*King Kong* chugged past the *Egadi*. The smell of rust, saltwater, and diesel fuel oozed from the rotting ship into the warm humid air. Anchor chains scraped against the barnacle-encrusted hull. No one on board the Italian vessel paid any attention to the tug. San Pedro was the only port on the island protectorate of Rio Bonita, and boats came and went at odd hours. In fact, there was no activity at all on the *Egadi*; she looked like a ghost ship. As they slowly cruised past, it became evident she was a virtual rust bucket.

Tugboat skipper "Warthog" Finley stood boldly on at tooth-grinding speed. After a while the tugboat came to the *Giove*. Her bilge pumps were pumping steadily and filthy sewage spewed from her side. A lone sailor was standing on the deck smoking a cigarette. He waved disinterestedly as the tug chugged past. Then he flicked his cigarette, which flew in a large looping arch over the rail.

All hands on Tugboat No. 1/*King Kong*, to include Raiding Force personnel, waved back, watching the cigarette sail in their direction as if transfixed. The people being towed in the dinghy crouched down as low as they could possibly go, hoping to make themselves invisible. The powder-keg-intense atmosphere ratcheted up.

Immediately ahead, the *Ems* towered four stories tall. *Major Robert Rogers's first Standing Order to his Rangers in the French and Indian War,* Major John Randal was thinking, *was "Don't Forget Nothing." Well, someone had sure as hell forgotten to tell me she was going to be this big.* To the stunned Commandos in the final stages of their attack run, the *Ems* looked as large as the SS *Queen Mary*. Whoever thought this up had made a big mistake.

Major Randal was seized by a wild momentary feeling of panic. He must have been crazy to think they could capture a cruiser-sized Q-ship with such a tiny handful of Commandos. Then he almost laughed out loud at the enormity of their mission.

Tugboat No. 1/*King Kong* was so close to the *Ems* now they could smell the tar and fresh paint on her salt-encrusted hull. Like the two

Italian ships, she was anchored bow and stern, with her bow facing out to sea. The distinguishing difference, besides her size, was that the giant German surface raider was definitely no rust bucket. She looked ready to put to sea—prepared to go to war—at a minute's notice.

Faintly wafting down from the *Ems* was the sound of music emanating from a gramophone being played somewhere on the upper deck. The song sounded vaguely like "Putting on the Ritz." The music made the approach movement completely surreal, like the Raiders were in a Hollywood movie.

Looked at from down below, the *Ems* appeared to be the size an aircraft carrier with the Statue of Liberty mounted on her deck!

Tugboat No. 1/*King Kong was* thump, thump, thumping its way unswervingly to the release point. Warthog drove his tug straight home to the objective, completely oblivious to the size of the target. The skipper clearly had ice water in his veins.

As Corporal Merritt cast off the towing line, Major Randal, mindful of how sound carries across water, commanded softly, "Make way together." There is such a thing as the point of no return, and tonight this was it.

"We are under way," Major Randal added needlessly, doing it the way he had been trained at Achnacarry. The Lifeboat Servicemen responded immediately with powerful rowing strokes on the first command, and the dinghy actually surged ahead, picking up speed despite its heavy load.

Tugboat No. 1/*King Kong* disappeared slowly from the dinghy's view into the darkness, down the starboard side of the *Ems*, and continued on its way to carry out its assigned mission. Major Randal and his men were all alone and on their own. Soon the small wooden plank deck below the boarding ladder swam into view. Up above, the gramophone was clearly playing a German language version of "Putting on the Ritz."

Lights from the strings of naked bulbs in the riggings reflected off the water. Up close the string of lights were not nearly as bright as they had seemed from a distance. The quality of light they produced was actually quite dim.

The dinghy glided alongside the boarding dock in the golden glow given off by the rigging lights. Major Randal leaped lightly onto the planks, holding his silenced High Standard .22 pistol at the ready in both hands. The rubber soles of his canvas-topped raiding boots did not make a sound when he landed on the dock.

Two pale faces appeared over the rail. The Nazi sailors on watch peered down curiously. Was some of the crew returning early from the party ashore? Not very likely, but still there was no cause for alarm. Nothing ever happened on board the *Ems*.

The sultry night was gently disturbed by a noise that sounded vaguely like two wooden matches being struck one right after the other. "Whiiiicccccccch, Whiiiicccccccch," quickly followed by the sound of watermelons being thumped in rapid succession.

Nothing happened for a long moment that seemed to the Raiders in the dinghy frozen in time. All eyes in the dinghy locked on the two Kriegsmarine sailors. Would they give the alarm? Neither Nazi made a sound nor did they move an inch. Slowly, the sailor on the left seemed to relax slightly; then his companion also seemed to relax. Gradually, one after the other, they leaned forward in slow motion before toppling down and slamming onto the boarding deck so hard that both men bounced. The bodies made loud, meaty thuds as they hit the wooden planks of the dock. One Nazi had a .22-caliber bullet hole in the center of his forehead. The other had one an inch below his left eye. The Germans were both stone dead.

"Secure those men," Major Randal ordered, never taking his eyes off the rail above, his silenced pistol at the ready. "Make sure they don't fall overboard and get left behind when we pull out."

Then, without waiting for a response, he bounded up the ladder with Corporal Merritt hard at his heels and the Lifeboat Servicemen chasing directly after them.

Royal Marines Hoolihan and McDonald, Mr. Terhune, and the commodore all worked rapidly to lash down the dead sailors.

"Let's go, Mr. Terhune," Royal Marine Hoolihan ordered after the German sailors were secured, leading the retired naval demolition man up the ladder after the Lifeboat Servicemen, "Time to do your stuff, sir."

"Right behind you, Butch," the old Royal Navy hard-hat diver barked gamely. "Keep that bloody great cannon of yours unlimbered. I reckon we'll be traveling in harm's way quick enough."

Watching the two disappear up the ladder, Commodore Seaborn was beginning to wonder why he had been so quick to volunteer for this insane mission in the first place. If he had not been so rash, right this minute he could have been safely out to sea in command of a squadron of corvettes awaiting developments, which is where he should have been.

He realized too late that standing on the boarding platform of an enemy vessel manned by hostile enemy sailors, waiting to go up the ladder, was no place for a big ship man.

Commando raiding up close and personal was proving to be a little more exciting than he had bargained for.

34

PUTTING ON THE RITZ

LIFEBOAT SERVICEMEN TOM TYLER AND HIS MATE JIMMIE DODDS bounded up onto the deck after Corporal Merritt and charged the bow, their Browning A-5s at the ready. They immediately un-slung their Bergens, unpacked the gun cotton explosives Mr. Ray Terhune had painstakingly prepared for this specific purpose, slapped the charge on the anchor chain exactly the way they had been taught, ignited the fuse lighter, and scurried for cover behind the bollard.

"KEEERBLAAAAAAM!" The blast of white light lit up the whole harbor for a split second. The sound of the anchor chain detonating charge was mind-boggling, even though the charge had been purposely constructed to be on the light side to prevent major damage to the ship. The anchor chain rattled free, slid down the side of the *Ems*'s hull, and splashed into the bay exactly as advertised by demolitions man and cutting charge designer Mr. Terhune.

Virtually in chorus, a twin explosion followed from the stern anchor, set off by the HMY *Arrow* ratings with the same satisfying result.

Both anchors rattled free down the side to sink to the bottom, as per plan. The anchor demolition team had accomplished their mission right on schedule.

The Lifeboat Servicemen then immediately came out from their hiding place, opened their Bergen packs again, and took out the fireworks stuffed inside. With shaking hands, the men attempted to ignite the fuse of long, thin, cardboard Roman candles. Suddenly the idea of actually lighting up and shooting off fireworks while standing on a ship they were in the very act of pirating out of a neutral harbor seemed a lot less reasonable than it had when briefed and rehearsed all those times prior to the mission.

Lifeboat Serviceman Tyler succeeded in getting his lit first. Waving the tip in a circle to build up steam, he shouted, "I feel like a blinkin' fool on Guy Fawkes Day!" The fuse sputtered and fizzled, but finally a big green fireball looped out weakly and arched limply over the rail before landing in the water below with a sizzling hiss.

While the two Lifeboat Servicemen shot off their fireworks, they kept a sharp eye out for the towline they were going to secure from Tugboat No. 1/*King Kong* to the bollard of the German cruiser the moment the tug moved into position to effect the tow. The men had to get it right first time. The towline was their lifeline, their ticket home. The two Lifeboat Servicemen had practiced the hookup maneuver until they had all the moves choreographed like a Russian ballet.

As Lifeboat Serviceman Dodds pumped his red, white, and green fireballs into the air, he shouted, "Our mates in the Lifeboat Service would never believe this story even if we could tell 'em!"

Unlike the other two vessels, the German cruiser was an actual ship-of-war and, as such, had considerably more crew on watch when Raiding Forces came aboard. When Major John Randal and Corporal Jack Merritt raced to the bridge, they unexpectedly ran head-on into an intermittent stream of German sailors rushing down the main ladder. No one had foreseen anything like that happening.

As the two Raiders charged up the ladder, they found themselves going against a human tide of Nazi sailors hustling to their duty stations.

"Putting on the Ritz" was still blaring, and a klaxon was going off: AH-OO-GAH, AH-OO-GAH, AH-OO-GAH. The element of surprise was dead and gone now.

The crew of the *Ems* on duty was so intent on hurrying to carry out their assigned tasks they failed to recognize the two Commandos as enemy combatants in the uncertain light. Though the German sailors had conducted immediate action drills for every conceivable contingency, no one ever actually expected any enemy action in San Pedro Harbor, and they were not looking for intruders.

It was not clear to the *Ems* crew what the signal to man battle stations was all about. After all, the ship was interned in a neutral port, located in a sleepy Portuguese backwater. Most of the officers were absent at a party. Probably simply another drill; perhaps the skipper had come back on board early in a foul mood and sprung the exercise on his crew simply to make their miserable life even more intolerable, as he had been known to do from time to time.

Since speed was of the essence and for lack of any better plan, Major Randal simply pumped two .22-caliber rounds from his silenced pistol into every enemy sailor who came past, and never broke stride. Behind him, Corporal Merritt deliberately fired another round into each man, center of mass, as he came abreast of the major's targets, regardless of whether the enemy seamen were staggering from the gunshots or had already fallen to the deck. Nazis were going down like bowling pins.

In the dark and the absence of the sound of gunshots, compounded by the flash and sound of explosions of fireworks going off and the klaxon blaring, the confused sailors never seemed to fully comprehend what was happening, not even the men who had been shot.

By the time the two Raiders arrived on the bridge, Major Randal had completely emptied one magazine, performed a rapid reload, and was halfway through a second. Bounding up on the bridge he encountered two startled Kriegsmarine watch officers and shot them both three times where they stood. When the two Germans went down, Major Randal realized, with no small amount of relief and a certain surprise, he had successfully taken his objective.

Reflexively, he reloaded the High Standard with his last magazine then holstered it in exchange for his Colt .38 Super. Never in his wildest imagination had he ever pictured using that much silenced .22-caliber ammunition. No matter how many battle scenarios you plan for, the real thing never turns out like any of them.

At virtually the same moment Major John Randal was eliminating the two sentries standing watch at the top of the boarding ladder, Tugboat No. 1/ *King Kong*'s skipper, "Warthog" Finley, had come about and slammed into the starboard side of the *Ems*. The worn-out row of old truck tires lashed to her sides cushioned the impact, but the tug ploughed in pretty hard. The salty old skipper fought the wheel, held fast against the *Ems*, and stuck like glue. The maneuver was a fantastic feat of seamanship.

Simultaneous with the assault on the bridge, grappling hooks flew up and over the starboard rail as the raiding party, led by Lieutenant "Pyro" Percy Stirling, was up and away, scaling the ropes and clearing the rail fast. The Raiders had endlessly practiced scaling steep walls at the Special Warfare Training Center in Scotland, and tonight all that hard training paid off.

Lieutenant Stirling and Sergeant Mickey Duggan ran full tilt to the *Ems*'s communications room, followed by their bluejacket and the German-speaking Commando. Having memorized the schematic diagram of the ship's plan, the Raiders had no problem finding the radio shack.

Their immediate goal was to capture any codebooks still lying around or possibly a radio operator who might have knowledge of codes, radio procedures, encryption devices, or anything else of high signal intelligence value. More to the point, the Raiders were hoping to persuade any German sailor they caught in the radio shack to lead them to the all-important clandestine radio. They intended to be very persuasive. Since tonight they were nothing more than pirates, the Geneva Convention was not in full force and effect. Not that either man had ever actually read it.

When the Commandos burst in, they found a radio operator in the act of attempting to set fire to a pile of documents. Unfortunately, in the heat of the moment, acting on pure reflex, Sergeant Duggan administered a short, efficient, horizontal butt-stroke from his Browning A-5 to the unfortunate Kriegsmarine signalman, pancaking him cold. He was not going to be any help.

According to orders, they handcuffed the unconscious Nazi to the bulkhead. Lieutenant Stirling grabbed the first passing Raiding Forces trooper he saw and ordered him to stand guard over the radio room and not let anything (else) unhealthy happen to their high-value prisoner.

After a quick survey of the cabin, Lieutenant Stirling turned to Sergeant Duggan and asked, "Now, where do you think the real radio is located?"

Muffled booms were echoing throughout the ship as Commandos blew in watertight steel doors in the process of carrying out their individual assigned tasks. The takedown of the *Ems* was proceeding with robotic precision. The disoriented Nazi sailors never had a chance to consolidate and organize any form of resistance. One minute they had been peaceably asleep in their hammocks, unhappy at missing the party ashore, and the next, hell had arrived. Speed and violence of action were carrying the night. The Strategic Raiding Force was on the scene and they were not to be denied.

Royal Marine Butch Hoolihan and Mr. Ray Terhune raced down deep into the bowels of the *Ems*. On the way down, almost without breaking stride, Marine Hoolihan shot three German sailors rushing up to reach topside. The 12-gauge Browning A-5 boomed and spouted flame in the confines of the metal ladder well.

Mr. Terhune proved to be a real trouper and did not have any trouble at all keeping up with his bodyguard. He never faltered, never hesitated to hurtle over the dead Nazi seamen. When they reached the bottom, the ex-Royal Navy man took the lead, finding his way with the help of a large six-cell flashlight. The ship was dark on the lower deck, but he knew exactly where to look and he found what he was searching for. The deadly scuttling charges looked cold and sinister in the beam of his handheld torch.

He had only just begun to dismantle the scuttling device that would have sent the ship straight to Davy Jones's locker with all hands on board when a determined three-man demolition team of Kriegsmarine sailors, led by a ship's officer, arrived on the run to arm it.

Chaos reigned temporarily in the confines of the walk space until

Marine Hoolihan sorted things out with his Browning 12-gauge. The A-5's "Boooom, Boooom, Boooom, Boooom, Boooom, Boooom" was deafening. The gunshots reverberated and echoed, the loud discharges resounding off the metal bulkheads. A foot-long flame flared out of the barrel, punctuating every round. Through the blue gun smoke they could see the three Germans strewn about like crumpled rag dolls.

"Reminds me of one of those old-fashioned blunderbusses, the ones with a bell-shaped muzzle," a wide-eyed Mr. Terhune observed, immediately turning back to his work. "Nice shooting, Butch!"

"The barrel has this little duckbill device," the husky young Royal Marine explained as the gun smoke began to clear away. "Makes the shot come out in a flat, oval pattern."

"Flattened those blokes," Mr. Terhune agreed approvingly, "fair dink 'em."

Meanwhile, Corporal Merritt went back down to the main deck, collected Commodore Richard Seaborn and his bodyguard, Royal Marine Jock McDonald, and escorted them up to the bridge over what appeared to the commodore to be a carpet of dead and dying Kriegsmarine sailors. The Navy officer knew he would never forget the sight of Major Randal coolly picking off the two sentries with his silenced pistol. Too bad he was never going to ever be able to tell that story. You could dine out on a tale like that for the rest of your life.

"Sir," Major Randal acknowledged the commodore absently, intent on absorbing the details of all the action taking place both on board the *Ems* and elsewhere in the harbor visible from the ship's bridge.

"I had no need of an escort, John," the commodore stated. "Simply follow the trail of dead men. They led straight to you. I almost feel sorry for these poor bloody Nazis."

"If they didn't want to get killed they shouldn't have joined up," Major Randal replied shortly. "Do some Navy stuff, sir. Time for us to get the hell out of Dodge."

Just then Lieutenant Stirling came bursting up on the bridge, almost out of breath. "We found it, sir, hidden behind a watertight door with a big red skull and crossbones painted on it and "DANGER ELECTRICITY" printed in about five different languages. We were afraid to blow the door, but not to worry, Breedlove, the able-bodied you assigned us, knew exactly how to unzip it like a tin of sardines."

"Outstanding!" Major John Randal clapped the high-spirited lieutenant on the shoulder. "Nice job, Percy."

"We hit the jackpot, sir," the Death or Glory Boy continued. "Inside we found a high-speed transmitter with an encryption device attached, a bookshelf full of what appear to be codebooks, and there is a chart pinned to the wall with what Sergeant Duggan believes are individual call signs of the commerce raiders and U-boats. We captured one of the ship's radio operators, too, though he's a little dinged up."

"I knew I could count on you, stud." Major Randal paid the young officer his highest compliment. "Go conduct a quick all-around inspection of the *Ems* for me. Then get back here as fast as you can with a sit rep."

"Sir!"

On shore, the San Pedro Defense Forces were at first alarmed by the blasts coming from the harbor, but when they stood to, they saw the fireworks. They concluded that the stir-crazy German and Italian sailors had to be drunk.

The fighting men of the San Pedro Defense Forces certainly were, thanks to the generosity of the ladies of the night (whom Captain "Geronimo Joe" McKoy had hired), who had arrived bearing gifts. The SPDF quickly decided that guarding the booze left back in their quarters with the hookers was more important than guarding the port. As Captain McKoy hoped, the defense forces' harbor contingent stood down for the night. Mission accomplished. The citizens of San Pedro could sleep well; their defense force intended to.

At almost the same moment the San Pedro Defense Force decided to repair back to their barracks, a massive fireworks display erupted from the red-light district in San Pedro's harbor area, where a wild street party was in full swing. Simultaneously from high in the hills above San Pedro, an equally massive barrage of fireworks exploded, coming from the vicinity of the Gun & Rod Club.

Captain Wolf Steiner felt a faint stab of alarm when the initial explosion occurred. The noise that penetrated his alcohol-sodden brain sounded more like a genuine "something just got blown up" type of explosion than fireworks. A trained professional can distinguish between the two.

His thoughts were distracted, however, when Captain the Lady Jane Seaborn and Royal Marine Pamala Plum-Martin suddenly materialized from the crowd in their sexy cowgirl outfits, both girls laughing invitingly and drinking straight out of a magnum-sized bottle of champagne.

Without a word, the girls took him by the hands and led him around the side of the club, through the palm trees, to the back of the gravel parking lot. There, a long black 1928 Packard touring car, which Captain "Geronimo Joe"McKoy had hired for the evening, was waiting for them. Overhead the red, white, and green sprays of fireworks were erupting, one after the other, in a breathtakingly spectacular display.

When the two cowgirls reached the car, they each took a belt from the big green bottle, needing both hands to muscle the magnum up to their lips. Then they thoughtfully passed the big bottle to the German skipper and climbed up on the front fenders of the Packard. The band out on the terrace had launched into an enthusiast rendition of "Pistol Packing Mama." The band was working hard. The fireworks were booming. The two cowgirls started stripping!

Captain Steiner realized he was having the most fun he had had since the day the *Ems* received the signal to sail to San Pedro. "KA-WHAAAAAM." Captain McKoy stepped out of the shadows, minus his jingling silver Mexican spurs, and slapped the German on the back of the head with a leather-covered lead sap. The *Ems* skipper's head hit the ground before his well-traveled sea boots even left it. The foaming magnum of champagne clinked on the gravel and rolled off into the dark.

The women jumped down off the car's fenders. Captain Lady Seaborn stuffed her silk scarf in the Nazi's mouth, then took a roll of heavy-duty tape from inside the Packard's glove compartment and wrapped it around and around his head, taping the scarf inside his mouth and also taping his eyes shut.

While she was working, Royal Marine Plum-Martin was busy taping his ankles together all the way up to his knees. Then she taped his hands. Then she taped his elbows to his chest.

Captain McKoy stepped around to the back of the Packard and opened the trunk. "You tape the man any more and you're going to make a mummy out of him."

He came back and together all three of them dragged the unconscious German to the rear of the car, heaved him in, and slammed the trunk shut. Captain McKoy climbed in behind the wheel and the women both slid into the front seat. Down the mountain they drove.

"You ladies are pretty good dancers."

"If you had taken much longer we would have been naked!" Royal Marine Plum-Martin squealed in mock protest.

"I was takin' my time—in a hurry."

The women laughed, giddy from the adrenaline rush they were both experiencing.

"The things we do for England," Captain Lady Seaborn chuckled. "Hope y'all enjoyed y'all's show, y'all."

"I sure did. And that's a fact, ladies."

The Packard sped through the tropical night along the coast road until they reached the small beach for their prearranged rendezvous with Jim "Baldie" Taylor. They pulled off the road, walked down to the beach, unfolded three cloth deck chairs, and built a signal fire. Then they waited.

In the trunk of the car, Captain Wolf Steiner slowly regained consciousness and began to realize that his miserable, rotten war had taken a turn for the worse.

35

SUPERMAN

TUGBOAT NO. 2/*SUPERMAN* TOWED A DINGHY MANNED BY Lifeboat Servicemen Dennis Horrell and Fred Jones, transporting Captain Terry "Zorro" Stone and Lieutenant Randy "Hornblower" Seaborn to their designated target, the *Giove*.

From their position on the flimsy deck of the towed dinghy they could not see much other than the stern of the tugboat. The dilapidated tug was moving steadily, slowly but surely, with heavy emphasis on the slow part. Tension onboard was mounting second by agonizing second.

Lieutenant Seaborn's heart was pounding so hard he was certain the crew on the *Giove* could hear it. The raid was not at all like in the movies: no heroic speeches or patriotic pleas to the men to give their all for King and Empire. No one was going to storm any deck tonight with a dagger in his teeth. While the young Royal Navy lieutenant had a lot on his mind, thoughts of being killed, maimed, disfigured, or spending the rest of the war in a ghastly Portuguese prison eating cockroaches were not among them. What was really worrying Lieutenant Seaborn was his assignment to con the *Giove* out of the harbor to the linkup point with the Royal Navy. Tonight's mission was a different proposition altogether from taking the

Arrow, a boat he had grown up on, across the Channel on a midnight raid or crashing the MGB 345 alongside a German E-boat. And increasing the pressure on the junior Seaborn was that his father would be on the bridge of the *Ems*, dead astern, observing his every move.

Captain Stone was a world-class leader of men, and though at the moment he was tightly focused on the mission, he could sense that the young Royal Navy lieutenant was uncharacteristically introspective tonight. Normally, in tight situations he was cool as an ice cube. "What are you brooding about, Hornblower?"

"I have never actually conned anything as large as the *Giove* before. Hate to make a hash of it with Father watching."

"Are you crazy?" Captain Stone actually laughed out loud "Forget the commodore. Those Italian sailors on board laying in wait for us right now are most probably going to shoot you deader than a stuffed mackerel before you ever even have a chance to lay a hand on the helm."

Lieutenant Seaborn glanced up sharply to see if Zorro was joking. He was.

"Remember," the Life Guards officer confided sanguinely, "it is always darkest before pitch black."

"Thanks, Terry."

Petty Officer Tim Corny and Able Seaman Milford Gould were riding directly behind them in the dinghy. Their assignment was to follow Captain Stone and Lieutenant Seaborn up the boarding ladder, turn left, secure the forward bollard, blow the forward anchor chain, set off fireworks, and make fast the wire to Tugboat No. 2/*Superman* as soon as her skipper, "Mud Cat" Ray, came back around to effect the tow.

They were both snickering at the exchange they had overheard between the two officers.

Behind them, waiting with oars shipped, sat Lifeboat Servicemen Dennis Horrell and Fred Jones. Their mission, after they rowed the dinghy to the *Giove*, was to follow Petty Officer Corny and Able Seaman Gould up the boarding ladder, turn right, proceed to the stern, blow the stern anchor chain, and set off fireworks. They were both curious as to what the two bluejackets were laughing about.

When Tugboat No. 2/*Superman* finally at long last thumped its way to the release point, Lieutenant Seaborn cast off the towing line. Captain Stone quietly gave the order, "Give way together."

In the dark African night, the men in the dinghy almost immediately lost sight of the tugboat as it disappeared down the starboard side of the *Giove*. The moon, tide, and weather conditions were perfect for raiding. The raiding party could smell steel, tar, rust, salt, bilge water, and the faint aroma of . . . garlic? Not a sound was coming from the *Giove*.

Every eye was focused on the small boarding platform. The ladder came closer and closer as the Lifeboat Servicemen smoothly and silently and oh-so-professionally slipped the dinghy alongside.

Captain Stone leaped adroitly from the dinghy across about three feet of open water and landed silently on the planks with his silenced High Standard .22 pistol pointed up at the railing. The move was a stunt the matinee idol of the silver screen Errol Flynn would have been envious of.

Lieutenant Seaborn was after him in a flash. There was still no sign of life on the *Giove*. Petty Officer Corny lashed the dinghy to the platform.

Captain Stone nodded to Lieutenant Seaborn and then dashed up the ladder.

Lieutenant Seaborn covered him with his silenced High Standard .22. The checkering on its black walnut grip felt sharp in his hands. He was tightly focused, dialed in on his mission.

Suddenly an Italian appeared at the rail above and peeked over. Lieutenant Seaborn touched the trigger. It broke clean like a thin icicle and the silenced pistol made a sound no louder than a match being struck.

The tiny .22-caliber missile was launched on its way in an instant, aimed straight at the enemy sailor's heart.

Luckily, or maybe not, the bullet struck a thin steel cable running just under the top of the rail. It disintegrated and splattered the unsuspecting Italian in the chest with microscopic slivers of hot lead shrapnel. The lucky part was that if the .22-caliber bullet had not exploded on the unseen steel wire it would have drilled the sailor clean through the ticker.

Not being killed outright was all the good fortune that particular Italian sailor had coming. He turned around and, without bothering to utter a single word of warning to the rest of his shipmates, dashed across the *Giove*'s deck, heading for the starboard rail. Before he even reached it, the terrified Eyetie launched himself headfirst like the comic book hero *Superman* skipper "Mud Cat" Ray had named his tugboat after. The sailor performed a classic swan dive over the side of the ship. He should have looked first.

Had he, the Italian would have seen six grappling hooks attached to the rail and Lieutenant Taylor Corrigan, accompanied by five psyched-up Raiding Forces Commandos, coming up fast. Lieutenant Corrigan and his band of jolly buccaneers were surprised, to say the least, to see such a large flying apparition unexpectedly sailing over their heads.

"Who is bloody invading who?" Sergeant Roy "Mad Dog" Reupart muttered indignantly, not slowing his assault.

However, not even the highly disciplined, single-minded men of Raiding Forces' Team 2, scaling the *Giove* with deadly purpose and evil intent, could resist pausing long enough to look over their shoulders when they heard a muffled thud from below followed by a loud sick groan. The poor Italian sailor was lying mangled on the deck of Tugboat No. 2/*Superman*, surrounded by a rough-looking mob of tugboat crewmen who were whacking on him enthusiastically with iron crowbars.

"I would have to give the lad a 3.5," Lieutenant Corrigan observed conversationally as they went over the *Giove*'s rail. "He had a solid take-off, his form was not all that bad, but the Wop kissed the pooch on his landing."

36

FORTUNE FAVORS THE BRAVE

ON THE *EGADI*, CAPTAIN JEB PELHAM-DAVIES LANDED ON THE deck of the boarding ladder with his team of Lifeboat Servicemen and Royal Navy Volunteer Reserve sailors. For his primary shooter, he had Rifleman Ned Terrance, one of Major John Randal's Calais Swamp Fox Force Green Jackets, a former member of the Rifle Brigades regimental pistol team. He was a crack shot with a silenced High Standard .22. Captain Pelham-Davies was the backup. No one was standing watch, so the Raiders dashed up the ladder in record-breaking time and proceeded to immediately carry out their assignments.

Simultaneously, up the starboard side of the ship, Sergeant Major Maxwell Hicks was leading the charge of the Raiding Force Commandos from Tugboat No. 3/*Big Toot* sprinting up the ropes.

Captain Pelham-Davies had informed his team that he intended the *Egadi* to be under tow within five minutes after they came over the rail. The former Commando School instructor explained to the tug's skipper, Mike "Wino" Muldoon, that he was expected to have his towing wire hooked up within three minutes of "Boarders Away."

Wino was not the kind of old African hand to be ordered about by an Army wallah half his age, or any officer for that matter, regardless of age, seniority, or branch of service, when he was standing on the deck of the *Big Toot*. However, he recognized a leader of men when he saw one.

"Count on it, Cap'n."

Captain Pelham-Davies' Raiding Forces team hit the *Egadi* from both sides so fast, and with such explosive, violent force, they did not have to fire a single shot. As planned, the capture went down extremely fast. Fortune very well may "favor the brave," as the motto of his regiment, the Duke of Wellington's, claims, but it also shows a marked preference for the well prepared and highly motivated who execute their plan to perfection.

Wino was true to his word. No one ever handled a tugboat any better. The capture and cutting out of the *Egadi* was a shining example of accurate intelligence, first-class planning, superb leadership, and flawless execution by picked men exhibiting precision teamwork.

The *Egadi* was secured to *Big Toot*'s towline with one whole minute to spare.

In San Pedro Harbor, a spirited fireworks firefight was raging. Multicolored Roman candle fireballs were blazing away, crisscrossing back and forth through the pitch-black African night. Hearing the explosions and fireworks coming from the *Egadi* and the *Giove*, the high-spirited Commandos on board the *Ems* grew bored with popping the Roman candles straight up into the air. Soon they amused themselves by strafing their fireworks-shooting counterparts on the stern of the *Giove*.

The anchor demo team on the stern of the *Giove* returned fire immediately, and an out-and-out Roman candle war erupted between the two ships. Soon the fireworks battle spread to the bow of the *Giove* and from there to the stern of the *Egadi*. Needless to say, this had not been part of the plan.

On all three enemy ships the anchors were aweigh, meaning their chains had been blown and were now resting on the bottom of the harbor. That part of the mission had gone like clockwork.

The *Egadi* was under tow, steaming toward the harbor entrance.

Captain Jeb Pelham-Davies, standing on the bridge next to Chief Petty Officer Derrick Welch, clenching a thin, unlit cigar in his teeth, was right on his personal timetable—last in and first out. Tugboat No. 3/*Big Toot* was huffing and puffing like the The Little Engine That Could. Huge black balls of smoke were popping out her smokestack as the mighty little tug strained against the tow wire and headed for the open sea.

In the bowels of the ship, down in the engine room, Raiding Forces Commandos and the attached bluejacket volunteers were shouting at the terrorized Italian stokers— alternating between threats of shooting them and lavish promises of money and women—to encourage them. The Italians were shoveling coal into the *Egadi's* furnace like crazed demons.

Behind them the *Giove* was just beginning to make way. Tugboat No. 2/*Superman* was straining like a hunting dog against its leash. Black puffballs of smoke were popping from its smokestack from the herculean effort. The towed ship was beginning to pick up momentum, but to the Raiders on board it seemed like it was taking a long time to actually gain any speed.

On the bridge, tapping a Player cigarette on his silver case and observing the scene below, Captain Terry "Zorro" Stone turned to his young helmsman and asked, "First prize, old stick?"

"Second. Percy and I captured the French fisherman, remember?"

"That's right, slipped my mind," Captain Stone said absently. "You're getting to be an old hand at boarding and cutting-out operations, Hornblower. Not such a good thing to get too much experience too quick, don't you know. It can make one jaded."

Lieutenant Randy "Hornblower" Seaborn, said wistfully, "Jaded, I kind of like the sound of that."

Taken off guard by the keenness of his reply, Captain Stone gave him a long, inquiring look. "Randy, you get us out of here in one piece tonight, and I just might be inclined to take you along on my next midnight ride with the 'mink and manure set.' Talk about jaded!"

"Promise, your word as an officer?" The young lieutenant could barely contain the quiver of excitement in his voice.

"As long as you give me yours, not to *ever* tell your mother, NEVER. Brandy would cut me dead if she ever found out."

"You have my word. I shan't tell, at least not Mother."

"Fair enough, old stick. By the way, you are over eighteen, aren't you?"

On board the *Ems*, no one was thinking about women, at least not at the moment. The deck lurched.

"We are under way," Commodore Richard Seaborn announced.

Major John Randal checked his Rolex to find they were right on schedule, almost.

37

FORLORN HOPE

THE FIREWORKS HAD GRADUALLY FADED AWAY. THE HARBOR WAS NOW silent. Because everyone's night vision had been destroyed by the explosions and the colored Roman candle fireballs, it became really, really dark. From the bridge of the *Ems*, it was difficult for the command party to make out the bow. The *Giove* and the *Egadi* had already disappeared out of sight entirely and were making for international waters. The *Ems* was all by herself in the harbor.

If anything went wrong now Major John Randal and his team were entirely on their own. No one could come to their aid. All of a sudden the few Raiding Forces and supporting personnel on the bridge and forward deck felt very alone. The realization was not a pleasant feeling.

Slowly, almost imperceptibly, the *Ems* began to make way. Tugboat No. 1/*King Kong* blew large black puffs of smoke from its stack as it strained mightily against the tow wire. At her wheel "Warthog" Finley pointed his tug straight at freedom.

Sergeant Mike "March or Die" Mikkalis made an appearance on the bridge, trailed by Lieutenant "Pyro" Percy Stirling back from his tour of the ship. The ex-Legionnaire reported all resistance had ceased and all German sailors were secured throughout the ship.

"Nice job, Sergeant Mikkalis."

"Not much to it, sir," the former Swamp Fox Force topkick said. "You and Merritt shot half of them."

"Lieutenant Stirling?"

"Sergeant Mikkalis has the situation well in hand, sir."

"Place additional security on both of the *Ems*'s radio rooms," Major Randal ordered. "Don't let anyone in. I want those two rooms completely secure. No souvenir hunting—clear, Lieutenant?"

"In Technicolor, sir."

"Does anyone know where the voice tube in the engine room is located?"

"I do, sir," Royal Marine Jock McDonald volunteered. Like all Royal Marines, he was familiar with naval craft.

"Lieutenant Stirling, take McDonald with you. Report to the engine room after you beef up security on the radio rooms. Take charge of the stoker detail and have the German sailors put their backs into pouring the coal to the boilers."

"Sir!"

"McDonald, you establish contact with us here on the bridge the minute you get down there and stay on the blower."

"Sir!"

"Recruit extra hands from the other prisoners if you need 'em, Percy. Let's give Captain Finley on the *King Kong* all the help you can," Major John Randal ordered. "I've spent all the time in scenic San Pedro I care to."

"Aye, aye, sir!"

The thought of spending the rest of the war cooped up in a Portuguese POW camp was a powerful motivator. Major Randal could almost feel the raiding party straining to will the *Ems* out of the harbor. Exfiltration seemed to be taking a lot longer than the slow-motion attack run in, and that did not seem physically possible. The atmosphere on the bridge was supercharged.

Out on the bow the men were chanting, "Go, go, go," at the *King Kong*. So much for noise discipline: If anyone in San Pedro heard them it is doubtful they would be mistaken for Italian or German sailors, not even drunken ones.

Although the *Ems* was gradually making way, it was not fast enough to satisfy the men of Raiding Forces. Going on a raid, all a Raider wants to do is close with the enemy and get stuck in. The feeling at the end of a mission is entirely different: All anybody wants to do is get out of there and be quick about it. Men brave as lions suddenly have a different priority entirely. The Commandos on the *Ems* wanted to go home, and right then.

"Engine room to bridge," Royal Marine McDonald piped over the voice tube.

"This is the bridge, go ahead," Commodore Seaborn responded, speaking into the intership communications device.

"How do you hear me, sir?"

"Loud and clear, McDonald. Stand by the voice tube, Marine."

"Aye, aye, sir."

Now the *Ems* seemed to be gaining traction; she was noticeably moving. They were not traveling fast, but the ship was sailing smoothly. They could just make out the flashing blue beacon marking the entrance to San Pedro Harbor in the distance. The troops on the bow were chanting, "GO, GO, GO, GO." Everyone on the bridge joined in: "GO, GO, GO . . ."

The flashing blue light became brighter and brighter. When the ship finally slid past, a cheer broke out on deck. Commodore Seaborn called down the voice tube, "Bridge to engine room, we have departed San Pedro Harbor."

Cheering in the *Ems* engine room could be heard wafting over the voice tube on the bridge. Euphoria swept the Raiding Force Commandos all over the ship. They were going to make it home free. Back slapping, shared cigarettes, lit with shaky hands, laughter, and relief broke out shipwide.

Victory felt GOOD!

"The *Giove* and *Egadi* appear to be heaving to," Commodore Seaborn announced. "Stand by, signaler."

Sergeant Mickey Duggan stepped up next to him with his Aldis signaling lamp at the ready. Up ahead a brilliant white finger of light pierced the night. With military precision, it played across the *Giove* and then the

Egadi. The light moved crisply making its inspection with a no-nonsense purpose of action.

"Your squadron of corvettes, Commodore?" Major John Randal inquired.

"Possibly," the officer at the conn replied tersely. "A bit early, actually. We have not achieved the three-mile international line quite yet. I ordered the squadron to be patrolling right outside it."

The light continued to probe the *Giove* and *Egadi.* The Raiders could see the two ships had slowed and were coming to a halt. Major Randal picked up the Zeiss night glasses that were hanging from a strap next to the helm. It took him a moment to focus the binoculars on the source of the light.

"Were you expecting a submarine escort, sir?" Major Randal asked. "That's the source of the light."

"Let me have those glasses," Commodore Seaborn fairly screamed, ripping the binoculars out of the major's hands.

After a cursory glance, sounding remarkably calm for a man only on his very second combat operation, the commodore announced, "German U-boat on the surface, dead ahead; she is cleared for action."

The men on the bridge stood in shocked silence.

The Nazis were not going to be any too happy to discover that the source of all their priceless target information had just been captured by British Commandos.

"What's a Nazi submarine doing inside Rio Bonita's waters?" Major John Randal said through clenched teeth. Getting captured by a U-boat was one contingency no one had ever imagined, much less planned for. *So much for expecting the unexpected!* Major Randal decided in disgust.

"What better place to surface and wait for the radio signal from *Ems*?" Commodore Richard Seaborn asked bitterly. "Probably the safest spot on the entire Gold Coast. A U-boat at periscope depth can spot a surface ship and dive without being identified, and no British warship is ever going to drop depth charges in neutral waters without a positive ID. Have to give that skipper credit."

"Why didn't he dive the minute the *Egadi* first approached?"

"My guess would be he recognized her," Commodore Seaborn replied, still studying the Nazi U-boat through the Zeiss night glasses. "The skipper has most likely lain out here at periscope depth night after night studying San Pedro Harbor. That's exactly what I would have done."

In the distance, the sailors on the bridge could hear a German voice shouting guttural commands over a mechanical hailer.

"Anyone feel like becoming a POW?" Commodore Seaborn asked in a chatty tone.

"Never happen prisoners of war," Major Randal said. "They were going to hang us for pirates, remember?"

"Well, we cannot outrun them and we do not have any guns or depth charges to fight with," the commodore pointed out, stating the obvious. "I fear that only leaves one viable option."

"Sure as hell looks like it," Major Randal said. "Lock and load, boys. All hands on deck. We'll attack the German boarding party the moment they come on board.

"Sergeant Mikkalis," Major Randal barked, "in the event anything happens to me, you take every man still on his feet, commandeer the German cutter after we take out the boarding party, then go capture that submarine. Is that clear?" His plan was simple. No matter what happened, his forces were to go down fighting and never surrender.

"As it gets," the tough Commando sergeant snarled. "Make sure nothing happens, Major. I prefer to have you up front leading the way if it's all the same, sir."

"Major Randal, ring for 'Full Speed Ahead,'" Commodore Seaborn ordered as calmly as if he were standing on the bridge of the HMS *Hood* requesting a cucumber sandwich from his orderly.

"Stand by to ram!"

With that electrifying command, he became the high seas, blue-water battle commander he had always aspired to be. A thrill of optimism shot though the men clustered on the bridge. Commodore Seaborn sounded like he knew what he was doing. They all hoped so.

Major Randal did not have the first clue as to how to ring for "Full Speed Ahead." He opened the voice tube and shouted down it, "Bridge to engine room."

"Engine room, sir."

"Put Lieutenant Stirling on."

"Lieutenant Stirling, sir."

"Percy, the *Giove* and *Egadi* are dead in the water directly ahead, stopped by a German U-boat. The submarine is on the surface cleared for action, and she is preparing to board us," Major Randal informed him. "Commodore Seaborn has elected to attempt to ram the U-boat rather than surrender. Pour on the coal, make those prisoners put their backs into it! I want the furnace burning hotter than that lighthouse you blew on Tomcat!"

"YES SIR! YeeeeeeHaaaaaaa!"

"The lieutenant's a 'Death or Glory' boy," Sergeant Mike "March or Die" Mikkalis said. "You can bet good money he will crack the whip."

The effect on morale of having a plan is incredible, even a forlorn hope like trying to ram a nimble Nazi submarine with a lumbering ship under tow. Any chance is better than no chance.

"We are one and all 'death or glory' boys this night," Commodore Seaborn replied resolutely, stepping up to his rendezvous with destiny. "Now hear this; it is vital that the next two orders I give be carried out instantly. Any time now the Germans are going to challenge us. We have no idea what the correct response is, but then there is no reason the *Ems*, bottled up in San Pedro for the duration, would know. When the U-boat challenges, Sergeant Duggan, on my command, using the signal lamp, authenticate with the letters E M S and keep repeating it."

"Aye, aye, sir. E-M-S."

"The sub knows this ship is the *Ems*, which should confuse her because E-M-S is not going to be the correct reply to the challenge. The response may buy us some time because the skipper is not going to want to fire on a German ship that is in the act of trying to identify herself. Every second we can stall is precious now because it's allowing us to close.

"Hoolihan, secure axes from the ship's lifeboats. Report to the bow and take charge of the detail there. Stand by; then, on my command, have the Lifeboat Servicemen cut the towline. If Captain Finley should heave to or the towline goes slack for any reason do not wait for my command; cut it immediately. Do you understand?"

"Aye, aye, sir!" The Royal Marine repeated the instructions. "Cut the tow on your command or chop it free immediately should the line go slack."

"Those are your orders. Severing that line may be the most important assignment you are ever called to carry out, Marine."

"You can depend on me, sir."

"Right man, right job," Major Randal said locking eyes with his Raider. "Get it done, Butch."

Royal Marine Butch Hoolihan started to rush off the bridge but Commodore Seaborn reached out and restrained the young Commando. "The instant the towline parts, bring everyone forward on the bow back here on the double, Hoolihan."

"Aye, aye, sir. On the double, sir," he shouted.

And then all there was to do was wait for the Germans to make the next move.

38

BEER CAN

IN THE HEAT OF BATTLE, IT IS OFTEN HARD TO APPRECIATE THAT the enemy is just as tired, hurt, anxious, dispirited, or confused as you are. The German commander of the U-boat had been lying up in a quiet, safe spot listening to mood music from Radio Berlin while waiting for the nightly traffic from the *Ems*. Observing the three ships being towed out of San Pedro Harbor was probably the last thing he ever expected to see. His information was that they were to be interned for the duration.

It was a safe bet the German did not know exactly what was taking place. In addition, the U-boat captain had to factor into the equation that his U-boat was trespassing in Rio Bonita territorial waters. While only a trifling consideration to a diehard Nazi submarine skipper, it was still something he had to take into account. His next move could cause an international incident for which he would be held accountable. And, since events were developing while the Nazi watched—coming straight at him, in fact—he did not have a great deal of time to make an estimate of the situation, calculate a course of action, or take steps to effect a plan.

An equally sure bet was that the U-boat's captain would get it sorted out sooner rather than later. A German naval officer does not get to be the commander of one of the Third Reich's most deadly fighting machines by being timid. The U-boat skipper was doubtless a good decision maker and a surefire man of action.

Commodore Richard Seaborn knew that confusion creates opportunity. What he was hoping for was a brief moment of hesitation on the Nazi commander's part while he put the pieces of the puzzle together. A split second of indecision that created a tiny window of opportunity, it should happen, and when it did the commodore was setting up to take full advantage of the one chance, if he could. In real tactical terms, the situation was as hopelessly lopsided against them as any Royal Navy sailor has ever had to face.

"Cast off the towline!" Commodore Seaborn shouted down to the Lifeboat Servicemen on the bow, who were staring in horror at the surfaced U-boat. The men's submarine recognition skills were a little rusty, but it did not take much of a nautical expert to recognize the fluttering red Nazi flag with the white circle and swastika unfurled from the U-boat's conning tower, especially since the German crew had gone to the trouble to illuminate it with a small floodlight. Royal Marine Butch Hoolihan raced up with the axes he had taken out of one of the *Ems*'s lifeboats, and the Commandos fell to chopping the tow wire with a will.

"John, on my command, hit the switch that turns on the lighting in the topmast rigging," Commodore Seaborn ordered.

"Standing by lights, sir."

The Lifeboat Servicemen were slaving away at the steel cable like supercharged maniacs, but the line did not want to part. The men on the bridge of the *Ems* watched helplessly as the Raiders struggled to cut it. Suddenly Marine Hoolihan shoved them out of the way, unlimbered his Browning A-5, and started blasting the stubborn strands point-blank. "BLAM, BLAM, BLAM . . ." He used all eight rounds, but the intractable towline failed to part.

"Grenade," Marine Hoolihan shouted, producing a No. 36 and charging it as the startled Lifeboat Servicemen scurried to take cover. The Raider wedged the hand grenade under the towline and dashed for shelter. Seconds later a sharp explosion reverberated on the bow and the wire snapped.

The moment Royal Marine Hoolihan shouted, "Tow away!" Commodore Seaborn put the helm over hard to port. The *Ems* was now running parallel to and astern of the four halted vessels: the two tugs, the *Giove*, the *Egadi*, with the submarine on the surface a short distance broadside off their bows.

The U-boat was flashing a challenge from the conning tower: the letters "O" and "G" in international Morse code. Royal Marine Sergeant Mickey Duggan was responding with the letters "E, M, and S": obviously, they were not the correct authentication response letters, but under the circumstances, they had to be confusing to the Nazi submarine's commander. They were the *Ems* and he knew it.

The U-boat's deck gun barked and a shell screamed across the *Ems*'s bow, blowing a tall geyser of white water high into the air. If the round was a warning shot it did nothing to discourage Commodore Seaborn. He spun the wheel all the way back hard to starboard. The massive cruiser heeled over at once and came around fast. Everyone on board had to grab hold of something to avoid being tossed to the deck.

The big ship ploughed into the turn, picking up speed. A sharp sound came over the voice tube that sounded suspiciously like a Colt .38 Super being fired in the engine room. Accidental discharge? Probably not.

Unknown to the people on the bridge, Lieutenant "Pyro" Percy Stirling had deliberately shot a giant Kriegsmarine petty officer in the side of the head. The German sailor had picked the exact wrong moment to stage a one-man rebellion against the order to shovel coal. The swift, precipitous action carried out in a vigorous military manner by a determined Raiding Forces officer intent on carrying out his mission instantly produced the desired effect. The petty officer was lying dead in a pool of blood and the rest of the prisoners were shoveling coal like madmen!

The officers on the deck heard the sound of the pistol shot through the intercom. Though curious, Major John Randal chose not interrupt his young lieutenant in the performance of his duties. There was no reason to waste his time or distract him by calling down the voice tube to make inquiries. He had full confidence in Lieutenant Stirling's ability to carry out his assigned task and left him alone to get on with it the best way he saw fit.

The U-boat fired a second cannon shot. The shell screamed down the starboard side of the *Ems* and blew up fifty meters astern, sending up a tall, white plume of water.

"They were trying to hit us with that one," Commodore Seaborn observed conversationally. "Stand by to activate the lights, Major."

"Roger, on your command, sir."

The *Ems* sailed through the gap between the *Egadi* and Tugboat No. 2/*Superman*. The crews and Raiding Forces personnel on both vessels were standing on the decks staring at her in open-mouthed surprise. The *Ems* was now headed straight toward the German U-boat lying on the surface, perpendicular to them. Commodore Seaborn was closing fast.

"Activate lights."

The lights in the topmast came on, turning the *Ems* into a gigantic, supersized Christmas tree. To the sailors standing on the deck of the surfaced U-boat one hundred yards dead ahead, she must have looked like the Eiffel Tower all lit up as she came bearing down on them. And that was the idea: Commodore Seaborn was using every trick in the book. Panicking her crew could not hurt.

"Keeeeeeerblaaaam!" The U-boat's deck gun fired again. The *Ems* was in such close proximity now the Germans were having difficulty getting their deck gun depressed low enough to hit her. The shell sailed harmlessly over the ship—too high but right in line. The round screamed the length of the vessel.

The Kriegsmarine crew was desperately cranking the wheel manually, trying to lower the deck gun's muzzle. Suddenly the dark blue-black African night erupted into artificial daylight as a brilliant star flare exploded high overhead.

"Where did that come from?" Commodore Seaborn shouted. "Did anyone get a line of sight?"

"It came from out there," Sergeant Duggan pointed out to the open sea. "Must be the Royal Navy or another U-boat, sir."

Royal Marine Hoolihan and the Lifeboat Servicemen came clamoring up onto the bridge.

"Nice job, stud," Major Randal said. The distance between the two vessels was narrowing rapidly. The commander of the U-boat, identifiable by his white skipper's hat, could be seen standing on the deck of the conning tower. There was a look of terror on his face as the looming reinforced steel hull of the enormous *Ems* bore down on his helpless submarine like a giant razor-edged battering ram. Suddenly it was too late for him. There was no room to maneuver, no time to dive.

Major Randal leaned out over the rail of the bridge and began deliberately firing his Colt .38 Super at the group of horrified German sailors lined up along the length of the submarine's deck. They began peeling off and going over the side at every shot.

"Stand by for collision," Commodore Seaborn announced, doing it by the book all the way.

"Crrrrrrackkkkkwhooooooomppphh!" The U-boat's deck gun fired again, and this time the shell detonated on the lip of the starboard bow of the *Ems* with a blinding flash and ear-splitting explosion. Shrapnel screamed. The big lumbering *Ems* absorbed the hit without even slowing down. Nothing was going to stop her now.

Just as Major Randal emptied his pistol, the *Ems's* reinforced steel, knife-blade-shaped hull slammed into the U-boat slightly to the port side of the conning tower, slicing the submarine in half straightaway. There was a hollow metallic "Cruuump!" that sounded vaguely like a giant beer can being stomped on, but the *Ems* kept right on going and there was not so much as even the slightest sensation that they had even driven over a speed bump.

"Now that's what I call crossing the 'T,'" Major Randal remarked as he inserted a fresh magazine into his Colt automatic and racked a shell into the chamber.

The star flare died out and the darkness closed in quickly after Major Randal hit the switch and turned the lights in the topmast back off.

"Make Follow Me—Line Astern," Commodore Seaborn ordered Sergeant Duggan. The Royal Marine signaler ran around the catwalk outside the bridge and signaled the *Egadi* and the *Giove* to fall in behind.

The U-boat had sunk in two sections, going down almost immediately. Strangely, her deck-mounted spotlight did not short out right away, and it could be seen eerily glowing, deep underwater, as the Commandos sailed past.

"Think you hit anything with your automatic?" Commodore Seaborn asked Major Randal.

"Never know, sir," Major Randal replied, holstering the weapon. "I make it a practice to shoot back when somebody shoots at me."

"Sir," Royal Marine Hoolihan protested, "the Germans were firing a cannon at us!"

"Do what you can, Butch."

Sergeant Duggan stepped out of the shadows and offered Major Randal and Sergeant Mike "March or Die" Mikkalis cigarettes from a crumpled pack he produced from the pocket of his Denison smock. The three former Swamp Fox Force men stood looking at each other through the cigarette smoke, enjoying the moment.

Sergeant Duggan mentioned chattily, "It's difficult to kill a mosquito with a sledgehammer."

"Not if you hit him with it," Sergeant Mikkalis pointed out.

"Nice to know you men were paying attention," Major Randal drawled laconically, "that day at Calais."

A second star shell erupted brilliantly. This time it was clear that the flare came from a ship standing outside the three-mile international limit.

"Make S-O," Commodore Richard Seaborn ordered. "If it is the Royal Navy they will respond with M."

Since they had all been trained in the rudiments of signaling, every man in the small crowd on the bridge strained to see the reply. A cheer went up when the hoped-for authentication letter "M" flashed back.

Major John Randal called down to the engine room. "Percy, we have rammed and sunk the German U- boat and are in visual contact with surface units of the Royal Navy at this time."

"Yeeeehaaaaaah!" screeched over the voice tube.

"Eloquently put," Commodore Seaborn commented. "The lad has a way with words."

After a while it became possible to make out the sleek outlines of Royal Navy corvettes. The corvette was a warship, purpose designed with only one task in mind: to hunt down and kill submarines. They were deadly, efficient-looking little ships armed to the teeth and ready to spring into action.

Tonight the Royal Navy was not taking any chances. The sailors were not in possession of the details of the Raiding Forces operation. What the bluejackets did know was that they had just observed a surface action within the territorial waters of a neutral protectorate. And their orders were to rendezvous with a ship or ships coming out of San Pedro Harbor. While the Royal Navy did not have any notion of what exactly had taken place or why, they had every intention of finding out, with their fingers curled on the trigger.

The lead corvette signaled, "Stand by to receive boarding parties."

"Signal, 'Standing by,'" Commodore Seaborn ordered.

As they waited on the bridge for the cutters to arrive, Commodore Seaborn turned to Major Randal and said, once more sounding stiff and formal, "We have several options to consider, Major. The three prizes will proceed directly from here to Cape Town. The idea is to move them as far away from the Gold Coast as quickly as possible to prevent, as much as possible, any blame falling on anyone there. The Navy is going to be rather vague about where and when they intercepted the three enemy ships.

"Royal Navy Catalinas out of Accra are in the air as we speak, awaiting instructions on where to rendezvous with us to land and pick up Raiding Forces for immediate transport back to the UK.

"You and Captain Stone will be returning to the Gold Coast with the tugs. As you know, the plan calls for the two of you to link up with Jane and her team in Accra and, after putting on the appropriate show of being completely bewildered by what took place here tonight, return to England the same public way you came out."

"Terry and I are good at acting confused, sir."

"What are your instructions for me, John?" Commodore Seaborn inquired suddenly.

The question caught Major Randal off guard. "Sir?"

"In your capacity as the mission commander, at this point you have three options to choose from with regard to my future actions, which we have never discussed until now," the commodore explained carefully. "I can return to the Gold Coast with you, fly home on a Catalina with the troops, or carry on with the squadron of corvettes escorting our prizes to Cape Town."

Major Randal instinctively realized that Commodore Seaborn preferred one option over the other two, but for reasons of his own, the commodore apparently did not want to come right out and say which one it was. All things considered, it would have been perfectly appropriate, as far as the major was concerned, for the commodore to simply announce his intentions.

For the integrity of the mission, it was probably best for the commodore to return to the Gold Coast and help them in their charade. On the other hand, the naval officer might want to fly straight back home on one of the Catalinas. Then it dawned on him: if the commodore proceeded to Cape Town with the corvettes and the prizes, he would be in command, actually pulling sea duty as a unit commander. Command time at sea in commodore grade would be invaluable to him later when the Royal Navy got around to sorting out his rank status.

"Sir, I don't see where we have any options," Major Randal disagreed in a take-charge tone, looking the commodore square in the eyes. "As the senior naval officer present, it's your responsibility to ensure our prize ships reach safe harbor. We didn't go to all this trouble to simply hand them over to some navy type we don't even know."

"Thanks, John."

"I read in the *Times* it's an automatic award of the Distinguished Service Order for any captain of a ship who sinks a U-boat," Royal Marine Butch Hoolihan piped up. "Do you reckon that policy is still in effect, sir?"

"I believe that it is."

"The award is the same," the young Raider persisted, "if a captain drops a boatload of depth charges on a submarine, or catches one on the surface and destroys her with deck guns from a mile away?"

"That is correct."

"Congratulations on your DSO, sir! You rammed yours, and that has to be even better."

"The regulation only applies to the captain of a Royal Navy ship, Hoolihan," Commodore Seaborn laughed. "I seriously doubt it was intended for cases of international piracy."

"I can almost guarantee, sir," Major Randal said, "it's in effect tonight."

Commodore Seaborn had won his sea spurs the hard way.

Word of the successful mission was encrypted immediately and flashed to London. The celebration and simultaneous rush to take credit for it was instantaneous. The Royal Navy, Special Operations Executive, Combined Operations Headquarters, and even the Secret Intelligence Service, MI-6, all staked claims. Operation Lounge Lizard quickly became the least secret Most Secret operation of all time.

A highly classified "Eyes Only" after-action assessment was prepared for the prime minister and circulated to select deputies even before all the Raiding Forces personnel had departed the West African theater of operations.

The conclusion: "Operation Lounge Lizard was a masterpiece of careful planning, sound intelligence, organization, inner-service cooperation, secrecy, rapid movement, brilliant leadership, and decisive action. The mission demonstrates how a small body of picked men, properly supported by national authority, can carry out strategic military operations that reap enormous rewards for the nation far out of proportion to the men, treasure, and resources expended."

Prime Minister Winston Churchill scrawled across the bottom of his copy, "Give me more like this!"

AFTER THE MISSION

39

THE MINK MARINES

AFTER A LONG FLIGHT BACK TO ENGLAND ON BOARD A FLYING Clipper—during which he spent virtually the entire time ensconced in compartment No. 6 with Captain the Lady Jane Seaborn and during which his career as a hard-charging bachelor had been brought to a screeching halt—Major John Randal was stretched out by the roaring fire in a huge leather bat-wing chair in his room at Seaborn House, toasting himself. He was wearing a camel-colored terrycloth robe over a faded pair of blue jeans and an ancient pair of cowboy boots he had worn in high school and college and had carried with him to the Philippines when he was in the U.S. 26th Cavalry Regiment. They were so soft they could be rolled up into a ball when packed for travel.

Chauncy had found the boots and jeans for Major Randal in a duffel bag he had not opened since he had arrived in England. The robe must have belonged to Lady Jane Seaborn's dead husband, Mallory, but he did not want to think about that right now.

After having just completed a long, hot soak in the swimming pool-sized bathtub, he felt like a contented prune. His boots were propped up on a large ottoman, and there was a stack of newspapers in his lap. He was relaxed for the first time in a very long time. There was only one thing on his calendar to do and that was still several hours off. Tonight, at long last, he was going to have dinner with Jane and her uncle, Colonel John Henry Bevins, MC, Hertfordshire Regiment, graduate of Eton, member of Pop, investment banker, advisor to royalty, and so on.

The estate was virtually empty. All operations had been stood down. The troops were on leave. They more than deserved it.

Captain Terry "Zorro" Stone and Lieutenant Randy "Hornblower" Seaborn, who was sporting the expression of a hungry Cheshire cat eye-balling a plump canary in a cage with the door left ajar, had ridden off into the sunset together. Major Randal wondered what that was about, but he did not ask any questions because he specifically did not want to be in possession of any of the answers.

Captain "Geronimo Joe" McKoy was at the Bradford Hotel check-ing on his assistant, Miss Lilly Threepersons. He was taking her a batch of Portuguese-language movie star magazines he had brought back from San Pedro. Miss Lilly Threepersons could not speak or read one word of Portuguese, but the captain explained it would not make any difference what language they were in because "she just looks at the pictures."

Captain the Lady Jane Seaborn was also away in London visiting the new offices of Special Operations Executive now relocated to No. 64 Baker Street. That had given rise to the organization's new nickname, "The Baker Street Irregulars," bequeathed by their not-so-friendly competitors the Secret Intelligence Service, MI-6, aka "Broadway," an organization also nicknamed after the street it resided on. She would be returning any time now with Royal Marine Pamala Plum-Martin. Which was something else he was going to have to sort out: exactly who and what was Pamala? Major Randal could no longer turn a blind eye to the fact that she was obviously something more than merely a Royal Marine private who served as Jane's chauffeur.

Chauncy buzzed in like a happy bumblebee flitting from flower to flower. He needed to be sorted out too.

"What are you, exactly, Chauncy? A sergeant major or a butler?" Major Randal demanded.

"I was a sergeant major, sir, before I became a butler. Then Lady

Seaborn put me back in harness again temporarily, so to speak. I would say I was your butler, sir, except for the time I am acting in the capacity as one of your sergeant majors."

"I have been checking up on the Green Howards," Major Randal continued, "looking into your military antecedents."

"Very good, sir."

"The Green Howards have a dandy record as a fighting regiment, called the Yorkshire Gurkhas. Certainly impressive handle—the Gurkhas are well known as a bloodthirsty crew. You must have soldiered halfway around the globe, Chauncy?"

"Saw quite a bit of the bad parts of the Empire, sir."

"Butler, sergeant major, butler; how am I supposed to know when you're what?"

"My status should not pose any significant difficulty, sir," Chauncy commented absently as he rummaged through the closet selecting the uniform the major would require for his evening engagement. He understood full well the implications of the night's drill and was determined to ensure that Major Randal made his best impression.

"If I call you Chauncy, I'm not respecting your rank, which you earned. On the other hand, I don't feel too great about having a sergeant major polishing my boots. You see what I mean?"

"No sir," Chauncy said, holding a shirt up to the light to inspect the collar. "I do not see any conflict,"

"You don't?"

"No sir."

"I see," said Major Randal, which meant, of course, he did not. "How about if I call you Sergeant Major no matter what capacity you're operating in?"

"I should be most pleased, sir." It was becoming increasingly clear to Chauncy he was going to have his hands full whipping young Major Randal into shape vis-à-vis the gentleman-to-gentleman's-gentleman relationship. He would not want the major to embarrass himself around the other servants. "I have always considered you as my C.O."

"Oh! Okay . . . that's good."

"By the way, sir, Lady Seaborn's automobile has turned into the drive."

"Sergeant Major," Major Randal continued, ignoring him, "it says in the paper here the Battle of Britain has ended. And it says while the battle was in progress, the Luftwaffe tried to make 'a flaming desert out of the 692 square miles of Greater London.' I don't get it; those were German bombers we heard flying over last night, weren't they?"

"Yes sir."

"What do they mean, then, that the Battle of Britain is over?"

"The Jerries have given up continuous bombing during the daylight hours, sir. Mr. Churchill said it was not the end, or even the beginning of the end, but it may be the end of the beginning, or something like that, sir."

"I see," Major Randal mused. "Who won?"

"We did, sir."

"Flaming desert, do you think that's a typo? Deserts don't flame. I've seen a flaming drink—"

"Sir, there is someone with Lady Seaborn."

Major Randal struggled out of the deep leather chair and walked to the window overlooking the circular drive. The Rolls Royce was just coming to a stop. The household staff was lined up on the drive. They looked cold out there.

First out of the Rolls was Brandy Seaborn, dressed like a member of the women's auxiliary of the Russian Cossack Cavalry. She was wearing a full-length golden mink coat, a matching mink Cossack hat, impeccably cut jodhpurs, and highly polished riding boots—Bloods from the look of them. She definitely got his vote for all-time greatest-looking mother of a Royal Navy officer.

Captain Lady Seaborn and Royal Marine Plum-Martin both were dressed identically except for variations in the shade of mink (mahogany and platinum, respectively) and their Royal Marine blouses. Mink Marines.

Something was wrong with this picture. Major Randal could not put his finger on it, but he felt the faint ding of an alarm bell cook off. The women were moving with a purpose. He noted that the shade of their minks matched their hair colors.

"Sergeant Major, you better find me some place to hide."

"Why ever should you want to do that, sir?"

"Brandy Seaborn is probably coming here to do me in for nearly getting Randy and the commodore rubbed out on the same night. Those women look awfully serious about something. Whatever happens, no matter what, don't say a word about Terry and Randy going off together. That's on a 'need to know only' basis. Randy's mother definitely does *not* have any need to know."

"My thoughts precisely, sir."

Major Randal added, "I wish I had gone with them."

He plopped back down into the leather bat-winged chair to await the ladies. "Do you know Colonel Bevins?"

"Who, sir?"

"Jane's uncle—Colonel John Henry Bevins."

"I have met him, sir. Dignified gentleman, very likable; the staff seems to get on with him. He is a big sportsman. Fisherman, I believe."

"I'm going to need a briefing on the Hertfordshires before I leave for dinner this evening, Sergeant Major."

"The Hertfordshires, sir?"

"John Henry's regiment. He won the Military Cross serving with them during the last war. I'll need something to talk about at dinner."

Major Randal opened the *London Times*. The banner headline blared, "ENEMY SHIPS CAPTURED, U-BOAT SUNK."

According to the article, three enemy merchant ships had been captured at sea somewhere off the coast of West Africa by a squadron of Royal Navy corvettes under the command of Commodore Richard Seaborn, RN, OBE, while on routine antisubmarine duty. The only available photo of Commodore Seaborn was an earlier one taken when he was still wearing the uniform of a staff commander.

Commodore Seaborn, the article went on, had boarded one of the three prize ships to inspect it when a German U-boat surfaced nearby. Immediately the intrepid, quick-thinking commodore sprang into action, took over the helm of the prize vessel, the German merchant raider *Ems*, and in a spectacular show of incredible seamanship, heroically rammed and sank the enemy submarine, U-237, sending it to the bottom with all hands.

All three of the captured ships had previously been interned in the

Portuguese protectorate of Rio Bonita. Commodore Seaborn speculated the three ships' crews had "grown weary of internment and mutinied." He stated there was evidence that led him to believe the escape had been "carefully orchestrated to coincide with a time most of the ships' officers were away at a party ashore."

The captain of the *Ems*, captured on board, had received a minor head injury possibly inflicted during the mutiny, when the crew took over the ship and took him hostage. He was not being cooperative with authorities. It was not immediately known if the *Ems* skipper had been part of the plot or had merely returned early from the party and been swept up in the mutiny. Commodore Seaborn was reported as being convinced there was a possibility the escape was the result of detailed advanced planning; he believed the rendezvous with the U-237 in international waters outside San Pedro's three-mile limit could not have been accidental.

An American stamp collector who had been visiting the island the evening of the ships' breakout, Mr. Joe McKoy of Flagstaff, Arizona, was quoted as saying, "Everything had been real quiet," but went on to add that a taxi driver told him, "there had been rumors floating around the waterfront the crews were tired of being cooped up and might try to bust out."

Radio Berlin was claiming British Commandos had boarded the ships in a neutral harbor and spirited them away. Lord Haw-Haw branded the action as an "act of piracy" on his nightly German radio propaganda show. Portugal was demanding the immediate return of the three ships to San Pedro. Mussolini was furious.

The British Admiralty scoffed at the German claim, adding, "As for returning the three prizes, there are no plans to do so since they were captured on the high seas outside San Pedro's territorial waters."

Commodore Seaborn was to be awarded a decoration for his heroic actions.

"Outstanding," Major Randal said approvingly. The article was a neat piece of misinformation. Lieutenant Colonel Dudley Clarke, Lieutenant Commander Ian Fleming, and Jim "Baldie" Taylor were obviously hard at work covering Raiding Forces' tracks. He wondered if they were actually fooling anyone—apparently neither the Germans, the Italians, nor the Portuguese.

Suddenly the three women thundered into his room. Major Randal looked over the top of his newspaper with some degree of trepidation.

'Hi," he said. Clearly the trio was not on a purely social call.

"John," Captain Lady Seaborn announced breathlessly, "we located the target you have been searching for all these months."

"Really? And what might that be?"

"A pub located in a secluded village on the French Coast, right on the water's edge, where German pilots go drinking at the end of the day's flying."

"No kidding." Major Randal put down the newspaper. He sat up straight.

"SOE has an agent in the place who sent a report there is to be a squadron party this very night."

"Show me."

40

HOW HARD CAN IT BE

THE WOMEN SAT DOWN ON THE FLOOR AROUND THE OTTOMAN in their mink coats. Captain the Lady Jane Seaborn spread out the map on the ottoman and pointed to the small village named St. Leigh. "The name of the tavern is the Blue Duck.

"The Luftwaffe has a landing ground approximately two miles west of St. Leigh. The squadron operating there flies JU-87 Stukas. There are no troops stationed in the village except for a small military police detachment at the dock to log arrivals and departures."

Looking at the map, Major John Randal noted that St. Leigh was a tiny coastal village with a single road running through it parallel to the coastline. The road made a junction in the center of the village with another narrow country lane that wandered its way toward the interior. There was a small dock and not much else. The place was located in the middle of nowhere, which made it vulnerable to a small-scale Commando raid.

"Exactly the target I've been looking for," Major Randal agreed, thoroughly disgusted. "Typical it would show up when there's no way to get there and no one to go raid it."

The three women exchanged looks. "I can run us over to St. Leigh,"

Brandy announced. "You forget the *Arrow* was my boat before the Royal Navy took her."

"The *Arrow* is off having torpedo tubes installed."

"I know, but the *Arrow* is not the only boat in the Seaborn flotilla. We have a twenty-five-foot Chris-Craft speedboat topped off and waiting at the dock. Jane called ahead and had it brought around from the boathouse."

"I see. What about navigation?"

"We have all boated over to St. Leigh numerous times. It is not at all like trying to find a tiny pinpoint you have never been to," Captain Lady Seaborn explained. "We used to sail over to the Blue Duck on summer evenings, have cocktails, and sail home. It was a fun excursion."

"I bet it was."

"I shall simply do what Father taught me," Brandy chirped. "Aim five degrees to port and when we hit France, turn right."

"The 'Razor' taught you that?" Major Randal asked skeptically. "So, what's the plan, ladies?"

"Brandy runs us over to St. Leigh to arrive about midnight. You go into the Blue Duck before last call and kill them all." Royal Marine Pamela Plum-Martin made the idea of doing it sound chillingly simple. "How hard can it be to shoot a few drunken fighter pilots?"

Major Randal wondered if she was serious.

"If we leave now we can make it before closing time," Captain Lady Seaborn added, calm and composed. The women had it all worked out.

Major Randal looked at them through narrowed eyes. The three must have endured at least fifty or more bombing attacks over the last months. As a matter of fact, Stuka fliers like the pilots who would be in the Blue Duck had sunk Lady Jane's husband's ship. Each woman had lost friends, killed in the air raids. Some of the people in their circle had lost children in the random attacks. Royal Marine Plum-Martin had probably chalked up a squadron's worth of fighter pilot boyfriends shot down by now, and Brandy most likely felt the Luftwaffe had wounded her when she sprained her ankle at the Bradford Hotel.

The three were dedicated, committed, patriotic women fed up with the terror bombing night after night, knowing they were on the Nazi death list in the event the Germans invaded England. For the first time since the war began, they saw an opportunity to hit back at their tormentors, and they wanted to take a crack at it. Raiding the Blue Duck was their chance. Who could blame them? These women wanted scalps.

And, with the element of surprise on his side, it really should not be all that difficult to arrive unannounced and unexpected in the middle of the night and shoot up a small bar's worth of hard-partying pilots. He had come to that same conclusion long ago after many nights spent in the Blind Eye pub watching the local "Gallant Few" drinking themselves senseless at the end of a day's flying.

"Well, hell," Major Randal said, "let me get my pistols."

"Jane said you would," Brandy whooped. "Meet us at the boat dock as soon as you make yourself ready. We have to shove off within the half hour."

The trio trooped out of the room and clattered back down the spiral staircase. Major Randal stood up and took off the robe and tossed it on the bed. He pulled a black turtleneck sweater over his head. Then he methodically checked both of his Colt .38 Super automatics. They were in perfect running order.

He strapped on a shoulder holster and placed his primary carry Colt .38 Super in it. Next he inspected his High Standard .22 pistol and its silencer. The pistol went into its belt holster and Major Randal buckled it around his waist, thinking ahead, planning his moves, and getting his equipment set up so that he would have the right weapon in the right place when he needed it. He slid the holster around in front until it was right against the belt buckle and locked it down. The holster rode high with the checkered black walnut grip of the High Standard below and to the right of the matching black walnut grip of the Colt .38 Super. Either pistol could easily be drawn with his right hand.

Major Randal had a brief pang of regret that he did not have his 9-millimeter Browning P-35 available tonight. Captain "Geronimo Joe" McKoy had taken the pistol off to receive the same hand honing treatment as the Colt .38 Supers. That was too bad; its high-capacity magazine of 9-millimeter rounds might have come in handy.

"I'll need my overcoat, Sergeant Major," he said as he pulled his Denison smock on over his shirt and blue jeans and then filled both bellows pockets with loose 12-gauge shotgun shells. Additional magazines for the Colt .38 Supers were stuffed into other pockets.

"Sir, are you sure this is wise?" Chauncy asked in a worried tone as he helped the major slip the supple cashmere Pembrooks overcoat over the parachute smock. He wrapped a scarf around the major's neck and tucked the long ends into the overcoat.

"Dumbest idea I've ever heard," Major Randal said. "You don't think Brandy is actually going to find St. Leigh, do you?"

"She might, sir. Mrs. Seaborn is quite the sailor. During the evacuation, she made something like five trips to Dunkirk in the family houseboat ferrying out troops, with only Mrs. Honeycutt-Parker aboard as crew."

"All she had to do was follow the other boats in the armada," Major Randal replied, putting his spare Colt .38 Super into the right-hand pocket of the overcoat. Two more fully charged magazines went into the left pocket. Last of all he stepped toward his 12-gauge Browning A-5 shotgun leaning against the wall in a corner and picked it up. The A-5 was fully loaded. He racked a round into the chamber and topped off the magazine with a round from his pocket.

"Contact Jane's uncle and cancel dinner, Sergeant Major," Major Randal ordered, taking a last look around to see if he had forgotten anything. "Tell the colonel we'd like a rain check."

"Godspeed, sir."

One of the kitchen staff was waiting downstairs to drive him to the boat dock. It was cold out, and he immediately wished he were back in his room in the bat-winged leather chair by the fire. When he arrived, Brandy and Captain Lady Seaborn were already on board the sleek mahogany speedboat.

Royal Marine Plum-Martin came striding up the boardwalk with her full-length platinum mink coat flying. She was carrying a Thompson submachine gun at the high port.

"Can you handle that cannon?" called out Major Randal.

"What do you think?" she replied and jumped into the boat.

Brandy was at the wheel impatiently revving the powerful engines. "Thanks, Commander Tweedleton," she called to the retired Royal Navy officer who commanded Lieutenant Randy Seaborn's maintenance support team.

"Good luck, Mrs. Seaborn," he said, clearly troubled. "Would you like me to come along to see after the boat?"

"Not tonight, Commander," Brandy responded cheerfully. "We shall be traveling fast and should not welcome the extra weight."

The instant Major Randal was aboard, the retired pensioner cast off the lines and Brandy roared away from the dock, throwing him back into the seat next to Captain Lady Seaborn.

"Hang on, John," the golden girl shouted over her shoulder, laughing in the wind. Brandy Seaborn was a competition-class open sea speedboat driver, and as soon as they came out into the Channel, she lined up the correct heading (five degrees to port), opened up the throttle, and headed straight for France. Brandy knew that she couldn't spot, much less avoid, any of the blacked-out ships navigating the Channel. She simply put the hammer down and trusted to luck. It was a gutsy move. There was no telling how fast they were flying.

Major John Randal was not exactly clear how he had allowed himself to be talked into this mission. Then again, a flying squadron hangout like the Blue Duck was the perfect high-value target, and he fair and truly did hate Stuka pilots ever since the bridge at Calais. A bar full of drunken pilots was his dream mission, only he had imagined coming calling with a handpicked team of Raiding Forces Commandos armed to the teeth, not three joy-riding women in mink coats and Thompson submachine guns out for a little payback.

He sincerely hoped the Luftwaffe pilots in the Blue Duck were pouring it down with both hands right about now.

"Look at this, John." Captain the Lady Jane Seaborn's voice interrupted his thoughts. She showed him the butt of the Thompson submachine gun she was holding cradled between her knees, with the finned barrel resting on the deck of the speedboat. A capital J, canted slightly to the rear, was branded deeply into the stock. "Captain McKoy said it came from a ranch called the 'Rocking J.'"

"Lovely," Major Randal said. "Have you actually fired a Thompson, Jane?"

"You know Pamala and I are fully qualified agents."

"How could I forget; you can kill an attack dog with your bare hands."

"If we should happen upon one tonight in St. Leigh," Captain Lady Seaborn said in a no-nonsense tone, "I intend to shoot it."

"Good plan."

A light fog began to set in. Visibility was reduced. Ahead, the faded purple coast of France swam into focus through the haze, a smudge in the night straight ahead. True to her word, Brandy did exactly what she said she was going to do back in his room at Seaborn House. Without the slightest hesitation, she wheeled the boat over hard to starboard running at full speed and paralleled the coastline. The speedboat was still going wide open. In no time they were laying off St. Leigh.

Well, Brandy sure called my bluff, he thought.

From the bobbing boat, the village looked like a little toy town with a little toy dock. A light snow that had fallen earlier still covered the rooftops, and the single intersection in the village added to the fairyland effect. According to the luminous green hands on his Rolex watch, it was 2345 hours on the dot.

Major Randal leaned forward and put his arms over the backs of the boat seats occupied by Brandy and Royal Marine Pamala Plum-Martin and said over the deep "warbling" of the speedboat's idling engines, "We can pull this off if you ladies do exactly what I tell you."

Then, with a hard edge to his voice that surprised the women, he added, "If you don't, none of us will be coming back."

"Aye, aye, sir," Brandy immediately responded, sitting relaxed with her arms casually draped over the wheel, awaiting developments, having performed her part of the operation to perfection. "Boat's captain standing by for orders, sir."

"Pam and I will follow your instructions to the letter," Captain Lady Seaborn assured him in a husky voice, leaning forward to share in the conversation, not sounding quite as confident as she had back at Seaborn

House. Lying off a hostile beach studying your intended target before taking it to the enemy with guns blazing has a marvelous way of transforming one's perspective.

"Pamala?" he demanded through clenched teeth, the steel still in his voice.

"To the letter, John," the Vargas Girl Royal Marine responded. "Yes sir."

"All right then," Major Randal said. "Brandy, ease in as quietly as you possibly can. We'll go ashore the moment you come alongside the dock. As soon as we exit the boat, you run her out, pull around, and back her in. Be ready for us to be coming quick, on the run."

"I shall be on full alert," Brandy replied confidently. "Ready for a fast getaway."

"Jane, you and Pamala follow me off the dock up to the road junction. I'll assign each of you a sector to cover while I go into the Blue Duck. Shoot anyone or anything that moves in your sector. Don't hesitate or try to take prisoners, just open fire. Is that clear?"

Both women responded, "Clear!"

"Jane, I'm going to assign you the sector with the Blue Duck. Cover me when I come out. I'll be moving fast; try really hard not to shoot me."

Looking him full in the eyes, to make sure he knew she had heard and understood, the well-trained Royal Marine captain nodded. She was letting him know, by making direct eye contact, there was no possibility of confusion about what was expected of her.

"Light up anyone who comes out after I exit, Jane, and be quick about it."

"Yes sir."

Major Randal paused for a few seconds to allow both of the women to absorb the instructions. Finally he asked, "Any questions?"

The only sound was the warbling of the engine.

"Let's go kill some bad guys," Major Randal said. "That's what we came for."

41

TABLE DANCE

THE CHRIS-CRAFT MOVED SLOWLY, WITH A THROATY WARBLE, TOWARD St. Leigh's little toy dock, undulating gently with the waves. The moon, now covered by light fog, bathed the snow-covered village in a pale blue light.

Major John Randal hunched forward between the two front seats, sandwiched between Brandy and Royal Marine Pamala Plum-Martin. Captain the Lady Jane Seaborn was straining forward hard against him, with one arm over his shoulder for support. He was clicked on.

The three women—being women and therefore sensitive to change in tone, inflection, vibe, aura, karma and things like that—picked up on it instantly. Their reaction was to focus on everything he said. Without consciously realizing it, they dialed in. He went over the entire impromptu plan again.

They were winging it tonight, which is just about the worst thing you can do on a military endeavor. The quickest way to get killed in combat, Major Randal, knew was to go on an operation and make up the plan as you go along. Then again, very few high-risk missions are things of precision, and besides, once the first shot is fired, the best of plans generally goes right down the tube anyway.

"As soon as we go ashore, come about and be ready for a high speed getaway," Major Randal repeated to Brandy in an easy conversational tone. "Remember, whatever you do, DON'T tie up at the dock. Maintain your station with the engine idling. And no matter what happens, Brandy, DO NOT GET OUT OF THE BOAT."

"Aye, aye, sir," Brandy replied, never taking her eyes off the steadily approaching dock. Major Randal had no doubts he could count on her to be ready to go when they came out.

"Now this is the tricky part, Brandy. If there is shooting in the street, look at your watch immediately and start timing. If we are not back on the dock in exactly three minutes after you hear the first shot, you shove off and go home. Is that clear?"

"I understand—three minutes."

"Can you see your watch?"

"Not, very well, actually," she admitted.

"Take mine then," Major Randal unbuckled his Rolex. "You won't have any trouble telling time on it in the dark."

Turning to face Royal Marine Plum-Martin and Captain Lady Seaborn, Major Randal continued his instructions. "Last thing, if either of you two ladies has to open fire while I'm inside the Blue Duck, aim low, hold the trigger down, and shoot up the entire magazine of your weapon so I'm certain to hear the gunfire. If I'm not out of the Blue Duck within one minute after you engage your target, both of you return to the boat. Two minutes after that, if I'm not in sight headed for the dock, go home. Is that clear?"

The girls did not like it, but both nodded in agreement.

"Let me hear you say it."

"Clear!" the women chorused.

"Lock and load, Marines," Major Randal ordered. He watched as the women inserted the magazines into the Thompson submachine guns and charged them. If they were scared, neither of them showed it. Their hands were steady, their movements precise as they went through the manual of arms.

Because of German blackout restrictions, not a single light was showing in the village. The only sound was the warbling of the speedboat. Brandy put the Chris-Craft alongside the dock. The instant they brushed the pylon, Major Randal stepped ashore with Captain Lady Seaborn and Royal Marine Plum-Martin hard at his heels. He had the silenced High Standard .22 pistol in his hand, down flat against his leg. He held the A-5 Browning in his left hand, concealed inside his unbuttoned overcoat, stock reversed, trigger forward. Both women were right behind him, concealing their Thompson submachine guns under their full-length mink coats.

A German soldier wearing the standard issue coal-scuttle helmet, with the distinctive metal military police gorget dangling from his neck on its chain, stepped out of a small guard shack at the end of the pier and walked over to investigate. He was not on any heightened alert. Pilots frequently arrived by boat to go drinking in the Blue Duck, and more often than not they had women accompanying them. Nothing one of Fat Herman's "Eagles" could have done would have surprised him.

Major Randal let the German approach to within a few feet and then quickly shot him three times in the face, just below the rim of the steel helmet, with the silenced .22 pistol. The policeman collapsed instantly, a pool of dark blood rapidly growing on the soft white snow. His steel helmet made a hollow metallic ringing sound when it hit the ground.

If there had been any question about the gravity of the night's enterprise, it was answered right then and there for the two Royal Marines. Looking a man in the eye while he is being shot dead has a way of putting things into tight perspective. They had definitely crossed over from the planning and transportation phases to the execution phase, a mental as well as physical transformation that occurs at some point on every single combat operation for mission participants, no matter how many they have been on before.

Tonight was turning out to be quite different from faking Texas accents or snapping photos of each other in their swimsuits in a sleepy neutral country. The women were definitely focused now. Mentally they were cocked and locked, though it still felt a little surreal for them to come to grips with the fact that they had actually invaded enemy-occupied France by themselves.

The intersection was less than fifty feet from the dock. The trio skirted around the dead sentry, feeling exposed, but there was no one else around and all remained quiet. No one in the village suspected that a German soldier had been shot dead at his post.

The sound of live music could be heard coming from the Blue Duck around the corner every time the door to the bar opened and closed. Nothing else even so much as moved in the village. The night was perfectly still. The German occupation forces had imposed a strict curfew on the civilian population. Anyone out and about at this time of night was a Nazi, a Nazi collaborator, or a Peeping Tom—all certified legitimate targets.

When the trio reached the end of the short dock, they flattened themselves against the side of the building on the right side of the street; then, moving like big cats, they eased their way slowly and carefully up to the intersection. Major Randal was in the lead on point followed by Captain Lady Seaborn carrying her "Rocking J" Thompson submachine gun, muzzle straight up, and Royal Marine Plum-Martin with her weapon at the high port.

When he reached the end of the wall at the intersection, Major Randal made a quick head check around the corner. There was a cluster of Mercedeses, Citroëns, BMWs, Peugeots, Volkswagens, four or five motorcycles, and a small truck parked at haphazard angles outside the Blue Duck. Obviously, the partygoers had little regard for St. Leigh parking ordinances. Two of the cars were pulled up over the curb with their wheels on the sidewalk. No gendarme was going to issue a citation. Not tonight, not ever, to any of the German Eagles, the untouchables.

Two Luftwaffe airmen, probably orderlies, were standing outside the Blue Duck smoking cigarettes.

Major Randal placed the High Standard .22 back in its holster on the front of his belt, reached back, grabbed the lapel of Captain Lady Seaborn's coat, and pulled her closer to the corner of the wall. He held up two fingers and pointed in the direction of the Blue Duck. "There is your area of responsibility," he whispered. "Two bad guys are in plain sight. Wait here until I have time to reach the Blue Duck and take care of them before you move up to assume your position."

Captain Lady Seaborn made full eye contact and gave him an exaggerated slow-motion nod to make it clear she understood. She must have learned something at those intelligence schools she had attended. The woman knew exactly how to conduct herself on a mission. And that made things a lot easier for him.

Next, Major Randal grabbed the lapel of Royal Marine Plum-Martin's coat and pulled her forward until the three of them were in a tight huddle against the wall. He pointed to where the road ran straight ahead and to the angle it made to the left, running away from the Blue Duck. She had two avenues of approach to cover. The female Marine also locked eyes with him and nodded slowly to indicate that she understood her assignment.

Captain Lady Seaborn produced a black cylindrical object from her coat pocket and handed it to Major Randal. "Never hurts to cheat," she whispered.

The black object was a No. 69 Bakelite concussion grenade. He stuck it in the left side pocket of his cashmere overcoat with the two spare magazines for his Colt .38 Super.

"Particularly when there ain't no Plan B."

He gave the two girls a wink, pulled the High Standard out of his belt holster, held it behind his back, then stepped round the corner and walked straight toward the Blue Duck. His well-worn cowboy boots hardly made any noise at all in the snow.

As he approached, the Luftwaffe airmen looked up warily from their cigarettes. Apparently they did not recognize his uniform for what it was, and not taking any chances, they quickly snapped to attention and saluted. "Heil—"

Without breaking stride, Major Randal quickly shot them both two times in the head with the silenced .22-caliber pistol at point-blank range before they could even drop their salutes. The two Germans crumpled to the pavement without a sound and lay glassy-eyed on the sidewalk next to their still-glowing cigarettes. As he walked past, he pumped one more round into each of the prone Nazis for insurance.

At the door to the Blue Duck, Major Randal paused long enough to slip the High Standard pistol back into its holster, and in one smooth, well-practiced motion, he drew the Colt .38 Super from his chest holster and cocked it. He kept the Browning A-5 in his left hand, tight to his side under the coat, trigger guard forward.

Then with the big Colt automatic held straight down against his leg, he stepped through the door, pushing aside the heavy blackout curtain behind it, and on into the bar. The small room was crowded, and it was almost completely dark inside. Major Randal stepped a half pace to the right and placed his back flat against the wall to allow him time to assess the situation and give his eyes a little time to adjust.

A combat flying squadron normally consists of twelve to fifteen aircraft. Stukas, having a single pilot, translated into twelve to fifteen flying officers per squadron. Allowing for combat losses, which had been excessive for Stukas in the Battle of Britain, pilots on leave, injured, or sick, or those who had other plans for the evening, Major Randal had not unreasonably expected to find no more than six or seven highly inebriated pilots at play in the Blue Duck.

To tell the truth, he had been counting on fewer than that.

No such luck, not tonight. The place was packed tight. There appeared to be a sea of men and a number of women in the tiny room, though that was only an illusion because the pub was so small.

Unknown to SOE, the Stuka dive-bomber squadron was being pulled out of combat and rotated back to Germany to refit after heavy losses. An FW 190 squadron flying the latest model high-performance fighters had arrived to replace them. As so often happens, the intelligence information was almost, but not quite, accurate. Major Randal had arrived at the Blue Duck smack in the middle of a change-of-command celebration, with the better part of two squadrons of pilots in attendance.

In the far back of the crowded, dark room was a small stage. A blonde torch singer in a black corset, garter belt, fishnet hose, and six-inch heels, holding a black top hat in one hand and a silver-headed cane in the other, was sitting on a tall stool doing her best with a Marlene Dietrich song. A small, round spotlight illuminated the vocalist. She was coming to the end of her rendition. The singer was not giving a particularly convincing performance. Marlene Dietrich was the personification of decadent and world-weary; the blonde looked young and pretty. She could sing.

Regardless of what flag they fly for, combat pilots at play are not known for restraint and decorum. The men were not paying much attention to the performance. The disheveled and partially disrobed women scattered around the room partying with them were even more raucous, intentionally attempting to distract the pilots from the good-looking singer. One, naked except for her black patent leather high heels, was dancing on a table. The shoes, Major Randal noted from the shadows, sported little yellow and black polka-dotted bows.

The Luftwaffe pilots were doing their best to drown with alcohol the high level of stress induced by modern air combat operations flown against a resourceful and determined enemy who did not seem to understand that they were defeated. The Nazi fliers had been drinking since long before sundown. There was not a sober person in the room. These Eagles were totally smashed, just as their counterparts across the Channel in the Blind Eye were right this minute.

One group of pilots in the bar was exhilarated and more than a little relieved at surviving a highly dangerous combat tour. The other was anxious and excited at taking up frontline duty right on the very tip of the Luftwaffe's aerial spear. As the song came to an end, the revelers cheered drunkenly.

Major Randal took it all in. The setup was exactly the way it had been laid out for him by Captain Lady Seaborn, except for the large number of pilots present. As he sized up the room, it was difficult not to reflect on something Captain Terry "Zorro" Stone liked to say from time to time when things were at their absolute worst: "It's always darkest before pitch black." Looking at all the Nazis packed in the room Major Randal concluded this must be what pitch black looked like.

The bartender asked him a question, which was most likely, "What would you like to drink?" Not speaking a single word of French, Major Randal said, "I'll have a Black Strap."

42

GUNFIGHT AT THE
BLUE DUCK

THREE HIGHLY INTOXICATED GERMANS STANDING AT THE END
of the bar turned woozily, shocked to hear English spoken in their presence. The men were the first live Stuka pilots Major John Randal had ever seen up close. He flashed back to the dive sirens screaming, the intentional terror bombing and cold-blooded strafing of civilians at Calais, and the skin on his cheekbones grew tight. He had the distinct impression of Captain "Geronimo Joe" McKoy standing right there next to him whispering in his ear, "Watch the front sight close, touch her off, and adios—take your time in a hurry."

Major Randal went straight to work.

In one fluid motion, he brought the Colt .38 Super up to eye level, aligned the gold bead on the front-sight post, and began to fire. One of pilots, he noticed, was wearing the Knight's Cross around his neck on a thick red, white, and black-striped ribbon. His first shot went straight through the Knight's Cross choker.

"Now that's a sore throat," Major Randal rasped.

The three haughty blond Aryan supermen leering at him went down in a tangled pile as he continued to fire.

Sliding the A-5 up on the bar, and standing with his back to it, he gripped his Colt .38 Super in both hands and shot the two startled pilots at the table closest to him. The lithe, auburn-haired woman sitting with them let out a high-pitched scream like a panther. Terrified, she jumped up and took a bullet meant for the pilot at the table behind her. The round went straight through her unbuttoned blouse and struck the pilot behind her, knocking him out of his chair.

Pandemonium erupted, men and women screaming in panic, and the room went blurry with movement. Suddenly the lights came on full bright, which was to his advantage. The last thing people who have been drinking long hours in a dark pub want is harsh white light shining in their eyes. Now he could see his sights clearly.

Shooting the way he had trained, Major Randal was taking his time in a hurry, careful not to move out of arm's reach of the A-5 shotgun on the bar, calling his shots. He would have preferred to be able to move around the room but was forced to stay near the bar; circumstances dictated a need to keep the Browning 12-gauge close at hand to repel boarders in the event the Nazis managed to get their act together and charge him en masse. And he needed to keep his back against something solid.

Major Randal was hitting what he was aiming at, firing rapidly but carefully picking each shot. Pilots jumped up and attempted to draw their sidearms or scrambled away like crabs to get out of the line of fire; when they moved, he shot them. Some pilots sat paralyzed; he shot them. Other pilots tried to take cover under tables; he shot them where they hid. One attempted to draw his Luger service pistol and was so frightened, intoxicated, or such a poor gun handler that he blasted himself in the stomach.

A pilot came up off the floor from behind an overturned table with a small Mauser pocket pistol blazing. Major Randal shot him in the forehead. Another pilot charged out of the latrine at the far end of the bar. As he ran, he was firing a P-38 as fast as he could pull the trigger. Major Randal shot the man twice, the bullets making little tufts to the left of the ribbons on the pilot's chest. Major Randal realized he was seeing things in slow motion, a sensation he had experienced before.

He reloaded for the second time. The first had been so fast and automatic he barely remembered it. Two senior officers, the JU-87 and the FW-190 squadron commanders, were crouching behind an overturned table firing their small Walther PPKs over the top. He shot them both through the wooden tabletop.

A stocky pilot wearing his crumpled hat cocked back on his head, his shirtsleeves rolled up, sat at the drums slightly to the right of the blonde singer, frozen in place, holding his drumsticks in midair. Major Randal shot him off the stage.

Three desperate pilots, apparently weaponless, grabbed beer bottles by the neck, lurched to their feet, and rushed him, drunkenly stumbling over overturned chairs and tables in an attempt to gang tackle and beat him to death. Major Randal reached back, laid the Colt .38 Super on the bar, picked up the 12-gauge Browning, brought it around, and shot the three charging men down, point-blank. The last man standing was so close to the shotgun's barrel when it discharged into his chest that his beribboned blouse caught fire and flamed briefly.

A bareheaded pilot tried to low-crawl out the door, and Major Randal shot him. Screaming incoherently, a tall blond pilot jumped to his feet and ran to the door, but then, inexplicably, he paused to claw at his overcoat. Major Randal shot him. *Why had that man stopped?*

Then, there was simply the sound of women screaming and the smell of cordite. Besides the screaming women, the only people left alive were the singer and the bartender, who was standing petrified next to the light switch. *Had he turned the lights up to give me an edge?*

From start to finish the fight could be measured in seconds.

"Are you totally insane?" the blonde on the stage screeched hysterically in English from where she was crouched in the spotlight. "You slaughtered almost two squadrons of Nazi pilots you bloody madman!"

By reflex Major Randal covered her with the Browning A-5 shotgun, both eyes open over the top of the stubby chopped-off barrel.

"I'm your contact, you idiot!" the torch singer shrieked, leaping off the stage. "Get me out of here before the rest of the murderous Nazi slime comes back!"

"Who's coming back?"

"Two carloads of pilots drove off over an hour ago to pay one last visit to their girlfriends at Madame Meme's bordello. We have to get out of here right now. "

Major Randal tossed her an overcoat from the rack inside the door. He noticed that a number of pistol belts were hanging on the pegs under the coats. *That had been a mistake.* He knocked the coats off the rack with the barrel of the A-5 then scooped off the pistol belts and slipped them over his left shoulder.

"Slow down, lady; don't put the coat on until I tell you to. Wouldn't do to get taken for a German out on the street; there's a couple of trigger-happy Royal Marines out there."

"They could not possibly be any worse than you!"

Outside, right at that moment, one of those Royal Marines detected a dim glow. The lights were the last thing she wanted to see.

"Car lights, twelve o'clock," Royal Marine Plum-Martin announced.

"I see them," Captain Lady Seaborn responded without turning her head. She was intently focusing on the door of the Blue Duck, both eyes open over the sights of the heavy Thompson submachine gun she was resting against the corner of the building. The muffled shooting inside the pub had ceased. She was deeply concerned. The gunfire had not seemed to go on for very long; in fact, the shooting had been over quite fast, which could mean John was in trouble.

"Wait until the car approaches really close, Pam."

The glow grew into the cat's-eye lights the German military favored for driving during blackout conditions. The vehicle was a field gray Mercedes sedan. When it reached the road junction, Royal Marine Plum-Martin raised her Thompson to waist level, locked it tightly into her hip, and caressed the Thompson's curved trigger. When the car was approximately thirty feet away, she commenced fire.

The monster .45-caliber rounds—each as big around as a cigar, triggered in short, crisp bursts of three or four rounds per burst—hammered into the luxury touring machine, chewing it into a smoldering heap of junk. True to her orders, she kept firing burst after burst into the passenger compartment of the Mercedes until she had emptied the entire magazine.

While Royal Marine Plum-Martin was changing magazines, a second vehicle—a dark BMW also equipped with cat's-eye blackout lights—materialized, swung around from behind, and pulled up next to the smoldering wreck. There was drunken singing coming from the car and then a dull, hollow "cruuunch" caused by what sounded suspiciously like a champagne bottle being dropped out the passenger window onto the cobblestone. The pilots inside clearly did not comprehend what had happened. The fog of war, compounded by many hours of hard drinking following a long day's combat flying, had the German aviators firmly in its clutches.

"Jane!"

"Cover the Blue Duck," Captain Lady Seaborn replied in a cool, poised, professional tone as she spun to her left, bringing the Thompson down off the corner where she had been resting it. She tucked the hard wood stock of the weapon into her hip the way she had been coached and commenced firing.

The windscreen spider-webbed from the impact of the big bullets, then it shattered completely. Steam shot up from the BMW's radiator. All jocularity inside the car's passenger compartment immediately ceased. The Thompson submachine gun hammered away in short bursts for what seemed like a terribly long time before finally running dry.

"Here comes John," Royal Marine Plum-Martin called out tersely. "You are never going to believe what he is bringing with him."

As he went out the door of the Blue Duck, Major Randal called back to the bartender, "If I were you, I'd hit the deck."

Clearing the building, Major Randal pulled the pin on the concussion grenade and tossed it back inside the bar underhanded, hoping to discourage anyone who might have been playing possum from getting up and trying to be a hero. Then he turned and headed for the dock. The torch singer, lugging the heavy overcoat, was struggling hard to keep up. She was having tough going on the cobblestones in the spike heels.

The two cut straight across the street, ignoring the two shot-up vehicles. Behind them came a short ugly "Whuuump" followed by the tinkling sound of windowpanes disintegrating.

The blackout curtains blew out of the Blue Duck's broken windows and dangled down outside. No one would be coming out of that bar for some time. And, if they did, their ears were sure to be ringing and they were going to be highly disoriented.

"Slow down, let me take these lousy heels off," the Marlene Dietrich impersonator complained loudly as she hobbled along at high speed.

"Hurry up, lady," Major Randal said. "We've got a boat to catch!"

As they came past Captain Lady Seaborn and Royal Marine Plum-Martin, Major Randal observed, "That'll teach 'em to bomb your favorite jewelry store."

Both of the Royal Marines shot him an exaggerated dirty look and then swung in behind, walking backward and opening fire on the parked vehicles in front of the Blue Duck to cover their withdrawal. This time they each held the trigger down, running their magazines to hose the entire area. The two .45-caliber Thompson submachine guns working in tandem produced an awesome amount of firepower. One of the automobiles caught fire from a spark caused by a ricochet off the cobblestone street, igniting a trail of gasoline that spilled out of the vehicle's bullet-perforated gas tank. Eventually the running flame spread to the nearly full tank. The car blew up as they went around the corner to the dock. The loud explosion echoed through the village.

The four pounded down the dock to where Brandy was waiting, gunning the engines in the Chris-Craft. As instructed, she was watching the Rolex, counting the minutes.

"Whoa, John," she shouted gaily when she looked up and saw the protesting woman in her corset and garter belt he was dragging along with him. "Leave it to you to take the time during a gun battle to strip-search the women."

"Get the hell out of Dodge, Brandy!" Major John Randal ordered through gritted teeth as they all piled haphazardly into the speedboat.

Giving Brandy Seaborn an order like that was dangerous. The Chris-Craft surged forward so hard it snapped everyone's head back. Captain the Lady Jane Seaborn and Royal Marine Pamala Plum-Martin were both laughing hysterically as the speedboat roared out into the Channel.

No one on board could actually believe they were still alive.

"What are you two laughing at?" the outraged singer demanded as she struggled into the liberated Luftwaffe pilot's overcoat. "I happen to be your contact—not some piece of fluff."

"Fooled us," Royal Marine Plum-Martin quipped. "Anyway, we are laughing at John, not you."

"He's a barrel of fun, all right. The lunatic killed practically everyone in the whole village, including the mayor's wife. I thought for a minute he was going to murder me," she raged. "What could this maniac serial killer possibly have done tonight you might think is even remotely funny?"

"John has a reputation for saying 'Let's get the hell out of Dodge' at the end of every mission, like cinema cowboys in the flicks," Captain Lady Seaborn explained, still laughing. "Everyone wants to be able to claim they were there and heard him say it. We just did."

"My lucky night," the singer snapped tetchily. "You people are sick!"

"Lady," Major Randal said, "you forgot your top hat."

What she said to him was not printable in three languages.

Suddenly, Major Randal slumped over in his seat. Captain Lady Seaborn screamed. She ripped open his cashmere overcoat, then the parachute smock, and saw to her horror that he was bleeding profusely from a tiny bullet hole in his chest. No one was laughing now.

The trip home seemed to take forever.

43

INVESTITURE

INVESTITURE CEREMONIES WERE TRADITIONALLY HELD AT Buckingham Palace and were rigidly scripted affairs, complete with a full basic load of pomp, ceremony, colorful uniforms, and pageantry steeped in ancient ritual. The king personally made the presentation of the award to the recipient. At least that was the way it worked in peacetime before the war. Now that the palace itself had been the actual target of a Nazi air raid, a lot of the pageantry was dispensed with. Tin hats and sandbags were much in evidence.

Even with London under constant air attack, certain standards had to be maintained. King George VI, the man who had never wanted to be king but was making a very good job of it, was determined not to let enemy action prescribe when or how he honored the nation's heroes. That simply was not done.

Two investiture ceremonies involving the Raiders had already taken place at the palace over the preceding weeks. The first ceremony was a highly publicized affair designed to boost public morale. The English people do like their military heroes, and even though they were going through extremely dark times while England stood alone against the Third

Reich, it was important for the public to know that its men were rising to the occasion and performing great feats of derring-do in the country's defense. Commodore (Senior Grade) Richard "Dickie the Pirate" Seaborn had stood before his king and received the nation's highest medal for valor, the Victoria Cross, for his part in Operation Lounge Lizard. Prime Minister Winston Churchill had personally lobbied for the upgrade of the award. It made the fairy tale he was telling the unhappy Portuguese ambassador somewhat easier to swallow.

All his life King George VI had never aspired to be anything other than a Royal Navy officer, and he happily would have been one still had his scalawag brother not unexpectedly abdicated the throne to marry a divorcée. As a young lieutenant serving incognito as "Mr. Johnson" on board the battleship HMS *Collingwood*, His Royal Highness Prince Albert had seen action as the second officer in Turret "A" the day the Grand Fleet sallied forth and fought the Battle of Jutland.

Mr. Johnson (the prince was not really fooling anyone) very nearly missed taking part in the battle in much the same way as had today's VC recipient. Alas, at the very moment the *Collingwood* sailed, he was ensconced in her sick bay, incapacitated by a surfeit of soused herring consumed at a party in the officers' mess.

Making a speedy recovery, spurred on by the prospects of action, the future king busied himself by preparing hot chocolate for the sailors manning the gun in his turret. At first blush, this might seem somewhat foppish; however, at the time it was a pretty cool move when you consider that the Germans were lobbing cannon shells the size of Volkswagen Beetles at the *Collingwood* as fast as they could reload.

Prince Albert's personal recipe for cocoa, called "kai" in sailor's slang, was this: cocoa paste he made by scraping a block of Admiralty-issue Pusser's chocolate, sugar, a pinch of custard powder (as a thickener to make the spoon stand up straight all by itself in the middle of the cup— the lower deck's mark of good kai), condensed milk, and hot water. It is not all that easy to perform simple mundane tasks when you are standing by to explode.

In the very public, much-publicized VC investiture ceremony attended by family, friends, high-ranking political, military, and intelligence

luminaries of every stripe, as well as a contingent from the Strategic Raiding Forces led by acting Major Terry "Zorro" Stone, the commodore
received his "gong" and became a national hero.

Pinning on the medal, the king observed, "The fleet did not sail without you this time, eh, Dickie?" There are simply some things a man can
never live down.

The second ceremony was a small, hush-hush, private affair. It, too,
was held at the palace, though not in the grand hall, and the press was not
invited. In fact, they were not even allowed to know it was scheduled. No
family or friends were in attendance. The recipients, all of whom were
awarded the Order of the British Empire, were: Captain the Lady Jane
Seaborn, Royal Marine Pamala Plum-Martin, Jim "Baldie" Taylor (who
had been ordered to leave the Gold Coast and never return), Mr. Ray
Terhune, three very hungover Gold Coast tugboat skippers (who at that
moment were the three most surprised men on planet Earth), and Captain
"Geronimo Joe" McKoy.

The citations all read, "For Service to the Crown." And that was all.

The third ceremony, to decorate the men who had carried out the
daring parachute raid on Tomcat, was a bit unusual in that an entire military unit was decorated en masse, a rare event in Great Britain. The occasion was highly publicized for maximum exposure, but the event itself
was relatively private, limited to the men involved: the Strategic Raiding
Force, supporting elements from No. 1 Parachute School, Whitley pilots
and crew, certain members of the Mountain Warfare School, two Landing
Craft Assault skippers, and two invited guests per recipient. No press was
allowed to attend, interviews were forbidden, and all photographs were
limited to those taken by the official palace photographer. The heads of all
the major services were present.

Raiding Forces, under the command of acting Major Stone, assembled within the walls of Buckingham Palace, out on the driveway, ready to
march into the great hall for the ceremony. Their invited guests and other
dignitaries from all the branches of the military and intelligence services
were waiting inside for the proceedings to begin. The Strategic Raiding
Force was about to become, for a time, the most decorated unit in the
British Armed Forces.

The ceremony was a major event. Every officer and man was to be decorated. Those who were not singled out for specific awards for valor or special service were being "Mentioned in Dispatches," which is a much-coveted honor indicated by the person mentioned being allowed to wear a small bronze oak leaf on his or her service ribbon.

He did not know it yet, but for his planning, forward reconnaissance, and gallant conduct in Operation Lounge Lizard (though, being classified information, none of that was a part of the official citation), acting Major Stone was about to be accorded the great distinction of being inducted into the Order of the British Empire in the rank of Knight Commander. Henceforth, he would be known as "Sir Terry."

In addition to the bar to his Military Cross that Major Sir Terry "Zorro" Stone was to receive for his part in Operation Tomcat, he was also being awarded a second bar for "destroying an enemy munitions train while conducting a small-scale pinprick raid somewhere in France."

Squadron Leader Paddy Wilcox was to receive the Order of the British Empire—one of the few decorations he had not already won—for his part in planning and executing Operation Buzzard Plucker.

Lieutenant Randy "Hornblower" Seaborn was to receive a first and second bar to his Distinguished Service Cross for operations Tomcat and Lounge Lizard.

Captain Jeb Pelham-Davies was to be awarded a first and second bar to the Military Cross he had won while serving in the Duke of Wellington's Regiment in the British Expeditionary Force for operations Tomcat and Lounge Lizard.

Newly commissioned Second Lieutenant Jack Merritt, Inns of Court Regiment (Armored Cars), was to receive the Military Cross for his actions on the *Ems*. Out of respect for the known wishes of Major John Randal, it had been decided that his direct commission be backdated to the day before Operation Lounge Lizard so that the former corporal could be decorated as an officer. (In the class-conscious British military system of awarding medals, generally speaking, majors and above receive the Distinguished Service Order, captains and below receive the Military Cross, sergeants and above receive the Distinguished Conduct Medal, while corporals and below receive the Military Medal.) He was also to receive a second Mention in Dispatches for Operation Tomcat, which made him the most decorated second lieutenant currently on active duty. The reason the former 2nd Life Guards Cavalry Regiment corporal had been commissioned in the Inns of Court Regiment was that he did not have the independent income required of all officers in the Life Guards. It was their loss.

Lieutenant Harry Shelby was to be rewarded with the Military Cross for his reconnaissance of Operation Tomcat prior to the raid. In addition, he would be receiving a bar for his part in Operation Lounge Lizard.

Lieutenant "Pyro" Percy Stirling was to receive the Military Cross for his actions on Operation Tomcat and a bar for his actions during Operation Lounge Lizard. (Since Operation Comanche Yell was an ongoing mission, there were to be no decorations awarded for it at this time.)

Lieutenant Taylor Corrigan was to receive the Military Cross and bar for operations Tomcat and Lounge Lizard.

Sergeant Major Maxwell Hicks was receiving a first and second bar to the Distinguished Conduct Medal he had won on the first Raiding Forces pinprick raid, for operations Tomcat and Lounge Lizard.

Sergeant Mike "March or Die" Mikkalis was to finally receive his Distinguished Conduct Medal for his actions at Calais and a first and second bar for operations Tomcat and Lounge Lizard.

Royal Marine Sergeant Mickey Duggan was to receive the Distinguished Conduct Medal for his part in Operation Lounge Lizard and the Military Medal for Calais.

Royal Marine Butch Hoolihan was to receive a well-earned Military Medal for his actions on the *Ems*.

Just as the moment arrived for the men to march in and meet their king, the gates opened and a Rolls Royce slowly rolled into the compound. Everyone turned to stare. The driver exited. She was a tall, striking brunette Royal Marine no one in Raiding Forces had ever clapped eyes on before.

The chauffeur went around to the back door and opened it. Out stepped a pale-looking Major John Randal followed quickly by Captain Lady Seaborn and Royal Marine Plum-Martin. The two Royal Marines each grasped an arm to keep him steady. Neither woman was smiling. Obviously, they did not approve of his being there today.

Major Randal was wearing his Pembrooks cashmere overcoat—Mr.

Chatterley had sent a note back with the perfectly restored garment, admonishing him to please not get any more bullet holes in it—and carrying a cane in one hand. When he caught sight of the troops, he turned and tossed the stick back into the car.

Raiding Forces wavered for a moment, then broke ranks and pounded down to the Rolls where they surrounded their commanding officer, all talking at once. They were a happy lot. None of them, except acting Major Stone, had seen him since he had been wounded. The word had come down that he might not make it, meaning die from his wounds.

"You didn't really think I was going to miss your big day, did you?" Major Randal laughed, sounding shaky. Well, yes they had, actually.

Flanked by Captain Lady Seaborn and Royal Marine Plum-Martin, Major Randal led Raiding Forces into the great hall at a slow march.

The king hung the Distinguished Service Order on the little metal hook that had been carefully pre-positioned on the pocket of Major John Randal's now loose-fitting Pembrooks uniform blouse. It would not do for his Royal Highness to be fumbling around trying to latch a pin. With just the slightest hint of the stammer he had fought since childhood, the monarch said, "You will notice, Major, that this ribbon has two bars on it, signifying the award of your second and third DSO."

Major Randal looked down in surprise.

"One is for your splendid parachute mission. The other, well, there is not much we can say about that one, is there? Operation Lounge Lizard aptly named after Major Stone, no doubt. Number three is for Calais."

"Your—"

"I realize, naturally, that as a citizen of the United States you do not actually regard me as your sovereign. However, Major, as a member in good standing of The Rangers, now a battalion of the K.R.R.C., I am quite confident you do acknowledge I am the colonel-in-chief of your regiment, a responsibility I undertake with the utmost gravity. In the course of my duties in that capacity, it has come to my attention you have indicated a desire to refuse any recognition for your service at Calais."

"That is correct, your Majesty."

"Major Randal, you looked after the welfare of your Riflemen at Calais and I am merely doing the same thing for one of mine now. Let no more be said."

"Yes sir."

"Lastly, if ever there should come a time when you should find your-self in need of a friend in a high place, as happens on occasion in the service, you need merely dial the number on the card I have ordered to be placed in the leather container that you will receive after the ceremony in which to store your medal. Say the code word indicated on the card and someone from my personal staff will accept the call."

"I'll try not to need it, sir."

Next, when acting Major Stone was given the order to "Rise, Sir Terry" after being tapped on his shoulders by his sovereign's sword, the king looked him square in the eye and said, "Princess Elizabeth asked me to convey to you her heartfelt congratulations. She would have dearly loved to be here today to deliver them in person, but her mother, the queen, forbade it, a salacious incident in the Life Guards mess involving a red-headed BOAC Clipper Girl recently having come to her attention. I should like to point out to you that my daughter, the royal princess, is only seventeen years old. Would not your best service to the crown, Sir Terry, be found somewhere in, say, the Middle East?"

Uh-oh!

After the ceremony, Captain McKoy walked a noticeably exhausted Major Randal and the two stone-faced women Royal Marines slowly back to the Rolls. The silver-haired showman was dressed in an ancient tuxedo. A pale blue ribbon flecked with tiny white stars and a five-pointed bronze medallion dangling on the end was draped around his neck.

"That what I think it is?" Major Randal asked, looking at the Medal of Honor. It was the first one he had ever seen worn by a recipient. "You must have really torn 'em up in Cuba."

"I wore it to honor my star pupil, young Major."

"Means a lot, Captain McKoy."

"Between you and me, John, I don't put much truck in medals. Who got what don't mean nothing most times. Besides, I didn't get this in Cuba."

"Captain, we need to talk; you've some tall explaining to do."

"Maybe we'll do 'er someday," Captain McKoy responded evasively. "Right now, before these two women drag you out of here, I've got a ques-tion I've been dyin' to hear the answer to. What did it feel like to wade knee-deep into a barroom full of Nazis and blaze away?" Captain McKoy asked. "I'd sure loved to have been a fly on the wall in the Blue Duck when you cut loose."

"A mistake."

"I've know'd the feeling."

In the car, when Major John Randal turned over the card in the leather zippered container, written on the back were the words, "DEAD EAGLES."

HISTORICAL NOTES
OF INTEREST

Chapter 2
Special Operations Executive was the first national-level government-sponsored guerilla warfare agency in history. It was designed to overthrow enemy governments by special means. They were charged by Churchill to "set Europe ablaze."

Chapter 3
The chief of the security detachment was rotating his men through No. 1 British Parachute Training School and the Special Warfare Training Center at Achnacarry, Scotland, two at a time so they would be as well trained as the men they were charged with providing security for.

Chapter 5
Vice Admiral Randolph "Razor" Ransom, VC, KCB, DSO, OBE, DSC, was a legendary retired naval officer who had recently been recalled to active duty to act as commodore to merchant convoys on the "suicide run" to Malta.

Chapter 7

On Operation Tomcat, ordered at the last minute to "blow the lighthouse," Lieutenant Percy Stirling had ignited the fuse on 125 pounds of guncotton that had been wedged under a two-story-tall acetylene fuel tank. This unwittingly created what might arguably have been the largest incendiary device on the continent of Europe, which when it exploded made him an instant living legend and earned him the nickname "Pyro."

After Raiding Forces' first raid—where in a stroke of fantastic good luck they captured Panzer General Ernest von Rittenhauser parked in his staff car on the beach with a French girl of questionable morals— Churchill went on radio and warned all Germans serving everywhere that they must be ever vigilant because there was a "hand of steel" that would come from the sea to pluck them from their post.

Chapter 10

It was later determined that the shots that killed Commander Sprague were the first fired between England and France in 125 years.

Chapter 11

Colonel Menzies, Lieutenant Commander Fleming, and Captain Stone were all graduates of Eton. Colonel Menzies and Captain Stone were also members of Pop, the 2nd Life Guards, and the Beauford Hunt.

In the quirky British military, what were described as German E-boats (the E standing for enemy) were called S-boats by the Kriegsmarine (the S standing for *schnell*, or fast). E-boats (S-boats) were equivalent to motor gunboats or motor torpedo boats. They had a crew of twenty-five-plus men.

R-boats (*Raumboots*) were small minesweepers, with a crew of forty-plus men.

M-boats (*Minensuchboots*) were minesweepers, with a crew of eighty-plus men.

Chapter 14

During No. 1 Parachute School, the men of Raiding Forces learned the Rebel Yell from Major John Randal. However, they confused the name and began calling it a Comanche Yell. No matter how hard he tried, Major Randal could never get the Raiders to refer to the Yeeeeeehaaaaaa!—which literally drove the instructors crazy—by the correct name. In the military, once a nickname is given, it sticks.

Raiding Forces had not had an opportunity to improve its woefully lacking training in demolitions. No one really knew how to blow up an E-boat. It was powered by diesel engines and diesel fuel was not thought to be particularly explosive.

Chapter 20
Operation Lounge Lizard was named in honor of Captain Terry "Zorro" Stone. Lady Jane had once described the legendary lothario by that term in pre-war days.

Chapter 23
The governor was called home to England within the next few months, and he retired from the service involuntarily. A worse assignment was eventually found for General Giffard in the China-Burma-India Theatre.

Chapter 28
Not one word of the disappearance of SS Colonel Doctor von Himmel and his wife ever leaked out publicly. The German couple had simply vanished. As for the Gyaman tribe crossing into the Gold Coast Colony causing an international incident, it infuriated the Vichy French, but no one in the Third Reich gave it so much as a passing thought.

Chapter 42
The Knight's Cross was worn on a red, white, and black choker around the recipient's neck. Receiving the coveted award was called "getting a sore throat."

Chapter 43
In the Great War, then Sub-Lieutenant Richard Seaborn had been ashore buying vegetables for the officers' mess when his ship sailed without him to fight the Battle of Jutland.

THE BATTLE OF
THE PLAIN OF REEDS

THE RAIDING FORCES SERIES IS DEDICATED TO THE MEN OF A COMPANY 2nd Battalion 39th Regiment 1st Brigade 9th Infantry Division.

After an intensive six-week campaign of airmobile operations in the Mekong Delta, Alpha Company played a key role in the climatic Battle of the Plain of Reeds, which resulted in the 1st Recondo Brigade, commanded by the legendary Colonel Henry 'Gunfighter' Emerson, being awarded the Presidential Unit Citation.

On 3 June 1968, the third morning of a four-day running battle in the Plain of Reeds, Alpha Company air-assaulted into a hot LZ; charged across one hundred meters of open rice paddy straight into the teeth of a dug-in main force Viet Cong regiment that was throwing everything at them but the kitchen sink; carried the enemy left flank, penetrating their first line of bunkers; and pinned the VC in their emplacements and fixed them in place until the rest of the 1st Brigade could arrive, encircle, and destroy them. This was accomplished despite A Company having landed outside the range of artillery support, with the company commander killed in the first few minutes, and fighting in 110-plus-degree heat—with no shade, no water—armed with M-16 rifles that would not function in those conditions. They were outnumbered more than ten to one. The initial air strike had to be called in on their own position to prevent A Company from being overrun, which was complicated by the lack of even a single smoke grenade or any other signaling device to mark their location.

One senior officer described Alpha Company's charge and refusal to allow the VC to break contact as the "finest small unit action ever fought"—and maybe it was.

Six Huey helicopters flew out all the men in the company left standing.